W9-ARC-324

THE SIEGE WINTER

ALSO BY ARIANA FRANKLIN

City of Shadows

Mistress of the Art of Death

The Serpent's Tale

Grave Goods

A Murderous Procession

THE SIEGE WINTER

Ariana Franklin and Samantha Norman

wm
WILLIAM MORROW
An Imprint of HarperCollins*Publishers*

This book is a work of fiction. References to real people, events, establishments, organizations, or locales are intended only to provide a sense of authenticity, and are used fictitiously. All other characters, and all incidents and dialogue, are drawn from the author's imagination and are not to be construed as real.

HarperCollins books may be purchased for educational, business, or sales promotional use. For information please e-mail the Special Markets Department at SPsales@harpercollins.com.

FIRST EDITION

Library of Congress Cataloging-in-Publication Data has been applied for.

ISBN 978-0-06-228256-9

15 16 17 18 19 OV/RRD 10 9 8 7 6 5 4 3 2 1

For Barry Norman,
for all his help and encouragement

THE SIEGE WINTER

PROLOGUE

AD 1180, Perton Abbey

IT IS A WOOD-PANELED ROOM of sumptuous size—the abbots of Perton have always done themselves well. The present incumbent, however, has stripped it of its tapestries and the gold leaf that once decorated the carved ceiling—they've been sold to benefit poor women of the parish. He's also replaced an elaborate, padded prie-dieu with a plain version that is hard on the knees.

This austerity has rather shocked his monks, who have also lost some of their comforts; they now have only three courses for supper rather than the seven that previously graced the table of their refectory. However, for all his asceticism, he's a good abbot as abbots go, rather more understanding of peccadilloes than some.

Anyway, he's dying.

He lies on a cot, propped up with pillows to aid his breathing, and so that he may look out the window opposite, which has its shutters open summer and winter. It is autumn now and the great oak in the garden beyond is beginning to change color. Only its top is visible to him, but he can tell from the sound of munching and grunting, and an occasional coarsening of the fresh air, that the monastery pigs are enjoying the acorns at its base.

He wonders whether he will live to see the last leaf fall from the oak, and knows that he must. He has something important to do. He has to record a tale of treachery and murder, also a story of courage and love, before he, too, twirls off life's tree, yet he is too ill, too weak, to write it himself.

To this end, a young scribe has entered the room and now sits on a stool beside the bed, a pile of wax tablets on the floor at his feet, one on his knees, stylus poised.

"You are too young to remember the war between the empress Matilda and King Stephen, though your grandparents will . . . ," the abbot says. He raises himself and fumbles among the parchments lying on his bed, finally extracting one. "I think, my son, that we can begin this chronicle by repeating the description by Orderic Vitalis in his Historia Ecclesiastica. *I have the quotation here."*

The young scribe rubs his hand with the skirt of his robe before accepting the parchment in order that, though he washed them only yesterday, his fingers should not sully its surface.

"'Thus troubles spread everywhere, far and wide,'" he reads out, "'and England was filled with plundering and burning and massacres; the country, once so rich and overflowing with luxuries, was now wretched and desolate.'"

He looks up. "It was as bad as that?" Either he has learned nothing from his grandparents, or he paid them no attention.

"Worse." Even the good Orderic had not the words for it, *the abbot thought. Anyway, he'd died in 1142 and the war had gone on for more than a decade. Fourteen years during which all decency fled the land, the powerful changing their allegiance this way and that to whosoever promised them more power at the time, forgetting their responsibility to those beneath them so that their private and foreign armies ravaged the common people like dogs pulling apart a living deer. Women raped, peasants hanging from trees by their own entrails. Nearly fourteen years of it, during which England's people said that God and His saints must be*

sleeping, since there was no answer to their prayers for deliverance.

"Then it is a most excellent beginning, my lord, and one that will contrast well with the present day, when a merchant may travel English roads with gold in his pack without fear of molestation."

Damnation. This boy was hired for his speed in writing, not his commentary, however cheery. Time, time. The leaves will be falling soon.

"I think," the abbot says, "that we need expend few words on the circumstances of the war's beginning, since everybody knows them."

"Er . . ."

Damnation again. Didn't they teach them history at Perton? "Its causes," the abbot says distinctly, "began with the death of King Henry the First of England in the year of our Lord 1135 in Normandy . . ."

"Dead from a surfeit of lampreys," the scribe says brightly, "I know that much."

The abbot sighs. "A man of voracious appetite, and not only for food. His bastards were legion."

"Shall I put that down, my lord?"

"I don't care. But it would be useful if you could mention the king's insistence that the nobles gathered about his deathbed should swear an oath that they would accept as their queen his only remaining legitimate child, the empress Matilda, formerly empress of Germany, but widowed by then and married again to the Angevin Geoffrey Plantagenet."

"The same empress who was the mother of our present king Henry?"

"The same. However, her cousin Stephen, hearing of his uncle's death, raced from Normandy to England and secured the crown for himself with the aid of some of the very barons who had sworn to support the empress."

"They never having been ruled by a woman, nor wanting to be?" asked the scribe helpfully.

"If you like, if you like. And now, my son, we reach the nub of my chronicle, when, in 1139, the empress Matilda invaded England with an army to fight for the right her father had granted her. By this time

Stephen had disappointed many of those who had so enthusiastically espoused his cause. Undoubtedly an affable man and, in war, a courageous one, he concealed a shifty cunning that caused him to break his word to the trustworthy in favor of men of the moment. His brother Bishop Henry—a stronger character than he—had helped him onto the throne, and might have expected to be made archbishop of Canterbury as a reward. Instead, Stephen alienated his brother and conferred the position on the little-known Theobald of Bec. Also, he dismissed the lowborn but clever men who had run Henry the First's administration and put in their place favorites who lacked the knowledge to govern efficiently. Arbitrarily, madly, he arrested three bishops, one of them the bishop of Ely, who had displeased him, taking their castles into his own hands, thereby showing that he had no care for the liberties of the Church."

The young scribe tut-tuts; he sets great store by Church liberties. "Such wickedness."

"He was a fool," the abbot says. "His kingship was tainted with foolish decisions, which, by 1141, had caused some of his erstwhile supporters to switch their allegiance to the empress and fight against him. Worse, it gave opportunity to wicked men who cared not who ruled as long as they themselves flourished." He draws a long breath. "It is at this point, my son, where we must begin our history, with the war in full spate. And for that we must revert not to the doings and battles of the great, but to an insignificant village in the Cambridgeshire fenland and to an eleven-year-old girl who lived in it."

"Commoners, my lord?" It is said with alarm. "Is this not to be an Historia Anglorum*? An account for the edification of future generations?"*

"It is indeed, but this one is an Historia Vulgi *as told through the mouths of ordinary people who, in turn, told it to me."*

"But . . . common people?"

The abbot wheezes with the irritability of the sick. "It is a tale of murder and treachery. It is the tale of the rape of a child, a castle and a country. Now, in the name of God, write . . ."

CHAPTER 1

Winter, AD 1141, the Cambridgeshire Fens

AT FIRST, NEWS OF THE war that was going on outside passed into the fenland without impact. It oozed into that secret world as if filtered through the green miasma of willow and alder that the fenlanders called "carr," which lined its interminable rivers and reed beds.

At Scutney, they learned about it from old Sala when he came back from his usual boat trip to Cambridge market, where he sold rushes for thatching. He told the tale in the village church after the celebration of Candlemas.

"Now yere's King Stephen . . . ," he began.

"Who?" somebody asked.

Sala sighed with the exasperation of a much-traveled man for the village idiot. "I told you an' told you, bor. Ain't Henry on the throne now, it's Stephen. Old Henry's dead and gone these many a year."

"He never told me."

"Well, he wouldn't, would he? Him bein' a king and dead."

As always, the little wooden church smelled of cooking from the rush tapers that had been dipped in fat. Scutney couldn't afford beeswax candles; anyway, rushes gave out a prettier light.

"Get on with it, will ee?" Brother Arth struggled out of the rough woolen cope he wore to take the services and into the sheepskin cloak that was his working wear in winter. "I got ditchin' and molin' to see to."

They all had, but the villagers stayed where they were—it was as well to be informed about what was going on in them uplands.

Sala stretched back his shoulders and addressed his audience again. "So this King Stephen's started a-warring with his cousin the empress Matilda. Remember as I told you old King Henry on his deathbed wanted his daughter, this Matilda, to rule England? But the nobles, they don't want no blasted female queenin' it over un, so they've said no and gives the crown to Stephen, old Henry's nephew."

He looked sternly into the standing congregation. "Got that, Bert, now, have you? Good. Well now, Matilda, she ain't best pleased with bein' passed over and seems she's brought an army as is a-fighting Stephen's army out there some'eres."

"That it?" Nyles asked.

"Enough, innit?" Sala was miffed that Nyles, the big man of the village because he owned more sheep than anybody else, hadn't been more receptive to the news. "I been tellin' you as there's a war goin' on out there."

"Allus is." Nyles shrugged.

"Excitin', though, Pa, ain't it?" asked eleven-year-old Em, looking up at him.

Nyles cuffed his daughter lightly about her red head for her forwardness in speaking in church. She was his favorite, but it didn't do to let females get out of hand, especially not this one. "Well, good luck to 'em, I say. And now let's get on with that ditchin' and bloody molin'."

But old Sala, irritated by the interruption, raised his hand. "And I'll tell you summat else, Nyles. And you'll want to listen this time. Want to be keeping a close eye on that one, you will," he said, pointing at Em. "Folk say as there's a band o' mercenaries riding round 'ere like the wild hunt and with 'em there's a monk, likes redheads he does. Does terrible things when ee finds 'em, too."

Nyles shook his head indulgently and turned toward the door. He knew old Sala with his scaremongering and preposterous tales of abroad, and yet he suddenly felt inexplicably chilly and, without realizing it, had reached out and drawn the child closer to him. Daft old bugger.

"That it then, Sala?" he asked. The old man looked deflated but nodded, and with that the men, women and children of Scutney trooped out of its church to continue their own, unceasing war—against water.

The North Sea, that great enemy, was always threatening to drown East Anglia in one of its rages, submerging fields and cattle, even lapping the just-above-sea-level islands that dotted the flattest land in England. In winter, the sluggish rivers and great drains had to be cleared of weeds or they clogged and overflowed.

Oh, and the mole, as big an enemy as the sea, had to be killed to stop the little bugger from weakening the dykes with his bloody tunnels.

No, the people of Scutney didn't have time to spare from their watery business to bother about wars between the danged nobles. Anyway, they were safe because just over there—over *there,* bor, see them towers in the distance?—was Ely, greatest cathedral in England.

Every year, the villagers had to deliver four thousand glistening, squirming eels to Ely in return for being protected by Saint Etheldreda, whose bones lay in a jeweled tomb within the cathedral walls.

Powerful saint, Etheldreda, an Anglo-Saxon like themselves, and although Scutney people resented the number of eels they had to catch in order to feed her monks, they were grateful to her for keeping them safe from the outside world with its battles and carryings-on.

Oh yes, any bugger who came a-trampling and a-killing in this part of the fens'd soon have his arse kicked out of it by good old Saint Ethel.

That's if the bugger could find it in the first place and didn't drown in the meres or get led astray by spirits of the dead who took the shape of flickering jack-o'-lantern flames in the marshes by night.

Folk allus said that for an enemy force to attack Ely it'd take a traitor to show the secret causeways leading to it. And who'd be so dang-blasted stupid as to betray Saint Etheldreda? Get sent straight to hell, he would.

Such was the attitude.

But a traitor was even now preparing his treachery, and the war was about to penetrate Scutney's fenland for all that Saint Etheldreda in her five-hundred-year-old grave could do about it.

THE FIRST THE VILLAGE KNEW of its fate was when soldiers sent by Hugh Bigod turned up to take its men away to build him a new castle.

"Bigod?" roared Nyles, struggling between two captors while his redheaded elder daughter batted at their legs with a frying pan. "We don't owe him nothing. We're Ely's men."

Hugh Bigod, newly Earl of Norfolk, owned a large proportion of East Anglia. The Scutney villagers had seen him in his fine clothes swanking it at Ely with their bishop during Christmas feasts and suchlike. Didn't like him much. But then, they didn't like anybody from Norfolk. Didn't like the next village across the marshes, come to that.

Nor was he their overlord, as was being energetically pointed out to his soldiers. "Tha's not law, bor. We ain't none of his. What's he want another castle for? He've got plenty."

"And now he do want another one," the soldiers' sergeant said, "in case Empress Matilda do attack un. There's a war on, bor."

"Ain't my war," Nyles told him, still struggling.

"Is now," the sergeant said, "and if them nippers of yourn don't cease bashing my legs, they'll be its bloody casualties."

For Em had now been joined by her younger sister, Gyltha, wielding an iron spit.

"Leave it," Nyles told his girls. But they wouldn't, and their mother had to drag them off.

Holding them tightly, Aenfled watched her husband and every other able-bodied man being marched off along the roddon that led eventually to Cambridge.

"Us'll be back, girl," Nyles shouted at her over his shoulder, "but get they sheep folded, an' don't ee sell our hay for a penny under thruppence a stook, an' look to that danged roof afore winter's in, and . . ." He had suddenly remembered old Sala's warning in the church. "Keep Em close . . ." And then he was too far away to be heard.

The women of Scutney stood where they were, their men's instructions becoming fainter and fainter until only an echo came sighing back to them and even that faded, so that the air held merely the frightened bawling of their babies and the call of geese flying overhead.

They didn't cry; fenwomen never wept.

THE MEN STILL HADN'T COME back by the beginning of Lent.

It was a hard winter that one, too. Birds dropped out of the air, killed by the cold. The rivers froze and dead fish could be seen enclosed in their ice. The old died in their huts, the sheep in their pens.

In the turbaries, spades dulled themselves on peat that had become as hard as iron, so that fuel became scarce and it was necessary for tired, overworked women and their families to venture further and further away from the village in order to retrieve the peat bricks that had been stacked a year before to provide fire for shepherds during the lambing season.

On Saint Valentine's Day, it was the turn of Aenfled and her children to trundle a barrow into the marsh to fetch fuel. They'd left nothing behind in the woolly line and the thickness of their wrappings gave them the look of disparately sized gray statues perambulating through a gray landscape. Their breath soaked into the scarves round their mouths and turned to ice, but a veil of mist in the air promised that the weather might, just might, be on the turn. The children both carried bows and arrows in case a duck or goose flew within range.

Tucked into Em's belt was a little carved wooden key that Durwyn, Brother Arth's son, had shyly and secretly shoved into her hand that morning.

Gyltha wouldn't leave the subject alone. "Wants to unlock your heart, he do. You got to wed un now."

"Sod that," Em said, "I ain't never getting married and certainly not to a saphead like Durwyn. Anyways, I ain't old enough an' he ain't rich enough."

"You kept his old key, though."

"Tha'll be on the fire tonight," Em promised her, "keep us warm."

They stopped; they'd felt the drumming of hoofbeats through their boots. Horsemen were cantering along the causeway behind them.

"Get into they bloody reeds," hissed Aenfled. She pushed her barrow over the causeway's edge and tumbled her children after it.

Horses were rare in the fenland, and those traveling at speed suggested their riders were up to no good. Maybe these were friendly, maybe not, but lately there'd been nasty rumors of villages sacked by demons; women raped, sometimes even murdered; and grain stores burned. Aenfled was taking no chances.

There was just time to squirm through the reeds to where the thick, bare fronds of a willow gave them some cover.

Her hand clasped firmly over the mouth of her younger daughter, not yet old enough to silence with a look, Aenfled prayed: *Sweet Mary, let un go past, go past.*

Go past, go past, urged Em, *make un go past.* Through the lattice of reeds above her head, she saw flicks of earth being thrown up as the leading horses went by. She bowed her head in gratitude. *Thank ee, Saint Ethel, thank ee, I'll never be wicked no more.*

But one of the middle riders pulled up. "Swear as I saw something dive into that bloody ditch."

"Deer?" One of the leaders stopped his horse abruptly and turned back. As he approached the wind picked up, lifting his robes and revealing the animal's flanks, which were lathered white with sweat and dripping blood from a set of vicious-looking spurs.

Keeping still as still, Em smelled the stink of the men above her: sweat, dirt, horses, blood and a strange, pungent smell that was foreign to her.

"Coulda been."

"Flush the bastard out then. What are you waiting for?"

Spears began thudding into the ditch. One of the men dismounted and started scrambling down, hallooing as he went.

Em knew they were done. Then her mouth set itself into the thin, determined line that her sorely tried mother would have recognized and dreaded. *No we ain't. Not if I lead 'em away.* She pushed her sister's head more firmly into the ground and leapt for the bank. A willow twig twitched the cap from her head as she went, releasing the flame-red curls that hid beneath, but although she paused briefly, she didn't stop for it. Now she was running.

Aenfled kept Gyltha clutched to her, her moans and prayers covered by the whoops of the men. She heard the one who'd come into the ditch climb back out of it and join the hunt. She heard hoofbeats start up again. She heard male laughter growing fainter as the riders chased their prey further and further into the marsh. She heard the faraway screams as they caught Em and knew her daughter was fighting. She heard the horses ride off with her.

Birds of the marsh that had flown up in alarm settled back into their reed beds and resumed their silence.

In the ditch Aenfled stopped praying.

Except for her daughter's soul, she never prayed again.

CHAPTER 2

February, AD 1141, Kenniford Castle, Oxfordshire

STANDING IN HER OWN CHAPEL in her own castle for her own wedding, sixteen-year-old Maud of Kenniford wondered whether they'd even have the courtesy to ask if she'd take this man, fifty-three-year-old Sir John of Tewing, to be her lawful wedded husband.

If they did, the honest answer would be: "What in hell else can I do?"

The question being put at the moment by the mud-flecked, out-of-breath priest in front of her was: "Who giveth this woman . . . ?"

At which point, one of the Beaumont twins grabbed her arm and pulled her forward. "I do, Waleran de Meulan, Earl of Worcester. This lady is a ward of our blessed king Stephen. In his name do I give her to this man. And for the sake of God, get on with it."

The earl, like this priest he'd brought with him, like the dozen or so knights surrounding Maud, smelled of sweat, horse and panic. They'd fled the Battle of Lincoln, which they'd apparently lost, to race here and marry her off to a man she'd never seen before in the name of a king who'd been captured—might not even be king anymore.

For all they knew the empress's forces were about to overwhelm the country, a disaster to be avoided at all costs because, as queen of England, Matilda would take away the lands of those who'd opposed her, *their* lands.

And one of the costs, to Maud at any rate, was a marriage that would put said Maud's castle, and, more importantly, the vital crossing it commanded over the upper Thames, into the hands of said John of Tewing, one of King Stephen's most loyal supporters, so that the empress could be denied access to the west if she came this way.

Matilda's own supporters, her head steward, Sir Bernard; her cousin Lynessa; and Father Nimbus, who were to be witnesses, were hemmed in by a group of Stephen's knights in case they objected—indeed, the Earl of Leicester, Waleran's brother, was holding a dagger suggestively near Father Nimbus's throat. Milburga, her nurse, had elbowed her way in, and not even England's foremost barons had been able to deny her, nor dared.

Sir Rollo, the commander of Maud's troops, stood in the bailey below with his milling soldiers, bellowing up at the chapel window: "Are you all right, my lady?"

No, I'm not, you stupid old pillock. Why in hell did you open the gates?

Strictly speaking, of course, Sir Rollo had had no choice, just as Lynessa, Milburga and Father Nimbus could make no objection as long as Maud gave her consent. Kenniford was already nominally held for the king, to whom, at the coronation, Maud's dying father had chosen to pay homage, leaving Maud and her inheritance in Stephen's wardship to be bestowed on whomsoever the king wished to reward.

Unlucky gifts for the bestowees, as it had turned out. It became known that to choose Maud of Kenniford as a bride was to choose one's coffin—a superstition that suited Maud down to her shoes. All Stephen's three choices for her had died before their marriage could take place; the first broke his neck in a hunting accident, ditto the second in a tournament, while the third, a five-year-old—Maud's favored choice because she thought she'd have no difficulty managing him—had shown deplorable carelessness by drowning in a well.

But John of Tewing was prepared to court bad luck. He was bad luck himself. She wouldn't be able to manage *him*, that was for sure. He was overlarge, grizzled, scarred, lumbering, rank like a bear. The man's manners were as boorish as his appearance; he had even brought his concubine with him, a sullen-looking, unkempt woman by the name of Kigva who was lurking in the corner of the room staring sourly at Maud.

Hello. The officiating priest was turning to her, opening his mouth, asking *the* question without which the marriage would not be strictly legal. "Do you, Maud of Kenniford, take this man . . . ?"

Maud turned to look at Father Nimbus, ever her confessor and adviser. Despite the knife at his neck, the little priest's eyes were urging her to say no. This was too rushed, too dangerous for her future. While they were being hurried up the stairs to the chapel, he'd managed to hiss at her: "Sweetness! The man's an absolute hog, just *look* at his fingernails. Tell them you want to be a nun. Tell them you'll enter Godstow convent. Tell them you're vowed to the Virgin."

Oh yes, that would go down well. Several female saints and martyrs had tried that one, and achieved sainthood through martyrdom because of it.

The only reason these desperate men around her were bothering with a marriage ceremony at all, and weren't taking over the castle willy-nilly, was that her own soldiers in the bailey outnumbered them two to one. Sir Rollo might not have been very bright, but his affection lay with neither the king nor the empress; it was Maud's. If she gave the signal, he and his men would fight for her. On the other hand, if she gave her consent, John of bloody Tewing immediately became their legal, and therefore not-to-be-disputed, commander. And hers.

The little chapel smelled, as it always did, of age and incense and whatever scented herbs the fastidious Father Nimbus mixed with it.

Her father had commissioned a monk from Abingdon to paint its walls, so that the child Maud could learn her Bible from the depictions of the Garden of Eden (rather jolly), the Ascension, the Wise Men worshipping a plump baby Jesus and the one that had always fascinated her—a depiction of virtuous Judith cutting off Holofernes's head, which Father Nimbus had wanted obliterated for being too bloody, but her father had said counteracted Salome and John the Baptist.

It was remarkable, Maud thought, how much her bridegroom resembled the bestial, drunken Holofernes.

The officiating priest was putting the question again: "Do you, Maud of Kenniford . . . ?" She felt Waleran's hand tighten on her arm.

"Wait, will you?" she snapped. "I'm thinking about it."

An arranged marriage at some time or another had been inevitable. Kenniford with its manors and lands was a valuable prize to bestow on anyone the king wanted to reward; Maud's own wishes had never been consulted, and never would be. While the present incumbent repelled her, so had the owners of the two broken necks, one a raving madman with a high laugh, the other a drinker never seen sober. Would this brute be so bad?

Maud considered it logically. He was old, which was in his favor; he would oblige her by dying, and, to judge from his choleric complexion, sooner rather than later. He was a renowned warrior—also in his favor, since he would spend much of his time away fighting battles in which somebody might kill him. With luck and the intervention of the Holy Virgin, to whom she would step up her praying from now on, he might rush off to war right away and save her the horror of the wedding night.

After all, even if she were allowed to adopt Father Nimbus's ploy and go into a convent, it would mean giving up Kenniford and her other lands forever. Which she could not do.

Since the age of nine, on the death of her father, Maud had ruled her estates and their people like a despot. She was lucky in that the blood in her veins came from both Anglo-Saxon and Norman nobility—she was descended from King Edward the Elder on her mother's side and Roger d'Ivry, sheriff of Gloucester, on her father's—which, until she should marry, gave her a legal right to command two castles (admittedly, one of them little more than a motte and bailey in Cambridgeshire and nothing to compare with Kenniford), five manors scattered around England and three more in Normandy, as well as the advowson of six churches, all of them acknowledging her as their overlord just as she acknowledged the king of England and Normandy as hers.

She had been well advised, of course; her father's head steward, Sir Bernard, was a loyal and wise administrator, but he had found in his young mistress a mind quite as shrewd as his own, capable of retaining in it a record of her every acreage of plowland, herd and grazing; which of her hundreds of tenants were free and which villeins; what dues they paid her; which of her knights owed her military service and which owed castle guard; those who, by tradition, must render her seven geese or embroidered gloves, etc., on which saints' days, or make some other service. (Maud took particular delight in the dues owed by William of Garthbrook, who held the tenancy of thirty Sussex acres and had to simultaneously perform a leap, a whistle and a fart at every one of her Christmas feasts.)

Never again to command her willing garrison, to order her kitchens, to sit in judgment on wrongdoers while rewarding the virtuous, to bully and physic the villagers outside her walls, to oversee the harvest, to dominate the Christmas feast . . . to change all that for incarceration in Godstow convent? Her soul would shrivel to nothing.

Yes, marriage would mean handing over her men and women to this husband, but she would still be around to protect them—a duty and a joy with which God had entrusted her.

Waleran's hold on her arm had become tighter; the knife at Father Nimbus's neck was pricking his skin. She could hear Sir Rollo gathering his men to charge the tower.

These were her people; she would not have one of them killed.

Marriage to this old lout would be a sort of death—but it had to be hers, not Kenniford's.

Maud came to the decision that she'd known from the first was the only one she could make.

"Oh, very well," she said. A murmur of relief flitted around the room like a breeze interrupted only by a howl of anguish from the Kigva woman.

DAMN THEM, THEY WEREN'T IN that much of a rush that they were going to gallop off into the night to put their castles on war footing without being fed first.

Maud, with a chaplet hastily made and crammed onto her head, sat with her new husband at the top table of her hall, miserable, but nevertheless congratulating herself and her kitchens for the efficiency with which the wedding feast had been prepared at short notice. Now that she'd done what they wanted, the Beaumont twins, on her left, were being fulsomely complimentary on the food, reverting to the gallantry they'd shown during her visits to court. Their charm had won them earldoms from Stephen—the king being susceptible to it. Waleran had even been given Stephen's four-year-old royal daughter in marriage, but the child had died soon after the wedding in the same month as Maud's infant fiancé, occasioning Maud and Waleran to exchange condolences, which she'd supposed—wrongly as it turned out now—had led to a coincidental and mutual regard.

"And your beef, lady. Is it Welsh? How do you produce such taste, such tenderness?"

"We hang it for two weeks like our enemies," Maud said shortly. Damned if she was going to be lured into a conversation on cattle breeding with them, interesting as the subject was.

On the other hand, they were the only ones she *could* converse with. Her husband was still not addressing her, preferring to quiz Sir Rollo about wall thickness and the siting of arrow slits, all the time spraying the poor man with food grabbed from dishes by his unwashed hand and chewed in his open mouth, lubricated with swigs of her best wine.

Maud passed him one of her linen napkins without comment and turned to Waleran. "After such a defeat at Lincoln," she said, rubbing it in, "what are we to expect? Why must Kenniford be in readiness? Isn't the king overthrown and the war over? Isn't the empress now queen?"

No, it appeared she wasn't. Again, Maud found herself excluded as the twins took the first chance they'd had since Lincoln to make a careful analysis of the situation, but she listened hard. Until today—politics were not her interest—it hadn't bothered her whether Matilda or Stephen ruled England as long as Kenniford wasn't threatened. Now that it was . . .

First, it seemed, Empress Matilda's claim had to be ratified by the Church. "And what's the betting that bastard Henry deserts Stephen and persuades the other bishops?" Waleran said.

"She's got the West Country, of course."

"She hasn't got London."

Maud managed to identify "that bastard Henry" as the bishop of Winchester, the king's brother, a papal legate, one of the most powerful churchmen in England next to the archbishop of Canterbury. Stephen had been crowned with his help but had then offended him, so which way said bastard would turn could only be guessed at . . .

The West Country was dangerous, it appeared. Gloucester, of which the empress's adoring half brother was the earl and another bastard, in both senses of the word . . . Cirencester . . . Wilton . . . Reading . . . Oxford . . . they'd all accept his sister, if she could get there, God burn each and every one of the shit holes . . .

But the empress would need London, and London was a commune—come back everything Waleran and his twin had ever said about bloody communes—to which Stephen, God knows why, had shown a liberality that the empress, autocratic cow, was unlikely to extend to it. Yes, London was hopeful . . .

Normandy now . . . what of Normandy? Would Geoffrey Plantagenet, the empress's new husband, conquer that dukedom? He was making a damn good job of it at the moment . . . Mind you, was he doing it for himself? Or for the empress? Husband and wife didn't get on.

Maud struck in, to bring a touch of lightness.

"There you are," she said brightly. "One of you make peace with Geoffrey and then, if the empress *does* become queen of England and *does* prove vindictive and confiscates your estates over here, you'll still have Normandy."

Until that moment she hadn't appreciated how despairing they were. Two handsome pairs of eyes turned on her and in them she saw calculation. They were considering it, oh God, *actually considering it.*

Taking that way out, they'd still survive as powerful men; the twins owned vast estates on both sides of the channel, while she, Maud, held only a few. Having now placed her firmly in Stephen's diminishing camp, they'd put her at the empress's mercy. Without Kenniford and her other, smaller English estates, she'd be left with only a miserable Norman manor or two on which to subsist like a damned serf.

You bastards, she thought.

The exchange had succeeded in attracting John of Tewing's attention. Throughout the meal he had been pawing at Kigva, nuzzling her grubby neck and squeezing her breasts in such a vulgar display that it made Maud's stomach churn. Suddenly he turned to them and spat: "That bitch'll never be queen."

"God grant she won't," Waleran said, "but I wish I was as sure."

"Yah, where's your balls, boy? God'd strike her dead at the coronation, even if I didn't. A woman? Not natural. Women are for fucking, and that's all they're good for."

Every head turned to him in the sudden silence. Men who believed what he'd said had been taken aback by its being shouted at a mixed table.

To Maud, it was like being punched by an opponent whose

strength she hadn't realized before; she'd known she was handing over control, but it hadn't struck her with the force it did now. She was in the jaws of a dog. She looked at Kigva to see how she had taken it, but the vacant expression on her slack features registered neither shock nor effrontery, changing only to spite when she saw Maud staring at her.

She looked away quickly—the woman was as sinister as Sir John was brutish—and found that her knees managed to stiffen enough to get her to her feet. "Ladies," she said clearly, "it is time to leave the gentlemen to their wine." Kigva, she noticed, did not rise, and since only a few of the castle's women had attended the feast, she was followed only by Lynessa and Lady Morgana, a Welsh aunt on a visit.

As they went, Waleran belatedly rose to toast the bride on her wedding night: ". . . and may God bless this union with happiness and many sons." There was a ragged, self-conscious cheer.

Outside, Lynessa took Maud silently into her arms.

"They'll be off to war tonight, won't they?" Maud begged into the woman's ample shoulder. "They'll take him with them, won't they?"

"I don't know, my poor dear."

There was a halfhearted attempt to follow her to her chamber as bridesmaids should. "There ought to be ribbons and things, posies," Lynessa said, weeping. "Shall I fetch some?"

"No." This was one marriage bed that needn't be garlanded. Maud pushed herself away from Lynessa. "Festivities are not appropriate. You can leave me."

The only person she really wanted was Milburga, the nearest of her dearest, except for Father Nimbus.

Milburga was waiting for her by the bed, the room's brazier giving her ample body an even greater shadow on the wall. "I heard."

"Jesus God, what am I to do, what can I do?" Maud clutched her forehead, where, for the first time in her life, she felt thudding pain.

"Well, a headache ain't going to stop him. What you got to decide is, do you want his babies or not?"

"*No.*" The wall hangings absorbed a cry of revulsion. "Not his, never his." It would be like giving birth to monsters. There'd be time to have her own children by another, better husband when this one was dead.

"Didn't think you would, so I got you these." Milburga's outstretched hand held a clutch of feathery little seeds. She poured them onto the little table beside the bed.

"What are they?" Her nurse was an enthusiastic herbalist; there was nothing she liked better than a patient, a diagnosis and her own prescription, but occasionally her cures were as distressing as the disease. On the other hand, despite an enthusiastic and varied love life, Milburga had avoided all but two pregnancies.

"Plant seeds, as'll put paid to his, the pig. But you got to chew 'em well, otherwise they'll go straight through."

Seed. His seed. The repulsion was such that Maud began to retch. "Perhaps—ooogh—do you think—oh help me, God—Milly, do you think they'll take him with them when they go?"

There was no answer. Like Lynessa, Milburga didn't know.

Maud looked up at her. "I had to, though, didn't I? I had to say yes."

Milburga nodded. "I was a-watching that other earl. He'd've cut Girly's throat"—Father Nimbus's effeminacy drove Milburga mad—"and Lady Lynessy's an' then mine iffen you hadn't." She sat down on the bed and put her arm round Maud's shoulders. "There wasn't nothing else you could do."

The older woman and the younger stayed side by side, one head leaning against the other, Maud marginally comforted by the fact that she'd had no choice but to save the lives of precious people.

Comforted, that is, until a noise in the hall sent Milburga to the chamber door to listen, and turn back in distress. "They're bringin' him up."

"Mary, mother of God, be with me now."

She reached for the pile of seeds and began munching.

CHAPTER 3

February, AD 1141, Another Part of the Cambridgeshire Fens

HE'D HAVE STOPPED THEM GALLOPING off with the girl if he could, but he'd lost control of the men by then.

He'd lost his horse and all, because he'd dismounted to have a piss and given its reins to Ramon to hold. Which he shouldn't have, because that bastard had just been waiting for the opportunity to get rid of him.

So they'd taken off with her. *And* his horse. *And* the crossbow that had been in its saddlebag.

His *crossbow,* for Christ's sake. With that weapon, he was one of the finest arbalists in Christendom; without it, he was as helpless as the child. And her only ten, maybe eleven years old, poor scrap. Brave, though; fought like a terrier . . . but redheaded, unlucky that; the monk liked a redhead. He'd seen the look on the bastard's face when he came back from the last one; hadn't been able to save her, either.

The suffering man standing amidst the reed beds and pondering on these matters was somewhere around middle age and middle height; the skin of his face with its graying stubble and the black, bloodshot eyes was that of a dark Celt. As always in fenland, he felt so exposed to the vast sky—though it was misty at the moment—as to be under the eye of God.

This was not a comfortable position for a mercenary who was automatically damned by his profession; Gwilherm de Vannes had lost his soul a long time ago and was aware that, owing to recent events, he had small chance of finding it again.

He had witnessed things lately enough to shock the devil—the plunder of Ely cathedral, the murder of monks and women and children—and although he had played no part in it, his mere proximity to the atrocities had been enough to damn him. No two ways about it, his soul was lost for good.

Nevertheless, he dropped to one knee in order to pray for the deliverance of the little girl he'd just seen abducted and, while he was about it, for the restitution of his crossbow so that he could kill the men who'd taken both.

He listened for an answer and heard only the rustle of wildlife in the reeds and the mocking *ke-ke-ke* of a hen harrier as it quartered the marsh.

Well, what did he expect? Rustling slightly himself—he wore a mail hauberk over boiled leather under his cloak—Gwil stood up, took off his helmet and looked about him.

Where the hell was he, apart from deeply in the shit?

He saw flatness, just flatness extending into mist; reed, marsh, black water—he'd seen little else since Lincoln.

Lincoln. The only pitched battle so far in this war of sieges—and they'd lost it. The last Gwil had seen of King Stephen, he'd been surrounded by the enemy, laying about him with an axe.

Brave man, Stephen, and a bloody dolt. William of Ypres had begged him: "Wait and send for reinforcements, my lord."

Had he? Oh no, waiting for reinforcements to come was against the royal manhood, apparently.

So they'd attacked the bloody castle and its defenders had come storming out, yelling like berserkers, and overwhelmed them.

A fucking rout, that's what it had been. Most of Gwil's contingent had made for the river and, to judge from their cries, drowned in it. He himself had mounted the nearest riderless horse and charged through Stephen's knights while they were still laying down their arms. All right for fucking knights; they got ransomed, enjoying nice dinners and comfortable beds while their knightly captors waited for the money to come in. Poor bloody mercenaries like him got hanged.

He and a group of others had ridden south with the empress's soldiers in full cry after them, heading for the cover of Lincolnshire's fens and then, throwing off the pursuit, further south into the even deeper fenland of Cambridgeshire, not knowing what fucking awful country it was. If he ever got out, he wouldn't come back there. You got lost in it; flickering lights tempted you to follow them at night, but if you did you were never seen again; bog that could suck rider and horse into it—and had. And *cold,* cold enough to shrivel your bollocks.

At first he'd more or less been able to command the small band of mercenaries. Yes, all right, they'd raided the occasional village for food as they went, but never more than they needed and there had been no killing; he'd never allow that.

Until that weird bloody monk had joined them, him and that bastard Ramon.

God alone knew how those two objects had teamed up. Ramon was only a bloody stone slinger for Christ's sake, lowest form of mercenary life. Who the monk was you couldn't tell; never gave his name, never removed his cowl, but he reeked of asafetida, of all things. It was a smell Gwil recognized from the old days when he'd been serving under old Sir Hugh d'Arromanches, a former crusader with bad digestion—an affliction he attributed to the rich food of Palestine—who spiked his every meal with it.

"Stops me breaking wind all the time, d'ye see?" he'd declared. "Great stuff for avoidin' embarrassment in front of the ladies, asafoetida." (Privately, his men had thought that ladies would probably prefer to be embarrassed than have their noses unremittingly assaulted by the all-pervading, pungent stink of the spice that enveloped the old knight.)

Taken individually, Gwil could have commanded Ramon and the anonymous monk, but together they'd radiated a powerful insanity that the others had mistaken for leadership. Terrorizing, ransacking every village they came to and leaving it on fire—it had been madness, as Gwil had pointed out: "What's the fucking point of setting every man-jack's hand against us?"

But he'd been forced to stay with them because it *had* set every hand against them; any mercenary caught on his own now wouldn't have bollocks left to shrivel.

And then Ely.

At first, even Ramon had balked at attacking a cathedral, but the monk had been set on it.

Ely's bishop, the monk said in that strange, thin voice of his, was still in exile for having supported the empress, and most of Ely's knights with him. Only a handful of monks guarded its treasures, he'd said. "And I know the secret causeway to it."

I bet you do, you bastard, Gwil had thought, *and got your own reasons for betraying it.*

But Ramon had heard the word "treasures" and that was enough.

So they'd gone in and plundered. Well, he, Gwil, hadn't. Not exactly *plundered.* With a mercenary's priorities, he'd gone straight to the kitchens to take food, a bottle or two, and a pinch or so of tinder fungus . . .

All right, *all right,* he'd called in at the bishop's empty house on his way and filched some coins from the money box—he needed it more than a bloody bishop—but he hadn't killed anybody.

Ramon had, though, along with the others. When he emerged, Gwil had found corpses of monks butchered on the steps of the cathedral where the poor buggers'd tried to protect the jeweled relics of the saints who lay inside it.

If he hadn't been doomed before, Gwil knew then that, by association, he was doomed now. They'd been powerful saints in there, Anglo-Saxon saints made more powerful by being in their own country.

Even Ramon had felt intimidated by what he'd done once the killing madness left him. Interestingly, the monk had not. And the pack mules they'd both acquired carried sacks that clinked with gold and jewels.

Anyway, they'd galloped away from the place with revengeful spirits breathing down their necks.

It was soon after that when the child had bolted up under their hooves from out of a ditch and into the reeds.

Gwil, horseless and stranded, had watched them go after her. *Run, run, girl, in the name of God run.*

But her hair had betrayed her as she went, bending low. It had trailed like a fiery comet through the reeds, the only color in the grayness. And even from this distance Gwil had seen the monk fix on her, like a hawk on a mouse.

They'd herded her, playing with her, cutting off her escape this way, then that.

Brave little devil, too; fought like a wildcat when they caught her—Ramon's nose wouldn't regain its shape for a week. Her screams had stayed in Gwil's ears long after he'd lost sight of them all.

"Lord," he begged again, "I'd have saved her if I could."

Again the marsh harrier mocked him, *ke-ke-ke*. It was right; no good dwelling on it; she was past praying for by this time.

And so are you, my lad.

He found that once more he'd fallen to his knees. He got up.

The appearance of a weak sun was clearing away the mist, allowing him to get his bearings. He looked about him again. And *shit*—something was emerging out of the sky to the northwest. Towers were formulating themselves as if out of cloud, giving the impression that they were floating above the ground.

Ely.

Either he'd been walking in a circle or the place was pursuing him. And him with some of its bishop's gold in the pack on his back.

Quickly, limping slightly, Gwilherm de Vannes set off southwest through the marsh, wishing he wasn't exposed as the tallest thing in it.

Wishing he could have saved the girl.

BY DUSK HE WAS NEARING the fen edge; he could tell that much because he was up to his knees in bracken, and the trees that darkened it here and there were beeches, signifying that he'd left peat for chalk. He'd hoped to strike a road by this time but couldn't even see a path.

The mist had been a false promise; the darkening sky was clear, every star showing, and the air freezing.

He blundered on, not wanting to build a fire he could lie down by in case he attracted unwelcome attention, but knowing that if he didn't rest soon he'd fall down and, in this cold, never get up again.

A few minutes later, he was in a clearing and approaching what had once been a small village set around a well.

To begin with he thought Ramon and the others must have come upon it; then he saw that the burned houses were an older devastation, an early casualty of Stephen and Matilda's war perhaps. Weeds had grown among the ash.

The only building left standing was a tiny church, a plain, unadorned rectangle of stone no more than thirty feet long. Its blackened patches showed the raiders had tried to put that to the torch as well but had been defeated by sturdy Saxon masonry. Though its thatch had gone, a nearby yew tree, its trunk almost burned through, had fallen sideways onto its roof and provided cover of a sort.

Sanctuary.

In the fading light, Gwil gathered bracken and what dry wood he could find to carry in. The church's interior was no warmer than outside and full of rubble. He had to clear a space to build and light a fire in virtual darkness, but he was an old hand and the tinder fungus from Ely lit at the first spark of flint on steel. Feeding it fronds of bracken, he began puffing . . .

Once he had his fire going, he looked around for something to make a tripod from which to suspend his helmet—it was also his cooking pot—over the flames.

Charred but serviceable beams from the roof had fallen on the rough stone table that served as an altar at the church's eastern end. They'd do.

He was taking his pick of the spars when his boot stubbed against something yielding. Bending down, he saw that an animal had crawled under the altar to die.

He took hold of one of its legs and pulled.

It was a girl, naked and filthy, cold as all dead things are. The long hair on its head was reddish under its dirt. Christ have mercy, it was *the* girl. They'd done it to her here.

He let go and turned away because the dried blood between the corpse's legs was as indecent as the crime that had caused it. He had to get rid of it. Bury it quickly to hide its shame.

It whimpered.

"*Don't be alive,*" he told it, shrinking backward away from it. "*Be dead.*"

He picked up its arms and dragged it near the fire. Put his cloak over it.

Then he went outside and interested his mind by looking for their tracks so that he could follow them and get his crossbow back.

It was too dim to see much, though enough to be sure that there weren't any tracks—at least, not of horses and men, only his own footprints and, where the girl had crawled, a trail of slime that led into the church.

For a bit, he followed that back into the bracken from which it had come, until it disappeared in the darkness.

Not here, then; they hadn't done it here. But not too far off; near enough for her to crawl to this place once they'd finished with her. That meant they might be camping only a hundred or so yards away. He listened and heard birds settling down for the night.

So they'd moved on; by this time they'd have been noisy with drink. Still, in the morning he could follow the track . . .

Gwilherm de Vannes. The voice came from the church behind him.

He didn't turn round. "What?"

She's still in here.

"I know, Lord."

You said you'd save her if you could.

He blustered. That had been then, when she'd still been whole and clean. Anyway, he didn't know how; she'd probably die anyway, and . . . oh *shit,* you had to be bloody careful when you invoked God; He could amuse Himself by granting what you'd prayed for . . .

He went back into the church, fetched his helmet and carried it to the well. The windlass was frozen but some water in the bottom of its bucket came out in a block of ice. In his pack there was a clean cloth—well, cleanish—that he kept for polishing the crossbow stock.

Inside the church once more, he built the tripod and hung his helmet from it, put in the ice to melt, took the cloth from his pack and, with reluctance, removed his cloak from the thing on the floor ready to begin the process of washing it . . .

SHE KEPT WAKING HIM UP with her whimpering, and then he'd prod her cheek to see if it was getting warmer, which it was.

In the morning she was still alive. By now his helmet contained a broth made with the beef he'd filched from Ely's kitchen, some salt and a good drop from Ely's brandy bottle.

He went outside to have a piss and gather some sage from an herb patch in one of the ruined gardens—he'd once heard that sage was good for feminine troubles. It added richness to the already rich-smelling contents of his helmet, but then came the problem of how to get the broth down her.

He consumed most of it while he thought about it.

In the end, going outside again, he used his knife to cut into the fallen yew tree and whittle a spoon out of its wood. He forced her lips open with it and let some of the remaining broth dribble in drop by drop.

Her hair bothered him; he supposed he should have washed that as well but there was too much of it, and it smelled disgusting—he didn't like to think of what. God, they'd done everything to her; there'd been blood round her nose, bruises all over. How many of them?

Yet he couldn't feel pity; she made him feel queasy—her, them, himself for having traveled with them.

Another thing he hadn't been able to clean was her right hand. It had something clamped in it so tightly he hadn't wanted to force the fingers open for fear of breaking them in the process.

In the bright afternoon—it was getting warmer—he followed the track she'd made and came across the clearing where they'd stripped her and afterward left her naked, to die in the cold. They'd taken her cloak and boots with them, those being salable items; the only things they'd left were her stockings and her underdress, tunic, kirtle, whatever females called it—a stained and tattered thing, but he decided to take it to her.

Hoofprints showed they'd then headed south. He nodded to himself; he'd come across them one of these days . . .

Back in the village, he stood in its center and wondered how long it would be before the survivors of its destruction—if there were any—came back to rebuild it, or knock down the church for its stone. Stone was so rare in fenland that, until now, the only bit he'd seen was an ancient stone where thrushes and blackbirds came from miles around to crack snails open against it.

She's still in here, Gwil.

"I'm coming, aren't I?"

His supper was a slice of Ely's loaf toasted—it was getting hard by now—and a few of the broth's chunks of boiled meat. He'd need supplies tomorrow. If the girl bucked up, her village would give him some when he took her back to it.

Throwing down the tunic where she could see it, he took a last look at her before he settled himself for the night, edging his cloak more closely about her with his foot.

Her fingers had uncurled and the object she'd been clutching now lay loose against her right palm.

He took it from her gently and held it toward the light of the fire to examine it. It was a scrap of good black worsted wool entwined around a wooden tube such as scribes used to protect their quills.

The wool was part of a cloak's inner pocket and smelled strongly of asafetida—the monk's without a doubt, torn off his cloak by the girl during the assault.

Using his thumbnail, Gwil prized off the tube's lid. No quills, but a piece of parchment that, unrolled, showed itself to be covered in writing. Gwil could recognize Latin when he saw it, even if he couldn't read it, but this wasn't Latin; the letters weren't the right shape and there were marks over the tops of some of them.

He rolled the thing up and reinserted it into the tube before putting it in his pack. Whatever it was, the monk had valued it, and the fact that he would be displeased when he discovered its loss was a good reason for him, Gwil, to keep hold of it.

Turning back to the girl, he saw that, alarmingly, her eyes had flicked open and fixed on him.

He'd practiced what he would say. "You, safe, now," he told her slowly and loudly in English. "I, am, Breton." He didn't want her to think he was a fucking Fleming. Whether they fought for Stephen or the empress, the Flemish mercenaries weren't exactly endearing themselves to the people of England.

Her eyes stayed on him. Not a child's eyes now; vicious and terrified, more like a cornered weasel's. He wished she'd close them again. "You hurt. You, all, right, now. Tomorrow, I take, you, home."

Nothing.

Gwil, whose travels had enabled him to get by in most languages, wondered if she spoke English. Nothing. He tried Norman French: "Where, you, from? What, your, name?"

Nothing.

In the end he placed his helmet with its remaining chunks of meat within her reach, crumbled some bread in it, added a drop or two of brandy after swigging some himself and retired to the nest that served him as a bed near the door on the other side of the fire.

For a while he continued the work of yesterday—shaping a bow out of the fallen yew's heartwood; he needed a weapon of some kind. Fletching arrows for it would be the bloody problem.

He was aware of the girl warily watching every move of his knife. Well, he could understand that; there'd been cuts around her . . . her underparts, showing they'd used a dagger as well.

Reassuringly, he stiffened his face into a smile, wagged the knife at her and then tapped it on the wood. "Make bow," he said, "shoot birds for pot."

Nothing.

Well, he'd done his best.

He whittled on until he fell asleep.

A thump in his chest jerked him awake to see her hobbling out of the church. He looked down at what had hit him, and there was his own damned knife sticking into the front of his hauberk . . . *Jesus Christ, she'd tried to stab him.*

She was making for the trees, his cloak clutched to her and tripping her up.

"You little bitch, what you do that for?" He launched himself at her, grabbed her as she stumbled once more and hauled her back into the church, throwing her onto the bracken bed he'd so kindly made for her. "You could've killed me."

She couldn't have actually and he knew it; it took strength to penetrate mail and the boiled leather beneath it, but she hadn't known that and she'd tried, the little cow.

He addressed the small cowering shape. "I should've let you go." He was tempted to do it yet. "See how far you'd get on your own in the dark. Tomorrow you go home. And where is that? Eh? *Eh?*"

In a temper, he started to interrogate her again. He didn't know what else to do. Who she? Where come from? He, good, man. *Good* man. Her, ungrateful girl. What her damned name?

Though she flinched with every syllable, her sharp little eyes never stopped watching him and eventually he gave up. "Go and good riddance." He flapped his arm at her. "You'll bloody perish out there, and see if I care."

Stumping back to his bed, he picked up the knife from where it had fallen, waved it at her and, with some ceremony, put it back in its sheath, which he placed in his pack. Then, using the pack as a pillow, he lay down and made great play of pretending to go to sleep.

You're just a man's shape to her, Gwil, no wonder she can't trust you.

"I don't care, Lord. She should mind her manners."

But—

"I'm not listening." And he put his fingers in his ears and began to hum.

SHE WAS STILL THERE IN the morning, curled up under his cloak in the bracken like a leveret in its form. He was aware of her watching him as he shaved, a job he'd not done for some days. Dipping the knife into the water of his helmet, he said: "Get dressed. Today I take you home."

Nothing.

It occurred to him—he congratulated himself for the delicacy of thinking of it—that she might be reluctant to wear an underdress that was as fouled and ripped as her body had been.

The well's windlass had thawed out and he was able to bring up a good bucketful of water, which he took in to her. "Laundry time."

She understood that, he noticed, and while he rasped the rest of his chin and cheeks with the blade of his knife, she raised herself enough to wash the thing, showing the expert twist of the wrist all competent females should have.

The interrogation began again. What was she called? Where did she live?

For the first time her face showed an emotion other than fear and hatred—it was puzzlement, bordering on panic.

She doesn't know who she is, the Lord said. *Remember when Ernous got that dint on his helmet? Couldn't remember his own name for days.*

Gwil experienced a panic of his own. "She's got to, Lord. I'm not getting stuck with her. What more d'You want of me?"

After all, he couldn't build a church like the bloody rich did when they needed forgiveness of sins, but this girl God had presented him with was alive, not dead, and all because of him. That should count for something when he encountered Saint Peter at the gates of heaven.

Enough, is it, Gwil?

He battled with the answer all morning while he finished the bow and made some arrow shafts.

In the afternoon he went out to look for feathers and found a pigeon dismembered by a fox. Pigeon feathers didn't make good flights but they'd have to do until he could shoot a goose.

He hoped she might be gone when he got back, but she was still there sitting quietly, draped in his cloak, her head in her hands. Her tunic was drying on the tripod; so were her hose, though not their bindings, and God alone knew where they were.

Gwil sighed and pulled a bowstring out of his pack, cut it in half and threw the pieces toward her, pointing to her thick, woolen stockings. "Tie 'em up with that," he told her.

He made himself scarce while she dressed herself. A right little tatterdemalion she looked when he got back, but at least she was decent beneath his cloak.

There was only water to drink now, and a cheese left in the cache from Ely; he gave her a quarter and ate the rest himself before settling down to an evening's fletching.

He made one last try before going to sleep. "What's your name?"

"Can't remember."

Holy saints, it spoke. "Can't remember your own name? Can't remember what happened?"

She hissed at him between her little white stoat's teeth.

He thought for a while, wondering what to do next, and decided on comfort. "You was hit on the head. It'll come back. You be a good girl, now."

In the night, he was woken by a touch on his body. He'd been careless; he'd put the knife back in the sheath on his belt rather than in his pack and those sharp little eyes of hers had seen him and she'd grabbed it. Only this time he wasn't her intended victim.

By the time he was on his feet, she'd escaped with it to the other side of the fire and with a jolt he realized that she was going to turn it on herself; women did that apparently, killed themselves when they'd been shamed.

He held out his hand. "You don't want that. Give it back to me like a good girl."

She began backing away toward the far end of the church and raised the knife to her throat—but to his relief, instead of slicing her flesh, she began hacking at her own hair. And all the time her gaze was on him, as if he ought to understand. Her left hand held a hank of the filthy curls; the right sawed away at them at ear level.

"Ain't a girl," she said as he gaped in astonishment. Now the right side had gone and she was groping for the hair at the back. "Ain't a girl."

She was mad, that's what it was. They'd sent her mad, and small wonder.

Small wonder if she doesn't want to be a female anymore, Gwil, the Lord agreed. *Would you?*

"Does she remember what happened then? Or don't she?"

But God, having as little comprehension of the feminine mind as any male, did not reply.

Yet the metamorphosis was extraordinary. The crop-headed little figure glaring at him in the tunic and bulky hose was transformed into a boy. What had been viciousness was now courage to be admired; the repugnancy of its survival had become a wounded soldier's endurance. He could cope with her better now that she was a boy.

And then, for an anguished moment, he was taken back to where, for twenty years, he'd done his best to avoid going: to the last sight of another little boy in a Breton doorway, trying to be brave as Gwil went off to war, waving good-bye and promising to be back within a year.

He'd returned in two—it had been a long campaign, that one, under the banner of the Holy Roman emperor. There was no son waiting for him, and no wife, either, only a rough, single cross with their names scratched on it in the paupers' graveyard.

You were away too long, Gwil.

"Stop telling me. I know, don't I? I've always known."

Look after this child, then.

"But it's not mine."

It is now. Look on it as your penance.

Defeated, he walked round the fire and took the knife away. "You made a mess of that," he said. "Let's do it proper."

The remainder of the long hair fell to the floor as he trimmed it and then shaved the neck up to the usual army level. "One thing," he said, "you ain't no family of mine. That clear?"

She nodded.

"All right, then."

CHAPTER 4

AD 1141, the Cambridgeshire Fens

BODY SIDEWAYS TO THE TARGET (drawn in chalk on the trunk of the heftiest of the beeches sheltering the grove). Feet same distance apart as her shoulders.

Lower bow to load it. Nock arrow with index finger above and next two fingers below, not too tight, not too loose.

Raise bow (smoothly, smoothly), draw back string to ear. Aim with dominant eye (she'd never known she had one).

Release.

"Well," Gwil said, walking forward to retrieve the arrow, his feet crunching the grove's frozen grass, "you hit the bloody tree at least."

Actually, this time she'd hit the outer rim of the target, but he was as sparing in praise as he was in condemnation.

She shot him a glance as if to ask what she'd done wrong; he was beginning to be able to read her now, to understand her even.

"Didn't follow through," he told her. She stamped her foot but more in frustration with herself than anything else.

Bugger. Didn't make sense to stay aiming after the arrow'd left the bow. But if he said it mattered, then it mattered; when he shot, he hit exact center every time and she would become as good as him if it killed her.

"Mind out the way, then," she said, and reached for another arrow from the quiver on her back.

"No you don't. That's enough for today." He reached out to stay her arm but she flinched from him. She would never allow him to touch her—not that he wanted to. Not like that anyway. He was tempted to slap her sometimes for her rudeness but never would. He had never been one for disciplining children; his wife had complained often enough how he was too soft on young Emouale . . .

He shook his head against the memory, lowered his arm and stood in front of her.

"Enough," he said patiently. "Got to remember that the back is the archer's friend, got to treat it kindly. Now get inside and see to that stew."

She hissed at him and he saw her mouth tense as the familiar guarded look clouded her expression once more. Practicing archery was almost the only time when she could forget whatever it was she'd forgotten, when the waves she could hear roaring beyond the seawall in her mind quieted a little and she wasn't swept away in the whirling, filthy, inexplicable terror like she was in her dreams. With a bow in her hand she could summon up a hatred and a concentration equaling the deluge that'd otherwise overwhelm her. When she shot, she was no longer powerless.

Didn't mind not knowing who she was; didn't want to. Sufficient to have been delivered a month ago into a ruined church by that old midwife Gwil, archer and arbalist.

All she knew for certain was that she was both very young and very old; that she was a girl and yet not female; that she was called Penda because that was the name by which Gwil addressed her but that she had once answered to another name that was even now being tossed to and fro like flotsam somewhere on the ocean beyond her mental seawall, beyond her grasp, beyond his.

"I'm going to have to call you something," he'd announced one day. "Can't go around being nameless all your life." And then he'd closed his eyes as if lost in thought and when he opened them again he was smiling broadly: "Penda," he said. "That's what I'll call you. Pagan warlord, was Penda, descended from Woden, or so they say. I think it suits you." She smiled, although she hadn't the slightest idea what he was talking about, but on reflection she thought it suited her, too. And that's all she knew, except that she must shoot and shoot, so the point of her arrow could one day thwack into the center of a human target and inflict a wound on it like the one in the gaping tunnel between her legs.

There was just one last thing she knew, too, that she could trust old Gwil not to come too close. Like he was standing off now, arm outstretched to take the bow.

She passed it over to him and went into the church to stir the stew, pausing in its arched doorway to peer forward and then behind in case . . . in case of what? Something terrible.

No, nobody there. She went inside and felt the uneven walls slip around her like protective clothing. He'd made a safe, warm home of it, old Gwil. Patched the roof; made stools out of its spars; grubbed in the detritus of the cottages and found a pail, scorched but serviceable enough for cooking and washing in; hung old bits of iron from the same source on hidden string between the trees so they'd clang an alarm that would give them both time to disappear through a tunnel he'd scratched out under the back wall.

And he'd made her a cloak out of the hide of a young deer he'd shot when it came blundering through the trees. Bit smelly but kept out the cold. When she was good enough, he was going to teach her to hunt.

Goose tonight. When Gwil'd said it was time she did some wildfowling, she'd spat at him. That awful sea was out there beyond the trees; she wasn't going to risk it sweeping her off. "Bloody won't. I'm a-staying here." Here, where he'd made her safe.

"Stay on your own, then," he'd said.

Hadn't been so bad, really; something near familiar and reassuring about it. Cold, though, bor. The air that Gwil had expected to warm up by now was icier than ever once they left the shelter of the trees.

Crouching with their backs to the great expanse of reeds that troubled her, they'd waited for dawn and the honking, whistling, fluting airborne invasion that came in with it out of the North Sea, displacing the air with a hundred thousand beating wings. Arrows speeding up from her bow hadn't been fired in hatred this time, more with wonder at the magic of flight and the need to bring some of it down to the cumbersome, featherless humans below.

Dead bodies had plopped about them, one with an arrow of hers in it. "Mine," she'd swanked as they picked them up, although she'd been bound to hit something, the sky being so thick with birds. "We'll have this un for supper."

"Long as you pluck it," Gwil had said.

Which she had, unsurprised by the ease with which she did it and the instinctive knowledge that, when she'd set it to simmer, a leaf or two of sage and a couple of wild garlic bulbs ought to go in with it. She could remember enough.

"Could do with some bread," she grumbled as she poured it out on the wooden platters he'd made.

"Come spring," he said, "when we go to Cambridge."

She began whimpering. "Don't want to go to Cambridge, Gwil. I want to stay here."

He knew she was terrified of going outside this deserted village; she'd only come wildfowling—they'd needed something other than squirrels to eat—because she was equally frightened of being by herself.

But they couldn't stay here; when the weather improved the village's former residents might come to rebuild or carry off the church's stone. It was lucky this long, drawn-out winter still hampered people's movements and had given her the solitude in which to recover—as much as she could recover.

It was strange, Gwil thought; she knew which call came from which bird and could tell one herb from another, but she didn't know her own name. She had no memory of what was personal to her, yet with common tasks, like cooking, like laundering, she retained the lessons somebody had taught her.

She was sitting on the other side of the fire—she always kept it between them—gracelessly stuffing food into her mouth as if it was a chore, her small freckled face displaying no pleasure in what was a good stew.

She doesn't show pleasure in anything, Gwil thought, except . . .

He waited until she'd licked the platter, then he said: "We'll get me another crossbow in Cambridge," and watched her come alive, as she always did when the subject was shooting.

From the moment she'd seen him practicing with the ordinary bow he'd made for himself, she'd nagged and nagged until he carved and strung one for her.

The way she'd handled it told him she came from a wildfowling family, though few wildfowlers possessed the potential she did; oh, he'd spotted that sure enough—the fury that launched itself with the arrow as if from the same bowstring had shocked him, at first making him wonder whether, in that strange little head of hers, she remembered more of her ordeal than she realized. She stood differently, too, with a bow in her hand, confident, more upright, and from the very first time she held one, he had seen that she had the makings of an exceptional archer.

Not that he told her so; when she was shooting her fear gave way to an arrogance that could lead to self-satisfaction—the ruin of many an archer who had stopped practicing because of it.

"And me," she said now. "I want a crossbow."

"No."

"Why?"

"Can't afford two."

He began telling her how much expense and preparation went into the making of a first-class crossbow; how the best prods (the bow itself) were laminated, and how the glue for that came from the shredded tendons of an ox's heel soaked for days to soften it. He explained how its heavier draw weight necessitated using a leather stirrup to pull back the string (usually hemp); how its arrows (bolts or quarrels) had tips (bodkins or broadheads) that could go through any thickness of armor.

"And it's slow. A good archer can loose off five times quicker than an arbalist."

"Why did you use one then?"

"Longer range," he said shortly, which was true, but the real reason was that it was the surer killer—near always fatal, whatever part of the body it hit. The strongest, most close-linked mail couldn't withstand a crossbow bolt, however much backing it had.

"How'd you lose yours?" She doted on the tales he recounted about mercenary life, the armies he'd served with, the battles, the crusade he'd gone on as a young man. What he hadn't told her, and, out of shame, never would, was that he'd lost his crossbow through being in the company of the men who'd raped her.

"In the flight from Lincoln," he said, which, once more, was true—in its way.

"Make me one. I want one."

"Maybe. When you're skilled with the short bow. Being an arbalist's easy; anybody can use a crossbow."

I'd have talked like this with my son, he thought. Then he thought: no, Emouale was lovable and he was damn sure she wasn't.

Again he was tormented by his last sight of a little boy waving good-bye from the doorway at Vannes.

She's not a substitute, Gwil, the Lord put in. *She's a penance for your sins. I never said salvation would be easy.*

She'd tired herself with too much archery practice and, unusually, slept late the next morning, so he took the opportunity to go back to the spot where Ramon and the others had assaulted her. The little quill case she'd had clutched in her hand when he found her intrigued him; he'd studied the document it held time and again, hoping the writing on it would turn itself into words he could understand, but its curious letters obdurately remained letters.

Nevertheless, he thought, *let's see if the monk and the others left anything else that'll help track the bastards down.*

The moment he stepped out of the trees, the vast fenland sky came at him with its endless underlay of reeds, a landscape in which nothing moved.

He had no trouble finding the site again; ice had frozen it exactly as it had been a month ago, and the crushed reeds still retained traces of her blood on them, as if the Lord had halted time itself in order that the evidence of what had happened here should be preserved for all to see. And weep.

Wait, though, somebody other than himself had been here since. And that somebody had brought along a broom of birch twigs, for here it was, discarded, where it hadn't been when Gwil had first investigated.

And that somebody had used the broom to sweep the area beyond the site, for here were reeds lying down in neat tracks where they'd been brushed flat. As if somebody had been searching for a lost object among the roots.

"He was nearby," Gwil yelled at his Lord. "He was nearby and alone, the bastard, and You didn't tell me."

No hunter, though, was he?

He supposed he had to thank God for that at least, because if the monk had possessed the craft of tracking, he would have noticed the trail the girl had left as she'd dragged herself toward the trees.

He could've brought others, Gwil. Come down on you and her like wolves on a lambing pen.

True, very true.

Are we sure it was the monk?

Gwil strode over to the birch besom and picked it up. Strips of black wool tied its twigs together. He ripped one off, sniffed, but could smell only the cold that stiffened it. Then, as his mittened hands warmed the material, there arose from it the faintest but unmistakable whiff of asafetida.

"It was him, Lord. And he wants that quill case real bad."

It was time to start tracking the bastard down.

CHAPTER 5

AD 1180, Perton Abbey

IN THE SCRIPTORIUM LAST NIGHT, when he had copied the scratches from his wax tablet onto parchment in the cursive script of which he is justly proud, the scribe was overcome with indecision.

Had the abbot gone mad? Should he tell somebody? What he was copying was not decent, an affront to God Himself. History could not be written from the point of view of a mercenary, a debased girl and—the scribe shudders—a woman, however rich, who had flouted heaven's law with an unnatural act against the rights of a husband.

He felt he was being dragged into a conspiracy imperiling his soul; indeed, at the description of the Kenniford Castle wedding night, with the husband ascending the stairs to the woman's chamber, he'd had to creep away from his desk to the lavatorium in order to plunge his heated head and . . . well, other parts, into the cold water of its trough, that his body might not commit a shameful act of its own accord.

And yet, and yet, with it all, he is fascinated, like a bird fluttering to its doom toward the antics of a gyrating stoat.

Perhaps, when the tale is finished, he could dare to go over the abbot's head and take the manuscript to his bishop. When it is finished . . .

In the meantime he has to know: "My lord, what is the document in the quill case? And does the mercenary succeed in finding the villains?"

"When the thaw came with the spring, Gwilherm de Vannes began tracking them, like a hound with its nose to the spoor of a wolf. He did not tell the girl he'd named Penda what he was about; he feared what it would do to her to come face-to-face with her abusers. Nevertheless, track them he did, and the trail led them both west and, at first, was easy to follow, for the mercenary devil Ramon left a path of destruction behind him. But as we shall find, that particular trail went cold . . ."

"Does Gwilherm pick it up again?"

"We shall see, we shall see." The abbot is discovering, somewhat to his surprise, that he is a born storyteller. "But for a moment, let us return to the political situation. Now, where were we?"

The scribe looks at the scratches in the wax. "We have King Stephen imprisoned by the empress," he says. "Is that how the war ended?"

"My son, we are only yet accounting for the year 1141; there is longer and worse to come. Yes, the king has been taken to Empress Matilda's fortress at Bristol and is fettered with iron rings—an unforgiving woman, the empress. She is filled with joy, for now she feels she has England in her grasp. Once she is received into the city of Winchester, which contains the crown and royal paraphernalia, she can plan her coronation at Westminster. But, first, to enter Winchester she must gain the permission of its bishop, who is Stephen's brother Henry."

"And he refused her?"

The young man gains a smile for his innocence. "How much you have to learn, my son. No, our good bishop Henry is on the toasting fork of indecision. Which side should he present to the fire? His brother has disappointed him sorely in not granting enough rights to the Church—that is, to himself. Will the empress be kinder? His price is high but Matilda pays it, as she must if she is to be crowned. In return he pledges fealty to her as lady of England, soon to be queen."

The abbot finds a scrap of parchment among the litter on his bed. "Here is the declaration made by himself and other bishops who were present at that extraordinary council. Read it, my eyes begin to fail me."

" 'We choose as lady of England and Normandy the daughter of a king who was a peacemaker, a glorious king, a wealthy king, a good king, without peer in our time, and we promise her our faith and support.' "

"And this," the abbot says, "issued by men who had once sworn fealty and allegiance to Stephen."

The scribe shakes his head at human perfidy. "Treason."

"Treason, indeed, unless you account as the original traitors the bishops and barons who swore to a dying King Henry the First that they would acknowledge his daughter and then did not." The abbot begins to cough and clutch his chest. "My medicine, boy. Quickly." But, after a sip, he throws the phial onto the rushes of the floor. "What in hell is this?"

"My lord, I mentioned the trouble with your sight to the brother infirmarian, and he felt that ground bats' eyes should be added to your usual marshmallow and honey."

"Did he, indeed. Well, you can tell the brother infirmarian that if he does it again, I shall add my boot to his arse, weak as I am. Now, where are we?"

"The king is in prison, my lord, and the empress triumphs."

"Indeed she does. Her armies go forth, and one of them, under the command of her mercenary Alan of Ghent, marches on Kenniford Castle, that strategic jewel on the Thames, which, as we know, is in the hands of King Stephen's man John of Tewing. As they near it that morning, they come across some small boys fishing in a stream known as Kingcup Brook . . ."

The abbot's eyes become inexplicably misty. The scribe pauses for a moment. "Kingcup Brook. There were fine trout in that stream; on a calm summer's day you could tempt them into your net merely by tickling." The abbot sighs and shakes his head at his digression. "Some of Ghent's men capture the boys—so that their parents may be persuaded into paying a ransom for them—and take them to their commander. One boy, especially, is richly dressed, though muddy. He refuses to tell them his name, but his poorer companions, being frightened, say that he is called William and that he is no less than the son of John of Tewing himself."

"God be praised, so the unnatural machinations by Maud of Kenniford did not prevent her bearing her husband a son."

"They did, actually," the abbot tells him. "No, this William is a son by Tewing's previous wife, who died giving birth to him.

"He is seven years old. And trying not to show how frightened he is—almost as much of his father's wrath when he realizes he's crept out of the castle that morning as he is of his predicament. Which, I have to say, is somewhat parlous. The commander and men of the empress's army march him to Kenniford and, helpless, he has to watch as they take up positions surrounding the castle. Then the commander—this Alan of Ghent—drags the boy to the riverbank opposite the castle walls so that Kenniford's sentries can see him. A gallows is erected, a halter put round his neck. Alan of Ghent shouts for John of Tewing to come to his ramparts and, when he does, threatens to hang the boy if the castle does not surrender . . ."

CHAPTER 6

AD 1141, Kenniford Castle
THE FIRST SIEGE

IN THE EARLY MORNING, PATROLS reported an enemy force heading for them, too large, they said, to risk the garrison going out to do battle.

Immediately, and with considerable efficiency, the castle made ready to be sieged. As the alarm bell began clanging, men poured out of the guardhouses like bees swarming from a hive. The half of the bridge that spanned the Thames from the Kenniford gatehouse was drawn up with nerve-scraping grinds and the even shriller "*Pull,* you bastards, *pull*" of the gatemaster until it fitted over the portcullis like a shutter over a window, leaving the far span stretching uselessly into midair. Archers raced to line the allure running along the top of the outer walls, carrying bundles of extra arrows. Two trebuchets with pivoting arms sixty feet long were trundled into position in the outer bailey and great baskets of stones put beside them ready to be slung. Water-filled buckets were stood in rows against thatched buildings in case the enemy used fire.

Maud hadn't given much thought to the realities of war; never having faced them, she hadn't believed she ever would—fighting was a men's game, something they played elsewhere. She hadn't been able to conceive of Kenniford, solid, safe, peaceful and homely for generations, subjected to burning and violent death.

Now here she was, ordered to stay in the keep with the castle's women and children and prepare to receive the wounded.

She wasn't so much frightened as amazed; instead of carrying domestic sounds, the air coming through her windows was assaulting her ears with shouts and clangs and heavy movement. Amazed, too, that even among her own household, she was not in control; she didn't know what to do.

The one who did was the eldest among them. Lady Morgana, here on a visit from her Welsh castle, had put the serving women to stuffing sacks with straw in order to make palliasses and organized Cousin Lynessa and Maud into tearing up clean rags and rolling them for bandages. "Where's the kitchen maid?" she demanded.

"Here, my lady."

"The sharpest knives, if you please—clean, mind. Where's Milburga, I want her to organize games for the children. Maud, don't just stand there. What have you got in the painkilling line? Brandy will do, lots of it."

Maud looked at the old woman, the arthritic hands. "I'm sorry, Morgana," she said, "so sorry you've been caught up in this."

She earned a smile. "My dear, when you're facing the Welsh, as we are in the Marches, this is quite a normal day."

A normal day, Maud thought as she went outside to go down to the cellars. *It's not normal for Kenniford. It's not right.*

Unfairly perhaps, she blamed her husband; he'd brought this . . . this horrifying vulgarity upon her home—and not only *her* home.

Oh dear God.

Somebody caught her arm. "Best get back inside, my lady," Sir Rollo told her.

She clutched at him. "The village. Have the villagers been let in?"

He shook his head. "He's ordered the gates shut."

She knew who "he" was. "They've got to be let in." There were more than one hundred men, women and children out there in vulnerable homes nestling against the walls, with every right to expect her protection.

"They'll eat up our food, see," Sir Rollo said. "That's what he says."

"Does he, indeed?" She began striding toward the bridge to the middle bailey.

Sir Rollo pulled her back, but as she struggled against him there came a scream from the keep and Milburga was running toward them. "William, it's William."

"What about him?"

"Ain't here. Not nowhere. And his fishing rod's missing. Little bugger, I'll flay his hide when I gets him."

Milburga was panicking, another astonishment of this dreadful day. *Dear Christ, protect him.* The boy had gone to Kingcup Brook, crept out of the castle before dawn as he usually did—and they had yet to work out how—to come back with a creel full of trout for his father's breakfast.

And Kingcup Brook was in the path the army had pursued on its way to besiege them.

"He's allus home by now," wept Milburga.

Dear Christ, dear Christ.

When Tewing had first brought his son to the castle and presented him to her—"Here's a stepson for you"—she'd kissed the boy, smiled and nodded but without warmth at first. She didn't like children much, and certainly not one sprung from her husband's loins; even less one who, if he lived, would inherit her castle.

The thing was, William turned out not to be at all like his father. She supposed the gentle face and features, the pale and floppy hair, were an inheritance from his dead mother, the unknown woman for whom Maud felt the deepest sympathy.

Expecting the boy to be given preference, as heirs were, she'd been taken aback to find him almost as much an object of Tewing's bullying as anyone else in the castle.

William, at the age of seven, had gentle manners, an aversion to bearbaiting and a leaning toward bookishness, all attributes of his late mother—a weakling, according to Tewing—that must be beaten out of him if he were not to become an effeminate, namby-pamby milksop who'd rather stay in m'lady's chamber playing a fucking lute than go to war.

Maud, having her own problems with his father, had stayed aloof for a while—everybody else in her household conspired to mother the child—and was only drawn in by an event that was afterward referred to with awe as "Milburga's victory."

It had taken place in the keep's kitchen. Milburga, passing through the tiltyard, where young William had been put to practicing sword blows against the battered tree trunk set up for that purpose, saw blood dripping from the child's right hand.

"You come along o' me," she'd said. She'd taken him by the scruff of the neck and marched him to the kitchen so that she could administer to a small palm on which the skin had been taken off by friction against the sword's grip.

When John of Tewing had found them there, his bellows of rage attracted half the castle.

By the time Maud arrived on the scene, Milburga, shielding William behind her, was squaring up to Tewing, equally tall and big, both faces puce with shouting.

"I'm his father, you fat cow. I know what's best for 'im. He'll learn swordsmanship if it kills him."

"Bloody sword's too heavy for him, you girt fool. Taken the skin offen his poor little hand."

"Get out of my way, bitch." Tewing raised a hand like a ham as if to strike her.

"An' don't you be calling me no bitch," Milburga had yelled back, "or next time they brings you your bloody soup I'll have pissed in it."

There was a sudden silence. The crowd round the kitchen door hunched its shoulders in terrible anticipation.

Then . . . the man's hand had fallen to his side, like Balaam's when the ass he was beating for refusing to move saw the Angel of Jehovah blocking their way. John of Tewing was giving a grunt of approval and the hand that he had raised in violence now stretched to ruffle his son's hair. Turning to Milburga he said: "You've got balls, woman, I'll say that for you. All right, if he wants to, he can leave practice for today."

Milburga had won.

But William betrayed her victory. Getting to his feet, he'd picked up his sword. "No. I'll go back, Father. I'm sorry."

As she watched the small, courageous figure go out of the kitchen, Maud had felt a rare pity and the early stirrings of maternal love.

Now, with Sir Rollo dumbstruck and staring at Milburga, those same feelings propelled her across the bridge, through the middle bailey, across the next bridge—not registering the sudden quiet, nor that the men by the trebuchets, the spearmen, the archers lining the walls, were now so still they might have been ossified.

In a world of concentrating silence, the only sound came from one carrying voice. ". . . we will hang your son."

Tewing was standing in one of the crenels on the outer allure glaring across the Thames to the Crowmarsh bank. He was in his nightshirt, having been drunk the night before and still asleep when the alarm sounded. His squire hopped beside him, trying to get him into his mail shirt and helmet. Stang, his second in command, was with them.

Panting, Maud joined them to look where they were looking.

It was a beautiful September morning with a light breeze fluttering the pennants of the besieging force. And, dear Mary, mother of God, a little boy stood in the midst of them with a rope round his neck that ran up through a ring on the crosspiece of a high, stout pole. The tall man standing beside him, one hand resting on the child's shoulder, his other arm through the guige strap at the back of his shield, was demanding Kenniford's surrender. At the far end of the rope were two more men, ready to pull.

In that instant, the pity Maud had felt for the boy transformed into something more agonizing. She'd never been so afraid—not of the castle's danger, not even for the crowd of people immediately below, cowering against the castle's gate, but of what the man at her side would do, or, more terribly, would not do. She knew him.

And the child, so small, so brave, so very pale. *Help him, God, I'll do anything, I'll build You another church, just save him.*

The call came across the river for the third time from the man with his hand on William's shoulder. "You will be given honorable terms if you give in, but in the name of Empress Matilda, I say again, surrender your castle or we hang your son." The guttural Norman French carried easily.

"Can you see if the bastard's got a dolphin on his shield?" Tewing's question was for Stang.

Stang squinted. "Some sort of fish, my lord, far as I can make out."

"That's Alan of Ghent, then," Tewing said. "Fleming. I'm not surrendering to a fucking Flemish mercenary."

"You must, we've *got* to surrender." Maud knew it was no good pleading with him—he'd never listened to her yet—nevertheless she had to.

"How many d'you reckon?" Tewing asked.

"Four hundred," Stang told him. "More among the trees maybe."

"Should've had that fucking wood cut down."

They were discussing it, *discussing it.*

"Tell the archers to fire," said Tewing. "Get the Fleming first."

"*No. Stop it.*" Clawing at her husband, Maud put her body in front of his, but he pushed her away.

Stang was reluctant. "We might hit the boy."

"You do as I fucking tell you. He shouldn't have left the castle, been told enough times. I'll parley with the bastards, and you fire when I say."

Tewing moved into the center of the embrasure, roaring. He lifted the front of his nightshirt and grabbed what lay beneath in order to waggle it. "See this, you fuckers? Do your worst. I've got the hammer and anvil to make plenty more sons." He turned to Stang. "Give the order, and hand me a bow, I'll kill that Flemish cunt myself."

Maud shut her eyes and heard the note that is like no other—the sound of multiple arrows displacing air as they crossed the river. Stang was pushing her under cover; the opposing archers were returning fire. She fought against him. "Is he hit?" she shouted. "Is William hit?"

She managed to grab on to one of the merlons and pull herself up to look round the embrasure next to it. There was no small body on the grass of the other bank. The Fleming who'd threatened to hang William was retiring backward into the trees with him, covering them both with his shield.

"Mary, mother of God. Thank you, thank you." With arrows clattering around her, she turned to look at the man she'd never forgive. "And you . . . you . . ."

He capered at the enemy. "Yah, you're all fucking eunuchs . . . ," he was shouting. Nevertheless she thought she saw just a flicker of relief in his expression as he watched the Fleming carry William to safety before he exhaled, clutched at his nightgown and dropped to the floor.

"He's hit." Stang left her to run back, but although he got an arrow in his arm for his loyalty, he still managed to drag his commander into the shelter of a crenel.

Maud crawled after him. There was no wound that she could see immediately, but her husband's face had gone lopsided and his mouth was working without sound.

With the help of one of the archers and keeping low, they managed to haul him down to the bottom of the allure's steps, where they could go no further for the arrows pouring down into the outer bailey.

It took a tortuga of men, protecting themselves, Maud and Tewing with their shields, to drag him across the outer moat's bridge, through the next bailey and across a further bridge into the comparative safety of the upper ward, where Milburga was waiting for them with a scolding for Maud. "I'll flay you. What you go racing into danger for?"

"They've got William, Milly. They're threatening to hang him. Not yet, though. They took him under cover."

Milburga wiped her forehead and turned her attention to Tewing. "So what's the matter with that bugger?"

"I think he's been hit."

Stang, the arrow still sticking out of his arm, gave orders and accompanied the two women as his commander was carried into the hall and lain on its table.

Milburga tore Tewing's nightshirt open all the way down, turned him over as if he were a roll of pastry and tore again. She rolled him back to peer into a face that drooped down one side. "He ain't hit, he's had a seizure."

"What's it mean?"

"Means he ain't going anywhere."

"He's crippled?"

"Can't walk, can't talk. Maybe never will."

Maud pushed her to one side so that she could lean over her husband. His eyes pleaded with her. Gurgles came from his mouth.

"It's all right. We'll make you comfortable," she said. It was an automatic response to a soul in terror. She felt no triumph that a man prepared to let his son and her villagers die had been reduced to a useless hulk, but she recognized God's punishment when she saw it.

The hall was becoming busy; wounded men were being brought in, one with an arrow sticking out of his nose being teased for it by another. Her head smith was holding his blackened, peeling hands up to her and grinning: "Got the fire out, didn't I, lady?"

What fire?

Lady Morgana was at the other end of the long table dealing with Stang. She glanced toward Tewing and Maud. "Better fetch Father Nimbus."

"Is he going to die?"

"Best be on the safe side."

Going upstairs for the priest, Maud's mind moved as fast as her legs. Yes, yes, it could be no worse than it had been. She could do that; she *would* do it.

Her seven months of marriage had not been happy. Any authority she'd held in the castle had been taken away from her. Yes, she was permitted to oversee what food was served—as long as the meat dripped blood. (She'd stopped attending the feasts because of the behavior of the men Tewing brought to them, nor had he cared whether she came or not.) Yes, she and her immediate household could take their meals in her solar, and remain there all fucking day as far as he was concerned; just stay out of his fucking way.

By the grace of God, and possibly Kigva, he'd come to her bed less often than she'd feared—from the first they'd had separate rooms, he having turfed Father Nimbus out of his—though the occasions when he did so disgusted, humiliated and appalled her so that she lived in horror of the next.

Bursting through her solar door, usually drunk, Kigva wailing for him outside it, he uttered not a word, just penetrated her and jerked up and down for a while until a grunt told her he'd been satisfied, after which he went away again. He'd never asked why, as he left her, she began furiously munching the seeds from a bowl she kept nearby, though—and this had been alarming—he'd begun to inquire: "Your belly swelling yet?"

For the rest, she was sidelined and could merely look on as what had been a functioning home of a castle became a fortified hell. Her orchard and herb beds disappeared into a new moat; guardhouses sprouted along the rose avenues. There was a barbarously early slaughter and salting of cattle, sheep and pigs in order to feed the increased garrison through a possible winter siege. Rents not due until December were called in early, while the coffers of money so carefully kept and accounted for by Sir Bernard, the chief steward, were put in the charge of one of Tewing's men.

All this might have been forgiven on the grounds that Kenniford had to be put on a war footing. What was unpardonable was the behavior of the mercenaries Tewing inflicted on the castle. They were mainly Brabançons, who, according to Tewing, had more balls than fucking Flemings, which may or may not have been true. What they did have was savagery.

It was like the Norsemen come again; if they didn't think their food rations were enough, they raided the storehouses. Thirsty? They were always thirsty—they raided the cellars. Women? No maidservant was safe. Maud's own men, outnumbered two to one, were jeered at for being amateur soldiers (which they were; knights, sergeants and guards did their duty as Maud's vassals for their three regulation months and then went home to see to the harvest, being replaced by an equivalent number once the crops were in) and set on if they jeered back.

After one fight between the two sides, so many of Kenniford's had been injured that Maud ordered Sir Rollo to bring all of them into the inner bailey and build yet another guardhouse for them, leaving the mercenaries to their own devices.

This, however, as she'd pointed out to her husband, defeated the purpose of feudal service. "My men can't patrol, can't drill, can't do anything, they've been rendered useless."

"That's what they fucking are. Get rid of 'em. My Brabançons are all we'll need in a fucking siege, they've got balls."

"But I'm sieged now," Maud shouted at him. "I can't go hawking or coursing without filth being shouted at my ladies."

He'd merely shrugged and walked away from her.

And now he was helpless, and she was once more Kenniford's

keeper. She had her castle back—if the empress's men didn't destroy it.

Father Nimbus was in his chapel, trying to comfort a sobbing, frightened Cousin Lynessa with one hand while, with the other, packing his chrismatory box, ready to take it up to the outer walls to give the last rites to whoever needed them. "Now, now, dear heart, don't take on so or you'll set *me* off, and we don't want that, do we? Today, we've all got to be brave little soldiers for the Lord."

"Tewing's had a seizure," Maud said. "Morgana says he might die." She didn't pretend to grief—with this priest she didn't have to.

He felt it, though; his little face screwed itself up into concern. "Oh dear, then I must go to him."

Father Nimbus suffered for anybody and everybody who was hurt, even for a man who'd constantly held him up to ridicule as a "flouncing fucking betty."

Cousin Lynessa clung on. "Don't leave me, Father. We'll all be raped."

"Oh stop it, Lynessa," Maud snapped at her; she was too strung up herself to countenance another woman's hysteria. As Father Nimbus began tripping toward the door, she held him back. "I'm going to surrender the castle."

The chrismatory box dropped to the floor and priest's rosebud mouth formed an O of shock.

"I've got to," Maud said desperately. "William's been captured, he slipped out again before dawn and they found him. They're threatening to hang him unless we give in. *He* was going to let them do it." Identification was unnecessary. "And he wouldn't let the villagers come in, so they're stuck in the line of fire. I've *got* to."

"Little William," moaned Father Nimbus. "Those dear people." His eyes were filling with tears; he cried often—a habit that caused people who didn't know him to dub him a coward. For years he'd fought for Maud's soul against her sense of her own worth, asking her to value more what was due to God than to the Caesar she regarded herself to be.

"Sweeting," he said, "are we sure we are giving up the castle for the sake of William and the villagers? Or are we tempted into exchanging one regime for another? In which case we may be jumping from the frying pan into the boiling pot, where neither William nor our people will be any safer. Is it revenge for a marriage that has made you unhappy? Let you search your soul."

She searched it. Saving William and the villagers, she thought, was the laudable act of a woman forced into submission out of love for those threatened. If, coincidentally, it provided that same woman with the opportunity to throw off a yoke that was hateful to her, God would surely forgive her.

"There's a bit of that," she admitted, "but I can't allow slaughter." She began to babble. "It won't be so bad, will it? It's just exchanging an invasion of a lot of damn mercenaries for another, and at least the one holding William had the decency to protect him when the arrows started flying. And after all, the war's as good as over with the king in prison. It's common sense to declare for the empress now she's won. At least she's a woman."

Father Nimbus flicked the tears off his cheeks. "Well then, sweeting, *what* is it we must ask ourselves?"

"*Would Jesus do it?*" It was a question she'd grown up with under his tutelage. "Yes, he would."

"Then so must you." He picked up his chrismatory box. "Take Sir Bernard with you. Oh, and wear the purple bliaut, dear; it gives you gravitas. *Must* have gravitas if you're dictating terms."

She was immensely comforted. This was the most far-reaching decision of her life; if Jesus's mouthpiece—for that was what this little man was to her—said it was the right one, then it was the right one.

His voice trilled up to her as he went down the stairs. "That's if those naughty Brabançons *let* you surrender, of course."

There was a thump that shook the keep, sending bits of ceiling plaster down onto her head. Cousin Lynessa shrieked and began scuttling around the room.

Maud ran to the window. A spurt of masonry dust was blooming two floors down while, way below, the ball of rock that had caused it still bounced around the bailey.

From here, she couldn't see what had propelled the missile from across the river, but obviously the besieging force had brought up its own engines.

Fear took the form of fury and illogic: "What's the point of firing at me?" she shouted. "What's the *point*? It's the outer walls you want down."

As if the enemy's trebuchet masters had heard her, another rock whistled through the air to fall shorter and harmlessly in the outer bailey. They were getting their range; the defensive walls would be next. And how long could *they* stand?

Kenniford's own trebuchets were being employed now; seen from the back, they looked like immense, skeletal dragons with a sadly drooping tail in the form of a net. As she watched, the counterweight of the head was released and its tail lashed upward, propelling the ball it contained into an arc across the river. Where William was.

Engineered stupidity, so that men could throw rocks at each other like apes. And hit William.

Grabbing Lynessa, Maud pulled her down the stairs. Halfway, they had to press against the curve of the wall to let by a party winding its way up. Tewing was being carried to his tower room, the woman Kigva tenderly wiping the spittle off his face as they went.

Maud barely gave him a glance and hurried on down. Father Nimbus had made a telling point; the Brabançons were unlikely to betray the man who paid them by surrendering to his enemy just on her say-so.

Stang, when she spotted him, was bandaged and slumped on a bench in the hall. In lifting his stricken commander, his mail sleeve had fallen back, allowing the arrow to bury itself in an unprotected wrist.

"Missed the artery, but the barb went in deep," Lady Morgana said cheerfully. "I had to cut it out. That's one mercenary not likely to use a bow again. Nor wield a sword, either. God's judgment, that is." Stang—a Tewing man through and through—had been little more popular with the ladies of the castle than his master.

"Did you tell him so?" she asked, glancing across the hall at the stricken man.

"He knows."

He did know it; always taciturn, his thin face had become bleak from pain and a future that no longer welcomed him—an incapacitated mercenary *had* no future. The act of courage he'd shown on the allure had served him badly.

If she'd disliked the man and his profession less, Maud might have felt sorry for him; as it was, she merely took his condition into her calculations. By default, Stang was now the Brabançons' leader; his despair and the bribe she was going to offer him gave her a better chance of procuring his cooperation in getting them to lay down their arms.

Nevertheless, she was surprised at how simple it was; she'd expected him to show more loyalty to the cause that Tewing had espoused.

"You do understand?" she asked, in case the medicinal brandy in which Lady Morgana had soused him was confusing his wits. "I will ensure that the Fleming allows your men to march out of here in safety and with honor."

"Honor?" His voice was flat. "Hell with honor, they'll want pay. Make him agree to take 'em into his army. Only way."

"Will he do that?"

"Yep. Good men, our men. Lucky to have 'em."

"And *they'll* agree? They'll switch allegiance just like that?"

Stang nodded. Apparently, mercenaries turned their coats for money as easily as they changed horses. He sneered back at the sneer on her face. "Lady, ain't that what you're doing? How's your poor bloody husband?" Then he shrugged. "Now, where's that property that's going to set me up for life?"

Sir Bernard and his scribe were sent for to bring the appropriate documents, and within minutes the Normandy manor of Saissons, near Caen, with its water mill, land for four plows, thirty-six acres of meadow, woodland three furlongs in length and three furlongs plus ten perches in breadth, four freeholds, eight villeins and two bordars, passed from Maud's ownership into the mercenary's.

"I am not happy about this," Sir Bernard told her. The fact that he said it in English, his native tongue, one he both despised and rarely used, showed how unhappy he was. A most un-Saxon-like Saxon, born Osric of Oxenford, he'd converted to Norman ways under Maud's grandfather, whose villein he had been. Thin, dry, precise, without any discernible humor, a genius with figures, a man who'd probably looked fifty at the age of ten, and would look fifty in his dotage, it was gall and wormwood for him to let go of any estate in his stewardship. "The fellow is base, and this is good land. Not happy at all."

"Well, I am," Maud said. Actually, the land wasn't *that* good. She'd visited it on her travels round her far-flung estates. Saissons looked better on parchment than it did in reality; its meadows flooded, the woodland yielded little beechmast on which to feed pigs, and its villeins, even for the Cotentin, were sullen pains in the backside.

It was no great loss, but Maud saw no reason to say so.

As Stang held out his good hand for the documents, she snatched them away. "When the job's done." She frowned. "How *is* it done? Do we put up a white flag?"

GRINDING LIKE THE MILLS OF hell, the drawbridge went down and conjoined with its span on the opposite side. The portcullis screeched as it was pulled up. Maud's herald, young Payn Fitzgilbert, in Kenniford blue-and-silver livery, with servants behind him carrying a trestle table and two chairs, advanced to meet the enemy's much shabbier representative in the bridge's middle and arrange a truce for the parley.

Maud waited for his signal in the shadow of the gatehouse, listening hard as Sir Bernard listed the terms she must ask for.

Both he and Stang were to go with her, as was Sir Rollo, but Maud had made it clear that she was to do the main negotiating: "*I* am the chatelaine."

From all her women, she'd chosen Cousin Lynessa to go with her for propriety's sake. A nun on leave from Godstow convent, to which Maud was a generous benefactor, Lynessa looked the ultimate in gravitas; the fact that she twittered with sentimentality as much as Father Nimbus and was prone to hysteria would not be apparent as long as she didn't speak.

Maud had dressed for maturity in the purple bliaut, hair invisible under a sober veil and circlet, with her black velvet cloak clasped at the throat by plain black frogging. No jewelry. After all, she was as good as a widow now; whether she could elicit the Fleming's sympathy remained to be seen, but if it played to her advantage, there was no harm in trying to get it.

Payn's trumpet sounded. Maud took a deep breath and marched out onto the bridge into the sunshine of a warm late afternoon, her party behind her.

From below, on its steps, her villagers gave her a cheer. There was silence from the ramparts, where the white flag flew and Brabançons sullenly lined the allure, their bows ready in case of enemy treachery.

The table had been set up in the middle of the bridge, the two chairs facing each other across it. The tall Fleming stood on its far side with two men behind him, one of them of proportions that would have dwarfed Milburga's.

He bowed to Maud—"My lady of Kenniford"—and gestured to one of the chairs, inviting her to take one. She gestured back; he should sit first; it was *her* table and *her* damn bridge.

He sat. She remained standing. "Before anything is agreed between us, Master Ghent," she said, "my stepson must be restored to me. Where is he?"

He got to his feet, put his fingers in his mouth and whistled. Immediately, a group of men on the Crowmarsh bank parted and a small figure stepped onto the far side of the bridge, and stopped.

Maud wanted to wave but didn't. "*Eagerness is to be avoided,*" Sir Bernard had said. "*It gives the enemy advantage. Lamentable it may have been, but Lord Tewing's attitude toward his son was on the right lines.*"

"Restored, I said," Matilda told the Fleming.

He was abrupt. "And I say a hostage."

First blood to Alan of Ghent.

Once again, he indicated, politely, that Maud should sit.

Once again, she refused. "Not while my lady cousin is forced to stand."

It was a ploy. She could have sent three chairs out to the bridge, but making the enemy provide one or otherwise appear discourteous was a move that put him in an inferior position.

While they waited for one of the Fleming's men to fetch the chair for Lynessa, Ghent extended his condolences: "I hear your husband has been taken ill, lady. I am sorry for it."

"I thank you." She was cold.

"Just how ill *is* he?"

A departure from formality. With something like patronizing amusement, as if dealing with a child speaking for its parents. An attempt to undermine her in case she was undermining Tewing. Asking if she, a mere woman, was in charge, and whether any treaty would be nullified if Tewing regained his strength.

Which, Maud had to admit, was the case, but it was still an insult.

It's my damn castle, she wanted to shout at him. Instead, she was icy. "That is none of your business," she said. "It is sufficient for you to know that his position has devolved upon me."

She knew now why mercenaries unnerved her, not only because they were dangerous in themselves but because they were outside the only system on which her society, *real* society, was built, whereby everybody owed duty to somebody under feudal law, just as her tenants, free and unfree; her knights; and her manor holders had to pay her in various taxes and service, just as she, their tenant in chief, had to render taxes and service to the ultimate earthly authority, the king. Mercenaries were unattached from the only mechanism that gave order to the world; they floated free of all responsibility except to those who paid them, like disgusting flies sucking at a sweetness to which they had not contributed.

That was why Maud did not see Alan of Ghent then. He was a representative shape to her. His Norman French was excellent but with a strong glottal catch that, to Maud's ear, reduced it to the speech of a peasant. Nor did she recognize the long, carved lines of the man's face and his intelligent, penetrating eyes as in any way individual; she saw only a tall figure who was repulsive and threatening, who hadn't shaved in three days—another Stang, someone to whom, in better circumstances, it would have been beneath her dignity to converse on equal terms.

"My people and I are prepared to acknowledge the lady Empress Matilda—" she began.

"Now that she has won the war," the mercenary pointed out pleasantly.

I don't care who won the bloody war. I wasn't for Stephen, I wasn't for anybody, I was forced into an allegiance by a forced marriage.

She went on: "To recognize her as our sovereign to whom we owe our fealty."

"And so say all of you?"

Yes, blast you, because the only man who would say differently lies dribbling in his bed. How to put it? "All of us who are competent to say it," she told him.

"Ah," he said, "I see."

There. She'd satisfied him because she'd had to, betrayed a sick and hateful husband to a man whom she hated more for forcing her to do it.

The mercenary raised his head to look at Stang. "And you? Do you and your men subscribe to this new allegiance?"

She was furious. Was she to spend her life as a child while men arranged matters over her head? "*I* speak for Master Stang," she said, "and, yes, he is willing to surrender to you as long as he and his men are allowed to do so honorably and without reprisals."

"And will Master Stang and his men fight alongside me for the empress?" Again that hint of amusement.

"I undertake that they will," she said bitterly, "as long as you pay them for it."

"Oh, I shall. Nobody but a fool fights except for money."

Base. It's the only word for the lot of them. "So I understand," she said, and hoped he heard the disdain in her voice.

Two Bibles were sent for, one Maud's own, beautiful and gold chased, the mercenary's a battered thing that smelled of sweat and campfires. She had to place her hand on both as she swore before God her allegiance to the now lady of England—the empress's title until her actual coronation—and future queen.

In the silence while she did it, she heard two blackbirds singing in the trees on the Crowmarsh bank and sighed with relief. *I shall keep this vow, Lord, because You have sent me a lucky sign to tell me I must.*

She flapped her hand at Sir Bernard to take over; her part was done, though she was going to stay and make sure the minutiae of the treaty didn't cost her too much.

If she'd hoped—which she had, though without much expectation—that the whole boiling lot would now go away and leave Kenniford in peace, she was disappointed. Until things were settled and any barons still ready to fight for the imprisoned Stephen were defeated, her castle must be garrisoned by some of Ghent's men.

Indeed, for a week, she must feed and pay all of them, Flemings and Brabançons.

She sat up. "All of you. A *week*?"

"My men have marched fast and fought hard since Lincoln, lady. They need rest. Also, as I understand it, when Master Stang and his Brabançons vacate your castle, they become my dependents." He reverted to informality again. "And *I'm* not damn well paying them. Or feeding them." He turned to Sir Bernard: "Twopence a day per man, sixpence for my officers, a shilling for myself, two hundred beeves, four hundred sheep, a thousand capons, two hundred casks of ale—"

"*What?*" Maud's shriek silenced the blackbirds.

"A penny a day, threepence and ninepence," Sir Bernard said quickly, "ninety beeves, one hundred and fifty sheep, five hundred capons, thirty tuns of ale . . ."

Even that was too much for a load of blackguards. "Will you ruin me?" Maud moaned.

The Fleming turned round in his chair and gestured for William to be taken back to the enemy encampment. Facing front again, he said: "And forty sack of grain, white for me and my officers, rye for the men, *with* vegetables—I must consider their bowels."

He'd winked. The bastard had winked at her. *I'll consider your bowels, put on a spit and roasted.*

Sir Bernard upped his figures slightly; Ghent lowered his not at all.

Sir Bernard threw in inducements: the officers to be entertained in the castle, with feasting, but only for three days. "After all, the war is as good as finished."

"Not over yet. *Seven* days. And twenty ells of good worsted cloth, plus woolen hose." He looked sadly at a tear in the stocking just above his right boot.

"And lace-fringed kerchiefs, I suppose," Maud said.

"That would be nice."

She withheld comment after that; irony was lost on the pig.

It went on and on. The sun descended behind the castle; the villagers meandered back to their cottages; blackbirds stopped singing, leaving the dusk to nightingales. The river reflected glows in its blackness as fires were lit on its opposite shore. Maud looked for William but couldn't see him. She nudged Cousin Lynessa sharply. The nun had her elbows on the table, cupped her chin in her hands, and was hanging on Ghent's every word as if he were spouting psalms rather than theft.

At last, settlement was reached and the Bibles once more employed, Maud vowing on hers grudgingly; Sir Bernard had done what he could, but it would be a thin winter at Kenniford now.

The mercenary nodded toward his end of the bridge, and William came trotting toward her. She stood up to hug him and walked off with him without a word of farewell to Ghent, nor to Stang, who was joining the Fleming's camp across the river. "Did they hurt you?"

"No. Master Ghent said he was only going to pretend to hang me and I wasn't to be afraid, so I wasn't. We played conkers and I won. Is Father all right?"

"Not well, darling, I'm afraid. Skip off and see him, but let Milburga feed you first."

As the boy ran ahead, Lynessa, Sir Rollo and Sir Bernard caught up with her. "It went well," the steward said. "He was not unreasonable; it could have cost us a lot more."

"Could it, indeed," Maud said, deprived and angry.

"He struck me as soldierlike," Sir Rollo put in. "A base rogue, of course, but I think we may expect more discipline in his men than from the Brabançons."

"I thought he was rather attractive in a dangerous sort of way," Cousin Lynessa said, clasping her hand. "Didn't you think so, Maud?"

"No, I bloody well didn't."

Alan of Ghent watched them go. His lieutenant, Bartolomeus,

looming beside him, expelled a breath. "Wouldn't want to put that little harpy on her back. Too big for her boots she is."

Ghent's eyes were still on the gatehouse. "Pretty, though, ain't she?" he said, gazing after her.

WHILE THE FLEMING AND HIS men were in situ, Maud kept herself removed. Reports came up to her of the good behavior, even courtesy, demonstrated by him and his officers—Morgana was in transports—but she refused to be beguiled. "Officers," she'd scoff. "Riffraff more like."

The empress's pennant now fluttered over Kenniford; Ghent had produced it—a somewhat tattered, grubby and hastily sewn version of that lady's personal seal, showing Matilda enthroned with a scepter in her right hand, held in such a way as to suggest she might bash somebody on the head with it.

That was enough. Maud was flying the empress's colors; no need to hobnob with the rabble that served the woman. The devils were eating her out of house and home as it was.

On the second day Morgana left. "Back to the Marches, my dear," she told Maud; "besides, I'll be one less mouth to feed." Maud bit back her tears as she watched her leave, already ruing the departure of one who represented such stolid comfort. "You'll be fine," Morgana said. "These things have a habit of blowing over."

On the third day, however, Alan of Ghent sent up a request for an interview. "More of a demand, really," Milburga told her, bringing it, "but put nice. Hurry up."

"He should come to *me,*" Maud said, and then decided that her solar should not be so polluted. Putting on her shoes, she asked: "What does he want?"

"He's going. They're all going."

Maud made a quick obeisance of gratitude in the direction of the cross above her bed and hurried downstairs.

The mercenary was in the hall, shaved, cloaked, spurred, with his helmet under his arm and an impatience that brought out the scent of the floor's rushes as he strode back and forth. He began talking before she'd reached the bottom of the steps. "We're pulling out, lady. I'm leaving fifty men with you—all I can afford at the moment, but I'll send more when I can. Lieutenant Bartolomeus will be remaining—"

"And why is that?"

"Why is Bart—?"

"Why are you pulling out? I am delighted to hear it, but why?"

He shook his head to get sense into it. "I should have said. There's a message come from the empress recalling me; the situation has . . . changed. Stephen has been freed."

Oh, Mary, mother of God, I've just joined the wrong side.

When the mercenary had gone, Maud gathered her people to tell them that the war was on again.

CHAPTER 7

AD 1180, Perton Abbey

IT WAS THE EMPRESS'S FAULT," the abbot says.

"In other words another sinful Eve," his scribe says happily.

The abbot shakes his head with an energy that makes him cough. "Not sinful; at least, not like that. Nobody ever ascribed uncleanness to that particular lady of England. Arrogance to the point of stupidity, yes, she had that, but not sin in the sense that you mean it. If she'd been in the Garden of Eden, Empress Matilda would have throttled the serpent for daring to address her. No, there she was, Stephen in her prison, the barons temporizing while they waited to see what would happen, England at her feet. And what does she do?"

The scribe giggles and dares: "Buggers it up?"

"Totally. Already she has alienated the bishops who'd gone over to her; she has been haughty to King David of Scotland, who was on her side, and to Robert of Gloucester, most loyal of half brothers. She has the crown in her grasp. All she needs to have it on her head is a coronation at Westminster Abbey, and all she needs for that is to treat the burghers of London as human beings: forgiveness for their

support of Stephen, some courtesy, a little liberality. Does she extend any of these things? No, they are commoners; they must crawl to her; they must pay her an exorbitant sum for their former recalcitrance."

"She pissed them off, in fact," the scribe says, giggling again.

The abbot's eyes are failing, but they can still quell inky young upstarts. "My son, we shall abjure these salty interjections, if you please."

"Yes, my lord. I apologize, my lord."

His superior nods. "Though the description is apt, I fear. The empress's behavior was so outrageous that the Londoners lost their temper and rebelled, pouring out of the city to take revenge on this new Messalina where she sat at a banquet in Westminster. She got away only just in time, riding astride and heading for her heartland in the West Country—"

"Riding astride, my lord?" The scribe is shocked.

"You try going sidesaddle on a horse with the hounds of hell after you. The point, my son, is that she escaped to the west, thanks to her half brother, who fought a courageous rearguard action all the way. Eventually, however, the earl was captured."

"One moment, my lord." The scribe closes the lid on his wax book, puts it down carefully onto the floor and takes another onto his knee.

"Your hand is not too tired, my son?" the abbot asks, for lifting the stylus to change the direction of a stroke in wax takes considerably more effort than setting a quill to parchment.

"No, my lord, I thank you."

"Consider, then, the empress's position: she is discredited, still uncrowned; her greatest general, Earl Robert, is in enemy hands. All she can do is swallow that bitter pill and agree to free King Stephen if the royal forces free Earl Robert in return. And she does; the two men are exchanged. But Matilda doesn't admit defeat; she still has two great assets. One of them is her husband, Geoffrey Plantagenet, who is in the last stages of conquering Normandy for her against crumbling resistance, presenting a cruel dilemma to men who own lands

on both sides of the channel." The abbot pauses. "And she has their young son, Henry Plantagenet."

"Henry Plantagenet." The scribe's voice treats the name very differently. "Who grew up to become the killer of Saint Thomas of Canterbury."

"Sadly true." And the abbot is sad for it. "But, you must admit, he has also been the bringer of a peace and an order to England such as it has never known." He turns to his scribe. "You see, nobody had sworn loyalty to Stephen's eldest son, Eustace. If, as many lords were beginning to think, the disasters of war that had befallen them were due to breaking their oath to the empress, all could be amended by recognizing her son as heir to the kingdom after Stephen died. I think it is why, at that stage, his father allowed him to join his mother and uncle in England. A wave of a flag."

The abbot pauses, his eyes return to watching the leaves of his oak tree and softly he repeats to himself: "Henry Plantagenet."

Nine years old the boy had been when his father let him make the dreadful channel crossing. Not much older than young William in fact. In the depth of winter. Into a country ravaged by war.

Geoffrey Plantagenet had known the risk, but he also knew his son was worth a battalion to the empress's cause. He was round faced, russet headed, stocky, sparking with intelligence, loving every minute of the danger, throwing a temper when his mother sent him back to Normandy; word spread that here, perhaps, might be the future answer to England's dilemma.

The abbot is returned to the present by his scribe's sniff of disapprobation. Time's a-racing. The sun entering his window is at a low angle, sending warmth onto skin that is becoming increasingly cold.

"Well, well," he says, "young Henry returns to his father's care. With their king back, Stephen's armies go forth again, and one of them entraps our poor, beleaguered empress in Oxford Castle."

"Forgive me, my lord." The scribe is cautious. "But you seem to be expressing sympathy for a woman who brought disaster on herself."

"Am I? It may be so, it may be so. Or perhaps I am feeling pity for a little girl who was packed off to Germany at the age of eight to marry the Holy Roman emperor Henry the Fifth."

"A fine marriage, I'd have thought," the scribe says; he is not an imaginative young man, not where the female sex is concerned. "Wedded to the Christian emperor of the Western world. And she seems to have been proud enough of the imperial title; she kept it, after all, even when she'd been widowed and then wedded to Plantagenet."

"Perhaps she needed it." All at once, the abbot is too tired to go on. "My son, I think that tonight we shall have to leave her besieged in Oxford Castle with only a few knights, while a blizzard drowns out the howl of wolves, human and animal, circling the walls to bring her down."

"And tomorrow?" The scribe begins packing his tablets away.

"Tomorrow we must return to the wanderings of our mercenary and his adopted child. Good night, my son, and thank you."

CHAPTER 8

AD 1141, the Cambridgeshire Fens

DESPITE THEIR LONG START, THE trail left by the monk and Ramon and their men was not difficult to trace. Tiny villages—Earith, Papworth, Gamlingay, Potton, Cardington—marked an erratic swath of looting, killing, rape and destruction that led south and west. Gwil and Penda, trying to find where the mercenary band had gone next, were met by people frantically trying to rebuild burned cottages and barns, and, almost invariably, the question "Where was God when this happened to us?"

Sometimes it was: "Where was the law?" For it seemed that the system of justice that had prevailed under King Henry I had broken down. In too many isolated places like these, manorial courts no longer functioned because the knights who administered them had been pressed into the army of King Stephen as it rushed around the country putting down one rebellion only for another to erupt somewhere else. Men who should have been able to defend their homes, or form the hue and cry that would have chased down the despoilers, had been forced into service to build unlicensed castles—despite the fact that even to fortify a manor with battlements without the king's permission was against the law—now springing up like so many hydra heads as men took the opportunity provided by the general anarchy to defend themselves and at the same time increase their power over their neighbors.

"Who we chasing, Gwil?" Penda had asked.

"Fellas that stole my crossbow," Gwil said shortly.

Oddly enough, the answer satisfied her. During their sojourn in a rented room in Cambridge, he had made a crossbow, buying the glue and tools in order to save time, but doing the shaping and laminating himself, a process producing an article of such beautiful craftsmanship that the girl, fascinated by it, could imagine no greater loss than to have it stolen.

"Ain't goin' to catch 'em, though, are we?" she said. "They're two months ahead of we."

"They're going to settle," Gwil told her. "Sooner or later, they'll settle." He was convinced of it. Ramon's daring was growing with each raid, and so was his booty; raging through countryside would become wearing; and eventually the man would attack some vulnerable motte and bailey, fortify it and establish himself over its land as a robber baron. He wouldn't be the first; disaffected mercenary bands setting up their own lordships were destabilizing England as much as the war itself.

"If peace ever comes, it's going to take a bloody strong king to put this country back together," Gwil said.

What he was going to do when he caught up with the gang, he had no idea; he wasn't going to let Penda come face-to-face with it, he was sure of that—to reencounter the men who'd damaged her so badly could only damage her more. Yet to let them just disappear without some sort of accounting for what they'd done would, he knew, cause a dissatisfaction that would never let him lie easy.

Actually, the girl was improving; she still had no memory of who she was and he'd stopped asking because the question disturbed her, but she was beginning to show interest in the world around her. While she insisted on being taken for a boy, there'd been a surprising display of femininity when, in Cambridge, it had come to buying masculine clothes. He'd expected her to wish to remain inconspicuous, shrinking into the sartorial shadows, afraid of being noticed. But no, at the secondhand outfitters he'd taken her to in the market square, she'd spent an age hunting through the racks until she'd found a stylish, slim woolen tunic in a color that made Gwil blink. "It's *scarlet*."

"I know. I think it's pretty."

It clashed horribly with her hair but the choice suggested that, as a male, she could gratify a delight in color that had been unsatisfied in the fens, where men and women only wore clothes dyed in woad, if they were dyed at all. He didn't have the heart to refuse her, though the bright green midthigh stockings she chose to cover the gap between sky-blue trousers and elfin black leather boots were, he felt, literally going a shade too far. So was the purple cap with a jay's feather in it. "Look like a bloody popinjay, you will," he grumbled.

"What's a popinjay?"

Gwil drew the line at a cloak that could have rivaled a rainbow and bought instead a hooded and voluminous thing in serviceable brown wool that concealed an otherwise eye-dazzling ensemble.

All this, with two sets of linen underclothing for her, a new cloak for himself, *plus* the outlay on the crossbow, *plus* the rent for the Cambridge room, *plus* packs in which to carry equipment for life on the tramp, *plus* food and drink while they were doing it—and prices were getting high—had severely depleted the stolen coins from Ely. Sooner, rather than later, if the search for Ramon and the monk was to continue, they were going to have to find the means of earning a living.

THE SEARCH FOR RAMON ENDED at Cainhoe. The village itself had been razed, but a string of corpses hanging from the crenels of a castle overlooking it from a Bedfordshire hilltop were not those of massacred inhabitants.

Gwil spent so long looking upward that the castle gatekeeper peered out through the grille in the door at him. "Friends of yourn?"

Gwil pointed. "I'm hoping as that black-haired bastard there is the one as stole a bloody crossbow off me."

"Crossbow, eh? Lucky that's all he stole. Want a closer look?"

Up on the ramparts, Gwil was able to peer down at the heads below. The eyes had been pecked out by crows and the flesh of the faces was in strips, but the long raven-black hair of Ramon was unmistakable.

"Thought we was easy pickings, they did," the gatekeeper said with satisfaction. He was a jolly man, made jollier by the rotting bunting strung along the walls.

The castle, it appeared, was one of several owned by the d'Albini family. Usually it was unoccupied except for a few servants, but on the day of Ramon's raid old Sir Nigel d'Albini and some of his men had just arrived in it from putting down a rebellion against Stephen, intending to rest and recoup before setting out again. "We didn't even have time to raise the flag to show Sir Nigel was in residence, see, so them bastards must've thought the castle wasn't manned. Fact our lads hadn't proper got out of their armor before we heard screams from the village and saw it was afire."

With d'Albini's bowmen firing from the allure and his men-at-arms pouring through the gates, Ramon with his fewer mercenaries had been routed, captured and hanged. "But not afore we had some fun with 'em." The gatekeeper's grin was evil.

"Was there a monk with 'em?" Gwil asked.

"Monk? Never saw no monk. What'd a monk be doing with a gang like that? Never saw no crossbow, neither."

"What about booty? I heard they'd been robbing churches."

"Some. Not much, couple of chalices, bit of gold plate. Nothing to say where they come from, so I reckon as his lordship'll regard 'em as treasure trove."

There'd been more than that carried by the gang's pack mules when they'd left Ely. Either Ramon had stashed the treasure somewhere, or the monk had got away with it. Gwil's money was on the monk; Ramon had been no match for that crafty bastard.

News of arrivals in the castle had got around, and Gwil and Penda were taken to the hall to be interviewed by Sir Nigel d'Albini, a man with a face seamed like ancient leather. "Crossbowman, eh? I could do with you in my service."

"Kind of you, my lord," Gwil said, "but the lad and me, we're on a quest like." The last thing he needed was to rejoin the war; he had to think of an excuse. "There was a monk with those as stole from me. He was with the renegades, but he ain't one of them hanging out there, so we still need to find him." He glanced anxiously at Penda; would she remember that a monk had been one of her rapists? Apparently not; the girl was looking around her with interest, as if she'd never been in a knight's hall before. Which, Gwil supposed, she hadn't.

The explanation was accepted, even approved; Sir Nigel was an eye-for-an-eye, tooth-for-a-tooth man. Nor had he a liking for the monastic system. "Monks." He spat. "Bloody leeches, even the best of 'em. God aid you in finding him, then. Send him to hell from me."

"Thank you, my lord."

They were invited to spend the night. The next morning, because there were archery butts in the castle tiltyard, Gwil took the opportunity to give himself and Penda some practice before they left. He'd given in and let the girl try with the new crossbow, with which she was becoming as adept as she was with the standard yew bow he'd made for her.

D'Albini came out to watch. "That's fancy shooting," he said. "You two should give exhibitions. When you've found your man, come back."

"What's ex'bitions, Gwil?" Penda asked as they set out.

"Mummery and such." Gwil had a low opinion of it. "Fire-eaters, jugglers and the like showing off their skills to amuse lords on feast days."

"What's fire-eaters? What's jugglers?"

When she'd absorbed the concept, Penda was quiet for a time. Then she said: "That old man said as *we* was skilled."

"Better than most, but don't you get proud now. Ruins your aim, getting too proud does."

"Do they pay, these exhibitions?"

"Suppose they must. Low way of living, though."

"Like our money. You said that was getting low. It'd be a way of getting about, Gwil, and we could ask if anybody'd seen a monk with your crossbow."

He looked at her; in her eagerness she'd tugged at his sleeve, the first time she'd ever touched him. Bless her, did she think the crossbow was the be-all and end-all in his hunt for the monk?

Give it up, Gwil, God said. *Take her back to Brittany with you.*

"And do what, Lord?"

Make a home for her. She can't wander forever, not dressed as a boy. It's not natural and one of these days she'll remember . . .

"Maybe she will, maybe she won't, but it ain't natural what they did to her, neither. What that monk did . . . he ought to suffer."

Vengeance is Mine, Gwil. He'll suffer when he gets to hell, I'll see to that.

It wasn't enough. Gwil saw his life, what life he had left, stretching in front of him, unfulfilled, wondering what the monk was doing, whether he was prospering, praying with steepled hands, chanting, being lauded for his sanctity, and all the time his sin seeping from him like filth, miring other young redheaded girls with its slime.

Then, and only then, did it occur to him that the thought of the monk had propelled his hunt from the beginning.

Ramon and the others? Animals on hind legs. Slaughtered animals now. The true monstrosity was the beast dressed in holy robes, an abnormality unfit to live.

"And there's a link between us, Lord," he said. "It was in the girl's hand. You left the quill case there so's I could find him through it. You meant it for a sign. Don't tell me You didn't. I know You did."

God remained silent; He couldn't wriggle out of that one.

"You all right, Gwil?" Penda asked. "You're muttering."

"I'm thinking."

"*We* could give exhibitions, Gwil. We'd earn money. I hit dead center every time now. I'm good at it, that old lord said I was. I like shooting." Penda's voice became a deliberate whine. "Only thing I do like."

She's playing on it, Gwil, the Lord said. *You're becoming fond, and she knows it. She's twisting you.*

Yes, she was, but that, too, like her affection for bright clothing, showed she was getting better. The dullness that had encased her like the patina on an old sword was beginning to rub off, allowing glimpses of the character beneath. And the talking; although she still shrank from strangers, around him she was almost garrulous, and what with her incessant inquiry, there were times when he was nostalgic for the days when she was mute.

"Bloody mountebank, that's what you are," he said, grumbling.

"What's a mountebank?"

THE DOCUMENT IN THE QUILL case went untranslated because, though he inquired of lawyers, notaries and priests, Gwil found nobody who could read it. His other questioning of everyone he met was treated as laughable. A monk? Monks were two a penny; most were confined to their monasteries, but there were enough traveling on monastic business, carrying letters etc. from abbey to abbey, as to make them unremarkable.

"This one stinks of asafetida, though," Gwil would say, persisting. It was no good; most of those he quizzed wouldn't have recognized asafetida if it had been shoved up their nostrils, it being a rare commodity in England. A knowledgeable little apothecary whose shop Gwil ventured into at Bedford was at least informative on the substance, if not the monk.

"Ah yes," he said, "so named from the Persian *'aza'* and the Latin '*foetidus*,' I'm told, otherwise known as 'devil's dung' or 'stinking gum' for its penetrating odor—it *is* a gum, incidentally, not a spice. I presume the person about whom you are inquiring suffers from flatulence? A splendid specific against flatulence, asafetida. Also boils."

"Where would he get it from?"

"Well, not from the likes of me; I haven't got a wealthy enough clientele. It is used in the richer kitchens, of course; I'm told that when cooked properly it can impart a pleasant flavor reminiscent of leeks. Your odorous friend must be using it raw."

"Yes, but where'd he *get* it?"

The apothecary shrugged. "If he is a religious, presumably from his monastery, which, in turn, would have access to a port trading with the Orient, where the gum comes from. London, Southampton perhaps, or any of the East Anglian harbors."

Ely. That's where the bastard had got it from. Ely wasn't on the coast but was lapped by rivers that led to it. He'd been a monk at Ely, which had enabled him to have the geographical knowledge to betray it.

"Though," the apothecary said, intrigued by the puzzle Gwil had set him, and pursuing it, "one wouldn't have thought that an ordinary brother would be able to treat his affliction with asafetida; too expensive, hardly in keeping with his vow of poverty. There are other, herbal methods, though less effective, of course."

"This is no ordinary monk," Gwil said grimly.

"I imagine not. He must hold some position in the monastic hierarchy; those functionaries always do themselves well."

Before he left the apothecary's shop, Gwil showed him the document from the quill case. The little man peered at it, shaking his head. "I'm a Latinist. I don't read Greek, I'm afraid."

"It's Greek?"

"I believe so."

Out of gratitude, Gwil spent one of his diminishing supply of pennies on a strengthening medicine of motherwort and rosemary for Penda before he left the shop.

Where to go now? Where was the monk making for? Did he need more of that bloody asafetida? If so, where'd he get it?

Not Ely, that was for sure. He'd never return to Ely, not after what he and the others had done there. He and Ramon had been going *away* from East Anglia before they'd separated, heading southwest, so maybe he was keeping to that same direction. London? Southampton?

There was no more success in finding out what the document said; readers of Greek were rare.

"Couldn't You've given me more clues, Lord?" Gwil groaned. "A stench and a piece of writing no bugger can decipher, what's them to track a man down by?"

Stick with them, Gwil, that's My advice.

At least the immediate problem of where to spend the night had been solved by the apothecary. "Try the convent at Elstow, just south of here," he'd said, "the nuns there take in bona fide travelers."

They set out smartly; the light was changing, evening was coming on, and it was too dangerous to camp in the open. After dark, a fire could attract men desperate enough to slit a throat or two for the food cooking over it. So far Penda and Gwil hadn't been subjected to attack, but they'd seen what happened to those who had been. Already the road was deserted.

Not quite, though.

From round a bend came the sound of screams and shouting.

Automatically, Penda and Gwil reached for the bows in their packs, he selecting a bolt from his quiver, she an arrow from hers, before stepping into the shadow of trees on the right-hand verge to begin moving quietly along it.

Five figures were silhouetted against the setting sun; the screams came from a woman pinioned round the neck by the arm of a thickset man whose other hand ostentatiously waved a knife. His equally big companion was shouting at two slighter men. "Cash and quick, or he slits her fucking throat."

The two archers moved closer while the male victims fumbled in the purses at their waists.

Gwil put his foot carefully in the stirrup and armed the crossbow. "Mine's the one holding the girl," he hissed at Penda. "You take the other." He looked at her; she was breathing heavily, her face white in the gloom of the trees, her grin revealing teeth that were even whiter. "Get him in the arse," he told her. "We ain't out to kill."

She nodded.

"Now."

Instantly, fletched feathers were sticking out of the shouter's backside, and the hand of the other man had lost its knife to the end of a bolt that sent it into the trees.

For an openmouthed second nobody moved, then, as the woman freed herself, one of her companions looped into the air, landed on his hands, and performed another half loop so that his feet connected with the jaw of the man who'd been holding her, sending him crashing down like a felled tree.

It took some minutes for the three travelers to comprehend that their rescuers weren't replacing the two robbers in order to rob them on their own account, by which time the thieves themselves were hobbling off down the road, the shouter supporting his half-conscious friend on one arm while, with the other hand, groping frantically for the arrow still sticking out of his backside.

AS A GROUP, THEY ALL looked too disreputable to be invited to attend evensong when they reached Elstow, though the nuns were prepared to provide bread, cheese, ale, and a barn with straw to sleep on. They ate by the light of a candle Gwil produced from his pack.

Pan, Wan and Waterlily still hadn't finished marveling. "Just to hit the knife," Wan said. "Didn't even scrape his fingers far as I could see. You *were* aiming at the knife?"

"He don't ever miss," Penda said. Gwil turned to look at her, astonished. It was the first time she had spoken since they met the group and he was relieved to see that the taciturn suspicion with which she had previously regarded them, as she did all strangers, was fading. He was also a little flattered that it had been her pride in him that prompted it.

Pan turned toward her and smiled. "And you!" he said. "An arrow, right plumb in the arse. From that distance!"

"That's the bit I liked," Waterlily said, clasping her hands in delight. "That bastard running off with feathers sticking out his arse. Keep me warm at nights, that will." Gwil watched as a broad grin spread across Penda's face, like the thaw of spring.

"And your jumping!" The words came out in a great rush now and she was blushing. "How come you can jump like that?"

Pan spread his hands. "It's what we do."

They were strolling acrobats, collectively the Sons and Daughter of the Great Chan, whoever *he* was. Their clothing declared that they were performers; the colors of their cloaks and caps—all of them feathered—outdid Penda's so that compared with them she was a dowdy peahen among three peacocks. In fact, they were Saxon Londoners all born into its rat holes with the enterprise to clamber out.

"It was the docks," Pan said. "All the world comes in on ships to the London docks, and as a lad I saw this sailor doing handstands, don't know where he came from, somewhere to the east I reckon, but he taught me a few flips and I taught Wan and we went on from there."

The two men were sharp faced, thin bodied and alike as peas in a pod although, in fact, they were cousins. Waterlily was a waif they'd found dancing on the streets for money; they'd trained her and added her to their act to give it feminine interest.

"And bugger me," said Wan, "she's turned out limberer than what we are."

Her long, wavy red hair reminded Gwil of Penda's before she cut it; indeed, from a distance, they looked remarkably alike, which, he supposed, was one of the things that first endeared her to him. A childhood in London's hovels had given her a resilience that was admirable; from the way she chattered she might never have been held at knifepoint only an hour or so previously, ignoring the fact that her hands still had a tendency to shake, clattering the many bangles on her wrists.

As the sound of female voices chanting the "Nunc dimittis" for compline came through the barn's slats, she demanded quiet so that she could listen. Her eyes filled with sentimental tears: "I'd like to've been a nun. Must be lovely, all that peace."

"Got to be a virgin for that," Wan told her.

Amiably, she threw a piece of cheese at him—obviously, it was a regular exchange.

The three traveled from castle to castle, where they were in demand for feast days by lords laying on entertainments for their guests.

"You'd think the way things are they'd be too busy fighting," Pan said, "but the rich always got time and gold to celebrate a knighting or a wedding or some bloody thing."

"Done us a good turn, the war has," Waterlily chipped in. "Ain't so many farcers around no more. Plenty of mummers, but when did you last see a proper fire-eater? All run off to somewhere safe, and them as stays is mostly bloody amateurs. We're popular, we are."

Pan nodded. "One chamberlain tells another. Word of mouth. Can't do better'n that."

"But we got to keep off the roads come evening, Pan," Wan warned him. "I've told you before, it's getting too bloody dangerous."

"Or," Pan told him, glancing slyly at their rescuers, "we ought to team up with a couple as could protect us."

"That's right, that's right." Waterlily clapped her hands in delight. "You two come along of us and give exhibitions."

Penda was triumphant. "See, Gwil? Twice in a week we been told that. It's a sure sign."

THE STRIPED BALLS STREAMED BACK into the jugglers' hands like red-and-yellow iron filings to magnets, their owners bowed to the applause, there was a roll on the tabors . . .

The chamberlain of Hertford Castle took the stage. "And now, my lords, ladies, mesdames, messieurs, may I present for your amazement that world-renowned marksman with the bow Master Vaclav of Bohemia, and his talented young assistant, Master Penda, lured at great expense from the court of King Vlatislav the Second."

Penda had asked, "Where's Bohemia? And who's King Vlatislav?"

"Don't ask me," Wan said, "Pan come up with them names."

You had to have an exotic title in this trade. Norman lords, who'd happily hack off the limbs of other races on crusade, liked their entertainers to be foreign. Magicians were invariably Abdul or Mustafa from the Orient, acrobats hired from China, dancers from Persia, yet the oaths exchanged as they all struggled into their costumes in the allotted and overcrowded changing rooms rarely came from further afield than Yorkshire or Calais.

The exception was the fools. Buffoonery had to be seen to be homegrown; fools kept the plain names of Wilfrid or Godwin or Oswald, Saxons to a man—as if finding comical the antics of a people they'd conquered reassured some hidden Norman unease at having conquered them. They were always the pièce de résistance; their drollery, especially their ability to fart tunes, had noble audiences rolling among the rushes. The Sons and Daughter of the Great Chan ran close in popularity, partly because their agility beggared belief, and partly because watching a skimpily clad Waterlily being twirled like a twig by Pan's upheld right hand brought roars of appreciation from male watchers, if not their less enthusiastic ladies.

Master Vaclav and his talented young assistant attracted little applause to begin with and only appeared on the first program above a sad-looking dancing bear.

"I told you an' told you," Pan explained wearily afterward, "every bugger in that hall uses a bow out hunting, an' every bugger in that hall thinks if he only practiced a bit more, he could do what you do."

Penda was indignant. "Bloody couldn't."

"Oh, you're clever, but there's no sparkle to the act. Got to have sparkle in this game."

So sparkle, somewhat to Gwil's disgust, was introduced.

Penda now ran down the length of the great hall—apparently carelessly, but in fact counting her steps to mark out the required distance of a hundred feet—and placed a large square straw target at the far end of the tables.

Another roll on the tabors. ("Always musicians at the entertainments; you don't need to bring your own," Pan had said. "Just give the taborer a halfpenny.") Penda twirled and bowed again—she was good at sparkling; Gwil, self-conscious, tended to lumber.

She came back to pick up her bow and sent an arrow into the dead center of the bull. Gwil took her place and aimed, splitting her arrow open through its fletched end. To show it wasn't a fluke, they repeated it, each time moving the target a further two yards away.

A candelabra was set on the top of the target and its branches lit. Gwil and Penda took turns to snuff out the candles.

"Ooh"s and "aah"s from the watchers began to punctuate the performance.

Now it was the turn of the glove; it had been specially made for Penda with slightly extended fingers. Pan had suggested it, saying it was worth the expense.

Penda took up position at the side of the target, extending her right arm so that her gloved hand lay against the bull.

Again the tabors drummed. One by one Gwil sent an arrow so that it lodged between each finger. (Louder "ooh"s and "aah"s, though in fact this wasn't as difficult a trick as putting out a candle flame.)

Now. The finale.

For the first time, Gwil took up the crossbow—until this moment they'd been using vertical bows. While he cocked it the chamberlain, as instructed, took the floor. "And now, my lords, ladies, mesdames, messieurs, Master Vaclav will perform a feat so dangerous that he begs your cooperation by not moving or calling out in case he is distracted in his aim. To this end, the doors of the hall will be shut to ensure that there is no draft." There was a sharp, collective intake of breath and a long roll on the tabors.

Penda took the close-fitting cowl off her head and replaced it with a conical Phrygian cap, settling it carefully so that its forward peak was three inches directly above her forehead. She bowed again and took up a stance in front of the target.

Gwil hated this bit. It wasn't that he distrusted his aim; he was shooting as well as ever, though there was bound to come a day . . . What worried him was that there were times when, for all her gaiety in front of an audience, a look came into Penda's eyes—she never shut them for this but stared straight into his—that told him she didn't much mind if the bolt went through her brain.

I don't care, it said, *not if it wipes out the memory I can't remember.*

It shocked him; he'd thought she was doing so well. When he tried to envisage what it was like in the girl's head—and he thought about it a lot—he saw a horizontal shutter dividing her past from her present, the darkness behind the shutter seeping through it like fog into a room, so that her present, no matter how brightly lit, was always shadowed.

The drumming stopped. There was silence.

The hiss of the bolt going through the air sounded in the ear in the same second that the Phrygian cap lifted from Penda's neat, boyish red head and hung, quivering, as if from a hook on the target behind it.

In the stamping and roars of applause, Gwil cocked and armed the crossbow again and turned to face the top table, aiming at it for a second, causing a gasp, before raising his sight and sending another shot through a ribbon attached to a beam above the hostess's head, separating it, so that the bunch of flowers it had been holding fell into her hands.

As they escaped the thunder of the hall, the Sons and Daughter of the Great Chan, dressed to go in for their act, clapped them on the shoulder. "That," said Pan, "is what I call *sparkle.*"

PAN WAS RIGHT; IN A country falling apart, its barons and knights still managed to observe saints' days, weddings, celebrations etc. with music and feasting, despite the growing poverty outside their walls.

It was their masters of ceremonies who were feeling the pinch. Roads were becoming unsafe for those without military escort, and too many itinerant performers had abandoned England to ply their trade in safer lands. Those who remained were sought out by anxious castle officials responsible for finding entertainment that wouldn't shame their lord in front of his guests. The Sons and Daughter of Chan, along with Master Vaclav of Bohemia and his talented young assistant, had only to turn up at the gates of a castle to be welcomed, their reputation from their visit to the previous one having preceded them.

They were assured of a night's lodging, sometimes two if the feasting went on long enough; a silver penny in their pockets; and all the food they could eat from the nobility's leavings.

Also, and this was even more valuable, they were kept apprised of the political situation: which area was in turmoil, which castle under attack—the war had become one of sieges—and, therefore, how to avoid them.

For more than a year the five of them, protected by Gwil and Penda's bows, were able to travel the roads in comparative safety from one end of the country to the other. Wherever they went Gwil inquired after the monk but without success. Sometimes he felt he was merely treading water; he just didn't know what else to do.

He hadn't told Penda's history to his companions. It was maintained that they were uncle and nephew. (Neither had claimed the closer relationship of father and son, Gwil because it would somehow be betraying the little boy in a Brittany grave, and Penda because she knew she'd had a real father and, for the same reason, felt discomfort at denying his existence.)

Whether Pan, Wan and Waterlily were aware of Penda's real sex, Gwil didn't know. Thrown together as closely as they were, he thought they probably did, but secrets were respected in their profession, and the acrobats paid lip service to the deception.

But although she and Pan and Wan got along well, she was jealous, and showed it, when Waterlily made a fuss of Gwil. "You steer clear of that one," she told him privately, "she's a slut."

"You watch your mouth." Gwil was cross; he felt protective of the girl. "She's one of us."

"She's one of anybody's."

Waterlily's relationship with Pan and Wan was undeniably anomalous. "None of our business," Gwil said brusquely. "Them's happy enough with the arrangement. And it ain't no skin off our nose."

"Well, you're too old for it, so don't you go joining 'em," Penda snapped.

However there were even times when Waterlily extended her range and disappeared for the night with one of the better-looking young lords from their audiences. After each such encounter, another bracelet, sometimes of gold, appeared on her wrist. What shocked Gwil on those occasions was not just the young woman's wantonness but the fact that both Pan and Wan shrugged it off as "Waterlily's way." He wondered how the girl avoided pregnancy and had to assume she was conversant with what he'd heard described as "Eve's herbs."

Originally, he'd hoped Penda would benefit from female companionship and that, as she reached puberty, she might gain instruction in the, well, *women's things* that awaited her, a responsibility that, he feared, might otherwise fall to him.

Not now, though; it was clear that Penda found Waterlily's exuberant femininity alarming and he was also aware that anything the girl had to teach wasn't what he wanted Penda to learn.

Still he was fond of her, and it was an amiable enough caravan—they'd acquired a mule to carry their equipment—that trudged, leapt and shot its way into early December. Faces, events and the names of their hosts tended to blur into one. So did the halls with their bright wall paintings, the glorious velvets of the clothing, the heat from hundreds of blazing candles, the silver on the tables and the food—such food: heaped dishes with overelaborate sauces, swan, crane, boar, pheasant, larks' tongues, all of it overlaid with the smell of men and women who'd overeaten . . .

Until they arrived back nearly where they'd started—at the castle occupied by the sheriff of Bedfordshire.

Their last.

ON THEIR WAY IN THROUGH the gatehouse, they were pressed back against its walls by the egress of a mounted party of secular clerics, very pious, very dignified, in their long, simple white tunics; only the quality of their horses, and the bejeweled brooches in the center of their thrown-back cloaks, suggested that they were Jesus's camels trying to get through the eye of a needle.

Gwil's and Penda's attention was distracted from them by Waterlily, whose behavior was never at its best when she was presented with the sanctimonious.

"Woo-hoo, lads, here come the Pharisees." She tossed her long red hair off her shoulders before turning her back and waggling her backside, her voice echoing around the walls. "Kiss my arse, gentlemen?"

The sheriff's chamberlain, who was seeing the party off, was outraged. "I hope this is not what we may expect from you players tonight. We are entertaining the king, *the king*, you understand . . ."

It was to be a royal performance. Having endured the chamberlain's lecture, Pan and Wan were cross with the girl for once. "In the name of God, Waterlily . . ."

She was unrepentant. "We-e-ll . . . did you see that sour-faced bugger riding the bay? Looked at me like he wanted to kill me. They're all bloody hypocrites, them clergy." It was said with feeling. "Fuck you soon as look at you, then pray for you—*you*, not them—to be forgiven."

The presence of Stephen; his son and heir, Prince Eustace; and a considerable force of knights was straining the castle's resources, which, perhaps, was why the clerics had departed from it.

The only space left for the entertainers to prepare and dress was in the sheriff's dungeons, or rather just *one* of his dungeons, the others being full of malefactors awaiting trial. The stink emitting from the crammed cells was enhanced in theirs by the presence of Ursus the dancing bear, who had a stomach upset, and by Harold, the fool, going into the contortions that forced air out of his anus in tuneful notes. In the face of protest, he said with dignity that he'd performed successfully for King Stephen before, had now composed a special lai for him and needed to practice.

Before they left for the cleaner air upstairs, Waterlily insisted on handspringing back and forth along the row of cells, bangles jangling, "to cheer the poor buggers up." Which, to judge from the prisoners' howls of delight and repeated requests for an encore, it did.

Gwil and Penda, who wanted to see the king, watched the first part of the performance crouched between the bars of the musicians' gallery, which, being over the entrance to the hall, had a view of the top table.

Penda's expectations of what a monarch should look like were fulfilled. "He's real king-y," she said with awe.

Stephen's hair was more grizzled than the last time Gwil had seen him, but its silver streaks complemented the gold of his circlet. The face was handsome, the manner amiable; he was putting his host and fellow diners at ease.

For Gwil, though, there'd always been a suggestion of playacting—*Is this what a king should do? Have I the right air, the proper gravitas, the charm, for this occasion or that?*

At Lincoln Stephen had assumed a lofty courage that, in the event, had been bravado. His eyes had lifted to a higher plane than anyone else's and he'd become stubborn, ignoring the pleas of William of Ypres to wait for reinforcements. "*We attack right away.*"

As the order went through the ranks, Gwil's fellow arbalist Odo had thrown his cap on the ground and stamped on it. "*That bugger'll get us all killed. And you know why? Because his pa was a fucking coward.*"

Everybody knew it. While on crusade, the late Stephen of Blois had abandoned the siege of Antioch and returned home, earning himself the reputation of a deserter. The fact that he was later shamed into returning to Outremer and getting himself killed did nothing to lift a dishonor resting so heavily on his son's shoulders that, ready or not, every challenge to battle had to be accepted.

Odo had been among the prophets; he'd been cut down in the first wave of the assault, along with too many other good men.

All because you wanted glory, you "king-y" bastard. And you—Gwil turned his attention to the young man sitting a few places along from Stephen—*what sort of commander will* you *make if you inherit?*

Eustace was eating with adolescent energy, but there was a set to his chin that suggested the boy had none of his father's uncertainties and that if, as was now being quietly suggested, the solution to the conflict would be to put the empress's son, Henry, on the throne after Stephen died, this particular young prince wouldn't take kindly to being passed over. Which meant that the war would go on until it had devoured an entire nation.

Well, he, Gwil, would take no part in it. Somehow he had to find a patch of this world in which Penda could grow up in a peace that would assuage the torment in her soul.

There was a burst of laughter from the hall; during his dance, Ursus had squatted to give way to one of his stomach upsets, causing high amusement in everybody except the servants who had to clear up the result before the next act.

Penda disapproved of Eustace's banging his drinking cup on the table in his transports. She didn't think royalty should give way to immoderate laughter like a commoner. "That's not very prince-y."

They extricated themselves from under the musicians' feet and went down the spiral staircase to take their place outside the hall doors, ready for their appearance after the next act.

Their performance, now honed to perfection, was received with exuberance. They were called to the top table to receive the compliments and coins the king scattered in their direction and were on their way out with them when they were called back.

The chamberlain was looking uncomfortable. "Prince Eustace demands that he be allowed to display his own prowess with the bow."

"I do, I do." The boy had drunk as copiously as he'd eaten. "I can do that. I'm a sup'lative archer. Brought down a buck yest'day, right in the eye. Put the lad against the target again and *I'll* shoot his damn cap off."

There was always one; they were used to it by now, though they'd never had to cope with a prince of the blood.

The sheriff of Bedfordshire looked anxiously toward his king. He'd already had bear shit on his floor; he didn't want a dead boy as well.

Gwil approached the top table and bowed to the king. "My lord," he said in what he hoped was a Bohemian accent, carefully rehearsed. "Nobody doubts Prince Eustace's skill, but my assistant and I have dedicated ourselves and our performance to our patron saint, Saint Sebastian, who takes particular care of us. Last time a gentleman raised his bow at my assistant, he was struck down with a seizure before he could fire the arrow."

Saint Sebastian had proved useful in these situations, yet why he was the patron saint of archers was problematic. True, because of his Christian faith, pagan Rome had sentenced Sebastian to be executed with arrows, but those hadn't killed him. In the end he'd been beaten to death and thrown into a privy. Over the years, Gwil had earned money betting on how Saint Sebastian died.

Stephen was kind. He winked at Gwil before addressing Eustace. "We must not offend Saint Sebastian, my son, must we? You are too valuable to us." He gestured to the chamberlain. "Let them go."

"And now, my lords, ladies, mesdames, messieurs . . ." The chamberlain's voice overrode Eustace's disgruntled protests as the two archers, bowing, started to leave the hall.

Usually, they had to sidestep as the Sons and Daughter of the Great Chan bounded through the doorway. But not this time; Wan stood alone in the screened passage outside looking anxious.

"Can't find Waterlily," he said, "Pan's gone looking for her."

The chamberlain came out, flustered. "What are you acrobats doing?" he said. "I've just announced you."

"Ain't ready," Wan told him.

"God's saints, I'm *paying* you for this." He gestured at a page. "Find the fool, tell him he's on." He went back into the hall to explain a change of program.

"Where'd she go?" Gwil asked.

"Said something about being summoned by Prince Eustace."

"When was that?"

"Two hours ago, three."

"Can't have been Eustace." The entertainment had lasted at least two and a half hours and in all that time, while Gwil and Penda had been watching from the musicians' gallery, the prince had not left the hall.

"Don't understand it, then." Wan shifted from foot to foot with worry.

"Maybe she's waiting for him somewhere."

"That being her way," Penda said spitefully.

"No." Wan was firm on this. "She was dressed for the act. She'd have come back on time, she ain't never missed a performance before; she's a professional is our Waterlily."

They split up to search the castle, asking fellow performers if they'd seen the girl, irritating overburdened cooks with their questions, peering into attics, cellars, guardhouses, stables, bumping into scurrying servants and each other.

"She ain't here."

"Wouldn't have gone outside the gates, would she?"

They hurried to the barbican.

Yes, the gatekeeper had seen her. "Some time back. Going down to the village she was. Daring little devil, ain't she? Pretty, too."

The gatekeeper, having witnessed Waterlily's baiting of the clergy, had contracted a fondness for her.

"Did she say why?"

"Anybody with her?"

But the gate had been busy with continual supplies being brought in for the feast; servants, squires and royal messengers going back and forth; petitioners to the king demanding admittance; beggars . . . The gatekeeper had lost track of the comings and goings, let alone having time to chat to Waterlily or notice if she'd been accompanied.

By this time, it was dark. "She won't have gone far outside," Pan said, "she's scared of the dark."

Gwil heard Penda sniff. "She would've if she thought Prince Eustace was waiting for her."

It was deeply concerning; the sympathetic gatekeeper not only provided them with resined torches but sent his son to show them the paths.

A breeze had come up, carrying a cold drizzle of rain with it so that the brands they carried hissed and flamed horizontally back and forth, sometimes casting their elongated shadows on the stone of the walls, sometimes on the ground, and somewhere in the distance a wolf howled.

"She wouldn't be out here," Pan said. But they carried on, splitting up to extend the circle, shouting Waterlily's name, stumbling over strip fields, encountering hedges and having to find the gates that led through them, pheasants squawking as they flew away from their feet, their own cries becoming distant from each other, always shriller and more desperate.

Gwil glimpsed a wet, pale face. "That you, Pen?"

"It's me, an' I'm cold. Can we go back now? We missed her, she's still in the castle somewheres, I'd put a wager on it."

Gwil looked around for the other torches and saw two wavering in the distance as their holders ran about. The third, a bit nearer, wasn't moving. He watched it for a moment. Still, it didn't move.

Jesus Christ, please no.

"You go on back, then," he said. "Get to bed. I'll gather the lads and be along in a minute."

She protested halfheartedly that she'd stay to help, but he insisted. He watched her progress until her figure, going in, was outlined against the flares of the gatehouse, then he headed for the stationary light. The other two torches began to converge toward the same point.

It was the porter's son, looking into the open doorway of a hut. As Gwil came up, he began stepping backward, making regular, barely audible little grunts in his throat.

Gwil pushed past the boy, lowering his torch to see what was inside.

It was the sort of rough wooden shack shepherds built for themselves in the lambing season. It still smelled of sheep, and at first he didn't see what lay among the straw on its dirt floor.

She was on her back, arms splayed, her bright clothes strewn around her, the long red hair tumbled, eyes staring upward toward the roof.

The light brightened as Pan and Wan joined him, so that the greeny-whiteness of the small body was intensified, reddening her hair, and showing up the blood that had issued from the vagina, and the purple imprints round the throat.

She'd been tortured as well as raped. Three fingers of one hand had been broken at the middle joint so that the ends stood upward away from the palm like snapped twigs.

They heard the porter's son running to fetch help and crying to his god. Nobody else moved. Pan and Wan might have been stone.

After a while, Gwil knelt and closed Waterlily's eyes.

It was then that he smelled the asafetida on her skin.

He went outside and rested his hands and forehead against the hut wall. The breeze carried a burst of laughter from the castle before taking it away again.

Her red hair had killed her. He'd thought she was Pen. He'd thought she knew where the quill case was.

The gatekeeper came, distressed, bringing with him a sack to contain the body. Gwil grabbed the man to stop him going in. He shook him. "Who was here? There was a monk here."

"What?" The gatekeeper's eyes were dodging toward the scene in the hut.

Gwil shook him again. "Who came to the castle today? *Was there a monk?*"

"Monk? What you talking about a monk?" He tried to free himself, but the sight of Gwil's face gave him pause. "Think a monk done for her? Never. Only clericals been near the castle today was that lot as came to get the king to sign something for 'em." He focused. "You saw 'em going out as you was coming in. Remember as she—? Oh Jesus, save us." He'd glimpsed what lay beyond the door.

Gwil let him go.

No, he hadn't seen the clerics, not to register them on his mind;

his attention had been on Waterlily and her antics. But one of them had noticed *him,* and the flowing red hair of the girl with him.

What had she said? Something about a sour-faced bugger riding a bay? "*Looked at me like he wanted to kill me.*"

He'd come back to do it. He'd wanted the quill case, wanted it so desperately he'd risked returning to Bedford Castle to find it.

Vaguely, as if from another world, Gwil became aware of a change up at the castle. The tabor that had been tapping for the entertainment was combining with other drums in a call to arms.

They're mobilizing the military, he thought, *we can catch him.*

But it wasn't that. One of Stephen's spies had brought wonderful news. The empress was not too far away. At Oxford, and only a small force with her. Quick, quick, the tattoo blared, at last we can trap the bitch. Gather the army and ride. Ride. Now we have her.

As Gwil and Wan carried Waterlily's body in its sack up the castle approach, they were nearly run down by an outrush of riders led by the king, his cloak ballooning with the speed of his going. Prince Eustace's horse passed so close that Wan stumbled in avoiding it, and the sack was upended into the gutter that drained the barbican of its effluent.

THE MOMENT THE CASTLE GATES opened the next morning, Gwil collected the mule from its pasture, lifted Penda onto it and jogged with both to Elstow convent, where he paid the nuns to keep her in their guesthouse, allowing her neither in nor out until he came back for her. "And no visitors, neither."

By the mercy of God, in the castle's turmoil caused by Stephen's going, the girl had learned only that Waterlily was dead, and was ignorant of the circumstances. Believing it to have been a killing in the course of robbery, she went with Gwil meekly enough; she thought she was being punished and deserved it. "I'm sorry, Gwil, ever so sorry. I was nasty to her. Sweet Mary, forgive me, I was so nasty to her."

She died for you, he thought. He said: "You got to learn charity, Pen."

"I will. I swear I will. Did they take her bracelets, Gwil? Was that it?" Waterlily's bangles had been a source of envy.

"Yes," he said, and left her.

Pan and Wan managed to raise a hue and cry, but the castle occupants, as well as those without its walls, were too busy gathering supplies and men with which to augment King Stephen's force at Oxford to institute a proper search for a man with blood on him. Nor was such a one found.

Neither was the sheriff of Bedford in situ to investigate the killing; he was traveling his hundreds, raising the militias for the same purpose. Instead, his duty was carried out by one of his reeves, a man also harassed by other duties.

Gwil, doggedly pursuing his own inquiries, found little that would substantiate what he knew to be the truth. The clerics who'd visited the castle that morning had arrived in the middle of preparations for the royal feast and gone more or less unnoticed in the hubbub. In effect, they'd been faceless.

The chamberlain, when pressed, was vague. "They'd come to see the king. Wanted him to sign a charter. Or confirm some appointment or another. I don't know. I was busy. A monk? No, no monk among them."

"Where did they come from?"

"Saint Albans, I think. Yes, Saint Albans."

A groom who'd helped the clerics to dismount had noticed a strange smell emanating from one of their number that wasn't just body odor. "Reeky, like a foreigner," he said, but could give no better description. "I was busy, and them God-botherers all look alike to me."

By the requirement of *lex murdrum* an inquest of sorts was held, but, apart from a prurient examination of Waterlily's corpse, the local jurors didn't exert themselves. The victim wasn't one of their own; she'd been a wandering female performer who, by all reports, was of lax morals. Since she'd chosen to exhibit herself in public and scanty dress, the blame for her murder rested a good deal on herself at a time when men had lost all restraint. The words "she asked for it" were not actually spoken but they might as well have been. Their verdict was "murder by person or persons unknown."

The reeve, entering the finding in the sheriff's rolls, shook his head. "There are too many such in these sad times."

Gwil, to his shame, said nothing. What *could* he say?

Sirs, the killer is a cleric from Saint Albans who visited this castle that morning.

Oh yes, master foreigner, and what proof can you, another wandering performer, lay against a respectable ecclesiastic? A smell? Smells are not admitted as evidence in a court of law.

As well shout at the moon.

Also, he was bound by the fetter that was Penda. To tell the whole story, which might or might not nail guilt on the monk, would, of necessity, expose her to a memory she could not bear, let alone parading her to a world in which a raped female was a shamed female.

Worse still, it would put her in danger. He and Pen were no longer pursuing the monk: the monk was hunting *them*. What's more, he had the resources to do it now. No longer a monk but a cleric connected to Saint Albans, one of the great abbey cathedrals of England, with a high position in its hierarchy, else why had he been among those sent to petition the king?

For the thousandth time, Gwil speculated on what the Greek letters on the quill-case parchment spelled out, making them so vital that a man was prepared to torture and kill for them. A guide to buried treasure? Proof that the monk was heir to a kingdom? Some naughtiness committed by the Pope that would put the Holy See in the monk's power? Each guess became more and more unlikely.

Pan and Wan had accepted the inquest's finding—another weight of guilt on Gwil's shoulders, though to have given them such clues to the identity of the perpetrator as he possessed would have left them as frustrated as himself, and with as little chance of being believed. Also, if the monk had realized, as he must, that he'd killed the wrong girl, he had also drawn the connection between Gwil and traveling performers, thereby putting Gwil and Penda at risk in Pan's and Wan's company, just as they would be at risk from the presence of Gwil and Penda.

The death had aged both acrobats. Spiritless, they would try to build a new life abroad. Wan found the energy to say: "Come with us."

But the spell that had intertwined the five of them for so many months had been broken by the loss of the one. It was time to go it alone once more: for Gwil to grow a beard like a countryman crusader, to cut Penda's hair more closely and hide it permanently under her cap, to dress anonymously. But first, Waterlily must be buried . . .

It proved difficult. No parish priest was prepared to let her share the same ground as the dead in his churchyard. An immoral traveling performer who'd died unshriven and, quite probably, unbaptized? She must not pollute the corpses of the faithful.

The sheriff's reeve offered a plot in a scrubby unconsecrated patch of land in which suicides were interred, but be damned to that. In the end they took her coffin back to the convent at Elstow.

The nuns, out of charity and at Pan's pleading, allowed her a Christian grave, though they drew the line at marking it with the pagan appellation of "Waterlily."

"What name was she born with?" Gwil was fashioning her cross.

"Hild, if I remember," Wan said, and Pan nodded.

"Hild of . . . where?"

"London," said Pan, "just London. She never had no parents we knew of."

They lowered the slight coffin into its hole. A priest intoned the "I am the Resurrection and the Life" antiphon and, without conviction, a prayer that the soul of Hild of London would not suffer too long in purgatory.

The four stood a long while in silence, the only mourners, sleet from a gray sky wetting their faces. Then they picked up their packs and said good-bye to Waterlily and each other.

"Where we going, Gwil?" Penda asked.

A pertinent question.

The hunters had become the hunted and a wolf was after them, and for the time being they must escape it, but fleeing abroad was more than Gwil was prepared to do.

Downhearted, afraid for Pen as he was, he couldn't rid himself of the conviction that sooner or later they would be granted justice. The mills of God ground slowly—too bloody slowly—but they ground exceeding small. Hadn't the Lord just supplied the clue of Saint Albans to the pile that would eventually uncover the bastard's identity?

Leave it to Me for now, Gwil.

"Going to bloody have to, aren't I? In the meantime . . . ?"

"London, maybe," he told Penda. They could find employment and anonymity in a big city while they recouped and waited for God to work on their problem. "But we're going by boat."

He wasn't going to risk their being espied on a main road anymore; for all he knew the monk could be employing agents to look out for them. River traffic was busy; nobody would notice a middle-aged uncle and his nephew among the teeming and various passengers of its shipping.

So they followed the road leading them south and west until they could join the Thames below Oxford, well below the point where King Stephen was besieging the empress.

Then came a blizzard, buffeting them away from the riverbank with snow that left its towpath and stream deserted . . .

CHAPTER 9

AD 1180, Perton Abbey

THE SCRIBE WAKES IN THE middle of the night, his head teeming with the abbot's story and images of the female acrobat's death forcing him to rise from his bed to douse his vitals in cold water. The girl's torture was extreme, of course, but God's just anger with unchaste women could be terrible. Look at the punishment He called down on Jezebel.

And the abbot, oh dear, the abbot sighed in telling the story of the murder like a man in grief for it. "May God and His saints give peace in heaven for little Waterlily," he said, as if that was at all likely, and then smiled to himself. "Perhaps the Lord has a place for acrobats in paradise as He undoubtedly has for Rahere, the jester who built the church for Saint Bartholomew."

But not for a whore, *the scribe thinks, and wonders if now is the time to take the manuscript to the bishop. And yet, and yet, he finds the adventures of these common sinners hideously involving.* Can I myself remain pure while writing them down? Yes, if I armor my soul with prayer; the Lord be my strength and my shield against corruption.

"What happened next, my lord?" he had asked, ashamed of the eagerness in his voice.

"We are about to see threads that join all our protagonists begin to draw together, my son."

With difficulty, the abbot had raised himself on his bed, his face taut with effort. "I must, I must be witness to the fortitude of the human spirit when it is confronted with pandemonium."

He reached out a hand and the scribe passed him the phial of medicine that the brother infirmarian had provided to ease his chest. He seemed a little better for it, and his voice was stronger.

"For, at this time, despite the fact that Stephen's men are besieging the empress at Oxford, the king is no nearer the victory he seeks. Indeed, it is further away. He may have the wife within his grasp, but the husband is triumphant. Superb warrior that he is, Geoffrey Plantagenet has finally conquered all Normandy and been acclaimed its duke in the cathedral at Rouen. It is a disaster for Stephen because it is a disaster for his barons, who now waver in his support. What are they to do? Those who have fought against the empress will surely forfeit their lands in Normandy, yet if they leave Stephen, he will take away their lands in England."

He gave a chuckle that made him cough. "Take the case of Waleran de Meulan, the elder Beaumont twin. He may be Earl of Worcester in England, thanks to Stephen, but Meulan in Normandy is his patrimony; it is the inheritance of his ancestors, his very bones. No matter how many baronies the English king may confer on him, he is Waleran de Meulan, not *Waleran of Worcester, and without that nomenclature few will know who he is;* he *won't know who he is."*

"He deserts, my lord?"

"He deserts. He and his brother agree to do what we saw them discussing at the marriage feast of Maud of Kenniford. Between them they back both mounts in this two-horse race. He goes to Normandy and crawls to Plantagenet in order to maintain his lands on that side of the channel—which he does, incidentally—while twin Robert, no

doubt loudly bewailing to the king his brother's defection, keeps the English domains."

"Perfidy." The scribe sighed.

"A perfidy that costs Stephen dearly, for he has lavished much love and many riches on Waleran, as he has on others whose support he has bought with it. Allies of the empress feel encouraged and begin attacking strongly in the west in order to draw Stephen's army away from the empress at Oxford, but for once he refuses to be diverted." The abbot paused and then added: "Oh, and it has begun to snow . . ."

CHAPTER 10

"IT'S SNOWING, GWIL," PENDA WAILED from several yards behind him. They had traveled a long way very quickly, and like the late afternoon light, their energy was fading. He looked back at the forlorn figure trudging reluctantly behind him but dared not stop; if the weather was coming in, and by the looks of it, it most certainly was, they needed to reach a town soon.

He drove them on through the thickening snowfall until, by God's mercy, they came across a charcoal burner's hut in a wood with a good supply of charcoal still in the kilns next to it, and settled down to wait out the blizzard. The wind came through a crack in one of the wattle-and-daub walls as well as the rackety door, and the hut's shape was hideously reminiscent of the shack where they'd found Waterlily, but they would have to stay there or die. For one thing, the river was nearby and there was a possibility of blundering into it, thanks to snow that blinded by sticking its flakes onto one's very eyelids.

"Like old times, this is, Gwil," Penda said with forced brightness.

It was something he'd noticed about her; she was more eager to please since Waterlily's death, not so manipulative, less concerned with herself.

She wagged her elbows like bird's wings to shake the snow off her and, shivering, tipped the charcoal held in a scoop of her cloak into the central fire pit. "Ain't warm out there, bor."

"Ain't warm in here." Gwil was battling to keep out the slicing draft by stuffing their empty packs into the wall crack. Snowflakes found their way through the roof but they'd need the hole in it to draw out the smoke when the fire was lit.

"Lucky we came on it, though. What we got to eat?"

There was a small cheese and a corner of ham along with a stale loaf he'd bought from a woman at Tiddington, and some ale she'd also sold him that she ought to have been prosecuted for.

The charcoal was slow to catch fire without kindling; they had to separate some of its friable strands with clumsy hands and blow on the tinder's spark from lips almost too cold to purse before it caught.

By the time the fuel was glowing, Penda had begun to nod. Her cap had fallen off and he noticed that her hair, which seemed to grow like wildfire, would soon need cropping again; in repose, in fact increasingly these days, she looked more feminine. He frowned as he took off her wet boots and rubbed her feet. He worried about her more nowadays; the time was coming, and he knew it, when he wouldn't be able to protect her anymore. It was like trying to hold back the tide. He yawned and took off his cloak and laid it over them both, and sat, listening to the shrieking buffets of the wind against the hut's northerly wall . . .

Penda nudged him awake. "Somebody out there."

"Can't be." Nevertheless he reached for his crossbow to cock it.

Then he heard them: disjointed shouts of argument over the wind between two men.

"A light, I tell you."

". . . risk it."

". . . have to."

"Shit," he said.

"Got to let 'em in, Gwil."

"I know." To deny shelter to whatever flickering humanity was out in that howling waste was callousness they couldn't live with.

Nevertheless, he gestured for Pen to arm herself before going to the door. Snow had piled up against it and he had to push hard to get it open.

At first he couldn't see them; their voices were very close but disembodied. Then the whiteness beyond the door resolved into three figures, equally white, like ghosts blown toward him by the wind. He crossed himself before stepping back to let them in.

"Bless you, God bless you, good sir. Bit chilly out here."

Two men were supporting a woman between them. All three were crusted with snow, their eyes like gashes in a mask, though those of the man who hadn't spoken—taller and older than the other—looked from Gwil's bow to Penda's, as his hand slid toward the hilt of his sword.

Gwil put his bow down and reached for the semiconscious woman to help prop her up on the edge of the fire pit. He was stopped. "Better leave her to us," the younger one said gently, " 'f you wouldn't mind."

Between them, they removed her boots as Gwil had taken off Penda's, rubbed her feet and face. She wore fine doeskin gloves, and those they left on. "S'pose there ain't anything to eat and drink, is there?"

Gwil handed over the remains of the ham and cheese—there hadn't been much to start with—and one of the bottles. The taller man tasted the ale first, spat and said: "It'll have to do," before pressing the spout to the woman's mouth. "Take some of this, my lady." It was said in Norman French; his companion had used English.

Their ghostliness wasn't just from the snow; all three were enveloped in white sheets—satin, Gwil noticed—that stuck wetly to the cloaks underneath. Nor did the hiss as the men moved come only from ice spattering off them into the fire; they wore mail beneath their surcoats, excellent mail.

Knights.

"Did you come on horses?" he asked in English.

"Matter of fact, we've, er, had to walk quite a bit," the younger one said. "Well, slide mostly. Down the river, you know. It's frozen over further up. Missed our way this last stretch. Saw your light."

Knights without horses; unheard of.

"How far have you come?"

The woman's eyes were closed but suddenly she spoke with effort in a high, harsh voice. "Impertinence. Tell him. Mind his own business."

The taller knight laughed suddenly, as if relieved to find she could talk at all.

The younger one smiled. "Better introduce ourselves. This is Mistress Mmm . . . Margaret. Fella over there is Master Alan and I'm Christopher. Three simple travelers, you see." His smile stretched into the triumphant grin of someone having overcome an obstacle. "You English?"

"Will," said Gwil. He pointed at Penda: "My nephew, Peter. *Two* simple travelers." Damned if he was giving information when he wasn't getting any. These men were Sirs Somebodys of Somewhere. They reeked of privilege—at least Christopher did; Alan had the look of an experienced campaigner. As for the woman, she was no more called Margaret than he was; Christopher had stumbled over the name.

Christopher beamed again. "Much obliged, Master Will, *much* obliged. God's blessing on you." His head fell forward abruptly; he was asleep.

"Better get out of those cloaks," Gwil said.

Alan was reluctant for a moment but nodded and accepted Penda's help in divesting first the woman, then Christopher and finally himself of their cloaks.

All three were soaked through so that the clothes underneath were patched with wet—a condition that didn't hide the quality of the woman's velvet, nor the jewels around her neck, nor Christopher's emblazoned surcoat and the ornate hilt of his sword in its gold-threaded baldric. Alan's surcoat was less showy, though very fine, like his boots.

The way he hung up the cloaks by using the struts of the roof, spreading them wide so that they would dry the quicker and at the same time add another layer to the hut's walls, was reminiscent of every soldier who'd camped in hard conditions without a squire to serve him.

Don't know what you are now, but you were a mercenary once, Gwil decided.

He watched the man settle down to sleep.

"They ain't simple travelers, though, are they?" Penda asked softly.

"No, they ain't."

Alan's eyes remained closed. "We mean you no harm," he said.

"Don't mean you any, neither," Gwil told him.

Yes, a mercenary for sure; always one ear open.

The storm outside became wilder, shrieking as if in fury that it hadn't killed the five frail creatures in its path, shaking the hut to try to get at them, but the uninvited guests slept the impervious sleep of the exhausted.

During the course of the night, Gwil got up to push open the door every so often in order that its movement outward would shovel away the snow that otherwise threatened to block them in. The blast of freezing air that came in each time was almost welcome; the fire and five close-packed bodies, as well as the insulation provided by snow piling up against the north wall where the crack was, created a toasting heat.

The third time he opened the door, he saw that he'd roused Mistress Margaret. She sat up.

Immediately Alan was awake. "*Domina?*"

"Boots," she said. "Cloak."

The process of passing her these things and helping her into them woke everybody up.

"Shall I come with you, lady?" Christopher asked.

The woman said nothing, but her look quelled him into staying where he was. She pushed past Gwil, who was still by the door, and went out into the night.

"Leave the door open," Penda said, beginning to get up, "I got to go, too."

"When she's back," Alan told her.

"I ain't going to go where she goes."

"When she's back."

"She better be quick, I need to *go*."

Moments passed in silence, Penda fidgeting and putting on her own boots to be ready. The men were tense until Mistress Margaret once more appeared in the doorway. Alan nodded at Penda; now she was free to enjoy the facilities afforded outside.

"Thanks so *much*." Penda was all sarcasm before she bolted through the door.

In the morning all cloaks were dry. Christopher collected them to make a bed and pillow for the Mistress Margaret, who slept on.

And the hell with anyone else, Gwil thought, amused. But then, with Penda a supposed male, this must have been what they called chivalry.

He went to fetch more charcoal. "We ain't going anywhere for a bit," he announced, coming back. It had stopped snowing, but the world outside was swirled with drifts. Not far away, the last, low hills of the Chilterns encircled them on three sides, topped with forest like untidy lace against a gray and threatening sky.

Alan went to the door to check. "I'm confused. Which way is the Thames?"

Gwil pointed east to the river valley that was as indistinguishably snow covered as every other treeless space. "Hard going," he said. "Storm might blow up again. I wouldn't try it, not with a tired woman in tow. Not yet."

Again Alan had to go and look for himself. On his return, he nodded. "We'll have to wait it out."

"Where you heading for?"

"South."

Gwil shrugged. That didn't tell him anything.

"Mistress Margaret is going to need food. Apart from what you gave us she hasn't eaten in two days," Alan said. "It's time to go hunting."

"With swords?"

For the first time, the man smiled. "I hoped a couple of simple traveling archers might come with me."

Christopher was to be left in charge of the still-sleeping woman. "Keep a good lookout," Alan told him.

Penda raised her eyebrows at Gwil. Lookout for what? The silence around them was absolute; no birds, no sound, just white desolation.

Gwil recognized the anxiety of all hunted things. Something was out there in the emptiness; these three were being pursued, just as he and Pen were, but more closely.

The war, bugger it, he thought, *somebody's after them, and me and Pen don't want to be around when it catches up. Stephen's soldiers or the empress's—nothing to do with us anymore.*

However, food was a necessity for them all. Booted and wrapped, they set out for the forest, three brown beetles against a white landscape, choosing windblown, erratic paths where they could, otherwise plunging through drifts on legs that sank above the knee with each step.

"You'd better go back, lad," Alan told Penda. Being shorter than the two men, she was panting with the struggle.

She shook her head, eyes lit at the prospect of using her bow.

As they entered the shelter of the forest, the going became easier. And now there were tracks, hundreds of crisscrosses made by birds; the padded, sharp-nailed print of squirrels; a four-toed imprint of a fox.

Deeper in, they came across the promise of a feast. A mass of slots in the snow and some damaged young beeches showed that a small herd of deer had stopped in its search for food in order to tear bark off the trees. The strips were fresh and Alan wagged a triumphant thumb in the air, almost immediately turning it downward as he looked again. Here and there, prints like those of big dogs were overlaying the slots.

Gwil knelt to examine them.

Wolves.

The number of prints was difficult to make out. He held up two fingers for the others to see, then three, to show that he wasn't sure.

They began to hurry; there were four-footed predators ahead that could go faster and snatch prey away from them, scattering the rest in flight. They had two advantages: approaching from the south, as they were, they were downwind of the creatures they followed, and they didn't have to watch their feet—the snow had covered any twigs liable to snap.

In silence, they began to lope, reduced to animals of the pack themselves by hunger and a concentration that discarded thought in favor of sight, sound and scent, the craft of wild things.

They heard the wolves finally, a sudden loud growling and rending—not too far away, either.

They ran; no need for caution now, the wolves would be too intent on the kill to hear them. The noise was tremendous, not just the growling, but the cawing of a hundred disturbed rooks circling the sky in protest.

It was a deer calf. One wolf had it by the nose, the other two had their teeth into its rump, worrying it, shaking it. As Alan, Gwil and Penda crept nearer, they saw it give up the ghost. Its eyes went dull.

Behind a tree, Gwil put his foot in the stirrup of the crossbow and slotted a bolt into place. Penda reached over her shoulder and took an arrow from her quiver. She looked at Gwil: *Which one'll I take?*

He gestured toward the two wolves growling and tearing at the calf's rump. *Scare them off. Mine's the one at the head.*

He stepped out into the open. The wolf he'd earmarked for his shot turned its amber eyes toward him but didn't release its prey; it was too hungry to give it up for a two-legged intruder. Gwil aimed at the spot between its ears and shot. It went down.

Penda, he saw, had got one of the other wolves in the side, the only angle presented to her. It whimpered and jumped round, trying to dislodge the arrow. Its companion realized its danger but, instead of running off, bounded toward her, growling, its beautiful teeth bared. It was big, as big as she was. Bless her, already she'd fitted another arrow in place and was aiming, but Alan stepped in front of her, sword raised so that the beast speared itself on it in the throat. The impetus threw the man backward onto the snow, a dead wolf on top of him.

Everything had happened in seconds, a moment's lifetime of killing and surviving. The air stank of wolf and blood, but they spent minutes breathing it in without moving, the terror of what had passed only coming to them now, when it was over.

The other wolf had gone off yelping, Penda's arrow still stuck into its side, for which Gwil was sorry; somewhere it would die in pain. Bad hunting, that was; a dirty kill, but nothing to be done about it.

He strode off to Alan and helped him struggle out from beneath the great gray corpse. "Big un, ain't he?"

"Don't I know it." Alan felt his ribs tenderly. "Good shooting, both of you."

"Didn't do so bad yourself."

They were still shaking, but triumph was taking over. They would eat because they were lords of the forest whom God had set in dominion over all beasts for their delectation.

Alan produced a poignard from beneath his cloak and bent over the calf to begin the gralloch. It was a male fallow deer; its face and rump were in tatters but the creamy brown hide of its body was untouched. Alan turned it onto its back and splayed its legs outward as far as possible to expose the throat. He made an incision just below the windpipe and ran the knife carefully along the belly with a sound like tearing soft material, stopping before it reached the pizzle. Immediately, the stomach came bulging out. Alan wiped his poignard on his cloak before putting it away. He inserted his hands carefully into the long cut so as to ease out the rest of the stomach. It plopped out, milk white and steaming, onto the whiter snow.

"Innards?" he asked, looking up.

"Keep 'em in for now. We can roast the heart for the lady right away when we get back. Take the liver out, though."

They must leave that as an offering to the god of the hunt and whichever of his creatures would feed off it.

He noticed that his opinion was asked for and listened to, a respect won for him by his archery. In return, he admired the man who'd stepped in front of Penda. A brave act, that one, and the way he gralloched the calf had been neatly done.

A considerable fellow, this. How old? In his thirties? Alan, eh? Alan of where? Both his English and his French, though fluent, were touched with a Germanic accent that meant he could be German proper, a Frieslander, a Hollander, a Fleming or even from Lorraine; Gwil wasn't expert enough to differentiate, but a suspicion was beginning to form that scared him.

Above them, the rooks continued to make a racket. "Oh, shut up," Penda shouted at them, which made Alan laugh.

With the deer lightened of its stomach, the two men took a hind leg each to begin the long haul home. At least, it was a home to them now. They were bonded by success; what they dragged was not just food for those left behind—it was a trophy.

As if to reward them, the sky had cleared, allowing the sun to turn the world into crystal. Penda began singing—not exactly a pleasant sound, but it delighted Gwil because it was the first time he had ever heard her do it.

"We been on a deer hunt, a deer hunt, a deer hunt, / We killed off the Frekies, the Frekies, the Frekies . . ."

Alan grinned at Gwil. "He knows the skalds, does he?"

"Skalds?"

"Freki was Odin's wolf."

He hadn't known, though he'd heard that fenlanders had Norse ancestors. In the first joy she'd known for a long time, Penda had reverted without thinking to the paganism of her forebears. A right little Viking, then; well, it accounted for her toughness, he supposed, and he was proud of her. Maybe the shutter was letting good memories filter in.

With a shock, he realized that if she remembered who she was, he'd lose her; she'd go back to her real parents and leave him in a loneliness he hadn't known since his son died. He found himself swearing. Bugger it, he'd got used to her.

The day was drawing in by the time they came in sight of their hut. The light of the fire inside glowing through the hole in its roof and the cracks in its walls gave it the appearance of a giant lantern set down in the snow to guide passersby.

"Shit," Alan said. "It can be seen from the river."

"Who's chasing you?" Gwil asked.

Alan glanced at him. "Bad men," he said.

Gwil shrugged. "No help for it, though."

"No." Their two options—to put out the fire, or to set off into the freezing night—were no options at all; they wouldn't survive either.

On the other hand . . . "These 'bad men' of yours," Gwil said, "they ain't likely to find you tonight, not after dark. They won't be traveling by night, not in this weather."

"We found *you* after dark."

"You was desperate."

"So are they. Jesus, they might have got to her already. Stay here." He dropped the leg he was pulling so fast that the calf's body skewed to one side. Gwil and Penda watched him go toward the hut, the snow forcing him to lollop, like a man trying to hurry through thigh-high water. He drew his sword as he went.

"It's her they're after, then," Penda said. "Who *is* she?"

Gwil turned to look at her and saw the same amazing thought come into her mind as had been in his.

"Can't be," she said, "*can't be.* Can it? She's sieged in Oxford."

"Oxford's north," Gwil said. "They came from the north."

"Sieged, though. A bloody great army round her. How'd she ever get out?"

"They wore white. Remember? They had sheets over 'em. *Satin* sheets."

"Gor, bugger."

They were both silent as images—very similar images—transfixed them. They saw three ghosts, unseen by the patrols, gliding through the surrounding enemy lines, only footprints denting the snow to show their progress—and those disregarded.

"*Gor, bugger,*" Pen said again. A grin of exquisite astonishment crossed her face as she remembered the incident in the night. "An' she has to go out into the snow and piss like anybody else." She clutched at him. "A empress, Gwil. We got a empress in our bloody hut."

"We got a bloody danger in it. If Stephen's found out she's escaped on foot, he's sent soldiers after her. That's what's gnawing Alan."

They saw the man emerge from the hut and wave to them. All well.

Penda took the deer's other hind leg and began pulling. "I like him. He was nifty with that wolf—not that I wouldn't have got another shot in afore it got me. We sort of owe him."

"*No we don't.*" Gwil was emphatic. "We ain't getting involved with their wars. Anyways, they owe us."

"An' that Christopher's nice. Soft, but nice. Polite."

"We ain't getting involved, Pen. Tomorrow they go their way an' we go ours."

The rest of the dragging was done without conversation, though Gwil could hear Pen whispering, "A *empress,*" under her breath.

She bolted into the hut the moment they arrived, leaving Alan and Gwil to butcher the calf, a process that, for efficiency, required it to be hung up. Christopher came out to look and admire.

"Got any string?" Gwil asked.

Alan was apologetic. "Sorry."

Huffing with annoyance, Gwil went inside to fetch some from his pack. *Didn't even think to bring any bloody string with 'em.* He knew he was being unreasonable; if these people were who he thought they were, and made the night escape from Oxford he thought they had, string hadn't featured high on their list of requirements. But he was both overawed and frightened by them. They were high politics, the highest, in a trouble as extreme as troubles got. *Me and Pen, we've enough of our own.*

He wouldn't look at the woman as he snatched up his pack and went back outside with it, but he was aware of Pen sitting opposite her, hands clasped, staring with voracious, eye-popping interest.

He tied the front hooves of the carcass together. Christopher helped him hook it to a branch of the nearest tree. They took the heart out to be roasted for "Mistress Margaret"—it would give her some of the deer's strength—and cut off both haunches to be cooked for the rest of them.

Christopher looked sadly at what remained. "If we leave it hanging out here, it'll be gone in the morning."

"No room for it inside," Gwil said shortly. Anyway, venison went bad quickly when exposed to high heat.

They worked quickly in the extreme cold under a sky winking with stars and a rising moon that gave them long shadows.

A tripod for the cooking was the difficulty; the branches of the trees were desiccated by frost and would burn faster than the food. In the end, Alan, with much reluctance, speared the meats on his sword blade and they took turns revolving it over the fire.

Christopher was suitably floundered by the story of the hunt. "Bolt right between the eyes, and that while the beast was moving. I call it handsome." He turned to Penda. "And you, Master Peter, composure under attack in one so young—handsome, very handsome. God's blessings on you."

He said a grace before they ate: "*Benedic, Domine, nos et dona tua, quae de largitate tua sumus sumpturi . . .*"

Mistress Margaret said nothing, thanking neither the Lord nor anybody else for the gift of food. When the roasted heart was passed to her on the end of the sword, she took it between a gloved finger and thumb with the expression of one who was used to better.

But you're scoffing it fast enough, Gwil thought, watching her white teeth tear at the flesh.

Penda didn't take her eyes off her, and when, after the meal, the woman once more went outside to answer a call of nature, she nudged Gwil with ecstasy, unable to get over the fact that empresses were subject to the same physical requirements as the rest of humanity.

Probably pisses vinegar, Gwil thought. If this *was* Empress Matilda, she had a reputation as a haughty bitch, well deserved, as he was discovering, and it was small wonder the Londoners had chased her out of their city. He wondered how men like Alan and Christopher could grovel to her as they did.

Yet it seemed that the hut shone the more brightly for her presence; he imagined it pulsing with a light that sent out the signal "Look who's here" for miles around. He remembered something from the Bible about entertaining angels unawares. That was what he and Pen were doing: entertaining a stiff-necked, glowing bloody angel with no manners, likely to attract the forces of hell to their door.

He studied the angel's face with its thin, high cheekbones and straight, somewhat overlong nose. Large eyes of clear hazel, along with the perfect complexion, should have given her beauty—except that the arrogance with which they looked out on the world, and the sour mouth, were not conducive to it.

Brave, you had to give her that. Again, Gwil imagined the flight through the lines at Oxford and the subsequent terrible trek along a snowbound river.

No ordinary woman could have done it. She hadn't whined about tiredness or hunger, neither—not that he'd heard.

She ain't going to draw us in, he thought with force, *she* ain't.

The digestive silence following the meal was broken by Alan. "May I suggest you sleep, *domina*? I think we ought to be on our way before dawn tomorrow, and we have to discuss . . ."

The hazel eyes directed themselves with meaning at Gwil and then Penda. *Not in front of these yokels.*

Alan turned to them awkwardly: "Could you leave us for a while?"

Too much.

"No, we couldn't," Gwil shouted at him. "We guessed who she is, and if you want to talk secrets, you can do it without us freezing our arses off in the snow; we ain't going to tell anybody."

There was a gasp from Christopher, and the empress's arched eyebrows arched even higher. Had her mouth twitched in amusement, or just a wider sneer?

Her voice rasped, "Can we trust these fellows?"

Alan smiled. "I think so."

"Then they shall come with us, we may have need of them."

No "please," just the royal "we" making a command. Gwil opened his mouth, but a nudge from Penda stopped him. "Be good, that, wouldn't it?"

She's been bewitched, he thought. *The magic of a grand title's got her spellbound. But this ain't no fairy-tale princess sitting there; this woman's a liability as'll pull us down with her.*

On the other hand, he'd found comfort in being in the presence of the two men, especially Alan. Something of the terrible responsibility he felt for Penda had been eased merely by their company. She'd been accepted as a boy, and a decent one; Alan had protected her in the battle with the wolves. Wouldn't do any harm to continue with them for a bit, maybe, as long as the hounds after 'em didn't catch up. In which case, he and Pen would be off.

So he said: "Where you heading?"

"Kenniford Castle," Alan said.

"Where's that?"

"Downriver a few miles, I'm not sure how many, but it can't be far."

The empress broke in. "Are we sure of this Maud of Kenniford? She is unknown to us."

"Like I said, lady, she swore on the Bible to be your vassal."

"A switched allegiance, and one made under duress you say."

"One she was happy to make, if I'm any judge."

It didn't sound a good proposition to Gwil, and the more it was talked about among the three, the less he liked it. A castle in the charge of an untried female, and one that, if it *was* held for the empress, was unique in a swath of England that was almost entirely under the control of King Stephen, an island lapped by a hostile sea . . .

"We suppose there is no alternative," the empress was saying.

Not for you, he thought. *But Pen and me have one. We ain't getting drawn in.* "How big's this Kenniford?" he asked. "And once you're in, how you going to get out? Lessen you're reckoning you got an army as'll come and rescue you."

"It's no mere motte and bailey, I can tell you," Alan said. "Properly prepared it could hold out for a year, but I don't intend my lady to stay in it that long. There was no time to explore it all while I was there, but a castle that size wouldn't have been built without a postern out of sight of any besiegers, should there be any. Once we've gathered intelligence, we should be able to reach our own forces."

The discussion between the empress and her knights continued. It seemed established in everybody's mind, except Gwil's, that all five should travel together.

Alan, he noticed, was edgy and insisted that weapons be kept within reach, and that everybody sleep with their boots on—"In case we have to make a quick exit."

Gwil shared his disquiet, respecting the man's instinct, and was later than the others in getting to sleep. A shuddering cry outside had him reaching for his crossbow before he recognized the call of a tawny owl out hunting.

After what seemed like only a few minutes from closing his eyes, he was wakened by growling just beyond the hut. That would be wolves, their noses having made the inevitable discovery of the hanging deer.

Christopher stirred and muttered: "There goes breakfast."

He heard the snap of the branch giving way as the beasts pulled the carcass down and began dragging it off.

Taking it back to their lair, he thought. And then: *Making a hell of a to-do about it—for the growling had changed to snarls that became louder and louder, now interspersed with the belling of different animals . . .*

Penda got to her feet. "Hounds."

Alan was at the door. Had gone out. Was back. "Up. *Up.* They've found us."

The grab for cloaks and weapons was a confused melee before Christopher could usher the empress through the door, Gwil pushing Penda after her.

The moon was clear and high, showing them a scene in which black, reflective shapes moved as if on a steel mirror. Men and dogs had disgorged themselves from two rowing boats on the river to head for the lantern of the hut, but between it and them were the wolves, eight at least, ready to fight for the deer's carcass. Men were yelling at the hounds, trying to divert them from the smell of dead meat to that of living humans, without success. Dogs and wolves clashed together in snarling, whirling balls of fur and teeth and blood.

For a moment the people from the hut stood outside it, transfixed, before Alan began pushing them toward the southern forest. "*Run.*"

They ran, while wolves held the line behind them against men and dogs. It wouldn't be long: the wolves were outnumbered; the men had spears.

They ran, dodging trees, falling over brambles, trying to keep to tracks made by animals whose prints might disguise their own. At their backs the tumult rose, then began to dwindle. They heard the whimper of dying animals and at least one human scream before there was silence.

Now the hunt was on. Alan, who was leading, paused at the edge of a stream. "Along here," he said, taking the empress's hand and pulling her into the water behind him. They began wading in the direction of the current so that their scent would be carried along with them and not left behind for the hounds to sniff. Christopher, Gwil and Penda followed.

It wasn't a deep stream, but by God, it was cold. At first they couldn't feel it, but once their boots had absorbed the water, their feet threatened to become unbending stumps that made louder splashes than before so that they couldn't hear what was behind them.

Then there were no more trees and the stream had gone down an incline, turning to ice in the process. All five slipped, bringing one another down like bowled ninepins so that they twirled ridiculously out into moonlight and space—to find themselves on a bank of a river so wide it could only be the Thames again. They'd made a wide arc that had brought them a bit further south, though probably not much.

Alan helped the empress to her feet, looking upriver and down. They listened for sounds of pursuit and heard only the suggestion of a disturbance somewhere back in the forest that might have been hounds or more wolves. Or both at once.

"Now they know we're going south, maybe they'll have taken to the boats again," Alan said. "They know we'll be following the river."

But they were too tired to tackle the forest again, even if they could find their way in it.

The bank they were on was lined with pollarded willows and promised better going than the other, which, being bare, was just an escarpment of snow—not that they could have reached it; there was no bridge to be seen.

"Are you all right, lady?" Alan asked.

They'd all fallen heavily, but while four of them rubbed their backsides, the empress stood like a rock, as if royal arses didn't bruise. She nodded, breathing hard.

To give her another minute, Christopher said: "Who was Saint Lupus?"

"A bishop or something," Alan told him.

"Well, if he's the patron saint of wolves, I'm going to build him a chapel all to himself. Those animals did us proud, bless them."

They set off downstream.

Gwil kept looking behind him. Alan had been right; if Stephen's men had any sense, they'd have taken to the boats, watching the banks as they went.

No point in thinking how tired they were, no point in hating every drift that impeded them and had to be struggled through; no point in anything but lifting one foot and putting it in front of the other. One, two. Again. One, two.

A swan taunted their lumberings by flowing past them like a beautiful white aquamanile gliding along a black and gleaming tabletop.

One, two. And again. One, two.

Penda's head was drooping; she looked terribly pale, too, as though she were sickening for something. "Don't get poorly on me now, Pen," Gwil muttered under his breath as he took hold of her hand and started pulling her along. *We been drawn in after all,* he thought, and wondered how it had happened. One, two.

They disturbed an otter that slid down the bank and swam effortlessly away from them.

The empress stopped. She said nothing, just stood still.

Gwil watched Alan pick her up, put her over his shoulder and stagger on, her head bobbing against his back.

Bloody woman. Her fault, all of it her fucking fault. What she want to be queen for? Must be—Jesus—nearly as old as me. Three sons by Plantagenet. Or is it four? They said she nearly died having one of 'em. Guts, you have to give her that. Bloody woman.

Penda fell and didn't get up. Gwil knelt, heaved her round his neck like a muffler and limped on.

A coot emerged from the reeds, pattering noisily over the water before taking off.

Easy for furred and feathered things; fucking difficult for two legs.

"Sanctuary." The cry from Alan made him look up.

Eternity *did* have an end. In the distance, on the opposite side of the river where it bent, was a great wall. With towers. A castle.

From behind them came a distant shout: "*There they are.*"

Wearily, Gwil turned and saw, being rowed downriver toward them, the boat he'd known to be inevitable.

It was coming too fast and the castle was too far away; she'd be captured, they'd *all* be captured.

No you fucking don't, he thought. *Not now we come this far.*

He heard his own whisper: "Get on," and managed to raise it to a yell: "Get *on,* leave it to me."

He didn't see if he was obeyed; his eyes were on the boat. He lowered Penda to the ground, still sleeping. Somehow he raised an arm to unhook the crossbow from his shoulder, somehow found a bolt for it—his last. Somehow put his foot in the stirrup and by a miracle had the strength to cock the thing. Went to one knee in the striped shadows of a willow.

From a quarter of a mile away, in the bright moonlight, the boat with its men and spears had looked like a massive hedgehog speeding along the water toward him. Now he could see the glint of Stephen's silver-and-gold-striped blazon on shields.

The man-at-arms standing in the prow didn't spot him; he was too busy pointing at the two burdened figures staggering along the towpath.

Gwil waited, watching the approach of the boat's prow as its rowers fought against the current to change direction and reach the bank ahead of Alan and Christopher to cut them off. Near him now. Unconsciously he worked out distance, angle, water resistance.

Forgive my sins and be with me now, Lord.

He shot.

There was a spurt of spray at the side of the boat, disregarded by the excited men in it and sounding to Gwil as weak as the *plop* of a rising fish. Oh Jesus, he'd miscalculated. The bolt had hit the boat below the waterline but bounced off. It had hit but hadn't pierced, plugging the side, not holing it. Too tired, too old, he'd missed altogether.

He was wrong. One of the rowers shouted, let go his oars and took off his helmet to start bailing. The boat skewed and slowly, very slowly, tipped to port as water rushed in through the hole by its keel.

Men were crying out. Some were clinging to the boat's hull. The river was claiming others who splashed desperately to keep afloat in its weakening cold.

God help them, he prayed, and began the trudge toward the castle. Shields and spears floated past him as he went and the cries behind him grew weaker. *Help the poor buggers, Lord, but what else could I do?*

There was no bridge to the castle. At least, there *was,* but it was drawn up over the portcullis of a gatehouse some sixty-five feet tall and eighty away across the river.

Alan, with the empress pressed against his side to keep her warm, and Christopher were standing on a quayside that had on it what looked like a tollbooth. Their voices were engaged in shouts with two others across the river, the argument making echoes skip back and forth across the swift-flowing water between them.

"Tha's all very well," a man's voice from the gatehouse was saying as Gwil limped up the quayside, "but iffen you don't know the password . . ."

There was an interjection from somewhere along the ramparts. "Don't think we got one, Ben."

The gatehouse guard was put out. "Ain't we? Still and all, we ain't letting just anybody in. I got my orders."

Gwil sat down and rested his head on his knees. This was sanctuary?

"Your orders come from Maud of Kenniford," Alan yelled, "who has sworn herself and this castle to the service of the empress Matilda. This *is* the empress. Let her in."

"Don't look like no empress to me," said the gatehouse guard. "Where's her crown?"

Christopher tried diplomacy. "If you would be good enough to fetch Lady Kenniford . . ."

"This time o' morning? She won't take kindly. Be a braver man than me . . ."

The empress detached herself from Alan's arm and stood tall. She took two steps forward and spoke. "I am the empress Matilda, lady of England and your sovereign. Open to me. *Now.*"

A thousand years of dominion went ringing across the Thames like a trumpet blast. Anglo-Saxon and Viking-Norman ancestry combined in a chord that had deafened and conquered nations. It expected the moon to bow the knee. If not, so much the worse for the moon.

The gatehouse guard made an arbitrary decision. There was a roar of clanking chains as the bridge lowered and thumped into place at the lady of England's feet.

Head up, she crossed over it, followed by the others, to be received into Kenniford Castle.

MAUD WAS SPITTING MAD TO hear that five more strangers had been admitted into the castle and was wondering whether she should add the blasted gatekeeper Ben to the list of people she'd quite happily hang at the moment, the herald Payn being top of it.

She'd discovered his latest slip after one of her rare visits to Sir John yesterday.

John of Tewing was still alive—paralyzed but alive. The left side of his face, from eye to chin, was lopsided, as if its flesh had melted and run downward. He had no use of his right arm or leg and had to be helped in and out of his bed. Yet, in many ways, he was as big a presence in the castle as he had been before.

What animated him was fury. The eyes in that ruin of a face, one of them pulled down to show a glaring red rim, bulged out at the world like an enraged bull's. The only intelligible sound he could make was "Uck-oo," and he shouted it over and over, "Uck-oo! Uck-oo!," with the regularity and force of a deranged *Cuculus canorus*, pounding his good hand against his useless one as if to hammer life back into it.

Despite the inconvenience to herself and everybody else who attended on her patient, Kigva had insisted on moving Tewing to the topmost room of the keep, with views to the north, east, west and south.

It had been built by Maud's father, a man distrusting his own people, that he might keep an eye on them from all points of the compass as they went about their business 120 feet below. Kigva had said that was where Tewing wanted to be, perhaps for the same reason, perhaps to give him an interest. Maud, wanting to do her best for the man, had seen no reason to deny it to him—and only regretted it when, with Kigva's delighted help, he managed to prop himself up against the window mullion and burst into "Uck-oo, uck-oo, uck-oo, uck-oo"s that could be heard throughout the castle baileys and beyond.

Nobody doubted that he was swearing, and that the word lacked an "f" in front of it, and a "y" after the "k," nor that it was addressed at his wife, though, after a while, it seemed directed at anyone he saw passing. "Uck-oo, uck-oo, uck-oo, uck-oo, uck-oo." Like blow after regular blow from a blacksmith's hammer, as if he accused all Kenniford, from Maud down to the kennel boy, of betrayal, blaming them for flying the empress's colors, for not being as helpless as he was.

They became used to this winter cuckoo, showed it respect by nodding or bowing as it called to them from above in much the same way that they acknowledged a magpie—"Hello, Mr. Magpie"—to ward off bad luck, but it engendered a guilty discomfort that made it a relief when, at night, it fell silent.

Everything that could be done for him was done. Maud had called in two doctors from Oxford who consulted over his urine and recommended frequent bleeding as well as cold baths to abate what hot blood they left him with, and potions made from seethed toad, mandrake root and ground ivy. The infirmarian from Abingdon Abbey was summoned and diagnosed demonic possession, attempting to cast out the evil spirit with prayer and holy water.

These administrations were met with a battery of "uck-oo"s from their patient. He threw his piss pot at the doctors and nearly strangled the infirmarian with the monk's own rosary. All three refused to return.

Before he left, still clutching his bruised throat, the infirmarian told Maud: "This evil is of the devil, be sure of it, else how could a sick man exert such energy? I believe it to be witchcraft by that hag who attends him. Turn her away."

Maud didn't like Tewing's mistress, either; on the other hand, Kigva showed a devotion to her patient that Maud, who was only prepared to expend monies on him as a wifely duty, shuddered at. It was Kigva who cleaned him when he fouled himself, Kigva who massaged the wasted limbs with linseed and honey to bring back their strength, who chewed meat into a pap so that he could swallow it, dripped strengthening drinks of her own concoction into the distorted mouth and kissed it. Murmuring like a lover, she could calm him out of the worst of his tempers—not that he exempted her from them. She interpreted the grunts he made. "My lord wants extra blankets," she'd say. "Get them." Or: "He says they bloody cooks put too much salt in his broth."

Maud had climbed the winding turret staircase to John of Tewing's room and paused outside the door to gather herself for its encountering stink. It was not the smell of farmyard with its tinge of sewage that pervaded the bailey—she hadn't noticed that; it was too familiar, too friendly—but that of a pustule. Kigva's idea of cleanliness was that of a sow's. Maud and Milburga had done their best to purify the room but Tewing had kicked over their bowls of scented water and thrown their herbal garlands in their faces.

Still, at least young William would be there; like the dutiful son he was, he spent much of his time these days sitting by his father's bed helping Kigva minister to him.

She squared her shoulders and went in. Three pairs of eyes were rounded on her, as if she had intruded into a secret meeting. Even William's, though his held . . . what was it? . . . Guilt? Well, that she could forgive; she knew he was fond of her but his fidelity, like that of all males, was to the man who had fathered him, and as a result she would never make her own claim on him, not wanting divided loyalties to tear him in half.

"And how are we today?" she asked Sir John brightly.

"Uck off."

"Now, we don't need to say that, do we?" She was convinced that Tewing was recovering speech and strength while hiding both from her. His face was still distorted, the right side of his body useless, but from her solar she had occasionally heard a limping step crossing and recrossing the ceiling above, along with harsh replies to Kigva's murmurs. He'd become mentally and physically stronger.

But if he thinks he's getting Kenniford back, he can think again.

"What would you like for supper?"

As she discussed food, she looked around. The place always made her shudder but there was something else here today.

Kigva kept the room in darkness and, as usual, was crouching by Tewing's bed like a malignant familiar. Her dark, dirty hair hung about a face that had sharp cheekbones, its beauty spoiled by eyes of such a pale blue that they were almost white. Maud refused to be afraid of her, but she daunted others. Maids sent up on errands were reluctant to go, and not just because Tewing threw things at them; the witch cursed them, they said. By night at certain phases of the moon, she gathered strings of milk thistle, ivy and mistletoe with which to decorate the room; people who saw her at it crossed themselves and went indoors.

Today there was a scrying bowl on the floor filled with what looked like urine. Only God knew what she dipped her rushlights in but it wasn't good animal fat.

That was it; *that* was what was different: there was another smell in the room, like a woman who's just left a place leaves a lingering trace of her scent, but this wasn't perfume, it was harsh, a riband of a different stink, and masculine. Maud couldn't identify it, had never smelled its like. Since the room was the same as it always was, and there was no one else in it, she assumed that it came from outside, though when she opened the shutters and sniffed all she could smell was the winter air.

Later that afternoon, as was her custom, she joined William and Milburga in the parlor. It was already dark outside and the comparative coziness of the candlelit room was a welcome retreat from the winter drafts that now ravaged the rest of the castle.

At a large table William was tucking into great mouthfuls of bread and sucking down a delicious-smelling pottage from a cup under Milburga's ever-watchful eye.

"He can eat, that one!" Milburga said, her arms folded proudly across her chest. "I'll say that for him."

William looked up briefly from the overladen trencher in front of him to direct one of his great beaming smiles at his stepmother.

Maud leant against the wall and sighed contentedly. She loved this leg of the day; after all the endless bustle of castle business, she could relax for once. It was satisfying, too, to be able to nourish the child, one of the few things, in fact, that she *could* do for him.

She was watching him now, itching with a desire to grab a cloth and wipe away the broth dribbling down his chin, knowing that she should not. He was growing up so quickly, she thought sadly, weaning himself away from the ministrations of all clucking, cosseting women.

In the background Milburga chattered on.

"Don't s'pose ee gets much food up there," she muttered. "And even if ee did who'd want to eat with those swine in that swill . . ." She burbled on and on until, unawares, Maud caught the tail end of a question: ". . . How d'you think ee looked anyway?"

"Sorry? What?" She had drifted off, lost in her own thoughts. It wasn't that she wasn't interested in what her beloved Milburga had to say, it was just that, on occasion, there was so much of it. "Sorry, Milly," she repeated. "Who?"

"His lordship!" Milburga said with exaggerated patience; she sometimes despaired of her mistress's powers of concentration. "How do you think he looked?"

Maud shot an anxious glance at William. She refused to discuss Sir John in front of him, out of deference to the child as much as anything. The boy, for reasons best known to himself, adored his father, and since she, Maud, could not be relied on to say anything kind about the man, she felt most things were better left unsaid. On this occasion, however, he seemed so absorbed in his food that he appeared not to be listening.

"Well," she said, lowering her voice and sidling closer to Milburga, "I thought, actually, that he looked a good deal better." She was about to add "unfortunately" when William piped up behind them, startling them both.

"Oh, he is," he said cheerfully. "A man came to see him today and Kigva thinks he might be able to cure him."

Maud turned abruptly.

"What man?" she asked, frowning. "A physician?"

"Oh no." William shook his head. "I don't think so, I've never seen him before. He looked like a monk and Kigva says he has powers and that he will use them to help Father." Maud was gaping so uncomprehendingly that he turned pink under the scrutiny.

A monk! What would a monk be doing in that unholy pigsty? she wondered, then remembered the delegation from Henry, the bishop of Winchester and Stephen's brother, who'd appeared at the castle that morning to persuade her to return to the king's side. He needed access to the river crossing that Kenniford provided.

At one point during the negotiation she had been tempted to cast aspersions on the bishop's own loyalties, which blew in the wind, as far as she could tell, but Father Nimbus had recognized the direction of the conversation and put his hand on her arm, so, in the end, she hadn't.

"A *monk*?" she said at last. "One of Bishop Henry's messengers who came here today do you mean?"

"I-I think so," William stammered. His stepmother was looking unusually cross.

"What did he want with your father?"

"He blessed him."

"Why?" Maud was confused.

"Kigva asked him to and it worked, Father's getting better already. The monk made her scry for him afterward and she said that she could see Father would be well soon. She said that he must come back again and that if he did Father would carry on getting better and better." He looked imploringly from Maud to Milburga and back again.

"I'll bet she did," Maud said under her breath. The woman was a primitive but sharp enough to know that without the patronage of Sir John, she would be turned out of the castle to crawl back under whichever stone it was she had crawled out from under in the first place and would, therefore, clutch at any straw to prevent it. She took a deep breath, torn between irritation with Kigva and pity for the boy.

"I won't have scrying under my roof, William. Do you hear me? If she does it again you're to tell me. Understand?" She had very little truck with magic and mistrusted those who practiced it. "And I won't have strange monks roaming my castle, come to that. Do you hear me?"

William hadn't liked it much, either. In fact he had been frightened out of his wits by Kigva's strange chantings and alarmed by the sudden appearance of the strange man, who had introduced a peculiar atmosphere into the room that emanated not just from the unpleasant smell he trailed behind him but something else, too, something clandestine and unsavory. And although he could never confess it to Maud, for fear of betraying his father, he had been more than happy to see him leave.

"Do you hear me?" Maud repeated, dragging his attention back to her with a stamp of her foot. William nodded and bowed his head. It was most unusual for Maud to get so cross with him—more often than not it was Milburga who did the scolding—and he couldn't understand it.

"Good," she said, her voice softening at last. "Then you may get down from the table."

She waited until he had gone before summoning the herald, who'd been put in charge of the visitors.

"What do you mean by it, Payn? Letting Bishop Henry's men rove the castle as they please."

Payn flushed almost as pink as William at Maud's admonishment. He took his position seriously and was ashamed; he'd been outflanked; there'd been a diversion. He'd settled the messengers in the barbican with an archer to guard them, had ordered them food and wine, sent their horses to the stables to be watered and seen to. While he was doing this, the visitors boldly walked out into the inner bailey, separating as they went. "I ordered them back, lady, but they didn't stop. I couldn't shoot them, could I? As messengers, they were under our protection."

He'd managed to round up the two knights and one of the monks, but it had taken time to find the other, who was eventually discovered in Tewing's room—and unceremoniously rejected.

"He was just a monk, lady," Payn said with all the contempt of a knight-to-be for a religious. "He was praying over Sir John. I hope there has been no harm done."

"I hope there hasn't. Don't do it again." As her herald reached the door, she called out. "Did he smell, Payn?"

The boy grinned. "Did he *not*? It was the same devil's dung my grandmother used to ease her wind. Terrible wind, my granny. We never knew which was preferable, her farts or the asafetida."

A stinking monk and now somebody purporting to be the empress. Whatever next?

CHAPTER 11

December, AD 1142, Kenniford Castle
THE SECOND SIEGE

SO IT WAS THAT, SHIVERING and in no good mood, Maud of Kenniford stumbled from her bed to follow her porter through the cold, dark baileys and their darker arches to the gatehouse. "Of course it isn't her, you numbskull. What would she be doing here? Last we heard she was besieged at Oxford. What do you think she did to get here? Fly?"

"Wouldn't put it past her," Ben, the porter, said. "You waits 'til she talks."

"Rubbish. You've let in a load of beggars again, blast you, and I'm going to have to feed them." Christ's injunction to succor the poor had to be obeyed, but it was a nuisance, especially in the early hours of a freezing morning. She paused. "Are they armed? Have you called out the guard?"

"Two's got bows, and two's got swords, but Daegal's guarding 'em with his spear."

"Very comforting. I told you not to let anybody in unless they knew the password."

"What *is* the password?"

Maud, who'd forgotten it herself, gave him a shove that allowed her to precede him into the gatehouse, where five tatterdemalions drooped against one of its walls.

Despite the poor light, she knew the tallest immediately. "Come to take another small child hostage?" she asked.

Alan of Ghent smiled and bowed—not to her, but to the wreck of a female beside him. "Lady, may I present Mistress Maud of Kenniford."

Maud surveyed the woman to whom she was being presented, rather than, as her position usually demanded, the woman being presented to *her*—the veil that showed straggles of hair, the torn and dirty cloak, the saturated boots. Then she looked into the eyes and, after a moment, dropped into the deepest curtsy she'd ever made.

"Welcome to Kenniford Castle, lady," she said, and to the porter: "What are you keeping my lady empress waiting here for, idiot? Escort her to the keep."

She ran ahead to wake the household.

THAT EVENING, SIR BERNARD BENT to his household account books to record the day's outlay, as a good steward must do every night.

"*To the two maids, Mildryth and Leola, 2d each for provision of baths.*" (They were entitled to extra pay for lugging jugs of hot water on a weekday, rather than on a Saturday, when they had to do it for nothing as part of their duties.)

"*To a gallon of wine for the empress's bath: 4d.*" (This addition to the water was because the lady was considered in need of strengthening.)

"*To messengers Picard and Bogo for travel to the West Country: 40s.*" (A large amount of money, but necessary for two men who were going to have to ride hard and fast to seek out the empress's supporters and gain information about where she might safely meet up with them.)

"*To good wool cloth and silk for the empress's new clothes to be made quickly . . .*"

"*To the accommodation of her companions . . .*"

"*To this . . .*"

"*To that . . .*"

At last Sir Bernard sprinkled sand over the page in order to dry the ink on what he had written, tapped shut the lid of the inkwell, cleaned and sharpened his quill to ready it for tomorrow and closed his book with a sigh. It had been an unusual and very expensive day.

Up in the solar, Maud sighed, too, and not just at the expense. For one thing, she was physically uncomfortable at having to sleep on a palliasse on the floor, her own bed now being solely occupied by the empress behind its heavy, drawn curtains.

(Milburga, whose palliasse it was, now had another outside the door, ousting the even-lower-ranking Tola from that position, and so on down the line . . .)

It wasn't the indignity Maud minded—an empress had a right to expect a lady of high degree to be her woman of the bedchamber. If anything, Maud admired the empress for not showing an ounce of gratitude for the trouble her presence was putting everybody to. She herself, she realized, was too easygoing and allowed her household to treat her with overfamiliarity. The empress was setting her an example, and by God, she intended to follow it.

No, by sheer lineage and the right Maud had granted her, this was the empress's castle. It was the danger the empress was putting it in that wouldn't let its chatelaine sleep.

Alan of Ghent had emphasized it with the vulgarity she'd come to expect from him, actually berating her. Red-eyed from fatigue, he'd shouted: "Great God, lady, I told you to have the place in readiness. You should have better lookouts than those clowns at the gate."

Before she could splutter a protest, he'd continued: "Once Stephen knows Matilda has escaped him at Oxford, he'll guess she's here. Where else *could* she go on foot? He will come and he will have you cinched so tight you cannot breathe. If God is merciful, he will not bring up his army for a few days, by which time she'll be rested, I will know the lay of the land and I can get her away. But he is coming. Like the wrath of God he is coming—*and you are not ready for him . . .*"

It went on and on. Where were the improvements to the curtain wall she should have made? What was Sir Rollo doing, apart from getting fatter? Where was the castle's postern?

This last floored her. There *was* a postern, a narrow defended back gate into the outer bailey that shepherds and cowmen brought their herds through from the fields to save taking the animals round by the river entrance.

But, no, he didn't mean that.

"A secret passage," he yelled at her, "a hidden way out. A tunnel. Before God, woman, there must be one."

Must there? To save her face she had spat in his for his rudeness—not ladylike, perhaps, but he'd made her furious—and stalked off. Yet he'd shaken her.

Now, turning and turning on her straw pallet, Maud alternated between anger, humiliation and downright fear for her castle and her people.

He'd dared to shout at her. Dared to insist that the males he'd turned up with should be treated and accommodated like nobility. Sir Christopher was obviously of good stock . . . but the mercenary? And that peculiar-looking redheaded boy he had with him?

Was there a secret postern? Bloody Ghent had implied that no castle worthy of the name should lack such a thing.

Jesus and Mary, but she was in grown-up territory now: sheltering a fleeing empress; about to be swooped down on by an angry king. The last siege had been child's play in comparison, and she'd been able to deal with it. The next, if it came, would bring real fighting, real death. And, as that bastard had said, she wasn't ready for it. She saw now why her husband had made such defensive alterations as he had—he'd known how important they were—whereas she, and stupid old Sir Rollo, had relaxed once the danger was past, thinking it wouldn't come again.

But a postern. Her father had never mentioned one. There simply wasn't one. Nobody knew the castle better than she herself, she who was, after all, familiar with every blade of its grass, every stone.

No, not *every* stone.

Sweet Mary, she thought. That's *where it is. Damn it.* But despite a reluctance that brought sudden shivers, she got up, put on her boots and an underdress, took her fur mantle off its hook, picked up a candle and went quietly out to kick Milburga awake. "Take my place for a bit," she told her.

"Where you going?"

"To find the secret postern," Maud told her. "We'll have to smuggle the empress out of it if necessary. Stephen's likely to besiege us any moment."

"I ain't never heard of it. Where is it?"

Maud told her.

"I'm coming with you," Milburga said.

Tola took Milburga's place in case she was needed, though, as Milburga said, anyone who snored as loudly as the empress was doing was unlikely to be woken by even the Last Trump.

KENNIFORD'S UNDERCROFT WAS A BEAUTIFULLY arched cave. It smelled of tuns of wine and brandy as well as the valuable spices and almost-as-expensive candles that were kept for chapel and hall in lead-lined boxes. There was also a tinge of pee from the cats that kept the rats down. Beyond this storeroom, it petered out into tunnels that followed the castle's foundations in a circle like a snake, becoming lower and narrower as they went. They provided massive storage space but it was rarely used, the castle's people being reluctant to visit them. They said they contained bad spirits, and it was true that the tunnels often reverberated with strange moans. Father Nimbus declared that the cause was drafts of air forcing their way through the narrow passages, but nobody believed him.

"Which way?"

"Right." The passage to the left would take them widdershins, i.e., against the direction of the sun, which was unlucky, and Maud was not inclined to court any more bad luck than she was facing already.

The lantern she had brought with her threw the two women's shadows stalking along the walls, foreshortening every time they passed one of the pillars holding up the roof, then jumping back to become gigantic. They were aware as never before of the massiveness of the castle above them, of the possibility of becoming trapped.

Weight-bearing archways led from one section to another until they were moving along passages where cobwebs broke against their faces.

"We're going in a circle."

"Must be following the underside of the curtain wall. And stop whispering."

"Same to you."

But to speak louder brought mocking echoes suggesting that they were waking things better left unwoken.

"Is this it?" Milburga asked. A great iron door with bars on the outside. A grille at head height in it provided a peephole.

"No." Maud hurried her on. She knew what lay behind that particular door and it wasn't a postern. Her one and only visit to it had been with her father when she was nine years old and she had never been back. Known as "the Wormhole," it was where extra-special prisoners had been lodged, men who'd offended old King Henry and required punishment from his sheriff in these parts, her father, Robert of Kenniford. Or had offended Robert himself. It was said of it that those who went in rarely came out, their screams being heard as far away as the village.

Her father had taken her to it to, as he said, "show you where to put your traitors."

A harsh man, her father, disappointed that, despite three marriages, the only child surviving to him, his last, had been a daughter. Affectionate to nobody, not even her, he had nevertheless done his best to equip her for life as he saw it.

"Will there be traitors, Father?"

"There are always traitors. Trust nobody."

It was his theme—perhaps because both were themselves descended from a traitor. Their ancestor Wigod of Kenniford, kinsman to the sainted King Edward the Confessor, had betrayed his country by going over to William the Norman the moment that England's conqueror had set foot on its soil. And done well by it, gaining a rich Norman bride, permission to build this castle and the shrievalty of Berkshire as his reward.

Since Maud, being female, could not inherit her father's position as sheriff, she would be absolved of coping with political prisoners, although she had a right to sentence ordinary lawbreakers in her own court.

Her father had been ill and she'd been frightened, as much by his harsh breathing and his attitude as by the dark tunnels, which seemed to her little legs to stretch for miles. Eventually they had come to the Wormhole's door. "Is this where we must keep the traitors, Father?"

"It is." With difficulty, for he was coughing badly, Robert of Kenniford had lifted the door's great bar.

At first she'd thought the cell was empty. So it was—of the living. Then her father had raised the lantern and she'd seen the skeleton hanging in chains set into the back wall.

"See there, Maud," her father had said. "Those are the bones of Walter Corbet, whom I caught betraying me with my first wife.

They have hung here for twenty-three years as a sign to other traitors of what they may expect if they cross me further. They are careful not to do so."

She could see why they wouldn't. The points of the blinding iron were still in Walter's eye sockets.

Keeping the light focused on the skeleton, Robert of Kenniford had once more recounted his creed to his daughter. "Betrayal is the natural tendency of men and women, child. Remember it. Brutus betrayed Julius Caesar, Delilah betrayed Samson, Judas betrayed Christ, and so on down the ages. Expect your servants to cheat you, your friends to go behind your back, your love to let you down. That way you will never suffer disappointment. Only show them, as I have here, that they cannot do it twice. Do you hear me?"

"I hear you, Father."

But Maud had looked from where Walter Corbet's eyes had been to those of her father and, young as she was, seen an equal emptiness.

"And now," Robert of Kenniford had told her, "should this castle itself betray you, I shall show you how you may thwart it."

They never got that far. As he tried to replace the Wormhole's bars, blood had gushed from her father's mouth, and Maud had scampered back the way they had come to fetch him help.

He died the following evening. She saw that he'd been aware that he was dying when he took her to the Wormhole, and that he'd felt the urgency of stressing his philosophy to her at the last. No final words of love, or of goodness, or of God; his legacy to her had been the truth as he'd seen it. "Trust no one."

It was not Maud's truth; she'd known it even then. His blood might have run in her veins, but so did that of Robert's third wife, the mother who'd died giving birth to her, a jolly woman apparently, much loved by her household. In Maud, the amalgam ameliorated the one and strengthened the other.

In that sense, his daughter was another who betrayed Robert of Kenniford. She took joy in being a stern but affectionate and confident ruler. Trust, she found, was a two-way business: give it and, more often than not, it was returned. Accordingly, she handed the keys to the undercroft storage to Sir Bernard and Milburga, knowing they would not cheat her, which they did not. Those who did received sharp punishment, like any other malefactor, but aboveground and in the open: at the castle whipping post, or the pillory, or the village lockup, where they could be abused by their enemies and fed by their friends—this last saving Maud money on their maintenance, always a strong consideration with her.

None of her prisoners went to the Wormhole, nor did she visit it herself, but she secretly sent Sir Rollo to transfer the bones of Walter Corbet to the burial ground. She'd wondered how her father had got away with flaunting them for so long—the murder, even of an adulterer, should have provoked inquiry, if not a trial. But that had been in the days of old King Henry, who'd been her father's friend and not above murder himself if the rumors about the death of his elder brother were true.

Whatever it was, the prison held a grimness for Maud, and she'd paid good money to nearby Abingdon Abbey so that its monks should pray for peace for Corbet's soul that his ghost might not haunt her, the child of his killer.

So large did the memory of the cell loom in her mind that, until now, she'd forgotten what else her father had taken her down there to show her.

What was it he'd said? *"Should this castle itself betray you . . ."*? Something about thwarting it. She hadn't understood at the time—how could a castle commit an act of betrayal?

But it could if it fell to an enemy. (How typical of Robert of Kenniford to blame even a building for failing its function.) In which case, it must provide a salvation for those it betrayed.

An escape route. *That* was where the secret postern was—if there was one at all—somewhere further along, and it behooved her, as its owner, to find it.

They kept on going along the gradually curving tunnel, hating it, wondering at the labor and expertise that had built it, passing no exit. The ground began to rise sharply, which suggested that it would eventually reach the surface.

There was a nudge from Milburga and Maud nodded; she, too, had heard the light steps behind them. God help them, the place was haunted after all. Terrified at what she might see, she swung round, raising the lantern to shine it on whatever creature or noncreature was following them—and saw a pale, small figure as frightened as herself.

William.

"Father sent me after you, lady. I think he worries for you."

Oh yes, highly likely. If John of Tewing's brain was still working, it wasn't for his wife's protection. More probably he, or perhaps Kigva, had wanted to know what was going on in the castle tonight and had sent young William to find out.

Time you went away, my lad, she thought now. He'd reached the age when boys were sent off to some other noble house to begin their training for knighthood. Secretly she suspected the boy would be more suited to the cloister with his gentle manners and ways, but he was determined to follow his father's ambitions for him and Maud had already entered into negotiations on the matter with Sir Robert Halesowen, a distant cousin, who held extensive lands in the West Country and Normandy. John of Tewing would not approve of that were he to know about it—Halesowen was an empress supporter—but then John of Tewing wouldn't approve of anybody who didn't beat knightly manners into his protégé's backside, whereas Halesowen, though strict, was a kindly man as well as a competent fighter.

She sighed. "What are we to do with you?"

"Bring him with us, I reckon," Milburga said. "Look at the poor little bugger shaking."

It had taken courage for the boy to face these dark tunnels on his own; sending him back to a maddened father was more than she could do.

"We are looking for a postern, William, a secret exit. Keep your eyes open."

"Is that it?" He was pointing some yards ahead to where there was a break in the form of an arch in the outer wall. The women hadn't seen it.

"Must be. Hallelujah."

By Maud's reckoning, they had circumnavigated well over half of the passage that lay beneath the castle; if they'd turned left out of the undercroft instead of right they would have got here sooner.

There was no doubt that this was an exit; for the first time since leaving the undercroft, they felt a cold draft.

"Where d'you reckon it comes out?"

"Let's see."

The arch led to a spur of the tunnel they were in, much smaller, lined with closer-packed stone, and considerably less daunting now that they were heading for fresh air. At the far end it had partly fallen in, making it impossible for someone of Milburga's size to get through. Maud sent her back to fetch men with picks and spades while she and William struggled through holes in the debris that, peculiarly, resembled miniature versions of the tunnels they were leaving behind.

"Oh God, what was that?" Something bristly and strong smelling had blundered against Maud's ankles.

"A badger, I think."

The light from Maud's lantern showed a gray, thickset body scurrying away from her on short legs.

"Poor thing, we frightened it," William said.

"Not half as much as it frightened me."

But some of the tunnels the badgers had built into their sett were of a size to accommodate a human child, so that Maud and William, both of them slim, were able to get through them by heavy scrabbling, heading for the dim light that now showed ahead.

Maud had been expecting the tunnel to end in a grille, something that could be raised or lowered, but if there had been one it had rusted away. Instead, bedraggled and scratched, they emerged out of a hole in a hedge. From here the ground sloped downward through a copse of rowan trees, leafless now but so thickly planted that their bare branches formed a roof hiding the approach to the postern from eyes scouring the castle walls from the surrounding Chiltern hills. The snow was trackless except for a tiny path leading from the sett behind them to where the badgers, cleanly animals, kept their privy.

William began to follow it. Maud dragged him back. "We're expecting visitors, boy. Unfriendly ones. Better that our footprints don't show them how to get into the castle."

"Like that one?"

She followed his gaze. To the east, where the dawn was touching the hilltops, was a rider. His outline faced the castle and was perfectly still, as if he were waiting for something. As she watched, another horseman joined him, then another and another, sprouting along the horizon like equine statues.

Taking William with her, Maud pushed her way back through to the main tunnel in order to alert her castle that it was again under siege.

CHAPTER 12

THAT MORNING, AS EVERY MORNING, Gwil had woken first, prodding Penda awake with his foot.

"Got to get up, Pen. We been summoned." Alan had appeared beside them only moments before to warn them that they would be needed.

The small recumbent body at Gwil's feet groaned and opened one eye, then closed it again quickly.

The truth was that Penda had slept badly if she'd slept at all; quite apart from the alien environment she now found herself in, yet another strange bed, there was also the matter of the unaccustomed, debilitating ache in her belly, a peculiar cramping that had begun during their flight from the charcoal burner's hut and now spread to the top of her legs, making her feel sluggish and sick.

"Ain't even light yet, Gwil," she pleaded, turning away from him to curl into the fetal position, which eased the pain.

"Tell that to Stephen's men, then," Gwil said, " 'cause I don't reckon as they know arse from elbow when it comes to timekeeping, an' they're right outside. You want to ask 'em to come back when you're ready or shall I?"

Suddenly she was wide awake, the top half of her body launching itself upright from the waist like the arm of a mangonel.

"We under siege then, Gwil?" she asked, her voice squeaky with excitement, the pain all but forgotten.

"More 'n likely," he said. "An' if so we'll need all the archers we got so you'd best rise sharpish."

He turned away and stood with his back to her.

He'd become more mindful of her privacy lately and sometimes, she'd noticed, it was as if it offended him to look at her. She couldn't blame him; it offended her to look at herself nowadays: her once neat and malleable body had become increasingly cumbersome, the fleshy mounds on her chest more resistant to their swaddling now, however tightly she bound them.

She gathered her blanket around her in defiance against both Gwil's back and the morning chill and stood up, but as she did so something warm and liquid seeped down her legs.

"Gwil!" The panic in her voice made him turn abruptly. She saw his face fall.

"Oh, Pen."

She followed his gaze to the wetness at her feet and saw, for the first time, the tiny rivulet of blood dripping from her ankle bone onto the floor, and suddenly the banks of an old memory burst like a dam flooding her head with a maelstrom of long-forgotten images, of unholy wounds and water and men on horseback, of pain and fear and blood.

Gwil caught her before she fell and laid her gently on the palliasse. When she came to, the memories had gone again and Gwil was kneeling beside her gesturing at her awkwardly with a fistful of strips of cloth.

"Here," he said. "For the blood."

She grabbed his arm. "Am I dying, Gwil?"

He smiled then and stroked her forehead.

"Not dying, Pen; just means as how you're a woman now. You'll grow accustomed to it, all women do, or so they say." He was trying to reassure her, hoping his features had arranged themselves into what might pass for benevolent reassurance; judging by hers—the downturned mouth, the large, anxious eyes—they had not.

"How do *you* know I ain't?" she croaked querulously, peering suspiciously over the blanket at him. "Dying, I mean." He stared back dumbstruck: what she needed now was a woman, not him, some kindly female who could explain the peculiar mystery of her sex to her, because he was damn sure he could not. But who? They knew no one, and besides, this morning of all mornings there wasn't time, either.

"Damn!" he said, recoiling from her and turning away as an unwelcome memory of his own began to play itself out, of a damaged child, a savage wound and a ruined church.

"And what do I do now, Lord, eh? Can't pretend she's a boy for much longer, can I?"

Protect her, Gwil, like always. You'll think of something.

But what? How could he protect her from herself, from the burgeoning femininity that would make her vulnerable once more? His confusion was making him irritable; besides, it wouldn't do to go soft on her now. She needed to pull herself together.

"Get up!" he said, his voice suddenly harsh. "Ain't got time for this now." He turned his back, was heading for the door when another unbidden memory thumped into his head, this time of his wife curled up like a baby, pale and suffering and bemoaning "the curse of all women." He had felt just as powerless then as now but he also felt pity infused with an overweening sense of duty.

It was God's fault.

He had made him take the girl on, which meant that, for better or worse, he had to see her right. He took a deep breath and turned back to her.

"Look . . . ," he said, struggling to find words he wasn't sure he possessed. "It's . . . it's what gives you power, Pen." He could feel the color rising in his cheeks. "It's . . . it's how you get to have a baby, see?" Judging by her blank expression she did not. "It's . . .

oh GodandallHissaints!" He clenched and unclenched his fists. "It's how your body gets itself ready to have a baby . . . And, Pen . . ." He paused, but it was too late to stop now. "Well . . . Thing is, see . . . There are them'll tell you it ain't clean and that it's wicked but it ain't, Pen, it's a blessing, a blessing in disguise . . . might not feel that way now but one day you'll come to appreciate it . . . or so they say. . . ." His voice trailed off as Penda's bottom lip began to quiver.

"But I don't want a baby," she wailed, and a slow tear rolled down her cheek.

Gwil knelt beside her. "Don't talk daft," he said tenderly. "Don't mean you're going to have a baby *now,* just means as how you could, one day, if you wanted." He stood up again. "Now, you use them cloths to stop the bleeding, replace 'em when they're wet. And hurry up about it, we been summoned, remember!"

She did as he said, stuffing the cloths between her legs, waddling uncomfortably behind him like a newly hatched duckling as he strode toward the door. She still felt sick and her belly ached like the devil but something of what he had said resonated with her: "the curse of all women," she had heard that somewhere before and somehow knew that it would be all right.

They arrived at the hall as a trumpet blew from a point high up on the battlements and suddenly the bailey swarmed with a throng of men and women chivvying to their various posts in the blue dawn light.

MAUD HAD CLEARED THE HALL of the servants who slept in its niches by night, leaving Sir Rollo, Sir Bernard and Father Nimbus, her advisers, to discuss the matter of the siege with Alan of Ghent and Sir Christopher. They sat clustered around one end of the great table, the flames of a large candelabrum shining on worried, tired faces.

The sharp eyes of the empress spotted Gwil and Penda as they entered, and to their surprise, she gestured that they should join her.

A vicious chill engulfed them all. The *cover-feus* that blanketed all fires at night had not been removed yet. Penda started to shiver, which exacerbated the pain in her belly, and while the others leant earnestly over the table toward one another, deep in conversation, she shrank back into her cloak, grateful for its warmth as she pulled it around herself tightly.

Outside the hall the castle bustled with activity. Somewhere below their feet, men with axes were enlarging the secret postern to fit horses and were doing it as quietly as possible among disgruntled badgers while others were filling great vats of water set at intervals round the cellars. Sapping was the danger. More than one castle wall had been brought down from having its foundation dug out by hidden miners. A shiver on the surface of the water vats would mean the enemy was digging somewhere.

After much chiding from his stepmother to be very careful, William had been allowed onto the roof to keep an eye on the enemy, reemerging every so often to report that its circle around the castle was thickening like a ring of scum around a bath. So far it had not attacked.

"What are they waiting for?" It was Maud who spoke.

"To parley," Sir Christopher said. "Stephen won't relish the idea of another siege this winter, and who can blame him? He'll want to negotiate a surrender."

"But we won't surrender, will we?" All eyes turned to Maud. "Surely we can't." She looked pale, Penda thought, less sure of herself suddenly, and she noticed that her hands were fidgeting in her lap as she spoke. "Kenniford will not be slighted. It cannot." It was more of a plea than a statement of fact and the timbre of her voice betrayed it.

For a while nobody spoke and then Alan broke the silence.

"There is no question of surrender, at least until the empress is safely out of Kenniford. But the question, madam, is how well you heeded my advice when last we met and how well provisioned you are for another siege."

Maud turned automatically to the reassuringly calm figure of Sir Bernard sitting beside her and put her hand on his arm. He cleared his throat.

"We are well prepared, sir." He looked steadfastly into the mercenary's eyes as he spoke, filling Maud with a sudden desire to throw her arms around his grizzled old neck in gratitude. Unaware of the emotion he had provoked in his young mistress Sir Bernard continued stolidly: "We have one hundred good men, including the fifty you garrisoned here previously. A good harvest means that stocks are plentiful, and as long, God willing, as there isn't another freeze, our water supply is sufficient."

Alan looked surprised but nodded. "Good" was all he said.

Hah! Maud was exultant. *Hadn't expected that, had he? Damn his eyes!* She sat up a little taller on her stool. Out of the corner of his eye Alan of Ghent, who noticed a good deal more about the chatelaine of Kenniford than she realized, also noted the change in her deportment and smiled to himself; then he turned to the empress.

"*Domina.* Last night two men were dispatched to Bristol. As soon as I have news of the reinforcements they will ask for we will leave here, but first you must rest." The empress acknowledged him with a slight inclination of her head and stood up.

She sure was calm, Penda thought, you had to give her that. On the other hand, though, this was probably a normal day for her, her entire life one long litany of battles and sieges won and lost; today was just one more, and she had the arrogance to assume that it wouldn't be her last.

The meeting ended to the scraping of wood on stone as they rose from their stools and benches. Just as they were about to leave the hall William and one of the guardsmen came rushing in with the news that three men from the enemy camp were approaching the castle gate.

"They're here! They're here!" he shouted.

Alan turned to Maud.

"Are you ready for the parley, madam?"

Maud nodded curtly. "Indeed I am," she said, pushing past him toward the exit.

Once outside Gwil grabbed Penda's arm and spoke to her for the first time since they'd left the keep.

"You stick close to me now," he said, swinging her round to face him, his hands gripping her so tightly that the metal links of her hauberk bit viciously into the flesh of her arms. She winced and tried to pull away but he maintained his pressure, glaring at her with an intensity that frightened her. "You don't make a move until I say so and you keep your eyes peeled. Understand?"

Penda glared at him sullenly as she fought to free her arms.

"*Do you understand?*" He was shouting now. She felt tears burning her eyes but could not raise her hands to rub them away.

"*Yes!*" she shouted back, hands clenched, cheeks livid with fury. "I understand! Now let go of me!"

"Good," he said, smiling at last. "That's better." Then he patted her roughly on the head and turned to follow the others toward the gate.

She followed him up the staircase to the ramparts, muttering under her breath as she went, cursing him, which made him smile.

He was glad she was angry. It was what he wanted her to be. She shot better when her blood was up, and today of all days he needed her sharp.

They reached the top of the staircase and stepped out onto the allure. Through the loophole in front of her Penda saw, for the first time, the reality of war.

The emissaries of death stood in rows on the far side of the river, the sun glinting blindingly off hundreds of metal helmets: in the front line the pikemen and slingers, shifting from foot to foot behind an interminable row of wooden pavises, bracing themselves against the cold and the bitter thrill of battle; behind them the archers—at a rough glance she counted close to two hundred, including around fifty arbalists—and behind them the knights, their bodies swaying with the movement of their horses shifting restlessly beneath them, their hooves pawing testily at the ground. And then beyond them all, like the background of a macabre tapestry, great plumes of smoke rose into the sky from the burning village. The king's men had not been idle that morning.

Penda looked toward Gwil, who occupied the merlon beside her, and saw him cross himself and mutter some incantation under his breath. She did the same, although her hands trembled as a bolt of fear and excitement shot through her.

"You're a brave little bugger, Penda," Gwil said, puffing hard as he slipped his foot into place in his crossbow's stirrup to cock it against the ground. "And I've taught you as well as I know how. But you've never shot more'n a wolf and I'm fearful for you. You stay alive, hear me? By God's eyes I'll do all I can to keep you that way but this ain't our war, ain't our siege. Our job's to survive and theirs," he said, gesturing toward the enemy lines in the distance, "is to kill us, and I mean *us,* not them." He was pointing now back down into the bailey, where the Kenniford knights were waiting. "Our lives is cheap, Pen, you gotta know that. Won't be no knights lost in all this; too valuable as hostages, them, but we ain't, and what's more we're a bloody nuisance and Stephen's men'll kill us soon as look at us." All the time he was ranting at her he'd been busying himself with the weaponry at his feet. When he had finished he looked up and saw her mouth quivering.

"No crying, now," he said with a sudden tenderness that made her want to sob out loud, but then checked himself, and the stern look and hectoring tone returned.

"Ain't no time for crying," he said, turning back to his loophole. "Ain't no place for crying in battle." He repeated it over and over again like a mantra until something in the dim reaches of Penda's memory echoed back:

"Fenwomen never cry."

She'd learned that once, someone had told her that once, but who and why she couldn't remember. She shook her head against the voice. *Not now, not now.* Whatever it was must not come back now. She couldn't afford to remember now!

The sudden screech and grind of heavy apparatus cranking into action dragged her back to the melee of the present, and the booming exertion of male voices drowned out the ones clamoring in her head. Then a loud creak announced the raising of the portcullis and from her vantage point she saw Maud, Sir Rollo and Father Nimbus walk out over the drawbridge toward the three men waiting for them in the snow-laden field.

CHAPTER 13

IT WASN'T EASY TO WALK confidently, Maud decided, in the snow. Standing behind the gate as Milburga clucked and fussed around her like a mother hen, waiting nervously for the signal to egress, she'd planned to do so as elegantly as possible. She was meeting the king, after all, and as the representative of her beloved Kenniford, she might at least try to win the battle before it began with a display of her own personal invincibility. If she could hold her head up and convince Stephen that she, and therefore Kenniford, was indomitable, there might be a chance of negotiating a mutually beneficial truce. After all, there wasn't much else she could do.

Deep down, of course, she knew it was futile, had known it since she'd first clapped eyes on Stephen's men on the far side of the river that morning and watched her precious village burn. Even Sir Rollo had flinched at the sight, and although, as she was fond of telling people, the man was dull to the point of eye-watering tedium and could probably bore several men to death at fifty paces, there was no denying that he was also brave.

"King Stephen has a reputation for goodness, you know," Father Nimbus had whispered as they waited for the herald's trumpet to sound. He'd sensed her nerves, bless him, and was doing his best to quell them.

And it was true that in the past Stephen had been reasonable, but it was also true that his reputation for leniency, which, according to his critics, had bordered on idiocy, had been hastily revised since the day, not so long ago, when he had hanged poor Ernulf of Hesding at Shrewsbury Castle along with four of his knights and eighty-eight other members of the garrison. This news coupled with the fact that he was famously kicking himself for allowing the empress to escape him twice—first at Arundel and now at Oxford—meant that he was unlikely to embrace clemency, especially as regarded Matilda, ever again.

As they stepped off the drawbridge the leather soles of her shoes began to move independently of her feet on the icy, rutted earth and she grabbed hold of Father Nimbus's arm to steady herself.

"There, there, my dear," he said, patting her hand, although he was slipping and sliding like a skater himself. "All will be well. Just keep putting one foot in front of the other and if we all remember to—whoops!—dreadful weather this!—er—just remember to, er, breathe in and out, God, I'm sure, will protect us."

He'd better, Maud thought. If she were perfectly honest, she was beginning to wonder where exactly God was in all of this. How many times must she plead for the safety of her castle and the people in it? Why couldn't they all just leave? Why, even the empress! She could simply go back to Normandy, or wherever it was she damn well came from, and Stephen could go . . . well . . . anywhere, actually, she didn't care, just as long as it was away from here. The anarchic spirit of the age had entered Maud's soul. After all, this was now a land devoid of loyalty, where almost every man and woman was for him- or herself first and for the king or the empress only as far as self-interest dictated. Why should she be any different? Why not capitulate? Why not emulate the bloody barons who changed sides as often as they changed horses? She owed nothing to either party! The king had foisted a drooling boor of a husband on her and the empress a bunch of foul mercenaries. There was quite literally nothing and nobody to prevent her from declaring a truce with the king right then and there, thus saving Kenniford and relieving herself of the burden of the empress and this damned impending siege.

And all this she might have done if it hadn't been for a blackbird trilling away in the distance somewhere on the Crowmarsh bank, reminding her of the oaths she'd sworn so poignantly not only to the empress but to God. And what was it she had said? *"I shall keep this vow, Lord, because You have sent me a lucky sign to tell me that I must."* And suddenly, for one rare moment in her life, devotion overcame pragmatism and she realized there *was* no getting out of it. Damn it!

THE KING LOOKED OLDER THAN she'd imagined, slighter somehow. The deep lines around his eyes spoke of a weariness that no amount of sleep could ever salve and the set of his mouth betrayed a cynicism that no man was ever born with, but to her relief, she saw no cruelty there. None either in the man to his left, whom she assumed was William of Ypres, Stephen's mercenary commander in chief. He was typical of his ilk, so cold and indifferent that he might have been hewn from granite, but she'd seen his like before and had his measure. No, it was the man to the king's right, a cleric of some sort judging by his robes, who frightened her most. Cruelty was etched into every line of his face and appeared to seep from every pore—she could practically smell it—and when she looked into his strange, pale green eyes she saw that they were as cold and ravening as a wolf's. A sudden chill, like cold fingertips along her spine, made her shiver, and she looked quickly away.

At that moment the king stepped forward.

"Lady Maud," he said. "Here we are in the midst of yet another godforsaken winter." He was looking down at the ice-encrusted hem of her cloak. "And only a madman—my condolences, by the way, for your husband's affliction; I have only just heard the news—would relish the prospect of a siege in these conditions. So let us waste neither time nor words nor leave this parley without making peace."

Maud opened her mouth to reply but Stephen raised his hand to stay her. "Look yonder, madam," he said, gesturing toward his army. "Surely you can see that you are outnumbered and that beyond even those men my resources are limitless?"

There was something in the weary authority of his tone that prevented her from replying even though her mouth had opened to do so. He continued.

"Of course you might hold out against us for a day, a week, a month even, but as surely as night follows day we will batter your defenses, destroy your garrison and starve you into surrender." He spoke in a strange monotone, and it occurred to Maud that this was merely a recitation of a speech he knew off by heart and had made countless times before. They were wearisome statements of fact, as far as he was concerned, nothing more, nothing less. He looked from her to Father Nimbus and Sir Rollo and back again. It was her turn to speak.

"My lord." She heard the strangle of nerves in her voice and hoped against hope that he hadn't. Only Father Nimbus and Sir Rollo knew her well enough to recognize it and they, thank God, were on her side. Nevertheless, she paused for a moment to put her shoulders back, as Milburga had taught her to in times of crisis, and cleared her throat.

"I have faith in my men," she said eventually, relieved at the clarity of her tone. "And, as a matter of fact, our provisions are quite plentiful, so we have no need to fear a siege. But apart from that, I have sworn fealty to the empress in the eyes of God and I will not break my oath." To stop herself trembling, she had screwed her hands up so tightly inside her gloves that her fingernails were biting painfully into her palms. She stopped speaking to stare defiantly at the king. His turn.

"And if I were to offer you and the empress a safe and unmolested passage away from here, what would you say then?"

"Madam." Sir Rollo, who'd been agitating beside her for several minutes, suddenly broke in. "May I speak to you a moment?" Maud nodded and withdrew a few steps from the king.

"I must advise you, madam, as is my duty," Sir Rollo whispered when he deemed they were far enough away not to be heard, "that these are very reasonable terms. If you should accept the king's offer, you will lose Kenniford, but you have other estates and other castles. The empress will be imprisoned, of course, but will survive, and *she* has other supporters. But if you reject these terms now and lose, you will incur the king's wrath and the price of any further treaty will be much, much greater. Of this I must warn you. However, if you choose to stand and fight, I will of course stand with you." She looked at his worn, earnest face and smiled.

"You're a dear man, Sir Rollo," she said. "But I have sworn fealty to an authority higher than either the king or the empress and I will not break it." He nodded; it was what he had expected her to say.

"So be it," he said, and bowed.

WHAT'S HAPPENING NOW, GWIL?" PENDA asked as they watched the three distant figures turn solemnly away from the king and his party and begin their procession back to the castle. "They're coming back now! What does that mean?"

"Means the parley's over, Pen, and less'n they've managed to agree a truce, which I doubt, we'll be fighting soon."

"And then what?"

"And then it's anybody's guess. First off they'll try and batter us into surrender, and then if that don't work they'll get the underwallers in, and if that don't work either they'll try and starve us out. That's the bad bit. On crusade I heard of sieges went on so long all the supplies ran out and the garrison took to eating the flesh of their own dead."

"Yuck." Penda shuddered. She was quiet for a while and then a slow smile spread across her face.

"Tell you what, though, Gwil. I promise you this: if you die and I'm starving, I won't eat you."

Gwil grinned. "Nor I you, Pen . . . Or, leastways not unless I'm really hungry."

ONCE MAUD, SIR ROLLO AND Father Nimbus were safely back inside the castle a trumpet sounded, the drawbridge rose and the metal teeth of the portcullis locked into place. An unaccustomed silence fell as everybody stopped what they were doing and turned to the small figure of the priest, who was now standing in the middle of the bailey.

"May the Lord keep you and protect you." His thin clear voice floated up to the battlements. Gwil stopped what he was doing and bent his head in prayer; Penda followed, squinting sideways at him through half-closed eyes to take her lead as to what to do next. Father Nimbus raised his hands: "And may His blessing be upon you now and forevermore . . ."

He stood silently for a moment looking around at all the bowed heads surrounding him. He wanted to embrace them all, to keep them all safe. The idea of war was anathema to him. All this bloodshed and conflict was simply too much for his poor old heart, not to mention the tricky question of who to bless and who not. Oh dear! He hadn't a clue what the papal edict on crossbowmen was nowadays. It was getting so hard to keep up. But whatever it was, as far as he was concerned they were all God's lambs, yes, even the arbalists with their beastly weapons, and therefore just as deserving of divine protection as anybody else. And with that, he raised his eyes to the ramparts and made the sign of the cross. "Amen."

There was silence for a moment or two and then the castle erupted with a resounding "Amen" and business resumed.

AS FAR AS PENDA WAS concerned siege warfare was a malodorous affair. Even if she hadn't been feeling quite so unwell anyway, the combination of smells wafting up to the crenels would have been enough to set her off all by themselves. Some of them she recognized: the boiled meat and vegetables blowing in from the kitchens, for instance, which weren't so bad; the fresh blood from the ox hides strewn over every piece of thatch in the bailey as a protection against fire arrows wasn't, on its own, too unpleasant, either; but there were others that made her retch—like the one seeping up in great plumes from the hideous gray liquid the carpenters were stirring, which smelled like an entire ocean of rotting fish.

"That'll be the glue, Pen," Gwil said, amused at the look of disgust on her face. "For the bows. Case they get broke."

"Oh," she mouthed weakly, hoping very much that hers didn't; proximity to the fetid stuff might finish her off, never mind the enemy. She turned gratefully back to her loophole; there may have been danger on the other side but at least the air was fresh.

In the distance the enemy lines moved in a cumbersome but inexorable advance toward the castle. In the time it had taken Father Nimbus to grant his blessing, they had gained considerable ground and crossed the river.

The pikemen came first, their deadly phalanx of ash poles crowned with vicious metal spikes glistening wickedly in the sun and closing around the castle ditch like a malignant forest. Behind them droves of men hauled vast siege engines on rollers, the mangonels and trebuchets with which to bring the walls down, while ox-drawn carts carried huge stone boulders and tree trunks shod in iron. Even from a distance, their exertion was visible in the puffs of breath etched in the cold air. Following behind the archers, anonymous rows of men in coifs and hauberks marched swiftly across the demesne, picking their way past the vicious spikes of the caltrops that had been thrown down on Sir Rollo's orders to delay them.

Sir Rollo himself stood in the bailey alongside his knights while Alan of Ghent patrolled the ramparts. When he reached Penda's position he stopped, resting his hand on her shoulder.

"Shoot as well today as you did the other day, Master Penda, and we'll have no need to disturb those idle buggers down there." He gestured below toward Sir Rollo and his knights in the bailey. Penda laughed. She looked up at him, grateful for his encouragement, and saw that the weary, gaunt face of an hour or so ago had been transformed by the prospect of a fight. She'd noticed the same change in Gwil, too, who, despite his ill temper this morning, was suddenly imbued with a vibrancy and excitement she'd never witnessed before.

"Remember now," Gwil said, popping his head around the merlon to grin at her when Alan had gone, "any bugger so much as looks at that wall old-fashioned gets an arrow in the chest. Hear me?"

She nodded.

"And don't look 'em in the eyes, neither. Don't see 'em as people; them there's the devil, Pen, and that's all there is to it, right?"

She nodded again and realized that this feeling, whatever it was, apparently raging around the crenels had infected her, too, and suddenly she could hardly wait for the battle to begin. She snatched up her crossbow and was about to cock it against the ground when Gwil popped up behind her again.

"Oh," he said cheerfully. "Forgot to mention it earlier but you might offer up the odd prayer to Saint Sebastian now and then, too; he can be quite handy at times like these."

She closed her eyes and put her hands together to do as she was told when she felt the sudden pressure of a hand on her arm. Gwil was scowling at her.

"But don't close your bloody eyes, you fool."

CHAPTER 14

THE FIRST FLURRY OF ENEMY arrows clattered onto the allure behind them and were met not with return fire but, to Penda's astonishment, a barrage of jeers and insults. And even as the first boulder shuddered into the walls with such force that it shook her bones, the men closest to it merely leant out through their embrasures in a show of mock outrage and dusted the damaged stone with their sleeves. The jeering and hectoring got louder and more raucous as aggression and fear combined to fuel the incendiary atmosphere among the men on the ramparts.

Penda's pulse was racing, although not from fear. It was something else. For the first time since they had parted from the acrobats, she felt a sense of belonging. Shooting was undoubtedly what she did best, which meant that this was where she belonged, here among men, a bow in her hands and a sense of freedom in her heart. Life or death? Kill or be killed? They were the only questions she knew the answers to for certain and was liberated by their simplicity. This was her destiny, the role Gwil had prepared her for. Only the dull ache in her belly, which persisted like a nagging wife, dissented.

Down in the bailey the atmosphere was less excitable but no less charged: the serious business of feeding and equipping a castle under siege was under way and Maud once again was marveling at its efficiency.

She, too, was enjoying a sense of freedom. Sir Christopher had dispatched the empress to the safety of the keep with Tola for company, and with her out of the way, she was able to breathe again and, best of all, resume control of her own castle once more.

She was standing next to Milburga, overseeing the transfer of great slabs of salted meat from the barrels in the storeroom to the kitchens. The sacking of the village meant the castle's numbers had swollen by almost one hundred men, women and children, increasing the number of hungry mouths they would have to feed. Gorbag the chef, temperamental at the best of times, was not best pleased, and she had spent a good deal of the morning trying to placate him.

It had been the same with Sir Rollo, who, once again, as the desperate villagers appeared at the gates, clamoring to be let in, was reluctant to admit them until Maud appeared to chide him and remind him that they were *her* responsibility and that *not one* should be turned away.

"Think of the cost, my lady! The useless mouths!" he implored, wringing his hands. "Think of the drain on our resources!" But his words, just as last time, had fallen on deaf ears and were met with a look he knew only too well.

"Just open those bloody gates," she had said, stamping her foot, "and let the buggers in."

They came in droves, the village's dispossessed hungry, cold and frightened, to stand in tatty, confused huddles in the bailey. But if Maud was merciful, sentimental she was not.

"Get them doing something!" she hissed at Milburga. "Good-for-nothing bunch of dolittles, making the place look untidy. Get them working." So Milburga and Father Nimbus were dispatched to organize them and put them to good use.

THE ENEMY WAS NOW FIRMLY entrenched on the counterscarp, shielded behind large wooden pavises arranged along its edge.

"They're going to try and fill the ditch, Pen, get to the wall," Gwil warned. "See them fascines?" he said, pointing to the large bundles of wood stacked beside the pikemen and slingers. "They'll chuck those in and keep chucking 'em until they're dense enough to walk across and then they'll bring the ladders in. So, if you see so much as *one* of them buggers put his hand to un, shoot."

Which is precisely what she did, Gwil's instructions echoing in her head at all times—"*Load . . . Aim . . . Don't think . . . Loose*"—as the men below her fell like flies. She watched dispassionately as their expressions of eager intent turned suddenly to shock and outrage as each head whipped round to her arrow's sting and acknowledged the impertinent barbs she buried in their flesh. She felt no pity, either. Kill or be killed. It was the formula Gwil had taught her and its primitive power surged through her now. She wondered, too, at the efficiency and dispassion with which she could take a man's life and the ensuing sense of power it gave her. She wondered if it was natural, whether everyone felt the same, whether she had been born with it.

They worked together: Gwil tied strings to his bolts, which he would then fire at the enemy shields. As his quarrel pierced their center he would pull sharply on the end of the string, lifting the shields and exposing the men behind them like ants under a rock, leaving them easy prey to the ensuing volley of Penda's arrows.

As the afternoon wore on, the unerring accuracy of her shooting began to draw attention from her fellow archers. News of her prowess spread along the battlements like wildfire and by the time the light began to fade the young redheaded lad with the fearsome aim was celebrated throughout the garrison.

"And I thought death was supposed to be the only archer who never missed."

The voice behind her was familiar and she turned to see Sir Christopher grinning at her.

"I hear you got quite a tally today, Master Penda," he said, patting her heartily on the back. "Now come and eat."

As she, Gwil and Sir Christopher descended the wooden steps from the allure to the bailey, she noticed Gwil limping slightly and rubbing his back.

"Bowman's back, Pen," he said, noting her concern. "Got to expect it at my age, but mind you look after yours."

It was the first time in a long time that she had thought of him as old, and it came as a shock.

When she had first clapped eyes on him in the ruined church what seemed almost a lifetime ago now, she had marked him as, if not old exactly, certainly elderly, but as time passed and she grew to know him, the years had slipped away. To her he was Gwil the invincible, the ageless protector and provider of all things, on whom her survival had depended for as long as she could remember. But now, all of a sudden she saw him as if for the first time and was shocked by the flecks of gray in his hair, the slight stoop of his shoulders and the deep, weary lines on his skin.

"You're not to get old," she muttered under her breath. "I need you. You're all I've got."

Even in the twilight the outer bailey still hummed with people and activity, the air booming with the remedial hammering of the smiths and armorers at one end and the shrill commands of the scullions and cooks at the other. From inside the huddled reed-thatched houses that covered the castle's walls like moss, tallow candles and rushlights flickered over the injured and dying as they were ministered to.

When they arrived at the great hall the empress once again summoned them to her table.

Her patronage was still a source of puzzlement to them both, and they looked quizzically at each other and shrugged their shoulders. Nonetheless they were grateful for it, not least for the proximity it gave them to the fire and its welcome scent of blazing cherry logs.

They sat opposite her at the other end of the table and were immediately ignored as she idly watched a chandler attending the large candelabrum in the middle of the table. The flickering light illuminated the elegant lines and hollows of her impassive face and made them even more dramatic. She sure was beautiful, Penda thought, but colder than winter. All this fighting and sacrifice in her name and not a spark of emotion to show for it. She seemed impervious to almost everything, to war, to people, perhaps even to God Himself.

By contrast Maud, who was sitting beside her, was unusually fidgety. The empress's presence unnerved her in a way that nobody else's could, throwing, as it did, the familiar hierarchy in which she functioned best to disarray. To Maud, Matilda represented trouble and danger, sieges and expense and a bloody great managerial headache, and yet there was something about the woman that made everyone in her presence want to please her. The fact that Maud herself was not immune was almost more irritating than anything. Why, even Gorbag! The most recalcitrant of cooks—of men, indeed—had put himself out quite obsequiously for their royal guest. She had watched in fascinated horror as a great pageant of servants was dispatched bearing plates of suckling pig seethed in honey, quail and pheasant stuffed with last year's almonds and apple, *and* his very own specialty of meat tile, all of which, he insisted, was to be washed down with large jugs of wine spiced with ginger and honey. It was largesse on an unnecessarily grand scale and if it continued, she thought bitterly, they would run out of food within days. She would have to have words.

She sighed gazing mournfully down the table at all the mouths she was going to have to feed for the foreseeable future and then, with another twinge of irritation, spotted Penda and Gwil. She couldn't put her finger on it but there was something about those two, something peculiar, especially that sharp-eyed redheaded boy, to whom she had taken an instant dislike.

"What are *they* doing here?" she hissed, digging poor Sir Rollo in the ribs.

"Who?" he replied, looking up reluctantly from the trencher he had been loading with as much food as it could hold.

"That redheaded tatterdemalion and the mercenary, oh, you *know*," she added irascibly. "The ones who arrived with the empress yesterday."

"No idea," said Sir Rollo blithely, "but *she* seems to like them."

"Well, I don't," said Maud, glaring at them bitterly.

Gwil, oblivious to the hostility directed at him by his host, was deep in conversation with Alan of Ghent, who, Penda noticed, had been remarkably solicitous of him since their arrival at Kenniford.

"How long do you reckon?" she heard Alan ask.

Gwil shook his head and shrugged his shoulders:

"Your guess is as good as mine," he said, taking another large swig of the malmsey whose advent he had fallen on with alacrity, announcing to the table as he did so that it was the only known cure for a bad back. "Depends on resources and the water supply. Who knows? We held 'em off all right today but who's to say what'll happen if they build that belfry of theirs and get it to the wall? There's a lot of 'em out there."

"Two to one?"

"Reckon that at least, and they ain't going to be short of reinforcements when they're gone, neither."

Alan leant closer and lowered his voice.

"My plan is to get the empress to Bristol at the first opportunity. And as soon as I receive word from the Earl of Gloucester that he's ready to receive her we'll leave. Then, God willing, the king will call off the siege and follow us west and you lot can all go home."

Gwil smiled.

"Be a shame that, though," he said. "Now that we're so comfortable here an' all and so looking forward to the hangman's rope."

Alan laughed, patting his companion's shoulder affectionately.

"Whatever happens, we're in your debt, Gwilherm de Vannes,

you and your boy there. And although she might not show it, the empress is truly grateful."

The bond between them was palpable, and might have been touching, Penda thought, if it hadn't also been quite so boring. Most of the time, or so it seemed to her, they made no sense at all, speaking in an unfathomable shorthand as impenetrable as a foreign language. To make matters worse, toward the end of what already seemed like an exceedingly long evening, as their tongues loosened and their speech became slurred by the malmsey, they began exchanging anecdotes about their various campaigns and crusades, battles and sieges, at which point Penda thought she was going to die. Quite apart from the tedium, her belly was hurting again and she was so desperately tired that she could have cried, and yet there was no respite. Every time she closed her eyes they were joined by yet more men, each more drunk and garrulous than the last.

And so it went on until one of them, the fat one with the explosively red face who'd pulled up a stool so close to hers that he almost knocked her off it, began gesticulating with such abandon that he accidentally clouted her on the side of her head.

"Shorry, young fella," he said, slurring his words, barely able to focus as he patted the air around her with a large, apologetic hand.

She mumbled a resentful forgiveness and turned to gaze wistfully toward the other end of the table where the women, Maud, Milburga and the kindly-looking nun whose name she didn't know, appeared to be having a more civilized evening. On the other hand, *anything* would be more civilized than this! Even Payn, the young herald, who had sung with such angelic sweetness after supper, had joined the ribaldry and was making bawdy jokes about his grandmother's farts.

"Fell a man at twenty paces, they could," he said, giggling like a baby. "Tried to cover 'em up with that asafetida stuff, too, she did. Hopeless! If you ask me, that smells worse than farts. And the funny thing is, I was reminded of my dear old gran the other day when I got a whiff of it off that monk who was here . . ."

Quite suddenly the entire mood changed and Gwil, who, Penda had assumed, was too drunk to notice much at all, suddenly jerked upright on his stool, eyes wide with fury, lunging across the table to grab the astonished herald by the throat.

"What did you say?" he shouted, pressing his nose into the young man's startled face and hissing at him with such venom that the boy began to tremble.

"I . . . w-w-was . . . j-j-j-just," Payn stammered, "talking about my grandmother's wind—"

"Not your grandmother's farts, you fool!" Gwil said, shaking him violently. "The monk! What did you say about the monk?"

Penda had never seen him so angry and, fearful of what he might do, leapt off her stool to try to prize his hand from the herald's throat, but Gwil was too quick for her.

"Let him speak, Pen," he growled, thrusting out his other arm to fend her off. "I need to hear this."

"Th-th-that's it," Payn said, struggling feebly against him. "Th-th-that's all th-th-there is! There was a m-m-monk here day before yesterday, w-w-went to see Sir John, smelled just like my grandmother. That's all. I s-s-s-swear!"

Suddenly Gwil let go, sending the boy stumbling backward gurgling and clutching at his bruised neck.

"Enough, gentlemen!" Alan rose from his stool, put his hands on Gwil's shoulders and spoke quietly to him. What he said, Penda couldn't hear, but after a few minutes Gwil had calmed down and apologized. They shook hands, and when Gwil had poured the still-trembling boy a drink and given him an avuncular pat on the back, the evening resumed as if nothing had happened.

Fortunately, though still longing for her bed, Penda was distracted by the sudden appearance of a rangy-looking lurcher who approached the table in search of scraps. He was nervous of her at first and shied away when she extended her hand to him, but after a while, as she sat quietly and patiently making soothing noises, he crept closer until he was near enough to take the morsel she held out to him and rewarded her by resting his elegant head in her lap.

She sat for some time, delighted by her newfound companionship, smoothing and patting the dog's rough coat, and as her fingers worked gently and methodically along its back, she recognized something familiar in the sensation and wondered, as she did about so many things these days, whether she had ever done it before.

A VOICE BESIDE HER JOLTED her back to the company of the men and frightened the dog away. She scowled, irritated by the interruption, but smiled when she saw Sir Christopher standing beside her.

"What I'd like to know, young man," he said, "is where you learned to shoot like that." She felt herself turn pink. She wasn't used to compliments and had adopted Gwil's mistrust of them.

"Gwil learned me," she said, trying hard not to stammer.

"Well, he learned you well," Sir Christopher said, grinning. "Learned you very well indeed in fact. Your fame is spreading, Master Penda."

"What?" Gwil's head whipped toward them. He had that furious look on his face again. Her heart sank. *It's like the devil's got in him*, she thought.

Sir Christopher stepped back calmly, holding up his hands in apology.

"I was merely telling Master Penda here that his fame had spread. A talent like that doesn't go unnoticed."

"That's all right, ain't it, Gwil?" Penda said, desperately hoping that it would be. Gwil stared at her for a moment or two and then his expression suddenly softened and she let out the breath she'd been holding.

"S'pose so," he muttered sheepishly. "But why you feel the need to draw attention to yourself I don't know."

The injustice of the remark combined with everything else that evening was suddenly too much and she wiped furiously at a large tear that had begun its sticky journey down her cheek as she watched Sir Christopher excuse himself and wander off.

When he had gone Gwil turned to her and put his arm around her shoulders.

"Sorry, Pen," he said. "Didn't mean to snap. It's just we don't need no attention. Don't need un prying into our business. You know that, don't you?"

"But I don't understand, Gwil," she whimpered. "*Why* don't we? What difference would it make? Is it because we don't want 'em to know I'm a girl?"

"That's right, Pen," he said, seizing on the proffered explanation with unusual enthusiasm. "That's *exactly* what we don't want 'em to know."

But it wasn't of course, or not just that. It was something else entirely, and he was kicking himself for having forgotten it. Beyond the siege, beyond the lines of Stephen's men, a greater danger awaited her, and he had allowed it to come too close. The monk now had access to the castle and would return. He reached instinctively inside his cloak and his fingers closed tightly around the now-familiar shape of the quill case.

"Time to act, Lord?"

No time like the present, Gwil.

CHAPTER 15

BEYOND THE CASTLE WALL IN the darkness footsteps—light, silent footsteps—edge out of the siege camp toward the forest.

He glides effortlessly over the snow like Christ across the sea of Galilee while the full moon lights his path, bathing him in the glory of God.

Nobody sees him. Nobody hears him. Nobody knows him.

Hush now, not a sound. A few more steps and he will vanish among the trees and then he can abandon himself to the chase and run. Oh, how he will run, and when he runs he will throw back his head and howl at the moon and his cries will ring through the forest but only she will hear him and know that he has come back for her, just as he promised he would.

He reaches the forest edge but the thrill of what he is about to do makes him gasp and catch his breath. His heart is thumping like the devil and he's dizzy, but deliriously so. He stops for a moment to steady himself against a tree and then leans into the darkness as if to drink it in. He must savor this moment, because in no time at all, it will all be over.

HE DIDN'T RIDE WITH THE king's men into the village that morning but pulled up unnoticed on the summit of the rise behind. The ironclad horsemen on either side raced on, oblivious to his absence, descending on the innocents below like the wrath of God. He amused himself for a while, watching the villagers, flushed from their warm beds by the iron men, scamper like rats from burning nests across the fields away from the baying knights on horseback.

In the half-light of the morning and from this distance, the villagers were indistinguishable from one another, but then he spotted the girl; not, perhaps, the one he sought, although this one would do for now . . .

The sun had risen, the clouds parted, and a divine light had shone down on the mane of red hair fanning behind her like a glorious flame as she ran for her life.

She was halfway to the castle by the time he reached her but too exhausted to run anymore, and had barely struggled as he leant down, took her in his arms and galloped off with her to the forest.

He pulled up in a clearing to set her down and hoped she would run again, but when he lowered her to the ground, her legs crumpled like a newborn fawn's and she fell to the floor and lay there, her pale eyes staring blankly through him and above him at the canopy of branches high above her face.

And then from somewhere in the distance a trumpet blew. The king was summoning his men. He had to leave her.

He wrapped her in a blanket and tied her to a tree, all the while combing and teasing her hair with his fingers and murmuring his promise that he would return for her.

And now he is keeping that promise and running, faster and faster through the forest, crushing the undergrowth like bones beneath his feet as he races toward her. Nothing will stop him, neither man, nor beast, nor God.

He reaches the clearing. She is still there. He knew she would be. He stops short of her, panting with excitement, to catch his breath, but when he looks up again he sees that there is something wrong. She is still, so terribly still, her tiny body unmoved, unmoving, still swaddled in the blanket, still slumped against the tree, just as she had been when he left her. He fears that she is dead and he kneels beside her, lifting her chin tenderly with his fingers, and when, revived by his touch, she opens her eyes and whimpers feebly, he thanks God. He buries his face in her neck, grateful for its warmth, and breathes in the scent of her skin and hair.

Then he cuts the ropes with which he bound her and pulls her to her feet. "Run," he tells her, "run," but she only sinks to her knees again looking at him beseechingly, clasping her tiny hands in prayer. And then he realizes that her hair no longer shines and that, in the darkness, it is not even red anymore.

He kills her anyway but there is no pleasure in it this time.

CHAPTER 16

A BELL RANG, ENDING PENDA'S torment and summoning the diners to compline. Outside in the bailey the wind whipped up clouds of powdery snow from the rooftops and sent them whirling and eddying into the faces of the worshippers. Penda lifted the hem of her cloak above the slush on the cobbles, drawing its collar around her face to protect it from the bitter cold that pinched and pricked at her cheeks like a bully.

The castle was quiet now; only the distant voices of the guards on duty high up on the ramparts could be heard, that and the howling of a lone wolf in the forest.

"Come on, Gwil!" she called back irritably over her shoulder at him. She was still cross with him for his earlier behavior, and besides, she was so cold and shivering so violently now that she thought her bones were going to break, so without waiting for him, she put her head down and hurried toward the chapel.

Within a few feet of the door a shape darted across her path. Startled by the sudden movement, she looked up to see the ragged figure of a woman pushing against the flow of traffic, her lank dark hair flapping down her back like a filthy veil as she scuttled in the direction of the keep.

"Looks like that Kigva woman," a voice behind her said.

Gwil had caught up with her and she turned to see him squinting into the darkness at the disappearing figure. "What's the betting that's holy water she's carrying?" he asked.

Penda shuddered.

She had overheard Father Nimbus complaining to Maud that somebody had been stealing water from the font for purposes of witchcraft, or so he had presumed, and had been unusually vociferous in his demand that a lock be placed on it. There had been no aspersions cast against anyone in particular—it wasn't Father Nimbus's way—but suspicion had fallen automatically on Kigva, whose *maleficium* was renowned in Kenniford.

Penda shook the thought away with a shiver, then grabbed hold of Gwil's arm and hurried him through the door into the sanctuary of the chapel.

Once inside she succumbed to the warmth of the atmosphere provided by the tightly packed bodies in the nave and was soon fast asleep with her head on Gwil's shoulder.

When she awoke Father Nimbus was administering the final blessing as a seething mass of exhausted worshippers scrambled toward the doors and to bed.

Only Gwil stood firm, facing the altar, bracing himself against the crowds as they jostled and pushed past them.

"Ain't you coming, Gwil?" Penda asked, tugging at his sleeve in an effort to pull him toward the door. "Ain't you tired yet?"

He shook his head. "You go, Pen, get some sleep," he said. "I need a word with the father."

As soon as she had left, and the last of the worshippers had disappeared into the night, Gwil took the quill case from his cloak and made his way toward the altar, where the elderly priest, his back to him, was attending the candles.

"Father!" Gwil called out as he approached, but the old man seemed not to have heard.

"Father!" he repeated more loudly this time, at which point the priest turned, clearly startled to see the man standing in front of him.

"Can I help you, my son?" he asked when he had recovered himself, regarding Gwil keenly. There was something in the mercenary's expression that disturbed and moved him equally; he saw kindness and penitence in that face but grave anxiety, too, as if this man carried the weight of the world on his shoulders—a dog of war with a conscience, perhaps? There were stranger creatures, after all. In the ensuing silence Gwil began to shift his weight awkwardly under the old man's gaze.

"Do you need me to hear your confession, perhaps?" Father Nimbus asked gently, sensing his discomfort.

But Gwil shook his head and swallowed hard.

"No," he said hesitantly. "But thank you, Father. It, it ain't that . . . ain't time enough for that, though Lord knows I got plenty to confess. It's . . . it's this."

He uncurled his fingers and held out the quill case, tipping it so that the tube of parchment, now looking tired from too much handling, fell out onto the altar in front of them.

"Just read me this, if you can, will you?" he asked.

Still staring intently at Gwil, Father Nimbus unrolled the parchment with his clean, small fingers, then moved toward a wall cresset for better light. "How unusual," he said, turning back toward Gwil. "It's Greek." He paused for a moment, his eyes scanning the words in front of him, and then cleared his throat.

"'*Fulbert,*'" he read, "'*by the grace of God archdeacon of the great abbey of Saint Albans . . .*'" He looked up at Gwil. "You *knew* Archdeacon Fulbert?" Gwil shook his head. Father Nimbus looked relieved. "Then you are fortunate, my son. This was a man who brought disgrace on the name of Christendom. Dead now, though . . . Poisoned, or so they say."

"Go on, Father."

Father Nimbus cleared his throat again and continued with the translation: " '*I, Fulbert of Caen, Archdeacon of Saint Albans, send greetings to Brother Thancmar, monk of Ely Abbey, that by full right and any means necessary you procure from Ely the bones of Saint Alban that were most wickedly and with sacrilege withheld from Saint Albans, their rightful home . . .*' "

Thancmar, Gwil thought, *so* that's *his name.*

"But the bones have been returned to Saint Albans, have they not?" Father Nimbus asked. "There was a massacre at Ely to get them."

Gwil nodded. "After the battle of Lincoln. Mercenaries led by this Thancmar. Nine monks killed." He clamped his teeth together and then, because he was going to tell this priest the whole truth, he said: "I was there."

Not a quiver of shock from Father Nimbus; more a look of compassion. "With blood on your sword, my son?"

"No. But I was there." And Gwil embarked on the tale he had to tell, omitting only the part that included Penda. The priest was kindly and good, he could see that, but the girl must be protected at all costs and her tragedy was not his to confide.

As the words tumbled out of his mouth, so the memories came back and he encountered waves of distress that threatened to drown him. *I've gone soft,* he thought. He was tossed by the guilt of Ely, where, even if there had been no blood on his sword, he had ridden with men from whose weapons it dripped.

Again, as in his every nightmare, the unbidden image of the little girl with the red hair lying bloodied in the marsh tormented him. He stopped, gasping for breath, and raised his eyes to the vaulted ceiling. When he had collected himself he wiped them roughly with the back of his sleeve and looked at the priest.

He saw the effect of his emotion reflected in the ravaged expression on Father Nimbus's face and wondered if this effeminate little man could withstand the onslaught of what he was hearing. However, though the priest's eyes shed tears, they remained steadily on his. Only when Gwil reached Waterlily's death was there an outburst of pain, a de profundis of the soul at man's capacity for atrocity. "That poor child," Father Nimbus said quietly, then bowed his head and stood in silence for a while, until, with a deep breath, he returned, reluctantly, to the parchment. " '*And if this should be done to the satisfaction of this abbey and I, Fulbert, be made its bishop, Brother Thancmar shall be raised to the post of archdeacon of Saint Albans, which will be in my gift . . .*' Dear Lord." He turned to Gwil suddenly, pale and shaking. "You know the story of Saint Albans?" he asked.

Gwil shook his head.

"No, I presumed not." Father Nimbus continued. "It is well-known among the clergy but there is no reason its contagion should have spread further afield. This Fulbert of Caen," he said, rapping the parchment angrily with his finger and shaking his head, "was indeed archdeacon of Saint Albans and had ruled that particular roost, showing himself a slave to avarice and ambition, ever since the old bishop died, extorting money from his churches to put into his own money bags. His robes were gorgeous, his plate of silver and gold, and he traveled with a retinue of brutal mercenaries whose doings were a scandal, as, indeed, were those of the women who shared his bed. And yet . . ." Father Nimbus paused and put his hand over his mouth. "And yet," he said again with emphasis, "King Stephen would anoint him bishop! Fulbert supported him, you see, against the empress, advancing a fortune to the royal treasury, putting his mercenaries at his disposal while wriggling among his courtiers like an eel in salt water." The exertion of such an impassioned speech had begun to take its toll on the little priest and he sank down on the pew behind them, breathing hard. Gwil sat beside him and for a while a hush descended on the chapel until Father Nimbus spoke again.

"But good will out," he suddenly exclaimed as if to reassure them both, "even in these desperate times, and the virtuous people of the chapter of Saint Albans sent to the Pope warning that this candidate for a bishopric, this Fulbert, was worthy only of the fire. And meanwhile the fortunes of the abbey were dwindling, and with them Fulbert's power.

"You should know, though you may not, that many, many years ago when Christian England was still being torn to pieces by the pagan Danes, Saint Albans sent its finest relics to Ely Cathedral, yes, including the bones of Saint Alban himself, asking them to safeguard them until the danger of the invasion had passed. This they did, and returned them, too, though reluctantly, when it was eventually deemed safe enough. However, all this time later, provoked, perhaps, by Fulbert's wicked and extravagant ways, Ely suddenly announced to the world that it had not, after all, returned the relics but had kept them, and that what had been returned were fakes. All of a sudden Saint Albans's profits diminished, and even more its reputation, along with Fulbert's own; pilgrims were no longer willing to pay, you see, for the privilege of touching the tomb of England's first martyr if it did not actually contain the bones of that brave Christian and could therefore no more grant them the miracles they asked for than some common skeleton dug out of a charnel house." Father Nimbus stopped speaking and turned to look directly at Gwil.

"This parchment," he said, "is Fulbert's pact with the devil . . . this . . . this Thancmar. The return of the relics would restore riches to Saint Albans and silence Fulbert's critics; why, even the Pope could not gainsay the man who returned the bones of Saint Alban to their rightful place." He paused again, raised his eyes to the heavens and rapped the parchment on the front of the pew. "This is a license to rapine and murder."

"I know." Gwil spoke for the first time, although he could not look at the man beside him. "I was there, remember? I witnessed the slaughter at Ely."

Father Nimbus made the sign of the cross, then turned to Gwil and took both his hands in his.

"Then you are in grave danger, my child," he said, his voice barely a whisper now. "Fulbert is dead, murdered, like all the other witnesses to this crime. Thancmar is archdeacon now and King Stephen has applied to make him bishop. You and this parchment are all that stand between him and great power. And he will stop at nothing to get it back." Gwil felt the priest's small, cold hands tremble as they held his between them.

"I know," he said. "I knew Thancmar."

"But you don't know everything," Father Nimbus said in a whisper, clutching Gwil's hands between his own so tightly that Gwil could feel the blood freeze in them. "He is close. He was here today. I saw him! . . . Outside the castle. It was *he* who attended the parley with the king!"

CHAPTER 17

IT WAS TO BE A busy night for Maud. After compline instead of retiring to the solar she and Milburga accompanied Sir Rollo and Alan to the castle's labyrinthine basement to inspect the work being done on the postern.

The improvements were considerable. A metal grille like a small portcullis, operated by a simple windlass, had been added to the entrance, and the tunnel, wide and tall enough now to accommodate both horse and rider, had been shored against collapse by timbers from the cherry orchard. The felling of it had been a bitter blow to Maud, for whom the pink-and-white blossoms of the trees were one of the great pleasures of spring, never mind the deliciously plump cherries she had gorged herself on every summer as a child. *Ah well,* she thought, *another sacrifice to the empress. It better be worth it.*

"Where does it come out?" Alan asked Ernulf, the guard.

"Other side of the ditch," he replied. "Middle of a copse of rowan trees. There's good cover there, won't nobody see you." He pulled proudly on the ropes that operated the winch and the grille lifted smoothly.

"Shall we?" Alan turned to Maud, his arm sweeping theatrically in the direction of the entrance. She nodded, although she refused to return his smile; took the lantern Milburga was proffering; and stepped, businesslike, into the tunnel.

Once she was inside the darkness was visceral, but as her eyes grew accustomed to it, she saw that though it was long, it was at least straight, the contour of its exit just about visible in the distance illuminated as it was by the pale light of the moon. She began gingerly stepping toward it, instinctively moving closer to the man beside her.

"Not afraid of the dark, are you, madam?"

In this light she couldn't see his expression, could barely see her hand in front of her face come to that, but knew, somehow, that he was amused by her sudden tentativeness. "Wouldn't like me to take your hand I suppose?"

"No, I would not!" she snapped, recoiling from him and stepping up her pace to prove a courage she did not feel.

He was, she thought, without a single shadow of a doubt the most impertinent man she had ever met, and nothing he had said or done since she first clapped eyes on him could persuade her otherwise. And so damned *pleased* with himself! The confidence of him! Didn't he realize that he was just another blasted mercenary? That she loathed him and all he stood for? Did he know his place at all? It appeared not.

The courage that up until that moment she had been feigning began to rise in direct proportion to her indignation, and eschewing the hand he offered, she pressed brusquely on into the damp dark void, vowing, as she did so, that she would never again appear vulnerable to him even if she were forced to follow him into the bowels of hell itself.

He watched her stride off into the darkness muttering under her breath as she went, which made him smile all the more.

They were halfway along the passage when her lantern's candle sputtered and died. The cloying blackness closed around her like a shroud and she was forced to stop.

She hadn't admitted it to *him,* of course, but from childhood she had been terrified of the dark, which was why the ever-vigilant

Milburga kept a candle burning in her room at all times, even waking in the night to replace it if necessary. *He* had a candle; she could hear his footsteps behind her but to wait for him would be an admission of weakness. No, there was nothing for it, she must swallow her fear and press on regardless. She took a deep breath and closed her eyes against the panic swelling inside her, and when she dared open them again was relieved to find that her sight had adjusted to the engulfing blackness and she could see the moonlight in the distance. Phew! She walked on, staring fixedly at the halo of milky light ahead until her boot suddenly caught on something, tripping her up and sending her stumbling headlong toward the cold dank earth of the tunnel's floor.

But, just as she had braced herself for the inevitable fall and the painful impact with the ground, she found herself unexpectedly upright again and Alan's arms around her waist, holding her tight. For a moment or two neither of them spoke and then:

"I hope you're not laughing," she mumbled, relieved that in this light he couldn't see her blush.

"Wouldn't dream of it, madam," he replied softly, with, perhaps, just the merest suspicion of a smile in his voice.

"Good," she was about to say, but couldn't because a peculiar feeling had gripped her, like an invisible ligature around her throat.

He was so close, so terribly, terribly close. His face just inches from her face, his chest so tight against hers that she could feel his every breath, every beat of his heart, as though they were her own. And not only was she rendered speechless, she was no longer able to think or move independently . . . And worst of all was neither did she want to.

She shook her head. Enough now! She must separate from him, push him away and move on, and yet the delicious warmth of his hands on her back was so horribly thrilling that her body refused to budge.

What was happening to her?

She thought about Sir John, the only other man she had been

physically close to, and the equally powerful feelings he invoked, but the gulf between the two experiences was overwhelming, like the distance between heaven and hell. She must *do* something . . . before it was too late . . .

And yet, despite her resolve, it was *he* who released *her* . . . eventually.

"Shall we proceed, madam?" he asked gently.

Did she imagine it or was there the merest hint of a caress as he withdrew his hand from her back? She stepped away from him, and although she dared not look at him directly, could nevertheless feel his gaze on her face like the warmth from a fire.

"Madam?" he repeated.

Still unable to trust her voice not to betray her, she simply nodded, allowing him to take her hand and lead her the rest of the way along the passage.

When, eventually, they emerged into the moonlit rowan copse he separated from her and she watched him walk to the outer rim of the trees, where he stood hands on his hips, staring intently in the direction of the enemy camp. She could hear him muttering to himself as he plotted the empress's escape, calculating time and distance and the likelihood of a safe passage through the trees, and Maud, who had previously only felt resentment for Matilda, felt a sudden, unwelcome stab of jealousy toward her.

When he had finished his calculations he turned back to Maud and stood looking at her for what seemed an uncomfortably long time.

"Perhaps we should go back?" she said, her voice still tremulous.

He smiled.

"Good idea," he said after a moment, and then took her hand as though it were his to take and led her back through the trees toward the postern.

Once back inside the tunnel they walked in silence until halfway along a lantern came swinging toward them.

"There you are!" Milburga said, squinting at them from the other side of the light. "Getting worried about you I was," she added, wagging an admonishing finger at Maud. "You been such a long time down here as I was beginning to fret as how you'd been captured or summat."

"I'm fine, Milly," Maud said, almost euphorically grateful for her nurse's timely appearance. "I really am fine," she repeated, wrapping Milburga's ample arm in hers and squeezing it tightly. "Let's go back, eh?"

BACK AT THE ENTRANCE Sir Rollo was waiting for them.

"How was it?" he asked as they emerged blinking like moles into the unaccustomed brightness of the cavern.

After a long silence in which he never once took his eyes off hers, Alan turned to Maud.

"As posterns go," he said, grinning, "it was an absolute beauty. In fact, I can't honestly remember when I liked one better."

"Oh good . . . er . . . very good," Sir Rollo replied, twiddling his chubby fingers nervously. "Yes . . . Very good . . . uh . . . Well, if you'll excuse me, long day and all that . . ." And he wandered off.

Maud, who was still clinging to Milburga's arm, felt the heat rising in her cheeks again and hoped to God it didn't show. This feeling, this, this . . . malady or whatever it was, would pass—she knew it would; it had to. She would come to her senses . . . eventually . . . And yet, however hard she tried there was nothing she could do to prevent her mind slipping back to that moment in the darkness when he had held her in his arms and made her feel so unexpectedly peculiar.

"Bed," she heard Milburga say, and felt herself propelled firmly in the direction of the keep. "You're looking a bit peaky, madam, if I may say so."

CHAPTER 18

HALFWAY BACK TO THE KEEP the composure Maud had prayed for returned like an enchantment lifting. She stopped abruptly.

William!

Amidst everything else she had forgotten since she almost lost her senses, she had completely forgotten about the boy and was suddenly anxious about him.

"What's the matter?" Milburga asked. "Acting very odd you are all on a sudden."

"It's William," Maud replied. "I haven't seen him today!"

"Oh, ee'll be all right," Milburga said. "Shouldn't wonder if ee's not up with Sir John. Saw 'im at suppertime. Certainly ate hearty enough. Wouldn't worry if I were you." But Maud did worry.

There was something about the boy that haunted her. It wasn't simply that he was a motherless child with a brute for a father; it was something about William himself, some intangible quality that drew her to him. It was almost as if he had been born without the protective carapace other people possessed, making him extra vulnerable, and she had long felt an overwhelming urge to love and protect him as though he were her own flesh and blood. But if this revelation had come as a shock at first, the intensity of the feeling had only increased with time and was still capable of surprising her.

"I just don't like the idea of him being up there all the time," she said. "It's not healthy to spend so much time in that cesspit with those two . . . all that scrying and nonsense . . . No! It's not right! I'm going to fetch him."

Milburga sighed and shook her head. It had been a long day, they were both tired, and to cap it all her mistress had been very peculiar since she came out of that blasted tunnel. On the other hand, as she knew only too well, once Maud got an idea in her head there was no shifting it.

"Don't know what you're fussing for," she complained to Maud's back as it marched off in the direction of the turret. " Ee'll be asleep by now and ee don't seem to mind 'em." But Maud was implacable, and as Milburga had decided long since that it was *her* role in life to love and protect her mistress come what may, she would have to go, too.

The stairs were punishing on tired legs and both women were breathless by the time they reached the top. Milburga, who carried a good deal more weight than her mistress, and several more years besides, could be heard chuntering and complaining of pain under her breath most of the way up.

"Bloody child'll be the death of me *and* you, if you ain't careful," she said.

"Shh," Maud hissed. They had just arrived at the door to Sir John of Tewing's chambers, against which Maud's ear was now pressed—as if by sheer force of will she could absorb William through it—partly because, after the unpleasant surprise of the other day, she wanted to know what the creature Kigva was up to before she was alerted to their presence.

Nothing, apparently, there wasn't a sound.

"Ain't I told you," Milburga whispered as, eventually, Maud raised her hand to knock. "Them'll be asleep. Let 'em lie."

Maud knocked anyway and this time heard footsteps scampering on the other side of the door but still no one answered. She knocked again, more loudly this time.

"Lady Maud to see her husband," she called out imperiously. More silence and then, after a few moments, the door finally creaked open, revealing Kigva staring warily at them out of the gloom.

They brushed past her into the room, which, Maud noted, still smelled foul, but it was only, thank goodness, the familiar foulness of its general decay—nothing to suggest anything of the olfactory untowardness of her last visit. Milburga wrinkled her nose, grimacing at the squalor surrounding them. Goodness only knew when those rushes had last been changed, or would be, that floor having probably never seen a broom. She lifted her skirts ostentatiously high above the reach of the filth and sniffed accusingly at Kigva, who was now crouching in the furthest corner of the room like a spider.

"I am here to see how William is," Maud announced loudly and clearly, as though addressing the profoundly deaf. She had long since decided that both her husband and Kigva were beyond the reach of most human understanding, and therefore, to communicate effectively with them one should speak up.

"I'm well, thank you," piped a voice.

Maud peered into the murk in the direction of the voice and saw William sitting on the other side of the room, by his father's cot, where he was attempting to feed him some slush of indeterminate color. One of Kigva's preparations presumably.

"Uck-oo!" Sir John said when he spotted Maud. Maud pretended not to hear but noticed that he looked even more robust than he had yesterday. As she approached the cot he sat bolt upright. "Uck-oo!" he shouted again, and, "Uck off!"

"Ooh," she heard Milburga mutter under her breath. "Adding to our repertoire I see! Perhaps we *are* getting better."

William leapt to his feet.

"Stay calm, Father," he said, gently trying to press his patient back onto the pillows, but Sir John was, by now, incandescent with rage and was thrashing his one useful arm so wildly in Maud's direction that he accidentally clouted the boy on his head. It was a heavy blow with an audible clunk, but although William's eyes smarted with the pain of it, he refused to cry.

"It's all right, Father," he said quietly, taking hold of the flailing hand. "You didn't mean to hurt me. I know you didn't." He looked pleadingly at Maud and Milburga. "He didn't mean to. Really he didn't."

"Of course he didn't," Maud said, moved almost to tears by the generosity of the child to one so undeserving of it. "Nevertheless it is rather late and your father's obviously very tired and in need of rest. So I think it would be best if you came with us. Come back tomorrow, though, if you like?" she added brightly, holding out her hand to him.

William got up reluctantly and walked toward her, glancing back anxiously every few steps at his father, who had finally calmed down and was once more staring blankly at the ceiling. In the corner of the room Kigva, muttering to herself, rocked back and forth on her heels, and the moment Maud and Milburga reached the door she scuttled over to the bed.

They hurried William out of the room and took him to his chamber, where they rubbed comfrey oil on the bump on his forehead—by now the size of an egg—and put him to bed. When at last he was settled they returned to the solar, where, once again, a bleary-eyed Tola was ousted from the mattress beside the empress to make way for Maud.

"Not that one, neither!" Milburga snapped when, still half-asleep, the poor girl crawled onto its nearest neighbor. "That's mine. You're over there."

Outside in the bailey Alan and Sir Rollo were making a final tour of the battlements, checking to see that all the guards and men-at-arms were awake and the castle secure. Satisfied that all was well, they, too, returned to the keep, Sir Rollo to his own room on the upper floor, as befitting his status, and Alan to his pallet on the floor in the guardroom, as befitted his.

MAUD SLEPT FITFULLY THAT NIGHT and Milburga, who had been woken by her mistress's turnings and murmurings once too often, made a note to slip her some catnip oil at breakfast in the morning to ward off any further disturbance the following night.

In her dreams Maud was happy, deliriously so, and standing in the now-defunct cherry orchard squinting out from beneath the delicate shadows cast by the blossom-laden branches into a beautiful spring day. All around her was peace and calm, the siege a distant memory and the air filled not with the cries of men and the clang of weaponry, but with birdsong and the scent of flowers, and she herself was swaying in a gentle breeze to the strains of a distant choir, in the arms of . . . of . . . *Oh dear God! . . . Alan of Ghent!*

She woke up sweating, gasping for breath, and in the grip of panic grabbed hold of Milburga's wrist, which woke her up again.

"Catnip for you all right, my girl," Milburga grumbled, prizing off the offending hand. "Hear me?" But Maud had already gone back to sleep.

Below them, in the guardroom, among scores of prostrate, snoring men, Penda was sleeping badly, too. The pain in her belly had got even worse and she felt sick. The blood, which was apparently endless, had once again saturated the cloths she used to stanch it. Earlier that day Gwil had directed her to the basement, where large bales of the stuff were stored, so that, with some stealth, she was able to replenish them, but in the dead of night it wasn't a journey she relished. Nope, all in all, she decided, being a woman, whatever that meant, was an uncomfortable business and she didn't like it.

She propped herself on her elbows and looked around the crowded room at the men surrounding her, envying them their pain-free bellies and their ability to sleep; even Gwil, whose behavior had been so strange that evening, looked peaceful now.

He had been an age returning from the chapel but she had waited for him nevertheless.

She had lain on her back for what seemed like hours, staring blankly at the milky patch of moonlight shining through the oiled cloth that hung over the tiny window on the other side of the room. More hours passed, the room grew silent and still he didn't come.

Then, just as she was beginning to despair that he might never return, she heard footsteps across the room, the familiar, involuntary groan as he lowered his aching body onto the mattress beside her and the soft, contented sigh as he eased himself into the warmth of its blankets.

She turned to face him, wanting, more than anything, to talk to him, to learn about his business with Father Nimbus, but although he turned toward her briefly and smiled, acknowledging the fact that she had waited up for him, he turned back again almost immediately and went straight to sleep. It was the way things were between them nowadays and deep down she knew that all inquiry was pointless, unwelcome and unwise.

All her life, or as much of it as she could remember, she had been content with knowing only those things that Gwil taught her. Nothing else mattered; nothing beyond them existed—as if he had simply conjured her into being one day out of the fenland peat. She had never questioned the tacit understanding between them that no good would ever come from knowing about her past and understood somehow that, by maintaining her ignorance of it, he was also keeping her safe. And yet . . . and yet, something *had* changed in her, as if a *cover-feu* had been lifted from the embers of her memory, sparking long-forgotten images to life. She subdued them when she could, as she had struggled to do this morning, but her defenses were weakening and in her dreams the embers would stutter and spark and sear their way into her consciousness. Most of the time they seemed meaningless, fractured images of a peculiar land where the sea and sky merged into one and strange birds wheeled and screeched and rushes grew as tall as men. But just lately she had dreamed of a golden-haired woman who held her in her arms and sang softly to her, and when she woke up, her heart was heavy with a longing she didn't understand and a loneliness she could hardly bear.

THE NEXT MORNING, AS DAWN broke over Kenniford, the business of the siege began again. Emissaries from both sides rode out into the no-man's-land between the castle and the enemy camp and shook hands on their mutual implacability, and the fighting resumed.

"Hope you slept well, Master Penda," Alan said as they took their posts once more on the ramparts. "We're going to need you sharp again today."

Penda grinned.

"Hear that, Gwil?" she asked, poking her head around the merlon to peer at him. "Alan of Ghent thinks I'm sharp." But Gwil only mumbled something under his breath and carried on as if he hadn't heard her.

She couldn't understand why he wasn't more pleased or, indeed, more proud that under his tutelage she had garnered such skill and reputation. It made her wonder, and not for the first time, what she could possibly have done to displease him. She shrugged; there was nothing she could do about it, he was being very strange. Besides, she couldn't think about all that now; she was going to need all her wits about her for whatever today held in store.

Once they had settled themselves in, crossbows loaded and cocked, bolts and quarrels organized neatly beside them, Gwil appeared behind her.

"Same as yesterday, Pen," he said. "But watch you don't get too proud of yourself. Ruins your aim, getting too proud does."

"Oh, does it!" she muttered, as she raised her bow to aim it through the loophole. Then she paused for a moment, turned to glare at him over her shoulder and then, turning back once more to the loophole, drew the string tight to her chest, released and made her first kill of the day. "Does it indeed!"

CHAPTER 19

STEPHEN'S ARMY SPAWNED ITSELF DAILY. Penda had heard about monsters who could do that. Row upon row of anonymous men in hauberks and helmets surrounded the castle. When one fell another took his place.

So great was its number that, despite the best efforts of the Keniford archers, within days the king's men had filled the ditch and dragged their siege engines through the hailstorm of arrows to the very foot of the castle walls, littering the scarp with their bodies but advancing nevertheless.

Their picks, rams and bores, brutal structures hewn from vast pieces of wood, were rammed against the walls by teams of men, shaking the castle so violently that its battery reverberated through the body of every man, woman and child inside.

With each blow a great cloud of choking dust rose up to the archers on the battlements as the ashlar slabs fell from the castle walls, exposing the soft underbelly of the flint beneath.

On the allure Penda felt each shock judder through her bones, rattling her heart in her chest. There was no doubt about it; unless something miraculous happened and soon, the walls would be breached and the king's men would invade.

And it was this that terrified her more than anything. A swift arrow through the temple from a distant archer would, by comparison, be a merciful death, and she was prepared for that, could face it with equanimity even, but the idea of invasion brought unimaginable horror and her nightmares were plagued by it.

Gwil had heard her lately, crying in her sleep, calling out to him, begging him to protect her from some invisible assailant, and every time she did so he was dragged back to his lonely vigil in the ruined church and was once more powerless to help her.

"It's all right, Pen. It's all right," he murmured softly through those nights until the crisis passed and she fell asleep again, but each one was a reminder that the sleeping giant of her memory was stirring and that danger crept ever closer.

"And what then, Lord? Eh? How can I protect her from herself?"

That's a tricky one, Gwil. That's the question. Even I can't help you there I'm afraid.

And Gwil shook his fist at the heavens and wondered what on earth he had ever done to deserve such torment.

She had been fine when the siege began. Oh, he had worried about her, watched her like a hawk from the moment she set foot out on the ramparts, fretting about how she might react to it all, whether the violence of battle would stir her memory. But to his relief she took to it like a duck to water, and secretly, he had been proud—though he refused to show it of course—of the pluck she had shown and the confidence with which she fought.

"Enjoying this, ain't you, Pen?" he asked one day.

"Not half," she replied, grinning. "It's like there's this fire in my belly, gets lit the minute I got a bow in my hand, Gwil; makes me feel strong!" The words tumbled out in a torrent; her eyes sparkled with excitement.

"You just keep that ol' feeling, Pen," he said. "Ain't nothing wrong with that."

She had, too. To his great relief, the enthusiasm with which she scampered along the allure to her post every day as the weeks passed remained undimmed.

"Think I done this before, Gwil?" she asked him once.

"Done what?"

"You know! Fighting and such . . . This!" she said, waving her bow at him.

"Don't talk daft. You was too little for a start. Ain't never touched a bow afore I learned you."

She stood there for a while, staring thoughtfully at the weapon in her hand. Gwil watched her nervously, anticipating the inevitable scrutiny he knew must come . . . eventually. It was pure luck that it had been staved off this far but he knew that sooner or later something in that strange little head of hers would snap and she would demand to know exactly why it was that, alone of all her sex—or as far as he knew anyway—she needed to fight.

She stared at him for a while, frowning, and then suddenly her face brightened.

"Ah but!" she said, wagging her finger at him triumphantly as another thought occurred to her. "*You* said as how I was in a really bad way when you found me. How d'you know I hadn't been in some sort of fight or something then?"

Gwil shook his head.

He could tell her now; perhaps he should. Perhaps, after all, he owed her the truth; but what to tell? That as a child she had been so brutally raped and battered that something of the steel of the men who did it to her had entered her soul? That he might have prevented it? He looked at the bright little face gazing up at him and simply could not.

"Like I said, Pen. You was too *little*." Then he lowered his voice and hissed: "And you was a *girl*, remember! *Girls* don't fight. God only knows what happened or how you was hurt other than somehow you bumped your head so bad it made you forget your own name."

"Mmm." She narrowed her eyes again, regarding him suspiciously. "Think I'll ever remember?"

"Don't know." He shrugged as he turned his back on her and pretended to busy himself with the arrows at his feet.

GOD'S EYES! IT WASN'T ALL that long ago but it already felt like an age, and so much had changed since then. Christmas had passed, and January. As the weeks went by the mood among the garrison had become increasingly gloomy. However much Gwil tried to shield Penda from it, it was hard to avoid the inevitable conversation about the fate awaiting defeated armies once their walls had been breached. None of it was good; the rule of thumb, as he knew only too well, was that the more enraged the king became—the more often his entreaties to surrender were refused—the more members of the defending force, especially among the lowly ranks such as the archers, were hanged in defeat.

No one was in any doubt by now that Stephen had greater resources on his side and that his patience was running thin. His casualties had been heavy, his demands for surrender rebuffed, and therefore revenge, rather than reconciliation and a safe passage out of the castle, was the most likely outcome for the majority of them.

"I think we should leave here, Gwil," Penda said one day. "Ain't our war, you said so, remember? We could just go." Her only loyalty was to him and she was increasingly worried for his safety. They could, she reasoned, return to the charcoal burner's hut where this whole sorry business began, take their chances with the snow and the wolves, only this time refuse sanctuary to any passing empress, no matter how nicely she asked. He listened patiently to her argument but shook his head.

"And go where, Pen? Ain't no such thing as a safe place these days." He was right and deep down she knew it. Beyond the siege the ravening forces of lawlessness and anarchy reigned far more efficiently than Stephen ever had. The whole country was devouring itself. God and His saints were asleep all right, and nothing, it seemed, could induce them to wake up.

UNLIKE GOD AND HIS SAINTS, however, Sir Bernard had slept very badly of late. His meticulous accounting, of which he was inordinately proud, was on the verge of ruin.

"I'm not happy," he told Maud one morning as she paced up and down behind him in the great hall. "I'm not happy at all."

"Never knew you when you were," she said, stopping to peer over his shoulder at the ledger in front of him. "But what do you suggest we do?"

"You know my position, madam," he said as patiently as he could. "And you don't like it, but the fact is that, sooner or later, we must dispense with some of these useless mouths. There's nothing else to be done, I'm afraid. If this siege carries on much longer, we simply cannot afford to keep them."

"And you know *my* position," she said curtly. "I will not turn innocent men, women and children out of this castle to be slaughtered or die of starvation. We'll have to think of something else."

Sir Bernard breathed a heavy sigh and put his head in his hands. He knew what was coming next.

"How much did you say we were paying those mercenaries?" she asked after a while.

"Twopence per day per man, sixpence per day for the officers and a shilling a day for their commander," he repeated wearily. They had had this conversation many times before. He could hear her making the calculations under her breath, toting up the number of men and officers, until all of a sudden she stopped and threw up her arms jubilantly.

"Well, there we are, then!" she said. "There must be a good deal fewer of them now, surely. We'll just cut down on the others' pay!"

Sir Bernard groaned, his head drooping into the crook of his elbow on the table—it had been so much easier dealing with her father.

"How many times, madam," he said eventually, "must I remind you that a mercenary without pay is about as useful as a colt in battle? If we do not pay them they will not stay and they will not fight. We need them and you must accept this fact once and for all, however much you may dislike it."

"Bugger!" she said, and sauntered off, leaving Sir Bernard to his books.

Outside in the bailey, pushing her way through a melee of men, women, children, dogs and cattle who now crowded the place like a load of ambulatory detritus, she nearly stumbled over a decapitated horse's head that had recently been catapulted over the walls by an enemy trebuchet. Looking around furiously, she grabbed hold of the nearest bystander and, startling him out of his wits, pointed at the object and shouted: "In God's name make yourself useful and get rid of this, damn you! Don't just stand there or it'll be your head over the wall next and I'll fling it myself."

After that she felt better and went to look for Milburga.

She found her, eventually, in the chapel with Father Nimbus and Cousin Lynessa, trying to organize a bunch of unruly children into sitting quietly.

"Now, if you'll just listen, children!" Cousin Lynessa was trying but failing miserably to raise her voice above the cacophony. "If you'll just, just listen. I said *listen*! . . . We can all play a nice little game." But it was a hopeless task and after a few moments she crumpled onto a pew, looking plaintively out from under a rather skewwhiff wimple. Milburga stood beside her looking equally despondent. Father Nimbus, it had not gone unnoticed, had retreated to the altar, where he was pretending to busy himself but was actually meditating quietly and gratefully on the merits of chastity.

"Oh dear," Maud said as she cupped her hands around her ears in a futile attempt to cut out the din, "such noisy little useless mouths," and wondered whether it was too late to tell Sir Bernard she had changed her mind.

She looked around her at the squirming, seething mass of children and realized that the only one not present, as far as she could tell, was William. She mouthed his name at Milburga over the heads of the others, and she mouthed back: "Don't know and don't care. One less little bugger to worry about."

Just then the castle shook as another boulder crashed against the walls. Cousin Lynessa, her nerves by now entirely shattered, leapt up from her pew with a cry; the children screamed; Milburga shouted; and Father Nimbus ducked beneath the altar. Maud decided it was probably time to leave.

CHAPTER 20

PENDA MADE UP HER MIND that afternoon that if she and Gwil could not leave Kenniford, the only way to prevent an invasion was to take matters into her own hands and kill as many of the trebuchet masters as she could. Her tally so far had been pretty good but there was one particularly awkward bugger who had stayed tantalizingly out of range. As the day wore on her frustration was mounting, but she promised herself that if it was the very last thing she ever did, she would get the bastard before sunset.

She was cursing broadly and had just lifted her crossbow to make yet another attempt on him when something tugged at the hem of her mantle. She swung round, startled to see the boy William standing beside her.

"I could've shot you," she scolded, wagging her finger at him. "What in God's name are you doing up here?"

"Wanted to see what it was like," he replied, grinning. "It's a bit boring down there."

"Well, bugger off," she said. "Ain't no place for children up here. You could get killed. Go back, go on." With the weapon still in her fist she tried shooing him away but he refused to move and stood his ground stubbornly.

Penda, who recognized an impasse when she saw one, and the obdurate stance of a small boy, began to wonder what on earth she should do next. Short of picking him up and carrying him bodily down the stairs, there wasn't much she could do.

"I brought these for you," William said brightly, holding out a fistful of quarrels.

"Where'd you get 'em?"

"On the allure when I was looking for you. They were just lying on the floor. From the enemy I think."

She snatched them from him and flung them onto the stack on the floor beside her and then turned back to the boy.

"They'll come in useful them, no doubt about it, but I can get my own arrows, thank you very much. Don't need your help." She meant to sound cross but there was something about the child that took the sting out of her tone.

She had noticed him often during her time at Kenniford, as he wandered aimlessly around the castle in search of company, occupation and goodness knew what, and had felt pangs of pity for him. He was another dispossessed soul and she, of all people, could empathize with that. However, this was no time for sentiment and the last thing she needed was to feel responsible for anybody else, let alone John of Tewing's only son.

"So," she said, prodding him with the toe of her boot as she leant backward down the allure to check whether anyone else had noticed him. "What you looking for me for?"

"So you can teach me to be an archer," he said, smiling, his bright blue eyes closing almost completely under the pressure of his round, freckled cheeks. It was quite a smile, and she felt the corners of her own mouth twitching to return it.

"Are you mad or something?" she asked, trying to sound stern. "What you want to be an archer for? You're going to be a knight, you. That's much better, that is; won't have to stand up here all day in the cold getting shot at."

He thought for a moment and scratched his head.

"Trouble with being a knight is," he said eventually, "that I don't much like horses. And anyway, I want to be like you."

"Blimey!" She realized she was blushing. After all, although she knew her reputation had spread beyond her peers and was almost embarrassed about the attention she received for it, she'd had no idea that it had reached the likes of William.

"Well, you wouldn't if you knew me better," she said eventually.

"But I would," he replied. "You're the best. Everybody says so. And that's why I want you to teach me."

She scowled, put her hands on her hips and was about to explain that she didn't have time for teaching small boys, what with there being a siege on and all, in case he hadn't noticed, when a large rock sailed through the embrasure beside them and crashed onto the floor with a loud thump.

Bugger! She really *was* going to have to do something about that blasted trebuchet! So instead of arguing with him, she took him by the shoulders and spun him round to face the boulder, which had skidded to within inches of their feet.

"You see that?" she said, shaking him vigorously. "That lands on you and you're a dead boy. Understand?" Then she pushed him onto the floor beneath the loophole and pressed his head below the parapet. "You stay down there, hear me? Don't move, don't talk and don't let nobody else see you and when I'm finished with that . . . that . . . *pillard* out there I'm going to take you back down them stairs afore Lady Maud misses you."

As it turned out she need not have worried about William being missed that afternoon because after a cursory search of his favorite haunts Maud had decided to forget about him for the time being. No doubt he would turn up sooner or later, as he usually did, and besides, she reasoned, he was probably up in the turret with his father. No, this afternoon there was something more pressing she must attend to and could postpone it no longer. It was time to pay a visit to the empress.

As chatelaine of Kenniford it was Maud's responsibility to entertain the castle's guests, and while most of the time it was an amiable enough chore, she wasn't looking forward to this one. Nevertheless it was her duty, and since duty was a burden she had never shirked, she found herself trudging, though reluctantly, toward the keep.

When she reached the entrance to the solar she stopped for a moment to pat down the stray strands of hair that had escaped her circlet and smooth her skirts; then she took a deep breath and knocked on the heavily carved door.

Tola opened it, swinging it wide, and as she did so the beautiful, circular room, which had always reminded Maud of heaven, or what she imagined it might look like, was revealed. She paused on the threshold, as though seeing it for the first time, and, as always, its chalk-white light and beautiful lines lifted her spirits until the ensuing pang of regret that it was no longer hers dashed them again. She sighed and walked in.

The solar's latest occupant was sitting in a large chair in the middle of the room, her head bent over a piece of brightly colored needlepoint in her lap.

"Oh, it's you," she said without looking up.

"Lady." Maud curtsied, wondering how she knew *who* it was if she hadn't looked. "I . . . erm . . . came to inquire after your health."

The empress lifted her piece to the light and squinted at it.

"I am tolerably well, thank you." She still was not looking at her inquisitor. "And having found me so, what do you propose to do now?"

Maud, not yet wholly accustomed to the empress's rudeness, was lost for words; besides, if it came down to it, this was *her* solar and *her* castle, after all, and so far she had not received so much as a breath of thanks for the provision of any of it. She opened her mouth to say something, found she was still unable to speak and closed it again. What was the point? Any dissent would, no doubt, be treasonable and was, besides, unlikely to cut any ice with the empress.

"Well?" Matilda said, goading a response.

"Erm . . . I—I thought I might sit with you awhile, perhaps," Maud stammered. "I, er . . . thought you might . . . be in need of company." The humiliation was cheek scorching. She had never been made to feel quite so redundant or so foolish in her life.

"Oh, good Lord!" The empress was unpitying. "Why not spare us both the agony? Go about your *business*, woman! I'm sure you have some. Isn't there a siege on? Besides, I have Lola here, or Tola, or whatever you call her, and she, at least, has the decency not to engage me in idle chitchat. No. I simply can't be doing with it." And waving her hand loftily in the direction of the door turned back to her embroidery.

"Well, if that's all . . ." Maud bobbed a hurried curtsy and was about to rush out when the empress said:

"Never mind. Not too much longer now."

Maud turned back.

"Lady?"

"I said: not too much longer now," Matilda repeated. "I'm expecting word from Robert any day. We should be leaving soon."

"Thank God," Maud said, but not loud enough for the empress to hear.

THE FIGHTING CEASED AS DUSK fell and when the trumpet sounded for supper Penda was finally able to persuade William to leave her.

"And I don't want to see you up here again, mind," she said, pushing him roughly toward the stairs. "Careful how you go, now, and don't let nobody see you or there'll be trouble for me." She watched him clamber down the steps to safety and smiled to herself. She had grown rather fond of him during the course of the afternoon, enjoyed his company even. At times he had proved useful, too, sparing her the effort of stooping for her bolts and handing them to her like a small apprentice. Whether she had been as effective an assassin as usual with him around was another matter but he had, at least, taken her mind off her worries, and just before the light faded, she had, finally, claimed the trebuchet master she had been aiming for all day.

When she saw him fall backward clutching at the bolt she had buried in his chest, she had yelped with delight and danced a celebratory jig, and so had William.

It had been fun, and she couldn't remember the last time she had had any, certainly not at Kenniford.

WILLIAM HAD ENJOYED HIMSELF, TOO, enormously in fact, and was most reluctant to leave; on the other hand he was pretty hungry by that time, and however edifying Penda's company was, it was no substitute for food.

Once back down in the bailey he made his way immediately to the kitchen, where, to his great relief, Milburga was much too preoccupied with problems of her own to make inquiries of him. She fed him but was clearly distracted keeping an eye on the melee of irritable scullions and cooks who, at Gorbag's behest, were charging hither and yon turning great carcasses of meat on spits or running between vast iron cauldrons bubbling with stews and soups for that evening's supper.

She had incurred the great chef's wrath once already that afternoon when she commissioned one of his precious cauldrons to heat the water for Maud's bath. His reaction to the request had been so explosive that she was anxious about provoking him any further. There were few people on God's earth capable of intimidating Milburga, but Gorbag in a temper was one.

It was all Maud's fault. She had returned from her sojourn with the empress in a stompingly bad mood insisting, most unreasonably in Milburga's opinion, on having a bath; since they no longer had access to the solar, it would have to be set up elsewhere, which had proved a good deal easier said than done.

First of all it meant requisitioning a spare corner of the kitchen, despite Gorbag's menacing insistence that no such thing existed; then a large canopy had to be erected, to preserve Maud's modesty, which had pleased him even less; and finally she had had to purloin a reluctant team of his scullions to hoist the great wooden tub down several flights of stairs—all of which was performed to the accompaniment of some really quite dreadful eye rolling and cursing from the apoplectic chef. To make matters worse Maud had insisted the water be fragranced, so Milburga had found herself scrabbling around the kitchen garden in the cold gathering herbs for the infusion.

When eventually it was ready and Maud installed, Milburga set about scrubbing her back.

"What you want to make such a fuss for anyways?" she scolded, lifting the hair at the nape of Maud's neck so roughly that it made her wince.

"Ouch!" Maud shouted, spinning round to slap at the offending hand. "You're hurting me!"

"Sorry," Milburga said, "but what you got so vain for all on a sudden?"

Maud rounded on her again. "Christ and His mother! What's vain about wanting a bath! I haven't had one—in case you hadn't noticed—since the empress arrived. That's all."

"Is it now," Milburga said under her breath. She knew better than to say any more but she also knew her mistress like the back of her hand and was sure that something was afoot. In fact she wouldn't have been at all surprised if that something wasn't a certain Alan of Ghent, whose mere presence seemed to bring out the color in Maud these days. Nobody but a fool could have failed to notice the frisson between them during the business with the postern that one night.

She had been discussing her suspicions only that very morning in the chapel with Cousin Lynessa.

"Well, he is rather handsome," the nun had said wistfully. "And, even if he is only a mercenary, he's infinitely preferable to that awful old Sir John. And Maud is so young and lovely, and so it goes, I fear, Milburga."

Maud was, by now, out of the tub and drying herself.

"And what are we going to wear?" Milburga asked.

Maud thought for a while and then said: "The blue bliaut and the gold circlet, I think."

"You'll look very pretty," said Milburga, trying hard not to smile. "Very pretty indeed."

CHAPTER 21

AD 1180, Perton Abbey

THE SCRIBE WAKES, AND IN no good humor, either. He cannot sleep. Every night his dreams are assailed by succubi, those voluptuous emissaries of the devil who taunt and tease him and from whom no amount of genital dousing, however cold the water, can make him immune.

He blames idleness; he has been sitting by the abbot too long, he thinks; or perhaps, and this is more like it, it is the fault of the abbot himself and all his talk of unchaste women.

He will confess and he will wear a goat's-hair girdle around his loins in the future and may not even go to the infirmary today . . . and yet, and yet, the compulsion to do so is wickedly strong.

"You are late," says the abbot when, sometime after nones, the scribe finally appears. "I thought you might not come today."

"I am sorry, my lord," the scribe replies. "I had other business." It is a half-truth but it will do. He coughs nervously while he readies himself with his tablet and quill. "We must not discuss the, erm . . . the . . . incontinence today, though, my lord," he says, rushing the words out awkwardly, hardly daring to look up.

"Then we will not," says the abbot, and smiles to himself as a

thought occurs to him: "You were a child of the cloister, my son?" he asks.

The scribe nods. "Indeed, my lord. Left on the abbey's steps when I was but a few days old."

"Ah," says the abbot. "I see." And he does. Without experience of the secular world, it is no wonder the young man is so discomforted by its revelations. He must remember to be more gentle with him.

"We will turn then instead to the empress," the abbot continues, "awaiting news from Robert of Gloucester, remember? The Earl of Gloucester? Her half brother, the illegitimate firstborn of Henry the First?" He stops, grins wickedly and raises an admonishing finger, which he waggles at the scribe.

"Yes, his begetting was indeed 'incontinent,' as you might say, but we will not dwell on that; besides, no matter his origins, the man himself was an honorable one. So much so, in fact, that when his father died, and the question of the accession arose, he resisted the not-inconsiderable pressure to make his own claim to the throne.

"In the early days he was, in fact, loyal to Stephen, and a powerful ally, too. But the king was blind to his qualities and quarreled with him foolishly, reneging on his promise not to forfeit the English and Welsh estates bestowed on Robert by his father. So, when Stephen razed his castles, Robert was provoked enough to break ranks, renounce his allegiance to the king and send orders to his undertenants to prepare for war. Thereafter he devoted himself unstintingly to the cause of his half sister, whom he himself brought to these shores from Normandy."

"I see," says the scribe, who, if the truth be known, cares little for Robert of Gloucester because, despite the chafing of the goat's-hair girdle, he still has half a mind on the Kenniford women.

"I hope so," says the abbot. "And so Matilda waits, her patience stretched almost to the breaking point, unable to move until she knows her brother is ready for her."

"And is he? Does he rescue her?"

"He does his utmost," says the abbot. "All the time she was under siege at Oxford he was trying to lure Stephen away by besieging Wareham, the castle the king had previously seized from him. But the plan failed and Stephen refused to move. When Wareham finally surrendered Robert fought on tirelessly, taking in turn Portland and Lulworth, all the time building up a vital stronghold for his sister in the west, but only when it is strong enough will he summon her partisans to meet him at Cirencester."

"But what of Maud and the mercenary?" The thought rushes out of the scribe's mouth before he has time to censor it. "If the empress leaves Kenniford, they will be parted?"

"They will indeed," says the abbot sadly.

CHAPTER 22

February, AD 1143, Kenniford Castle

AS MAUD WALKED THROUGH THE hall that evening to take her place at the high table, all eyes turned to her. She looked beautiful.

Alan of Ghent, who was talking to Gwil as usual, forgot what he was saying midsentence and gaped openmouthed as she passed; even the empress turned her head to nod approvingly, and Milburga, walking behind her mistress, mopped up the attention like a sponge, barely able to contain her pride or suppress her giggles.

"Look at 'em all," she whispered. "All them men! You're turning 'em into fools." But it wasn't just the men. Penda, too, was transfixed by her.

During her time as an entertainer before they came to Kenniford, she had seen young women of nobility only from a distance, beautiful in their dress, accomplished, but with a sameness that involved high-pitched giggling except when men spoke, at which times they dutifully fell silent and listened as if in rapture. Maud was different.

Like the empress, Maud was the one who did the speaking. Her command over the castle was total, yet with it all she maintained a graceful feminine charm.

Penda, who'd always brushed her teeth with the frayed top of hazel twigs, had discovered, by eavesdropping on Milburga's conversations, that Maud used an ivory toothpick on hers and kept them white and her breath sweet by an infusion of parsley and mint. Now, minus the expensive toothpick, Penda did the same. She had even begun to wash her hair, when she washed it at all, in fern ash, spring water and rosemary, like Maud did. If she had to be a woman, she wanted to be one like that.

Most of the time she was content in male garb, but every now and then femininity beckoned seductively even though she knew its pain and recognized its siren song, which, should she succumb to it, would render her vulnerable to something appalling—and yet, and yet, there were times when she envied Maud's clothes, which, even when old, looked elegant.

Whenever Maud appeared Penda would stop what she was doing and watch her swish across the bailey, wondering how it would feel to sweep around in a beautiful skirt instead of lumping about in leggings, or to show the swell of one's breasts beneath an embroidered bodice instead of binding them tight with linen bands so that they didn't show. And then Maud vanished and a memory of Waterlily took her place, and she would change her mind. On second thought, better to cling to manhood for as long as she could. It was safer.

"You all right, Pen?" Gwil was nudging her. "Looks like you seen a ghost or summat."

"Sometimes I think I have," she said, gazing into the distance.

WHEN EVERYONE WAS SEATED A throng of servants bearing dishes entered the hall and was met by a great murmur of appreciation from the hungry diners. During grace an obedient hush descended on the hall until the final "Amen," when the drone and hubbub of conversation began to rise again.

Maud, who was sitting between the empress and Father Nimbus, noticed that the old priest barely touched his food and was fidgeting nervously on his stool. She was worried about him. He had been behaving peculiarly all day: distant, more anxious than usual.

"What is it, Father?" she asked when he showed no sign of settling. "You're not yourself today. Is something the matter?"

He was staring blankly into the distance and appeared, at first, not to hear her. She laid a hand on his arm.

"Father?" she repeated.

"Oh, I'm so sorry, my dear," he said, shaking his head as though to clear it. "No, no, I am quite well, thank you . . . there is just a matter which has been drawn to my attention and which is of great concern. In fact"—he put his hand over hers, staring intently at her—"In fact . . . I must speak to you . . . but first I must . . ." She saw him become agitated again and then rise from his stool to scuttle around the high table to where the mercenary Gwil de Vannes was sitting. After a brief exchange they left the hall together. She went on staring long after they had vanished, wondering what possible business they could have with each other. She would talk to Father Nimbus on his return and get to the bottom of it. Something was afoot and it worried her.

Once outside the great hall the two men walked in silence across the inner ward toward the chapel. When they reached it Father Nimbus turned to Gwil.

"In here," he said. "We'll have more privacy here." He looked nervously around him, then ushered Gwil inside and closed the door quickly behind them.

Father Nimbus lit a candle in one of the wall sconces then gestured toward a pew near the altar.

"I have been thinking," he said in a low voice as he shuffled in beside Gwil, "about everything you told me; indeed, I am almost unable to think of anything else."

Gwil nodded; he knew the feeling only too well.

"We must act," Father Nimbus continued. "We cannot, must

not, allow these crimes to go unpunished; we cannot allow a man such as this to gain yet more power, and . . ." He looked around conspiratorially, lowered his voice even further and whispered: "It is my fear that Stephen is considering this Thancmar for the archbishopric of either Canterbury or York."

Gwil's heart began to thump.

"But how?" he asked. "How can we prevent it?"

"Well, you see, this is what I have been thinking about," Father Nimbus replied. "With your permission, of course, I propose to speak to Lady Maud. We have the parchment as proof of Thancmar's crimes at Ely. We could send an envoy to the Pope. We could expose him."

Gwil laughed bitterly. He was loath to offend this gentle man but the idea was absurd.

"And then what? 'Part from the fact that it'll be almost impossible to get a messenger through enemy lines, what's the Pope going to do, slap 'im on the wrists and tell 'im he's been a naughty boy?"

Father Nimbus was crestfallen but Gwil was right and he knew it. There would be no justice. Even if they were to get a message to Rome—although the odds against it were great indeed—and even if they could convince the Pope to take action, in ecclesiastical courts, a cleric who committed a crime, even a killing, escaped the justice imposed on laymen by the procedure known as "benefit of clergy." The Church would insist on the privilege of dealing with him, and although it might banish him, defrock him, take away his living or even excommunicate him, it would go no further; it certainly would not hang him. He could literally get away with murder and be free to kill again.

They sat silently, heads bowed, staring blankly into their laps.

"Tell me one thing, Father," Gwil said after a while. "Tell me he'll suffer in hell forever. Give me that comfort at least."

But Father Nimbus shook his head.

"There *will* be forgiveness, penitence and redemption at the last, my son; after all, Christ came to take all our sins on Himself. No, I'm afraid I can't promise you that. The only consolation I can offer is that in his case it will take a long, long time."

"Then I will pray for natural justice." Gwil spat the words and rose sharply, but then, in recognition of the burden they now shared, paused to lay a pitying hand on the old man's shoulder before making his way back to the hall.

Because of the siege the after-supper entertainment to which Kenniford was accustomed was almost nonexistent; none of the itinerant entertainers—the mummers, minstrels, acrobats and jugglers—on whom they usually relied were able to reach the castle, so Payn had been prevailed on to sing again and was doing so quite happily when he spotted Gwil in the doorway. All of a sudden his gentle tenor began to warble off-key as, in round-eyed terror, he watched his former assailant making his way across the hall.

"What's up with him?" Gwil asked, resuming his seat beside Penda.

"Probably thinks you're going to try 'n strangle him again, I shouldn't wonder," she replied. "You're not, though, are you?"

He shook his head smiling. "Not tonight, Pen," he said, taking a large gulp of ale. "Don't know what got into me that night."

"Could've been that," she said, pointing at the cup in his hand.

He laughed, accidentally spluttering some of the ale out of his mouth.

"Could've been," he said, wiping his wet chin on his sleeve. "Could be right there."

He knew he had frightened her with his behavior that evening and was sorry for it; nevertheless he would rather sacrifice her good opinion and have her believe him a drunken fool than allow her to know the truth. After Payn's revelation there was no getting away from the fact that the man who had deprived her of so much already was even now on the threshold of the castle waiting to take her life.

CHAPTER 23

DURING THE SMALL HOURS OF the next morning a lone messenger arrived at the castle gate on foot, weary and disheveled but in possession of both a letter, bearing Robert of Gloucester's seal, and the correct password. And Ben, who was particularly cautious about entry to the castle these days, especially after the tongue-lashing he had received because of his last security breach, was sufficiently impressed to open the portcullis and brave enough to summon Maud and Sir Bernard from their beds.

"Kept 'im 'ere just in case," he said, eyeing Maud warily as he opened the door to the gatehouse. "Can't be too careful nowadays but least he knew the password. Can't gainsay a password when it's spoke, now, can I?"

The visitor was sitting on the cobbled floor, his back slumped against the wall, eyes closed. If he *was* an enemy spy, he seemed far too exhausted to pose much of a threat.

"Looks like he could do with some food and water," Maud told Ben. "Better get him some."

At Sir Bernard's approach, the man opened a weary eye, reached inside his mantle and offered up the letter. Sir Bernard took it, backing toward one of the wall sconces to read by its light.

"Well, well," he said, looking up at last. "The Earl of Gloucester, it seems, is ready for the empress. He asks that we provide her with a safe passage from here."

"Oh, is that all?" said Maud. "Better go and tell her then, I suppose."

Some moments later Gwil and Penda were shaken awake by Alan of Ghent and summoned to the conference in the hall to discuss the latest developments.

Tiptoeing across the still-dark guardroom, they wove their way as silently as possible around the pallets on the floor so as not to disturb the men who slept on them. They knew little about this morning's business, but enough to understand that these recumbent bodies would need as much sleep as they could get.

In the hall, the conference was already under way. The empress, Maud, Sir Rollo, Sir Bernard, Sir Christopher and Father Nimbus sat huddled in their cloaks like ducks on a frozen pond. Despite the bitter chill that morning no fire had been lit so as not to alert the enemy.

"We'll form a cohort and barge through with her," Sir Rollo was saying.

"No." Sir Christopher rubbed a bleary eye. "We stick to the plan."

"Too dangerous otherwise," Alan said. "My lady might be injured—a stray arrow . . ."

Father Nimbus, who always thought the best of everybody, said: "Surely we may depend on Stephen to ensure his cousin isn't shot at. We can trust him that far."

Alan closed his eyes: "I wouldn't trust Stephen to wipe my dog's arse."

At this Penda glanced anxiously at the empress to see how she took it, but Matilda's face was expressionless, only her cold eyes were animated as they flicked from one speaker to the next, leaving Penda to presume that anyone who'd spent as much time among mercenaries as she had was used to their colorful imagery.

Alan put his hand on Sir Christopher's shoulder. "I'd be doing this instead of you if I could, my friend, but I'm too tall."

Christopher simpered. "You don't look near as pretty in a veil as I do."

"What they going to do?" Penda hissed under her breath.

"Not sure," Gwil whispered back, "but it sounds as if they're going to send the empress out under cover of a decoy."

Alan stood up.

"Time to go, then," he said. The benches scraped back as the company rose.

Only the empress delayed and, looking directly at Maud, said: "Fetch three of your young and good men to the bailey."

Outside, though it was still dark, the entire castle was alert, every man and woman at his or her post. Maud hurried out of the hall to summon one of the men-at-arms, and before long, three anxious young men had been lined up on the rim of the bailey's pond and the empress was helped onto a mounting block.

"Hear me, you people." Her voice immediately cut through the hubbub and everybody stopped what they were doing to watch her in silence. For a moment or two she just stood there, surveying the crowd with an air of satisfaction, and then she turned to Gwil.

"Kneel," she told him, and as he knelt in front of her she held out her hand and turned to Sir Christopher. "Your sword, if you please."

What's she doing? For a mad minute, Penda thought that Gwil's head was to be cut off in some tradition that only the empress followed. Instead, the flat of Christopher's sword tapped each of his shoulders as the empress's voice rang out again.

"You and Master Penda here have performed a great service for me, and risked your lives in the doing of it. Were times as they should be you would be rewarded with lands. As it is, we must wait until I come into my own. In the meantime, I shall do what I can. Arise, Sir Gwilherm de Vannes."

She's knighted him, Penda thought, and whooped. *She's only gone and* knighted *him.* Sir *Gwil. Blimey, I'll never let him hear the end of it.*

Sir Gwilherm de Vannes got to his feet, looking bewildered.

The empress spoke again: "Know, you people, that on this day . . . what day is it?"

"Saint Valentine's Day, I think," Sir Christopher volunteered.

"On this, Saint Valentine's Day in the year of our Lord 1143, I appoint Sir Gwilherm here as military commander of this castle of Kenniford with Master Penda as his squire and assistant, both to receive emoluments according to their rank."

What's emoluments? Penda wondered. They sounded rich. *Oh gawd.* This strange woman, this granddaughter of William the Conqueror, whom she had thought to be nearly inhuman, was seeing fit to repay a debt as only royalty could.

"Sir Gwilherm's commands will be my commands during my absence," the empress continued, "his directions my directions. He is an experienced soldier in whom I put my trust."

Couldn't be anybody better, Penda thought, and then glanced toward the superseded Sir Rollo to see how he was taking it. He looked shaken. So did Maud, who was standing beside him. Neither had known that was coming. But there was nothing they could do; they had recognized the empress as their queen, therefore this castle was basically hers and she could appoint whom she liked to command it.

The empress's harsh voice rang out again. "You three men, do you hear what I say?"

The lads on the edge of the pond nodded.

"Shall you remember it?"

Yes, yes, they would remember it.

"Let us be sure. Tip them in."

Grinning wickedly, Alan and Sir Christopher strode along the line of the three young men, pushing them into the pond as they went. There were gasps of cold and a crackle of ice. It was the traditional way to impress a matter of importance, should it ever be questioned in a court of law, on the memory of men who could neither read nor write. They wouldn't forget this. If Gwil's position was ever doubted, each of the trio could say that on such and such a day he had witnessed it being bestowed on Gwil by the empress, and given a ducking in the process. Granted, the custom was usually carried out in warmer weather, but each of the three was awarded a silver penny for his trouble before being taken home to dry by the fire.

AT THE REAR GATE Sir Christopher, now mounted, was patting his veil into place under a circlet. "You sure it suits me?"

"You'd look better in yellow," Alan said. "Match your complexion." Around them, men and horses shifted in tension as they waited for the command.

Alan saluted. "Good luck and God go with you." And then he added: "If you get through we'll meet at Salisbury." Then he left to join the empress in the secret postern. As he did so Sir Christopher turned to Penda.

"Time for you to take your place as well, Master Penda," he said. "We shall be depending on your bow when we're chased." He smiled at her. "It's been a pleasure, young sir."

"Thank you," she said meekly; she would miss the courteous Sir Christopher and was anxious for his safety but still rather confused about what exactly was about to take place. However, clutching her bows and quarrels, she set off to the ramparts to position herself among the other archers who would be sending arrows down on Stephen's pursuing troops when they saw the pseudo-empress ride out.

That was the plan. To lure the enemy away from its encirclement by an apparent attempt to escape with the empress, actually Sir Christopher bewigged and veiled. To outride it if possible. To stand and fight if not. To give time and space for the real empress and her chief mercenary to emerge from the secret postern, leaving only two sets of horse tracks in the ground to indicate where they had gone. Which would be due west.

Below the castle, in the prickly passage that smelled of bushes and badgers, with grooms holding the two horses the empress and Alan would ride, Maud was also feeling confused and anxious. Her castle had been invaded and put in danger by the autocratic woman who stood beside her, waiting to desert it. Poor Sir Rollo had been offended—very well, he had his faults, but his loyalty to Kenniford was unquestionable—and a mercenary of low degree put in his place. What's more, and the thought struck her like a thunderbolt, if, as everybody expected, Sir John was going to die soon, the empress would most likely signal her gratitude to Gwil by bequeathing Maud and all her estates to him.

Perhaps Matilda was aware of the seething resentment emitting from her, for she suddenly said: "You have asked for nothing."

"I want for nothing," Maud said, and then added, "Except perhaps that, if I am to be widowed, I would ask that you don't marry me off." It was a spontaneous reaction.

All at once they were creatures together, sleek, rich breeding machines with leashes round their necks. Maud had been married off without consultation once, the empress twice.

She looked at her. Was that sympathy she saw in Matilda's face, sudden amusement, even comradeship? If it was, it changed quickly into calculation. If and when she became queen, the empress might need to award the prize that was Maud of Kenniford to gain a useful alliance. And she would do it. Oh yes, she would do it. Her sudden smile was quite inscrutable.

"But you are not yet a widow" was all she said. It meant nothing.

A rustle behind them announced the arrival of Alan of Ghent. He pushed past Maud and out of the tunnel, hiding in the rowan trees to peer beyond the castle walls to the lines of the enemy.

"Not long now," he said after a time. "Up you get, my lady." He came back and formed his hands into a stirrup. The empress put her left foot in it and swung her right leg across her horse's saddle.

Alan went outside again and this time Maud joined him. All was calm and quiet, the distant men encircling the castle as silent as those inside it.

"Why aren't they moving? Why aren't *we*?" Maud said. "In the name of God, why doesn't somebody *do something*?" The wait was almost unbearable.

"Nervous?" The mercenary's eyes were on the castle gates.

"I'm not nervous . . . nerves aren't something I suffer from. Will there be a signal?" But her teeth were chattering, and from something other than the cold.

"Soon. Gwilherm—sorry, *Sir* Gwilherm knows what he's about. But I warn you, it's going to be noisy."

The mounting suspense was terrible; unable to stand it, Maud went back through the tunnel to where the empress was twisting in her saddle to arrange her cloak into decorous folds. She reached up to help her, deftly tying the scarf strings of the empress's hood more tightly under her chin so that it should not be blown back to reveal either the gold circlet round her hair or the jewels in her ears and at her neck. In her outer clothes, she looked like any male winter rider; underneath she was fully equipped to bribe her way through enemy lines.

And how many of those enemies would be encountered on the terrible ride ahead of her? "God go with you, lady," Maud said, and was surprised by how earnestly she meant it.

Whether the empress replied, she didn't hear, because at that moment a great noise broke out at the castle gates. Maud rushed out of the postern to join Alan among the rowan trees and watch her contingent emerge from the rear gate making a racket of whistles, boos and shouts; there was even a trumpet blast. In the middle of them all a slight figure, its veil blowing in the wind, was screaming in a high falsetto.

"What in God's name are they *doing*?"

"Attracting the enemy's attention. They need that circle to break. Leave a gap."

Maud thought it unlikely that Stephen's men would believe the empress was being taken out with such furor. They'd suspect a trick. She said so.

"Stephen might, but I don't think he's here yet. Come on, you bastards, come on. Break ranks. Come and pick that nice fat plum for your king."

So far, the ring was holding, though some of its men were becoming restless at the jeers coming from the castle ramparts and were having to be commanded back into line by their lieutenants. Gwilherm, followed by the castle contingent, had turned round and was circling the enemy so close that he was in arrow range. He was shouting, though what he yelled, Maud couldn't hear. Sir Christopher's taunts were like the screams of seagulls.

The temptation was too much for Stephen's troops; they could take the empress, and they might even take the castle, with a reward for both. One by one the ring's sections crumbled, its pieces surging forward in ragged attack.

Gwil wheeled away from them and headed for a gap that had opened in the southeast toward the hills. Christopher and his men galloped after him.

The delay had cost them dear; the enemy was at their heels. One man was outstripping the others, a morning star with a wickedly flanged head flailing in his hand, ready to bring down Christopher's horse.

"Shoot him," Maud whispered. She was holding on to a tree trunk so that her knees wouldn't give way. "Kill him."

Whether anybody did or not, she suddenly couldn't see, because a troop of Stephen's men who'd been holding the ring to the west came past to join the melee, their horses plowing through the mud with a rocking action that scattered the earth.

"Bless 'em," she heard Alan say. He went back into the tunnel to get mounted and fetch the empress. "Our way's open, lady."

When, both mounted, they reemerged, Alan reined in among the trees and looked down at Maud. He had looked at her like that once before, almost on this very spot, and was having the same effect. *Oh no!* she thought. *Not again!* But this time she held his gaze and lifted her face to him.

"A farewell kiss?" he asked softly. "It is Saint Valentine's Day, after all." Afterward Maud tried to convince herself that she was about to protest but before she could say anything he had scooped her up and kissed her with an energy that sapped all hers and then lowered her gently to the ground again. Her heart pounding like a sack of frogs, she could only watch as the empress and her mercenary captain clamped their legs against their horses' sides, galloped off and turned right, away from the hubbub behind them.

"Impudence," she whispered, raising her hand to her cheek, when her head finally cleared. But because her knees were shaking, though this time from something other than fear or cold, she found another tree to hang on to while she watched two figures disappear behind the fold of her fields that led to the west.

ON THE RAMPARTS PENDA'S EYES followed the soldier with the morning star. He was chasing Christopher so closely that their horses were almost alongside each other. She could hear, or thought she could, the whistling displacement of air as the weapon flailed inches away from the laboring rump of Christopher's horse. Another attempt like that and the animal would be brought down.

Penda sighted the arrow in her bow. It was going to be a long shot, a very long shot; the man was only just in her range. "Swerve, you fool," she told Christopher under her breath. He did, his pursuer swerving with him, the gleaming morning star raised for another thwack.

It never came. The weapon dropped onto the field and the man fell forward onto his horse's neck as Penda's arrow went into his spine.

Sir Christopher looked round, saw her and raised an arm in salute before he made for the gap in the enemy ranks and disappeared.

CHAPTER 24

AD 1180, Perton Abbey

AND DID SHE ESCAPE? DID the empress get away?" the scribe asks.

"Oh yes," says the abbot, "after many adventures on the way, she arrived at her stronghold in the southwest, where she was reunited with young Henry at Bristol, but much of the fight had gone out of her; she was, after all, over forty years old by then."

"So the war was over then?" the scribe asks, rather too casually for the abbot's liking. He raises his eyebrows but the scribe is too busy writing to notice.

"Not quite over," the abbot says with emphasis, too tired to berate him properly for his ignorance today, "not yet . . . and anyway the Anarchy was just beginning. You see, in a strange way Stephen needed the empress as his enemy; her very existence had given his barons a straight choice: support me, the king, or you will be ruled by this domineering, unpleasant woman. Without her as a contrast, he was left naked as it were, his faults exposed, of which the greatest was weakness." The old man pauses and clears his throat to ensure he has the scribe's full attention. "Now, I'm not saying Stephen wasn't courageous or even a fine general—he could move an army around England faster than anybody—and he was even kindly if they'd let

him be, but he wasn't a"—he looks out at his oak tree to find the right word among its diminishing leaves—"a nailer."

"A nailer, my lord?"

"A nailer. Effective. He seemed unable to administer the finishing touch. A job was never quite completed, a rebel never totally reduced. The empress's supporters, who were still fighting, could tempt him away from one siege by an attack somewhere else, to which he would immediately respond. His word, though generously given, could not be trusted.

"Under Henry the First, a much harsher man, there had been a strong government, an efficient tax system, a rule of law. People knew where they were, even if they didn't like it, but under Stephen these things disintegrated; he had no time to apply himself to them, though I doubt if he would have had the administrative ability to do so if he had. Wrongdoing went unpunished. Barons who were concerned not with putting the empress on the throne but creating their own little kingdoms saw that they could defy his authority. They became savages, invading their neighbors' territory, torturing the landholders into revealing where they kept their money, taking men to build castles for them, stripping the fields of harvests so that peasants died in their thousands from starvation."

It has been a long speech for a dying man. He lies back on his pillows, gasping. The scribe administers a spoonful of medicine and tells him to rest. "We can continue tomorrow."

But there is one more question he has to ask. "My lord, what happened to Kenniford after the empress had gone? Did it give in?"

"Give in?" All at once the abbot is invigorated. "Give in? There were great hearts in that castle, its chatelaine not the least of them. No, my son, only treachery could take Kenniford." The abbot's eyes close again and his scribe sees tears creeping from under them. "The treachery of that grand dragon, that ancient serpent who leads the whole world astray, who was hurled to the earth, and his angels with him . . ."

The scribe creeps out of the room, leaving his master to murmur from the Book of Revelation.

CHAPTER 25

February, AD 1143, Kenniford Castle

EVEN WITH THE EMPRESS GONE and the dawn not yet broken, the battle raged. Stephen, thwarted by Matilda for a third time, was wreaking revenge on those responsible for his latest humiliation.

From Penda's vantage point on the ramparts, there seemed an added ferocity to this morning's attack, as if it were somehow personal this time.

Arrows rained down in great arcs, clattering onto the allure behind her, while the castle itself shuddered and shook as if, at any moment, it would crumble to dust under the relentless assault.

Gwil was no longer at her side; his duties as the newly appointed commander in chief had taken him elsewhere and she missed him. On the other hand, she was grateful, too; the archer who had taken his place had received an arrow through the eye and was lying faceup, dead on the allure behind her. Such was the mercilessness of the enemy fire that nobody had been able to risk attending the body.

All around she could hear the cries of men either wounded or dying as the Kenniford casualty toll rose. She herself had only narrowly avoided being hit when she turned briefly away from her loophole and an enemy bolt came whistling through, and with such force that it embedded itself in the stone wall behind her.

"I'll get it for you, Penda." A child's fluting voice, incongruous in the brutal noise of battle, wafted through to her.

It couldn't be! Surely it couldn't be!

She spun around but saw nothing, and comforted herself that she had just imagined it. After all, fear and panic did strange things up here. Perhaps it was her memory stirring—but then the voice came again, only this time, when she turned round, she saw him.

He was standing with his back to her, his feet set firm and wide, arms reaching high above his head, as he struggled to tug the bolt that had so nearly killed her out of the wall.

William!

"Get down, you idiot!" she screamed, terrified by the storm of arrows whistling through the air around him. He was going to be killed and it would be all her fault. It was *she* who had encouraged him yesterday when she should have summarily booted him back down to safety; it was *her* pride, the very thing Gwil had warned her about, succumbing to the flattery of a child, that had put his life in danger. My God! She had even praised him for his bravery and thanked him for collecting arrows for her, and now she would be punished for her sin with his blood on her hands.

"*Get down, William!*" Another voice screamed in unison with hers and Penda watched as a woman rushed toward the child.

He had freed the bolt now and turned triumphantly toward her, grinning with delight, innocent of the chaos and panic around him as he held it aloft.

"*Get down! Get down!*" But he seemed not to hear.

Maud reached him almost before Penda had a chance to move. She grabbed him, clutching him to her, weeping into his neck and scolding him bitterly with relief that he was safely in her arms. She, too, was oblivious to everything except the boy for whom she was prepared to risk her life.

Another arrow shot past them, perilously close this time, shocking Penda into action. She dropped her bow and rushed out from behind the safety of the merlon toward the woman and child. Whatever the risk to herself she must get them out of the line of fire and down into the bailey as quickly as possible.

Spreading her arms wide, she reached around the two crouching figures, mantling them in her cloak, to shield them with her body as best she could from the raging storm of arrows before forcing them back toward the stairs and safety.

"*Go back now, go back,*" she repeated over and over again as they stumbled in a ragged phalanx toward the stairwell.

When, at last, they reached it she pushed them through the gap in the wall and watched, as if her gaze alone could provide sanctuary, as they stumbled down the steps. Only when they were safely beyond the arrows' reach did she allow herself to breathe again.

They were down. Thank God!

She had just stood up, settled her mantle straight across her breast and prepared to return to the loophole, when she felt something strike her just below her right shoulder.

At first it felt as though she had been punched, and shocked at the audacity of the assault, she wheeled round, fists clenched, ready to confront whoever it was, to hit back if necessary, but there was nobody there.

She shrugged and carried on walking toward the merlon until suddenly her legs were too heavy to move and she stumbled as the pain in her back, little more than a dull ache at first, grew in intensity, surging through the right side of her body like a branding iron. She staggered toward the nearest wall, struggling to breathe, and then her knees betrayed her and she collapsed.

MAUD REACHED HER BEFORE SHE lost consciousness completely.

Having safely delivered William safely into the arms of Milburga she had turned around to look back at the strange redheaded boy who had just risked his life for theirs. He was still standing on the battlements watching over them, seemingly oblivious to the danger behind him, and therefore unable to see, as Maud could, the arrow that came winging its way over the castle wall to bury itself in his back. The moment she saw him fall, Maud picked up her skirts and raced back up the steps to the allure.

When she reached him he was lying down, arms by his sides, eyes open but unseeing. Maud knelt beside him and put her ear to his lips. He was still breathing, but only just, though judging by the crimson tide creeping over the stone beside him, his blood loss was already considerable.

Think, think! She reached out tentatively, hands shaking, to the arrow protruding from his back; it had to come out, she knew that much, but to remove it would cause yet more bleeding and she dared not, could not touch it; to inflict more pain and damage was somehow repulsive. She needed Milburga, she needed Father Nimbus. She raised her face to the heavens. *Oh help me, Mary, mother of God!* But there was no time to invoke anybody's help, because when she looked back at the stricken creature on the ground beside her, she saw that his eyes were closing, and his breathing was becoming shallow. He was dying and she could only kneel beside him and watch.

The castle shook again, rocking her sideways, as another huge boulder ricocheted off the wall. She had to get him out of here, had to do something! She scrambled to her feet, ran to the stairwell and screamed for help.

CHAPTER 26

IT WAS GWIL WHO CAME.

Despite the ferocity of the fighting and his new responsibilities, he had managed to keep half an eye on Penda all day and, wherever he was, whatever he was doing, would glance across every so often to check on her. When he saw Maud waving so desperately on the allure on the opposite side of the castle close to Penda's position, his instinct was to drop everything and run.

As he rushed toward her, darting through the crowds in the bailey, weaving his way around the archers on the ramparts, he hoped against hope that his instinct was wrong and that the casualty, if there was one, was not her. But as he reached the small, still body lying on the ground his hopes were dashed.

He lifted her up and carried her down the steps through the bailey to the keep.

The journey seemed to take an age. And it felt as if the very ground was conspiring against him as he jostled his way through the crowds carrying the unconscious Penda. Maud ran in front screaming at anyone who stood in their way, pushing and shoving when necessary to clear their path.

When eventually they reached the solar Father Nimbus and

Milburga were summoned, Father Nimbus queasy at the sight of so much blood and suffering, Milburga bristling with efficiency.

"What you all standing around for? That there needs to come out," she said, pointing at the arrow shaft protruding from Penda's back. "No good lookin' at it. Ain't going to pull itself, is it?" In times of crisis, as Maud knew only too well, Milburga's default position was one of supreme bossiness.

"But which way?" The very idea of removing the arrow was appalling; any decision taken now would be crucial to the boy's survival.

"We'll see." Milburga frowned as she peeled back the blood-sodden clothing from the wound.

"Can't see no barbs," she said, turning her head this way and that as she examined it. "But likely it's too deep. Pull it backward an' it'll rip more flesh and he'll bleed out." She stopped the examination for a moment to wipe her bloodied fingers on a cloth, then sighed, stood up straight and, with an emphatic nod of her head, said: "I say for'ards."

The decision was made.

Father Nimbus quailed and turned a peculiar shade of green, then stumbled toward the bed, laid a trembling hand on the mattress to steady himself and, for want of anything more constructive to do, began unpacking his chrismatory box.

Milburga stamped her foot.

"Put that away, Girly, you old fool. He ain't dead yet!" And then, spinning around to the rest of the room, hands on her hips, glaring at them fiercely, demanded: "Now, is you lot just going to stand there flapping, or you going to help me? You!" she said, pointing at Gwil. "Sit 'im upright, won't lose so much blood that way." And to Maud: "Send to the kitchen. We'll be needing a jug of wine, some yarrow leaves and some comfrey. And don't be long about it, neither."

As Gwil lifted Penda into his arms she whimpered and half opened her eyes. He felt the warmth of her blood oozing in sticky rivulets over his hands.

"I'm sorry, Pen, I'm so sorry," he murmured as her head flopped onto his shoulder and her eyes fluttered closed. The only sign that she was still alive was the shallow rise and fall of her chest against his.

"Stay with me, Pen, stay with me," he pleaded. "Don't go dying on me now. Not now."

He dared not look at her but stared fixedly instead beyond her through the window as though the dying girl in his arms were merely asleep.

As a professional soldier he had seen arrows pulled from bodies many times before with varying degrees of success. His only comfort now, the fact he would cling to desperately, was that she had not been hit by a crossbow bolt, which would have driven deeper and would almost certainly have been fatal.

Milburga and Father Nimbus heard him muttering under his breath and assumed he was praying; in actual fact he was berating God.

"Ain't she suffered enough, Lord? How much more you going to heap on her? How much more, eh?"

But God was in a contrary mood. *Did I fire that arrow, Gwil? Did I rape her? That was man's work, surely. So, my answer to you is itself a question: How much more will you heap on yourselves?*

In other circumstances he might have wept but desperation had dried his tears; besides, Penda needed all his strength, undiluted by any self-pity.

Maud returned from the kitchen breathless, having run there and back, and handed Milburga the supplies she had asked for.

"We need to strip 'im, get 'im clean afore I do anything," Milburga said, and before Gwil had time to consider the implications of removing Penda's clothes, they had lifted her out of his arms, stripped off her hauberk and peeled back the blood-soaked chemise and bandages that bound her breasts.

"God and all His saints!" Maud said, stumbling backward, as Penda's naked body was revealed.

"Well, bugger me!" Milburga put her hand to her mouth.

"Oh my goodness!" said Father Nimbus. "That poor child!"

Then three pairs of eyes swiveled on Gwil.

"So she's a girl!" he spat defiantly. "Still dying ain't she? In God's name help her!"

Milburga was the first to pull herself together and, with a shake of her head, began to tend the seminaked body now lying facedown on the bed.

"This might hurt a bit, my lovely," she said tenderly. "But, forgive me, I got to do it."

Penda lost consciousness completely at the first pressure from Milburga's hand and appeared to feel nothing as the arrow gnawed its way through flesh and sinew, scraping bone and piercing muscle, until, finally, its bloody head emerged through the skin just above her right breast.

When it was done Milburga cleaned the wound with a cloth soaked in wine and dressed it with yarrow leaves and comfrey while Father Nimbus poured some more wine onto a clean cloth and pressed it to Penda's lips. All the time Gwil stroked her hair and cheek softly, willing her to survive.

He wanted to stay with her, as if by sheer proximity to him she might absorb his strength, but Milburga had other ideas.

"You get on now, Sir Gwilherm," she said. "You got other responsibilities now. This here's women's work."

She was right and he knew it. He rose reluctantly, took one last look at the insentient patient and left the room.

WHEN HE HAD GONE, MILBURGA, Maud and Father Nimbus stood around the bed staring in amazement at the creature lying on it. Now that the arrow had been removed they had time to consider the implications of what they had just witnessed.

"So he's a girl." Father Nimbus shook his head. "Who would have thought it?"

"Might make no difference what it is," said Milburga, "if it don't live. A corpse is a corpse." She looked at Maud, who was still white with shock. "You'm quiet, my lady! Cat got your tongue?"

Maud was, indeed, dumbfounded and wrestling her conscience for an appropriate reaction. The confusion of it all was making her head ache.

At one point, and only moments ago it seemed, she had felt gratitude to the peculiar redheaded boy whom she had never liked terribly but who, nevertheless, had risked his life for hers and William's. Indeed, in that moment on the allure she had acknowledged an enormous debt to him; but now that this same boy had been unmasked as a girl, with all the duplicity and unnaturalness such a revelation entailed, she was overcome by feelings of revulsion and anger. And yet, and yet, she was still in his, or, damn it, *her* debt, and *still* grateful; yet the disorderliness of it all was appalling, especially to one who admired order above all things.

What she wanted most was to close the curtains around the bed, hide the pathetic abomination lying on it from view and forget about it. She couldn't, of course, so instead she turned away and started pacing the room; she had always done her best thinking on the move.

"What do you suppose we do now?" she said eventually, her feet crunching rhythmically over the rushes.

"Pray that she recovers, of course," said Father Nimbus. His conversation with Gwil that night in the chapel, never far from his thoughts, was foremost now. "I have a feeling that this child's physical injuries are perhaps the least of her suffering," he added.

Maud stopped pacing and glared at him. What did he know about her suffering? Did everybody keep secrets from her these days?

"What on earth do you mean?" she snapped.

"Judge not, that you be not judged," Father Nimbus said vaguely, aware that he was in danger of revealing too much.

"Well said, Girly!" Milburga nodded approvingly. "After all, can't blame 'er, traveling the length and breadth of the country like her and Gwil did. No female safe. Course she dressed as a boy. Who wouldn't?"

They were silent for a while until Milburga added: "Besides, boy or girl, she's a bloody good archer, or so they say, and if that lot out there carry on like this much longer we can't afford to lose her."

CHAPTER 27

AS THE LIGHT BEGAN TO fade and the fighting died down Penda developed a fever. Maud and Milburga attended her unstintingly and did their best to quench it, bathing her burning limbs with cold, wet cloths, encouraging her to sip water from a horn cup they held to her lips, but she was soon consumed by it.

In her delirium, she would wake, and her unseeing eyes would suddenly open wide as she arched her back and convulsed against the bed. Then she would cower into the pillows, her skinny arms mottled with fever writhing in front of her face as though fending off an invisible assailant.

As each crisis passed and the fever dipped temporarily Maud and Milburga took it in turns to stroke her brow and speak soothingly to her until the advent of the next one.

It was grueling to watch, made even more so by the fact that it was now obvious to both women, from the things she cried out in the grip of it all, that her torment extended, as Father Nimbus had warned, far beyond her physical wounds.

Watching her suffer so terribly, Maud's initial feelings of abhorrence for this peculiar changeling began to dissipate, replaced by an overwhelming sense of pity.

She had known death and seen injury before, plenty of it in

fact. During his lifetime, her father had insisted she learn the basics of medicine and the healing properties of herbs, as any chatelaine worth her salt must, but she had never before witnessed the process of dying and realized that her ministrations to Penda, inspired at first by a sense of duty, now sprang from another place entirely.

"Will she live?" she mouthed anxiously after one particularly bad episode.

Milburga shrugged. "Don't know," she said. "That's in God's hands now, that is. We can't do no more but wait and see."

Father Nimbus, who had left them, though reluctantly, to attend the wounded and dying elsewhere—and there were many that day—looked up from his duties every now and again to offer up a prayer especially for the girl. Cousin Lynessa did the same, crippling her aged knees on the cold, hard flagstones of the chapel as she prayed for Penda's soul.

The patient herself was oblivious to everything, however. Some part of her soul had sprouted wings long since and flapped away through the solar window; whether it would return she neither knew nor cared.

In her delirium she returned to the strange, flat, watery lands she had so often dreamed about but this time found herself in a warm wooden hut, standing on a floor of freshly strewn sweet-smelling herbs and reeds.

A man stood beside her, a kind one, judging by the look of him, and next to him the woman with the long golden hair who had appeared to her in dreams before. A little girl was sitting by the fire chattering away like a jackdaw, and all the time strange but familiar names drifted through her memory like blossoms on a breeze. Nyles, Aenfled, Gyltha. Yes! The little girl was Gyltha! She remembered now! Her little sister, Gyltha! And the man, Nyles! And the woman, Aenfled! Her father and mother. This was home.

No sooner had she recognized it than her wings flapped again, and she was transported to another place.

Now she found herself crouching in the marshes, huddled against her mother, little Gyltha whimpering fearfully through the hand her mother held over her mouth.

She looked up through the latticework of reeds above her head and caught a glimmer of the vast gray sky beyond and the shadows of the marsh harriers flying overhead. She could hear the wind rustling in the reeds, the raucous voices of the birds calling to one another and the slopping of water all around.

Then, suddenly she heard horses' hooves in the distance and harsh male voices, danger so close she could smell it filtering through the reeds with accents of men and horse sweat and another stench, the very worst one. And the next thing she knew she had broken away from the huddled figures and was running for her life through the marsh, knowing only that she must draw the men as far away from her family as she could. Her legs burned with exhaustion but she willed them to carry her further and further until finally, inevitably, one of the men, the monk, plucked her off the ground by her hair, pulled her onto his horse and carried her away.

She was soaring above the land now like a seagull on the wing, watching as they sped toward a ruined church; two men, two horses and a redheaded girl, tiny specks on a vast, shimmering landscape.

She could no longer see her mother and Gyltha cowering in the ditch from here, but her heart ached for them and hot tears coursed down her cheeks, scorching her flesh and melting her wings, until finally she was spinning out of the sky back down to the watery earth.

They raped her as she lay there, both of them. She remembered it now. But only the monk had beaten her, too.

She had fought back at first, tearing at his face, using her hands like claws against him, but it was futile. Eventually she gave up and lay impassively beneath him as he robbed her of her soul.

She saw his eyes spark as he smashed his fists into her face and ground himself inside her as though he could split her in half, and when she began to bleed he became frenzied, howling like an animal as he thrust his hands between her legs into the wound he had made to smear her blood into her hair.

He had admired her hair, she remembered that, too.

"A redhead!" he had called back to the other man as he snatched her up. "Thank God for a redhead!"

When they had finished with her she lay as still as a corpse on the cold, damp ground while they prepared to leave.

"She dead?" she heard one of them ask. Then she felt a searing, sickening thud as the monk, or so she presumed, kicked her in the ribs to make sure. When she made no response they mounted their horses and rode away.

Time passed and when she could move again it was already dusk. She felt nothing, remembered nothing and knew nothing except for one damned thing, that she wasn't going to die out here in this godforsaken marsh.

She groaned as she dragged herself first to her knees and then, slowly, agonizingly slowly, to her feet and began to stagger toward the church in the distance.

She would die there, she decided; it was as good a place as any. She clenched her fists against her pain and as she did so became aware of an unfamiliar object clutched in the palm of her hand.

CHAPTER 28

THE NEXT MORNING BROUGHT TWO unexpected gifts to Keniford: the lifting of the siege and Penda's recovery.

Having vented his spleen on the castle, in the aftermath of the escape, the king's appetite for another siege in the barren climes of winter, never strong exactly, waned completely. The cost was prohibitive, for one thing, and there was the discomfort, for another, so, with his unrivaled ability to move an army at great speed around the country, he moved them west in pursuit of the empress.

From the battlements, in the blue half-light of the morning the men on watch witnessed the welcome sight of hundreds of human backs and horses' rumps retreating into the forest, and the castle awoke to the cacophony of their celebration.

"Enough to wake the bloody dead," Milburga muttered, peering through the solar window to see what was going on.

And in a sense, of course, it was. When she turned back to the room, Penda had opened her eyes.

She sent for Gwil, who arrived almost immediately, disheveled and unshaven, having not slept all night. As he burst through the door, he barely acknowledged the faithful nurse, but pushed past her, his eyes searching frantically for the tiny, wraithlike figure in the bed.

"Thought you'd gone and died on me," he said, as he removed

his coif and dropped to his knees beside her. "You'll be all right now, won't you, Pen?"

To his horror, she shook her head.

He reached out to touch her forehead. "Fever back is it?" he asked, turning around anxiously to Milburga, who shrugged. Penda shook her head again but smiled this time.

"Not *Pen,* is all," she said, her voice barely a whisper. "I'm *Em.* My name, Gwil, it's *Emma.*"

Milburga saw the look of alarm on the mercenary's face, suddenly as pale as the girl's. "Don't take no notice. Been saying strange things all night," she said, tapping the side of her head to imply that the fever had affected Penda's brain. "Made no sense, most of it. Fever talk, 'ats all. It'll pass."

But Gwil knew exactly what it meant.

"You've remembered, then," he said quietly.

Penda nodded and stretched out her hand to him. "But also how you saved me," she said.

And to Milburga's further surprise, the newly appointed commander in chief of Kenniford Castle buried his face in the palm of the girl's upturned hand and wept.

AND HIM TOUGH AS OLD boots, I thought," she told Maud and Father Nimbus after Mass. "Crying like a baby!" But Father Nimbus was unsurprised and merely nodded.

"As I suspected," he said. "That child's suffering extends far beyond our understanding and Sir Gwilherm knows it."

"Well, that's as may be," said Maud brusquely, "but it's all a bit much if you ask me. And what in heaven's name are we to make of it? Is she Penda? Emma? Boy or girl? It's as if we've had some sort of changeling thrust into our midst."

Now that it looked as though Penda would recover, Maud felt it reasonable to vent her irritation with her.

"And another thing," she added. "What's to be done with her? She can't sleep in the guardroom now, surely?"

They all agreed that she certainly could not and there was much scratching of heads until Milburga suggested putting her on a pallet next to Tola in the corridor.

"I can keep an eye on her that way," she said.

AS THE DAYS AND WEEKS of peacetime passed the number of people in the castle grew fewer. Most of the "useless mouths" Sir Bernard and Sir Rollo had complained about returned to salvage what was left of their village. Many of the mercenaries left, too, of course, going where they could get better pay—their talents being in demand by warring barons—taking their women with them. Some of Maud's men sent their wives and children into service with the nuns at the convent of Godstow downriver, accompanied by Cousin Lynessa.

Maud wondered aloud one day whether Penda could be dispatched, too, but Father Nimbus raised a reproving eyebrow.

"Kindness at all times, my lady," he admonished gently.

One bright morning not long afterward Maud stood at the solar window delighting in the fact that it was hers again, looking out onto the castle to assess those who remained like pieces on a chessboard.

In the topsy-turvying caused by the siege, the complexity of feudal status in the castle—of villeinage, serfdom, free men, of who owed what to Maud, their overlord, and what service they must perform—had all been overthrown.

For instance, in the old days Godwifa, the laundress, down there in the drying court hanging out clothes with her big red-chapped hands, had been paid a penny a day, a pair of shoes at Easter and a cottage near the keep as long as her husband plowed Maud's north field when it was time. But her husband had been killed in the war, and, with three children to bring up, Godwifa was asking to be allowed to stay in her cottage anyway.

"I suppose I still have to pay her," Maud had said to Sir Bernard bitterly one morning during their discussion of manorial business. "What about my plowing?"

"She's a good laundress, lady."

"She can't plow."

"She can launder."

So Godwifa stayed in her cottage as, secretly, Maud had intended she should all along, but it entailed harness-maker and mender Merrygo plowing for her instead, so that he complained he didn't have enough time to do his proper job, let alone his own plowing.

"It's against custom," Merrygo grumbled. Custom was the law at Kenniford; its people lived by it, their memories of what they owed to its lord and what they were due in return going back for generations.

"It may have escaped your notice that we're at war, and that we've just been besieged!" Maud snapped at him. "Just work harder." Pampi the gooseherd had also complained at extra duty because his geese were let out at night to patrol the walls and give a cackle of alarm if they heard an enemy approach. (Father Nimbus said it was how Rome had been saved from the Gauls.) She'd allowed him an extra penny for that—she couldn't afford more and felt she'd been generous enough.

It was a fine March day she looked out on, almost as warm as late spring. Daffodils were nestling in the fields' balks and rooks were building nests in the elms on the Crowmarsh bank.

Around the castle itself there were few birds, apart from some sparrows vying with the hens for insects in the moss between the cobblestones. The stone dovecote by the pond with its beautiful louvered turret of a roof was empty. After the bad and hungry winter, not one of its birds had remained uneaten. Gorbag had even cast a rapacious eye toward the mews, but Maud had told him that if any of her hawks were touched he would go into the cooking pot with them. Hadn't her peregrine brought down a heron only that morning as a contribution to the communal stew?

She still grieved for the cherry trees, but the apple orchard behind the church still stood and some early bees were emerging from the skeps in the outer bailey to buzz round the small plumes of blossom emerging on its twigs.

Despite lack of fodder for the castle's stock during the winter, they'd been able to save a few animals from the annual slaughter—the rest were now in pieces packed in barrels of salt—and a decent-sized herd was now grazing on the pasture down by the river bend under the eye of Wal, the cowherd, who was equipped with a handbell to be rung at the first sign of enemy horsemen, the threat from which was still present. In the sties, piglets were suckling from a fat, indolent sow.

Bart the dairyman (sixpence a week and a seat at the hall table at Michaelmas) had set his daughter to turning the churn handle while he practiced his archery in the outer bailey, and the *clunk-clunk* of forming butter inside it made a bass counterpoint to the *tang-tang* coming from the smithy, where Jack the armorer (eighteen pence a week and four ells of cloth at Christmas) was mending hauberks. And here, with long strings of trout over their shoulders, came Tove and his son fresh from the river.

On the whole, it was a satisfactory scene, considering. The gardens of the huddled reed-thatched houses that arched together down one side of the bailey were planted neatly with herbs, half of which had to be given to Maud's kitchens. They emphasized the gimcrack cottage of the napper, where weeds sprouted even on his sagging roof. She'd had him whipped for laziness and drunkenness more times than either of them could remember, a punishment he'd taken in good part and without improvement, yet an exasperated fondness for him held her back from turning him out. On form nobody could make tablecloths and napery for the hall table like him, but his real genius when sober—after all, who needed napkins these days?—was for poaching. Keep him away from ale by day, and by night, he could creep out unseen and pheasants would come scurrying into his sack like ducklings following their mother.

"Your sack, *my* pheasants," Maud said, taking all but one off him.

Nevertheless, she thought, though they complained, not one of these people with her had ever begged her to desert the empress's cause and go over to Stephen for a quieter life. She was their overlord; they distrusted any other.

The empress herself was now safely ensconced in Bristol, reunited with her son under the protective wing of Robert of Gloucester.

"Good," Maud said when the news reached her. "Hope she stays there." Which wasn't strictly true; yes, she would be happy, for all the fealty she'd sworn, never to see the empress again, but there was a certain mercenary she missed more than she would admit.

Since the night he had galloped away, the ever-faithful Milburga had noticed that a certain spark had been extinguished from her mistress and that the blue bliaut in which she had been so gloriously vain was never requested again.

MEANWHILE, PENDA'S PHYSICAL RECOVERY CONTINUED apace thanks to Milburga's excellent nursing and no little fuss from Gwil. Her adjustment to life as a woman, however, was proving more difficult and she was haunted by an enormous sense of loss. It had, she realized, been a privilege to have shared in the lordship that belonged to all men, even the meanest, and now that she was forced to embrace the vulnerability of all women—and Penda had known the most extreme form—she was frightened.

During her early convalescence she and Gwil spent many hours weaving together the threads of her story, each consolidating gaps in the other's knowledge. The only detail he withheld from her was the significance of the quill case, because he still felt the monk's ever-present threat deep within his bones like an impending storm.

Only once did she ask about the strange object she remembered clutching as she staggered to the church, but when she did so he affected a sudden vagueness and pretended not to remember.

"Blimey, Pen! Can't expect me to remember every last detail; you kept me pretty busy that night." And bless her, she was easily diverted, never once connecting the curious scroll he carried with him at all times with the object she remembered.

Sometimes, when the memories got too much and he saw the sadness in her eyes, he would tease her. "You was a proper webfoot"—an inhabitant of the fens—"when I come across you."

"Webfoot," she said wonderingly, "I was a webfoot." It made her smile.

She needed an attachment, he realized, like a boat eddying in a storm needed an anchor to hold it fast, and he promised her that as soon as she was well enough and conditions were safe, they would leave Kenniford and head to the fens to find her family. She talked about them a good deal these days, now that she could remember, and clearly longed to see them again. Whatever the future held, he could not deprive her of that.

"Oh, could we, Gwil? Could we really?" she asked, her eyes lighting up. "I so want to. We could settle there, you and me, go wildfowling like we did before . . ." And then she stopped midsentence, suddenly crestfallen. "I'm being selfish again, ain't I?" she added, staring miserably at the ground. "You're happy here now, ain't you? Important. What would you want to come away with me for? . . . I should have thought . . ."

He took her hand. "Course I do," he said, and meant it. "Don't forget, Pen, I'm a mercenary first and foremost. Never been one to stay in one place too long. Give it a little while longer, though, let it all settle down out there, an' then I'll take you home." She brightened again. It was settled.

Inevitably the news that she was, in fact, female spread around the castle like wildfire, as she was afraid it would. She had dreaded most the reaction of her fellow archers, but oddly enough, they had greeted the discovery with I-told-you-so-no-you-never nudges at each other. For a while she had been unable to face them but it was Father Nimbus who reassured her that she should and told her that they'd be happy for her.

"I think it came as something of a relief," he said one day, taking her aside after matins. "They were becoming concerned by your lack of beard, the unbroken voice, afraid it might be a demon who outstripped them, which would bring more shame than to be outstripped by a woman. You brought quite a disturbance to some who had begun to question their own desires, my dear . . ." Father Nimbus heard confessions; he knew almost everything. "Yes, all in all, I think you need not be afraid; the most you will have to bear is banter."

And banter there was, heavy-handed some of it, too: heads adorned with women's bonnets, mincing walks, yes. But no molestation; they had been comrades too long.

"So she's got tits," they rationalized among themselves. "Still the best archer we got." And eventually even the bantering died down and they accepted her.

For a long time, however, she refused to give up her boys' clothes.

"It's time," Milburga announced one morning before breakfast as she cast a scornful eye over her. "Getting on people's nerves, you are, pretending to be what you ain't. Father Nimbus, now, everybody knows he's more womanish than a fella and they don't mind a-cause of his goodness, but bein' a boy don't suit you."

"Well, I think it does," Penda muttered.

"Not anymore it don't," Milburga said firmly. "Now, I got a nice piece o' scarlet worsted as I can get sewn up pretty into a kirtle for you. I was saving it but my old broadcloth'll still do—we ain't got grand guests round here no more anyways."

When it was ready, some days later, Penda was summoned to the solar to try it on but when the call came she was so reluctant that Gwil had to go, too, cajoling her all the way.

"Get off!" she hissed, shrugging his guiding hand off her shoulder.

"What's up, Pen?" he asked, grinning. "Don't you want a nice dress? It'll make you look pretty. Want to look pretty, don't you?"

"No," she said truculently. "I don't." But he pretended not to hear as he followed her up the stairs and chivvied her into the solar.

Inside the room Maud and Milburga stood side by side proudly holding up a kirtle of such vivid scarlet that, to Penda's eyes anyway, it looked more like a sheet of flame. She flinched and started backing toward the door. And yet, even as her feet were dragging her to freedom she knew she must change; for one thing the reflection in Gwil's highly polished shield, which had always acted as her mirror, had begun to show a distortion that was not simply due to the shield's convexity. There was no doubt about it, she was becoming odd looking, her face too old suddenly, too knowing for the juvenile cap and short cloak that supported its pretense. And the lumps on her chest, now that she was no longer able to bind them flat—Milburga had confiscated the strips of cloth with which she had done so and forbidden their replacement—looked like a malformation. "You've gotten weird," she told herself, and yet, somehow it was an image of weirdness she wanted to cling to.

And now here she was blinking like a baby in the bright light of the solar, before another weird image, helpless as a hare in a trap as the women advanced toward her waving the kirtle like a weapon. Suddenly she was in the grip of panic, and although she could see their mouths moving around words they uttered as they approached, she was unable to hear their words beyond the cacophony of the blood pounding in her ears.

She was going to faint. She was going to faint like a bloody stupid girl and there was nothing she could do about it. But as her legs buckled and she turned to Gwil to save her the bastard grinned, shimmied sideways and disappeared through the door like a thief.

"Stop screaming!" Milburga said, grabbing her firmly by the shoulders and shaking her. And suddenly Penda could hear again. "Making such a silly fuss. Ain't going to kill you." They both had hold of her now and were dragging her into the middle of the room.

"Now, you take off them silly clothes and we'll turn us backs if that's what you want, and put this on." And, pressing the garment firmly into her hands, they turned their backs, folded their arms and stood waiting.

Slowly, reluctantly, Penda took off her clothes to the accompaniment of two pairs of feet tapping impatiently behind her.

Even the air felt hostile on her naked skin, cold, uncompromising; she could feel the goose bumps rising and began to wonder slyly whether they would notice if she kept her braies and stockings on underneath the dress. On the other hand, as she knew only too well, there was not much that escaped Milburga, so, with a heavy sigh, she removed those, too, dropping them onto the discarded pile of rags that lay at her feet like a shroud.

"I'm ready," she announced eventually when she had fought her way through the mysterious, seemingly endless folds of worsted. She felt strange, wrong; she felt as if she were drowning.

Both women turned around and gasped.

"Well!" Milburga said with emphasis.

"Well!" echoed Maud.

Penda squinted at them, trying to read their expressions, but they were looking at her in a way she didn't recognize, and they were smiling.

The look on their faces wasn't pity, she was pretty sure of that; not mockery, either, she was familiar with that as well. No, it was something else, something kindly, something warm, and suddenly it occurred to her that if she didn't know better, she might mistake it for admiration or something very like it. The realization made her blush.

"I think we should get Sir Gwilherm back," Maud said, turning to open the door, and before she knew it Gwil was standing there, too, and *he* was smiling at her in just the same way, and when he spun his shield toward her she saw why.

She was transformed. Her reflection now showed an elegant,

sleek creature whose neck—though perhaps a little too sinewy from shooting—nevertheless added grace to the delicate head it upheld, and a face, a woman's face, framed by a dramatic cascade of scarlet curls.

"I'm pretty!" she said, amazed.

"Very," said Maud. And when Penda started to cry it was Maud who stepped forward to comfort her and put her arms around her and hold her tenderly while she sobbed.

"I'm not sure I can do this," Penda said.

"Yes, you can," Maud said gently. "And I'll help you."

SHE KEPT HER PROMISE, TOO, surprising everyone with her patient pursuit of Penda's rehabilitation. It was Maud who helped her dress in those early days, when it was still her instinct to rise before anyone else and slip into her boys' garb hoping no one would notice. Milburga was all for confiscating the pile of rags that she kept bundled beneath her pillow "just in case," but Maud insisted they were retained for comfort, if not for wearing. It was Maud, too, who, from her own wardrobe, provided the long linen chainse for her to wear beneath the bliaut, and it was she who instructed her how best to tie the double belt of cloth around her waist to make it fit more snugly.

Inevitably there were occasions when her patience was tested, as when Penda, quite deliberately, in Maud's opinion, eschewed all femininity and reverted to trudging about the castle with a masculine gait and shoulders bowed.

"You have breasts, woman!" she would shout at her, poking her sharply in the back. "Stick them out."

Gwil watched the metamorphosis from a distance, sometimes with amusement but often with a sense of loss. Although she kept the name he had given her—she still didn't feel like an Emma, she said—she was different now, beyond him somehow, and there were times when he caught sight of her across the bailey, a solitary, vulnerable figure, head bowed, kicking resentfully at the hem of her dress, and it made his heart break.

"What now, Lord, eh?" he asked.

Up to you as always, Gwil, the Lord replied, *but you know what's coming. You know* who's *coming. So if I were you I'd get her away from here before it's too late.*

CHAPTER 29

AD 1180, Perton Abbey

WHO'S COMING?" THE SCRIBE ASKS. "What did he mean?"

His visits have become more frequent, more necessary, as his interest in the tale rises and the abbot's health declines. He must hear the end of the story before the old man draws his last breath, and yet it is a race against time. The breathing is more labored now; the abbot tires more easily and the ever-watchful infirmarian is increasingly solicitous of his patient and disapproving of the scribe.

The scribe sits closer to the bed to hear the abbot's voice, which has become more faint; he dares not miss a word.

"The devil, that's who," the abbot replies, but the effort to speak, even to raise his head, exhausts him. He collapses back into the pillows with a heavy sigh and the infirmarian, on the other side of the room, looks up and scowls at the scribe. He disapproves of this business and will speak to the prior before the day is out. All this talk, all this questioning; it is too much for such a sick old man and should be stopped before it kills him. The scribe feels the disapproval emanating from him like the wrath of God, but although he shudders and shrinks a little he continues his interrogation anyway.

"But the . . . er . . . siege, my lord." He is whispering now, which

irritates the abbot who has to crane his neck painfully to hear him. "It is . . . er . . . lifted, is it not? The castle is secure at last?"

"Speak up!" the abbot says sharply, revived by a sudden flash of temper. "Yes, yes, Kenniford is indeed secure for now. *But let us not forget that it has thwarted the king once too often and that he cannot forgive. Remember, my son, he is vengeful." He gasps, gesturing weakly to the cup beside him, which the scribe lifts to his lips, cradling the old man's head in the crook of his arm while he sips from it.*

"Thank you," the abbot says at last. "And now, I fear, we must prepare for the worst time. Beyond the brief peace at the castle, there is total anarchy. Private wars, a thousand or more unlicensed castles like a plague of deadly mushrooms sprouting over the countryside . . . plunder, pillage . . . devastation, starvation. And in the middle, hated most of all by a king and a fiend in the shape of a churchman, there is, alas, Kenniford."

CHAPTER 30

Spring, AD 1143, Kenniford Castle

EIDER DUCK!" SHOUTED FATHER NIMBUS, hopping about so furiously in his skiff that he was nearly in danger of tipping himself into the river.

"That were yesterday's," Ben shouted back, "I ain't letting nobody in on yesterday's."

Gwil went down to the gatehouse to cuff the porter round the ear and set in motion the ponderous machinery that opened the gate. The traffic to and from the castle was flowing more freely again after the necessary restrictions imposed during the siege but was not without its frustrations.

"I am not a man who would deprive another of his employment lightly," Father Nimbus said as between them they pulled the skiff high onto the grass path that led round to the entrance, "but I do feel that Ben could be given a more suitable occupation than that of porter."

Gwil shrugged. It was a hereditary post; Ben's grandfather, great-grandfather and great-great-grandfather had held it before him. Therefore, infuriating though he was, Maud would no more deprive him of it than she would uproot herself. Gwil knew that;

Father Nimbus knew that. The fact that the priest was bothering to raise a much-raised issue was because he was postponing bad news; Gwil recognized the anxiety in his face.

"Come to the buttery for some ale and then a meal," he suggested, but Father Nimbus shook his head.

"Let us take a walk before Lady Maud finds us."

They went to the ramparts, where the priest looked back the way he had come. He and his fellow confessor, the estimable Father Sandford of Godstow, still met regularly, but they did it at a halfway point between Kenniford and Godstow, using the river so that Stephen's garrison at Oxford should not see Father Sandford giving information to a priest who would be considered the king's enemy.

How Nimbus's puny arms managed the long pull up the Thames, Gwil never knew, but the little man said he enjoyed the drift back and that it was safer to be midstream in a boat than walking along the banks, which were roamed by gangs of robbers desperate enough to steal anything, even the ragged robe off a priest's back. The belief that God would keep His clergy safe from predation had been exploded now that altars were rifled on an almost daily basis and their keepers killed if they tried to intervene.

"The king is consolidating his plans to make Thancmar archbishop of Canterbury or York," he said finally when he was certain they were out of earshot.

"Archbishop," Gwil said quietly, the color draining from his face. And then: "Seemed to me only the Pope could confirm an archbishop."

"That used to be true, but it looks as if Stephen is reverting to the old custom from before Anselm wrested the right of investiture solely for the Pope. He needs an archbishop who will anoint Eustace and secure his throne for the boy. Bishop Henry has summoned a meeting that he hopes will agree to Eustace's crowning, though the Pope has forbidden it." He sighed. "If he succeeds, we might yet see a rapist and killer at Canterbury or York."

Gwil had never told anyone, not even Father Nimbus, about what had happened to Penda. A raped woman was too often adjudged culpable in the crime against her—certainly shamed by it—and now that Penda had become a respected member of Kenniford's household, he wasn't going to do anything to change that. Yet somehow, Father Nimbus knew. He took Gwil's hands in his own and gripped them tightly.

"You must take her away from here," he said. Gwil nodded.

When Father Nimbus left he went looking for her and found her in the bailey, where she and the other archers were doing some target practice.

She was easy to spot among the men, incongruous in her long, colorful skirts and her thick red hair, which, now it was no longer cut, fell in abundant scarlet curls around her shoulders.

"Stick out like a sore thumb you do," he told her. "Why don't you wear one of them wimples or a veil or something like Lady Maud?" For her own safety he wanted her to look as unremarkable as possible, just in case . . . But Penda shook her head.

"Ain't doing that! Too hot for one thing," she said. "Means I can't shoot straight for another." She cocked her head and grinned at him. "You'd suit one, though," she said, jumping backward smartly to avoid a cuff around the ear.

"A nice, pretty yellow one," he heard her call over her shoulder as she ran off laughing, hotly pursued by the small entourage she had collected, consisting of the lurcher she had befriended, whom she had named Spider, and William, who was even more enamored of her now that she was a girl, and a pretty one at that.

They sped past Maud, who turned to watch as they laughed and jostled their way through the crowds.

She had become fond of Penda, no doubt about it, admired her even, and was eternally indebted to her, but there was no getting away from the fact that the girl was still peculiar, which meant that she had to question whether it was good for William to spend so much time in her company.

He was getting older after all and ought to start his training for knighthood, not be chasing around the castle on Penda's skirt tails. And yet, as Milburga so wisely pointed out, if it wasn't for Penda he would doubtless be wandering off somewhere getting up to mischief or, worse still, cooped up in the turret with Sir John and Kigva. It had been a very hard decision to make, but all things considered and after much agonizing, she had come to the conclusion that the boy must leave Kenniford. To that end she had finalized arrangements to send him to Sir Robert Halesowen's household near Bristol from whom she was expecting an envoy any day.

Besides, his father's health had taken a turn for the worse recently after another seizure and the limited speech he had regained after his first collapse, even the "uck-oo"s and "uck-off"s, had been lost entirely, along with all movement of his limbs

Only a couple of days ago William had come rushing into the solar in a panic.

"Please come, please come," he had begged, grabbing Maud's hand and dragging her toward the door. "It's Father; something's happened to him again. You must come quickly!"

When they arrived at the turret Sir John was lying motionless on his cot, the only sign of life the erratic rise and fall of his chest and the fearful expression blazing in his eyes.

Maud stood in the middle of the room unsure what to do while William rushed to his father's bedside to hold his hand. At his son's touch Sir John made a peculiar grunting sound, a muscle twitched in his cheek and a rheumy bloodshot eye blinked feebly; he was trying to speak.

"Him need the priest." Kigva was rocking back and forth on her haunches, her face buried in her knees from her customary position in the corner of the room.

Maud nodded, speechless, transfixed by the living corpse on the bed in front of her. "I'll send for the physician," she said when she had collected herself, "and Father Nimbus of course."

Suddenly Kigva shrieked and leapt to her feet.

"Not him!" she screamed, rounding on Maud, her pale eyes flashing venomously. "The other one! That other priest."

Maud shook her head. She didn't understand.

"But there isn't another one," she said, frowning. "Father Nimbus is the only priest we have here."

At the mention of his name something peculiar happened to Kigva and she threw back her head, howling with such ferocity that Maud found herself shrinking toward the door.

"Time to leave, I think, William," she said, trying to sound calm, but the boy did not move.

"William!" she called again, more sharply this time. She had reached the door and her hands were fumbling nervously behind her for the latch. "William, please!" There was an unusual urgency in her tone and this time he responded, rising, though reluctantly, and making his way toward her. When he was within reach Maud grabbed his arm and pulled him through the door behind her.

Once outside, she closed her eyes, let out the breath she had been holding and rested against the wall until her heart had stopped pounding. She did not understand the scene she had just witnessed or the reason for Kigva's anger, but its mystery was as frightening as its passion and she was keen to forget it.

Inside the room, as soon as the door closed and Maud had vanished from view, a rare smile spread across Kigva's face and she turned calmly to her patient.

"Him'll come," she said, pressing her mouth to Sir John's ear as she whispered softly to him. "Don't you worry, my luvver. Him'll come, you'll see."

AT THE BOTTOM OF THE stairs, Maud sent William in search of Milburga while she made her way to the chapel to find Father Nimbus.

For the boy's sake and his alone she would keep Sir John alive as long as she could, but there was nothing more anyone at Kenniford could do for him; what he needed now was a doctor or infirmarian. The trouble was that all those who had previously attended him had left as quickly as they had come, vowing never to return.

Father Nimbus looked stricken when she told him the latest news. "Poor, poor soul," he said, shaking his head sorrowfully.

"Oh for goodness' sake, spare your pity!" Maud spat; there really were times when she wished he wasn't quite so indulgent of everybody. "He absolutely refuses to have you anywhere near him, or at least Kigva does. He doesn't need pity, doesn't deserve it. He needs a doctor or an infirmarian or something but I've run out of them."

"Then we will send to Godstow," Father Nimbus replied, unabashed. "The infirmarian there is very good. I will send for him at once."

WHAT DO YOU SUPPOSE SHE meant by 'the other one'?" Maud asked Milburga as she prepared her for bed that evening.

"I told you an' told you," Milburga said, shaking out Maud's discarded bliaut and hanging it on the hook beside her bed. "Woman's mad. Lord only knows what she means half the time!" Then she stopped and thought for a moment before adding: "Less'n she means that other bugger . . . remember? The one who came before the siege?"

"Oh," Maud replied as the memory dawned on her. "The one Payn let in? Smelled funny? Well done, Milly! . . . Well, I'm damned if we're having *him* back."

CHAPTER 31

THE MAN IN QUESTION HAD other ideas.

News of Kenniford's female marksman with the astonishing red hair had reached the garrison at Oxford long since and spread quickly among the king's men, bringing shame to those who bore the scars of her arrows. It rose, like smoke, ever upward to the men of power, seeping into the court and finally the ear of the bishop of Saint Albans.

Other news has reached him, too, of a mercenary called Gwilherm de Vannes, who was knighted by the empress before she fled and is now military commander of the castle.

He shook his head and smiled wryly when he heard that.

"Well, well, Gwil," he said to himself, and chuckled. So *she* was close. There would be no mistake this time.

Not that he regretted his mistakes, not at all. The killing fueled him, sated him, if only briefly, and drove him ever onward in his inexorable rise to greatness, and greatness, in the form of the archbishopric, is within his grasp now. Canterbury or York? That is the only question left.

Only one obstacle remains, and although he is almost beyond its power now, the inconvenience its revelation might cause would be irritating indeed. Far better to wrest it back and destroy it, along with all those who know its secret.

He speaks to the king, bewitching him with his serpent's tongue as he spills his poison against Kenniford, reminding him of its perfidy, its position of value on the Thames. Its women! It should be ours, my lord, he says. It was once yours, remember?

But Stephen, though hating Kenniford as he does, has no stomach, no time, no money for another siege; besides, Matilda is elsewhere now, and what with the anarchy, the warring barons and the damned bishops—present company excepted of course—he has enough to think about.

But, my lord, he persists. Supposing there was to be no further siege? Supposing we had access directly to the castle? What say you then?

Then I might think about it, says Stephen.

CHAPTER 32

Spring, AD 1143, Kenniford Castle

WILLIAM!" MILBURGA'S VOICE RANG THROUGH the bailey like a herald's trumpet, assaulting the ears of all it reached. Her regular pursuit of the boy had become something of a joke at Kenniford and cries of "Wiw-yam!" echoed frequently around the castle in mimicry of her.

"Wake the nuns at Godstow, that could," Gwil said, shuddering. "What's the poor little bugger done now?"

Penda shrugged. She hadn't seen him all morning and, like Milburga, had no idea where he was. She stood up straight, grimacing as she flexed her aching shoulders.

Her wound had healed almost completely now but she was still stiff across her chest and arm, and today she had been helping Gwil de-rust the hauberks, a process that involved bundling them into large leather sacks filled with vinegar and rolling them around the bailey until they were rubbed clean. It was heavy work and she was paying for it.

"Phew!" She wiped her brow with the back of her hand.

"Tired, Pen?" Gwil shoved his sack hard with the toe of his boot, sending it bumping over the cobblestones. Then he, too, stretched, arching his back to relieve the habitual pain in that. "Me an' all," he said. "Let's stop for a bit."

They sat together on the stone wall round the pond enjoying the sun's warmth on their backs, chatting idly and watching the bubbles from the fish blistering the surface of the water.

Milburga, who until a few moments ago had been merely a disembodied voice on the other side of the bailey, came scurrying up to them now, puffing hard, her face red and beaded with sweat.

"You seen William, Pen?" she gasped.

Penda shook her head.

"God and His saints!" Milburga said to no one in particular as she cast anxiously around the bailey. "Lady Maud wants un and ee's nowhere to be seen *again*!"

They watched, amused, as she picked up her skirts and hurried off in a brisk waddle toward the gatehouse.

Ben hadn't seen him, either.

"Ain't been through here," he told her, shaking his head solemnly. "More'n me life's worth to let 'im an' all. Lady Maud says on no account ee gets through 'ere less'n ee got company."

Ever since the first siege, when he had been taken hostage, it was considered too dangerous to allow William to roam outside the castle anymore, an edict that was unlikely ever to be lifted.

"He'll wish he was more'n missing when I've done with 'im," Milburga growled through gritted teeth as she set off back whence she had come to break the news of the boy's latest disappearance to her mistress.

Maud, however, wasn't thinking about William just for the moment; instead she was sitting beside Sir Bernard, who was doing his best to quell an excitable rabble in the hall, which was packed to the rafters for the monthly manorial court.

On the dais beside them a hen squawked raucously, flapping its wings in panic and sending clouds of feathers into the air as an elderly man tried to encourage it to jump onto a stool.

"What, pray, is he doing to that bird?" Maud whispered to Sir Bernard, who was watching the spectacle with great interest.

"It's a tithe hen, madam," Sir Bernard replied solemnly without taking his eyes off it. "I say it's sickly but he says it is not. I say if it has the strength and wherewithal to jump on that stool—as any healthy bird should—then I will accept it; if not I won't."

Eventually, harried almost to death, the hen half jumped, half scrambled onto the stool, where it slumped to the accompaniment of a great cheer from the crowd. Sir Bernard looked disappointed.

"Oyez! Oyez!" he shouted to no avail, trying to make himself heard above the clamor. But it wasn't until he rose from his stool and slammed the side of his fist onto the table in front of him that the room fell silent at last.

Glaring into the crowd of Kenniford's villeins, squinting menacingly at anyone who met his eye, he took a deep breath and announced: "Let the court of Kenniford commence and let every soul tell the truth as it stands in the fear of God."

"And any bugger who speaks out of turn gets hanged," Maud muttered under her breath for her own amusement and to no one in particular.

"Rents!" shouted Sir Bernard, heralding the next item of business. A long litany of rents and debts to be collected was read out as Sir Bernard ran his finger down the notches of his tally and each person stepped forward to slap his coins on the table in front of him. When all dues had been received the business moved on.

"Appeals!" he shouted, but this time nobody moved.

"Be quick," he insisted, yet still no one came forward.

The siege had introduced a certain solidarity among the people of Kenniford and nobody, or so it would appear, had offended anybody since the last court. Nobody's animals had broken a hedge or trampled a neighbor's crops and nobody had been assaulted.

Maud looked around the room, a skeptical eyebrow raised; it wouldn't do for her people to think she could be cuckolded, even if, deep down, she was relieved not to have to sit in judgment on them today. After all, they had probably suffered enough for the time being.

Sir Bernard, however, was disappointed. Maud had long suspected that he rather enjoyed playing Solomon.

"Boons!" he called out, moving, with obvious reluctance, to the next item on the agenda.

Once again there was no response and nobody came forward.

Out of the corner of her eye Maud could see, by the way he bristled and shifted on his stool, that her steward was becoming irritable. He scratched his head, took a deep breath and bent forward to consult his ledger again. Such was the hiatus that the crowd grew restless and before long the hall began to fill with the sounds of shuffling feet, low murmurs and ostentatious coughing that gradually rose and swelled and threatened to become deafening.

Maud leapt up from her stool. "Silence!" she shouted, and sat down again.

And finally peace was restored. Sir Bernard looked up at last, surveyed the room with abject disappointment and reluctantly dismissed the court, at which point the hubbub resumed as a hundred people all gathered up their belongings and prepared to leave.

"Madam!" a voice called out to her from the other side of the hall, and Maud looked up to see Milburga advancing on her in full cry complaining bitterly about William's latest vanishing.

"Oh dear," she said. "I was hoping to see him this morning. There is something I really must tell him. Not with his father I suppose?"

Milburga shook her head.

"Penda?"

She shook her head again.

"Where in God's name does he get to?"

WAL THE COWHERD KNEW.

He happened to be sitting by the riverbank, not far from

where William was fishing, enjoying the spring sunshine. Wal was watching over his cattle up to their hocks in rich pasture chomping the grass and giving suck to their calves while his own son, a couple of years younger than the boy, ran along the balks scaring away the devouring corn buntings.

"Caught anything yet, Master William?" he called out as he always did when he saw him.

"Not yet," William called back. "But I will."

Wal was one of the few people who could be trusted not to haul him back to the castle and get him into trouble with Milburga.

"Mind how you go, then," Wal said, tapping the side of his nose conspiratorially. William grinned.

Besides his father, fishing was what William loved best, even if he did have to suffer the agonies of the damned every time he crept out of the castle to do it. As young as he was, he had a natural aversion to lying; the fact that he did so was testament to not only his passion for the sport but also the pleasure it gave him to present a fish or two to his ailing father for his breakfast.

And yet, despite his conscience, he found a rare peace among the reeds, screened from the world by the sentries of willow trees, listening to the birds; left to his own devices he could happily stay there all day. Indeed, the only time he remembered being happier was in the days before Sir John's illness, when they would come to the river together to sit in companionable silence watching the water flow by.

It seemed such a long time ago . . .

The sun was unusually warm for so early in spring, too warm for the clothes he was wearing, so he took off his shoes and stockings to dig his toes into the soft, cool mud at the water's edge.

A moment later a heron landed gloomily on the opposite bank and he sat up abruptly, flapping his arms at it until, eventually, it made its cumbersome retreat; then he cast his line, just as his father had taught him, and settled back on his elbows to wait for the fish.

The heat made him drowsy, time passed and the next thing he knew, Wal and his cows were mere specks in the distance on the other side of the meadow and the sun, much too warm for comfort now, was directly overhead.

Midday!

Milburga was bound to have missed him by now. He would have to rush back.

He packed up his things and put on his stockings and shoes in a hurry. He was disappointed not to have caught anything but the river was flowing too quickly today and, despite the occasional glimpse of a trout or two flicking languidly through its depths, had refused to offer him anything at all. Oh well.

He stood up, visible once more above the rushes, brushing at his mantle to remove the telltale signs of the riverbank detritus clinging to its threads, and was about to set off when he heard someone call his name.

Damn! It would be terribly bad luck to get caught now . . . If he could just manage to disappear before whoever it was got to him . . .

He scurried up the bank, hardly daring to breathe, bent as low to the ground as possible. If he could only get to the meadow he'd be able to disappear into the long grass and run home before they reached him . . .

He had almost made it, too, when the voice came again.

Too late!

He stopped, stood up straight and looked back, only this time he saw a skiff bobbing along the river bend bearing a figure in dark robes who was waving at him enthusiastically.

His heart sank. Whoever it was was still too far away to make out clearly but it looked suspiciously like Father Nimbus on his way back from one of his Godstow trips. *He* was bound to tell Milburga where he had found him, which meant—as she was so fond of threatening—there would be "hell to pay." Ah well . . . He stamped the toe of his shoe truculently into the muddy bank with a heavy sigh. Nothing for it now but to wait politely for the old man to reach him.

YOU NAUGHTY, NAUGHTY LITTLE BUGGER!" The moment she spotted William, Milburga's voice cut through the din of the busy kitchen like a knife; even Gorbag flinched.

During his sojourn on the riverbank he had missed both breakfast and dinner and was hungry by the time he got back to the castle. Hoping to find something to eat, he had made immediately for the kitchen, only to find Milburga lying in wait for him. If she didn't yet know how he made his way in and out of the castle—although it was a mystery she was working on—she was at least familiar with the tyranny of a growing boy's stomach and where that would lead him.

It was even worse than he'd imagined.

"Been chasing round looking for you all bloody morning," she shouted, grabbing him by the scruff of the neck and swinging him around to face her. "Disappear like that one more time and I'm warning you . . ." She was wagging her finger furiously. "Worried sick I was, and so was Lady Maud. Wants to see you, too, and sharpish." And, with her talons still locked tightly around his neck, she marched him off to the keep.

"Oh, William." Maud sighed as Milburga shoved him in front of her. "You'll have to stop this, you really will. It's very bad for Milburga's nerves . . . not to mention mine! Now, sit down, there's a good boy," she said, gesturing toward a stool in the corner of the room. "I've got something I need to talk to you about." She looked unusually serious. William felt his heart thump.

"The thing is . . . ," she began with unusual hesitance. "Well . . . the thing is," she repeated. "Well . . . it's time you left Kenniford . . . Now, it's not that we don't want you here because you know how we do and how terribly we'll miss you, darling, but you're getting big now and it's time you started your training."

She watched his eyes well, saw his bottom lip quiver. She hadn't expected him to relish the news exactly but wasn't prepared for quite such misery, either.

"I'm sorry about it, darling, really I am. But, apart from anything else, it's what your father would want for you." At the mention of Sir John a silent tear began its slow progression from the corner of his eye down his cheek.

Maud knelt beside him and took his hands in hers, but he brushed her off and turned his face away. She got up again and walked over to the window to look at anything but the stricken boy.

"So," she said after a long silence, "I have arranged for you to go to Sir Robert Halesowen's household near Bristol." As she said this, she turned to look at him but he was staring at the floor, his head bowed. "And this afternoon he is sending some delegates to meet you and take you back there."

Another plump tear rolled down William's chin and splashed onto his knee, yet still he made no sound. In the awful silence of the room Maud thought she could hear her own heart breaking.

"Oh, darling, please don't cry. You can come back in the holidays . . . It's for your own good, really it is." She looked in desperation at Milburga, hoping for reassurance, but saw, to her dismay, that she was crying, too.

"Oh, bugger!" she said.

CHAPTER 33

SIR ROBERT HALESOWEN'S MEN DID indeed arrive that afternoon and at the sound of the herald's trumpet Maud set off to the gatehouse to meet them.

As she made her way through the outer bailey in the blazing sunshine three tired, sweat-lathered horses were led past her by a groom.

She was surprised to see three horses, having assumed Sir Robert would send only two men; however a third was, of course, more than welcome—another pair of eyes, after all, to keep William safe on the journey back to Bristol.

Ben looked pleased with himself as he admitted her to the gatehouse. "Think they're the gentlemen you been expecting, my lady," he said, making a great show of unlocking the door with care. "Got the password right anyways."

"Thank you, Ben," she said. "My, my, security has improved!"

He beamed with pride. "One of 'em's a friend anyhow," he added, which Maud found baffling until the door opened.

Alan of Ghent made a very low bow. "At your service, madam," he said.

At that very moment Maud realized she had never been more pleased to see anyone in her life. She felt her face light up and noted with relief the responding look of delight in his. For a moment or two neither spoke; it wasn't necessary.

The truth was that since he had left she had thought of little else.

She'd known that it was unlikely they would ever meet again but had amused herself, nevertheless, in her quieter moments by imagining her reaction to him if they ever did.

At first she had been angry with herself for allowing him to kiss her and, worse still, to steal her heart like that and gallop off with it and the empress into the night. Had he turned up any earlier she might have punished him for the pain he had caused her, might well have greeted him then with an attitude of haughty froideur, to show him how little she cared, or was hurt; to make it quite clear that his existence barely even crossed her mind. But then the hours had turned into days, the days into weeks, and her longing for him grew like ivy.

And now here he was, standing there smiling like that, as delighted to be in her company as she was to be in his, so that any pretense at ambivalence was futile. Instead she found herself fighting the urge to run to him, throw her arms around his neck and beg him never to leave again.

However, many generations of good breeding and a natural reserve—though neither haughty nor froid—prevailed, so instead she offered him her hand, which he took and kissed and with such undisguised tenderness that once again she felt that strange, unstable sensation around her knees and feared she might sink to them in front of everybody.

"I am happy to see you," she whispered.

"And I you, madam," he replied.

"But it is a surprise," she added quietly. "A pleasant one, but a surprise nonetheless."

"Sir Robert is a close ally and neighbor of the empress, lady," he said. "News travels fast, so when I heard young William was to be sent to Bristol I volunteered to be part of the dispatch. Besides, the empress doesn't need me at the moment; things are pretty quiet in the west at present." They stood gazing at each other for some considerable time until behind them, two sets of throats cleared ostentatiously.

"Forgive me." Alan grinned. "A mercenary's manners are almost always found wanting, as well you know, my lady." He winked at her. "But may I make amends by introducing Sir Percy Bellecote and Edward Gilpin, whose company I've kept and, I must say, enjoyed immensely on our journey here."

The two young men smiled and bowed and Maud was suddenly reminded of her duty and sent them off immediately to be fed and watered.

She spent the rest of the day with Alan discussing everything that had happened since they last met. She told him about the final day of the siege, about Penda's injury and the shock of discovering that she was, in fact, a girl and how, although poor old Sir Rollo was still smarting from Matilda's insult, Gwil had proved an excellent commander. He in turn told her about their escape, the arrows he and the empress had only narrowly avoided as they galloped away from the castle and his fears for Sir Christopher, who hadn't appeared until well beyond Malmesbury but was still wearing the empress's veil when he did. Maud laughed.

"He is well, I hope," she said.

Alan nodded. "And your husband, madam?" he asked. "He is well, too?"

"Not exactly," she replied, "but still alive . . . just."

"I see," he said.

In fact Maud had been to the turret earlier that day because William had rushed there after their conversation in the solar and she wanted to make sure that he was all right.

When she arrived, however, the boy had refused even to acknowledge her and without his usual cheerful greeting the room felt even gloomier than usual. All that could be heard in the heavy silence was the labored rasp of Sir John's breathing interspersed with groans of pain.

He lay motionless on his cot, just as he had the last time she had seen him, and yet his face—bestially contorted on one side and as slack as an imbecile's on the other—was turned permanently toward the door as though he were expecting someone at any moment.

Kigva was kneeling beside him, murmuring softly, her back to the door, filthy naked feet splayed out behind her. Every now and then she tossed her head to free her face of the long damp strands of hair covering it to guide a cup to her patient's lips.

Maud shifted uncomfortably in the middle of the room and cleared her throat.

"Well, I shan't be staying long," she said, although the visit was fleeting even by her standards. "But if there's anything you need . . ." She was half expecting Kigva to round on her again like a wildcat.

But to her surprise she did not.

"No thank you, madam," she said instead, and although the woman still had her back to her, Maud realized that it was the very first time she had ever addressed her properly. It was strangely disconcerting.

"Well, if you're sure . . . ," she said, glancing over at William once more who was still refusing to look at her.

"Oh yes," Kigva replied, only this time she did turn around, the strange pale eyes staring directly into Maud's. "We've got everything we need now."

It was a peculiar sensation, but long after she had left the room, Maud could still feel Kigva's eyes on her back.

CHAPTER 34

AD 1180, Perton Abbey

THE ABBOT ATROPHIES DAILY AS though an invisible creature is eating him alive from the inside out.

It is the scribe's fault, *the infirmarian thinks as he puffs and clucks around his patient, muttering darkly that all this talk will do him harm; yet still the young man comes, armed with his instruments of torture to drain the old man's soul. And still the abbot welcomes him.*

It is morning and the scribe is sitting, as usual, at the bedside poised to write.

"It was a rare and joyful time for Kenniford," the abbot says. "After the siege and the fighting, its people had survived, triumphed even, and on the evening of Alan's arrival there was, for the first time in a long time, music and dancing, and greatest of all, there was love, at last." He sighs wistfully, causing the scribe to shuffle uncomfortably on his stool. He doesn't approve of music or dancing and certainly not the "love" of which the abbot speaks. He mutters to himself, gives the coarse girdle around his loins a peremptory rub to prevent any stirrings and stops writing.

The abbot looks up irritably.

"Oh for goodness' sake, boy! I will spare you the details but in God's name, write, I'm nearing the end."

CHAPTER 35

Spring, AD 1143, Kenniford Castle

WITH AN EXQUISITE PANG PENDA realized that today had been the happiest of her life.

The epiphany struck at suppertime as she looked around the hall at all the munching, laughing, chatting heads and understood that she loved them—well, not perhaps *all,* but definitely the idea of them and certainly most.

She could, at last, love the place with impunity now because her time there was coming to an end.

She and Gwil would soon be leaving, to take to the road like old times and head east to find her family if they could. It was this idea and also, perhaps, the delicious spiced wine—of which she had drunk rather too much—that had suddenly brought everything into such sharp relief.

"I love you," she told Gwil, resting her head on his shoulder and gazing up at him in woozy affection. "And I love you, too," she said, turning to Father Nimbus on her other side. The two men exchanged amused glances.

"My dear child, you are a most generous soul," Father Nimbus said, patting her hand. "And I am very fond of you, too. May the good Lord bless you and keep you always. You will be much missed at Kenniford."

"Ease up on the old wine a bit, Pen," Gwil said, nudging her in the ribs, but he was smiling and she could tell that, although displays of emotion embarrassed him, he was secretly pleased.

Earlier on they had bumped into Alan of Ghent, whom Maud had obviously primed so well that he did not betray the least surprise to see Penda in feminine apparel; instead he had complimented her on her beauty, adding that he hoped she was still as handy with a crossbow. Best of all, though, had been Gwil's reaction:

"Certainly is," he told him proudly before Penda had a chance to open her mouth. "Best I've ever seen."

It was a prize beyond rubies and she would remember those words for the rest of her life.

After supper there was dancing.

Penda sat on her stool, her feet tapping furiously to the music, watching the twirling dancers on the floor. Gwil, however, seemed oblivious to the merriment and was instead staring into his lap fiddling with the quill case like it was a penance.

"Could get bloody irritating that could," she piped up, when she could bear it no longer.

He looked up, startled.

"What could?"

"You fidgeting with that thing all the time. What is it anyway?"

He sighed wearily.

"I've told you an' told you. It's nothing . . . it's just a . . . thing . . . a mercenary's answer to rosary beads, that's all. Anyway, mind your own business."

She pursed her lips and shrugged. He could be a miserable bugger sometimes and this evening was turning out to be one of those times.

Her previous euphoria succumbed to a sudden stab of guilt. Perhaps it was all her fault! She should not be taking him away from here, not when he, of all people, had so much to stay for. Of course *she* could be happy, *she* was going home, most likely to be reunited with her family, but his family was dead! No, she was a selfish girl even to have suggested it, not to mention a stupid, conceited one to think that she alone could make him happy, and yet, from the very first, he had leapt on the idea with alacrity.

"I'm done here, Pen," he had assured her. "Siege is over. We done our bit. I'll hand back to poor old Sir Rollo and no harm done. Be like old times, won't it?"

Back then she'd thought he had meant those words but now she wasn't so sure. Look at him! He had hardly touched his food all evening and was so preoccupied with whatever it was that there wasn't so much as a flicker from him when a pair of blackbirds flew out of one of Gorbag's pies. All the other diners gasped and applauded but Gwil just sat there as if nothing had happened.

She was beginning to despair when Milburga, wearing a smile of grim determination, came bearing down on them and sashayed around the table to bully him to his feet. There was no doubt about it; he blushed a terrible color and affected huge reluctance, but at long last Penda could see that deep down he was rather pleased.

"I've often wondered about them two," she confided to Father Nimbus as they watched them dance.

"Really?" the old man replied, turning toward her in surprise. "Milburga? Oh, yes, yes, I see what you mean. Well, there is no doubt that she is a very, er, fine woman, a very fine woman indeed. But it would take rather a brave man, don't you think?"

"None braver than my Gwil," she said proudly.

At the other end of the table another couple, also giving many cause to wonder about the nature of *their* relationship, sat deep in conversation oblivious to all but each other. Penda could hardly take her eyes off them. It was the first time she had seen a couple in love and it made her curious.

From the way they behaved it looked a bittersweet experience, and although she could overhear very little of what they said, she could tell by the way Maud intermittently lowered her eyelids—very un-Maud-like—and the inclination of her head that it was not inconsequential. She watched spellbound as the exchange went back and forth until suddenly Alan reached out, pressed his finger to Maud's lips, clasped her hands in his and began to tell her something with such intensity and passion that Penda gasped and had to look away. When she looked back, some moments later, Maud's expression was one of rapt attention. Whatever it was they were discussing, this was the crux, but although she tilted her stool this way and that, and to quite a perilous angle at one point, craning her neck until it hurt, they spoke so softly that she could barely hear a word. And then, as if the sentence had been carried to her on a breeze, she heard Alan say:

"I *will* come back, my lady. As soon as this damned war is over I'll be back at Kenniford before you can say 'God save the queen.' "

The evening ended as the sun went down. The hall emptied and a host of hiccoughing fuzzy-headed revelers made their way obediently to the chapel for compline and then to bed.

CHAPTER 36

AD 1180, Perton Abbey

THE ABBOT IS MUTTERING ONCE more from the book of Revelation:

"His name that sat on him was death. And Hades followed with him . . ." He repeats it over and over again.

"Whose name, my lord?" The scribe leans forward to hear him more clearly. "Who is death?"

But the abbot puts his finger to his lips.

"Shhh," he says as his eyes cast wildly around the room. He is shivering.

Outside the light is dim for so early in the afternoon and thunder growls in the distance. A storm brews and through the window of the infirmary the scribe can see the trees on the rise beyond the abbey bend to a sudden gust of wind as dark clouds chase across the sky like warlords on horseback.

There is a hush broken only by the abbot's sudden gasp.

"He was waiting, you see, in the rowan copse, as he said he would, standing in the shadows, waiting." The old man is struggling for breath. He makes no sense; the scribe is frightened.

"But who, my lord?" He must press him; time is running out. "Who? Tell me who."

"The monk," the abbot replies, his voice barely audible now. "That fiend in cleric's robes. It was he who was waiting."

"But for whom, my lord? For whom did he wait?" He is desperate to wring the ending of the tale from the old man before he goes entirely mad or dies, yet death is breathing hard upon his scrawny neck.

"The serpent. The betrayer of Kenniford," the abbot hisses. "He alone who knew its underground labyrinths; he who could come and go through them unseen like a will-o'-the-wisp.

"It is he *who leads Death to the postern, guiding him like a shepherd along its narrow path to where another passage, unknown to all but he, converges.*

"They do not speak but the monk, crawling on his hands and knees through the low, dark tunnel, mutters unholy things beneath his breath.

"And still he leads him on to the Wormhole and through the rusted grille into the castle itself . . ."

The scribe rocks back and forth upon his stool, hands writhing in his lap, his face tilted to the ceiling as he implores God to give him patience.

But the abbot has turned his face to the wall and is silent once more, while outside the thunder executes its threat, bouncing angrily over the hills as the rain lashes hard upon the abbey's roof. It is colder suddenly and the scribe shrinks deeper into his robe.

"My lord?"

The abbot turns toward him and his face is wet with tears.

"While God and His saints slept," he sobs.

CHAPTER 37

Spring, AD 1143, Kenniford Castle

AS THE REVELERS STUMBLED TO their beds and the servants settled into their various niches in the hall, Gwil made his way to the ramparts for his final patrol of the evening.

It was a cold, clear night and the watchmen stamped their feet, their arms flapping like the wings of a murder of crows to keep themselves from freezing.

"Good night, gentlemen," Gwil said, nodding at each in turn as he made his way along the allure behind them.

"Night, Sir Gwilherm," they mumbled through frozen mouths, their warm breath etched in the chilly air.

Gwil shivered. It made him cold just to look at them and not a little grateful that before too long, duty done, he would be tucked up under his blankets in the comparative warmth of the keep.

"Keep warm, mind," he called back over his shoulder as he headed for the stairs.

A breeze arose as he picked his way down the icy steps to the bailey, mischievously gathering the hem of his mantle and sending it wafting about his shoulders. He grumbled to himself as he pulled it more tightly around him and set off at a brisk trot through the bailey.

Most of the buildings in the inner ward were in darkness, their occupants asleep, the only light a candle guttering in the chapel's window.

Weary and by now extremely cold, he was in a hurry to complete his rounds, but since Father Nimbus had obviously not retired yet, he would need to make a detour of the chapel to check on him.

As he opened its door he was met with the familiar smell of incense, beeswax and damp stone that had emanated from all the churches he had ever set foot in and typified, for him at least, the very essence of God.

The hinges on the door creaked as it swung wide, making the old priest jumped at the sound.

"Oh, Gwil," he said, patting his heart theatrically when he saw him. "I wasn't expecting visitors. I'm afraid you rather startled me."

"Sorry, Father," Gwil said from the doorway. "Just looking in to say good night. All well?"

Father Nimbus smiled and nodded, and satisfied that indeed it was, Gwil ducked back into the night and set off toward the keep.

One last duty to perform and then he could climb the stairs to the guardroom and curl up for the night as he longed to, but first he must go down into the undercroft to make sure old Ernulf, the postern guard, hadn't fallen asleep on duty. Not that he would, mind, good man, Ernulf, but it was just as well to make sure.

The darkness in the tunnel was almost tangible and the brand he was carrying made shadows on the walls strange enough to tease even an imagination as solid as Gwil's. Water dripped noisily from the ceiling while thick cobwebs brushed against his face and from all around his feet came the scratching of rats' claws.

An inhospitable bloody place, this, he thought stepping up his pace. Wouldn't do to spend more time than was strictly necessary down here. He was relieved when, a few moments later, he rounded a bend and emerged gratefully into the well-lit cavern at the entrance to the postern.

Ernulf, the guard, was leaning against the grille contemplating the toe of his boot, looking as weary and cold as Gwil felt. At the sound of approaching footsteps he looked up sharply, automatically reaching for his sword, but when he saw Gwil emerge out of the darkness, he smiled with relief.

"All well, Ernulf?" Gwil asked.

"All well, Sir Gwilherm," he replied. "Quiet as a grave down here tonight."

"And twice as cold," Gwil said, blowing on his hands. "Keeping warm, I hope."

The guard nodded.

"Well, good night then."

"Good night."

ERNULF WATCHED, WITH NO LITTLE envy, as Gwil turned around and walked back along the tunnel the way he had come.

"Quiet as a grave." Ernulf could have kicked himself for that! Didn't do to mention graves and such in the middle of the night in a place like this; didn't take much to pique the imagination down here. Besides, it was Ernulf's belief that loose talk was all it took to conjure up things best left unconjured. He'd heard too many stories about the dreaded Wormhole and the ghost of Walter Corbet, who could still be heard, or so they said, rattling his chains and moaning at midnight—not to be superstitious.

He shivered, stood up straight and stamped his numbing feet. He would go for a walk, keep his blood flowing, show himself willing, though what for he didn't really know. Since the siege ended there hadn't seemed much point in a vigil down here; nobody but a handful of people even knew about it. On the other hand duty was duty and keeping moving might take his mind off old Walter.

He took a brand from the wall and followed the tunnel to his right, which lead to the wine stores. He might not be able to drink the stuff, not on watch anyway, but at least he could smell it, and anything was better than the stench of dead rats and cats' piss that assaulted his nostrils otherwise.

Time passed, though how much he didn't know, but it was almost certainly past midnight when he started to hear things.

He had stopped for a while and was leaning against a broad wooden pillar, just about to close his weary eyes for a moment or two, when a sound that seemed to come from somewhere in the direction of the postern jolted him awake.

He was used to strange noises down here, what with all the rats and cats and even the occasional snuffling of a badger, but this was different; footfall, and human at that, the soft, furtive tread of someone trying not to be heard. As slowly and as quietly as possible he took his sword out of its scabbard and began to make his way back to his post.

But when he reached the postern there was nobody there. And the noises had stopped. Ernulf scratched his head; must have been imagining things. He looked around again. Nothing.

He had just replaced his sword when he heard it again, the unmistakable sound of footsteps, only this time closer and coming from somewhere on the other side of the grille.

He lifted his brand and approached the bars. It was too dark to see much but somewhere in the recess of the tunnel something or someone was moving; he could feel it. His heart began to race.

"Who goes there?" he called, his voice sharp with fear.

The footsteps stopped.

"Who goes there?"

And then, from behind him, came a scream—high-pitched, hysterical, every note resonating with terror—and then a man's voice.

"Quiet," it hissed.

Two people, then.

And Ernulf was about to spin around to face whoever it was when he felt the cold steel of a knife against his throat.

THE MONK SMILED AS HE ran his knife across the guard's throat, spilling his blood in spurting rivulets onto the earth floor. There was no noise, no fuss, just an almost imperceptible hiss as Ernulf's artery yielded to the blade and spewed out its contents. And when he crumpled to the floor the monk knelt beside him peering curiously at him as he watched him die, aping the movement of his mouth with his own as it gaped fishlike, desperate to breathe.

On the other side of the grille scores of men wove and paced like ravening wolves waiting to be let loose on the unsuspecting sleeping castle. He took the keys from the dead man's belt and opened the gate, then stood back as they rushed past in a great wave flooding out into the undercroft.

Three Kenniford men died with arrows in their backs before anyone had a chance to raise the alarm, and by then it was too late.

FATHER NIMBUS HAD STAYED LATE in the chapel, remaining there long after Gwil's visit to pray, because, he felt, it was the least he could do now that divine providence had delivered Kenniford from the siege and restored it to such robust good health and happiness.

But as he knelt before the altar to offer his heartfelt, unconditional thanks to God, it dawned on him quite suddenly that something was very badly wrong.

He had never been a superstitious man, but this dawning took the form of a sensation more than anything else, like an ill wind lifting the hair on the back of his neck, making him rise abruptly and rush to the door.

Outside everything was backlit in an orange glow. There were half-roused, half-dressed people running hither and thither without purpose and in a panic he couldn't understand.

Perhaps he was dreaming.

He stood blankly in the doorway, then rubbed his eyes with the heels of his hands and looked again.

And eventually, through the mist of disbelief, a vision of hell emerged.

Bodies littered the ground, some smoldering still from the fire arrows that had melted their clothes and flesh, others twitching, mutilated and bleeding, and as each piece of the diabolical tableau filtered through so, too, did the accompanying sounds: the screaming, the roaring of the flames and the clash of steel on steel.

And then, on the opposite side of the bailey, something else caught his eye.

He moved beyond the sanctuary of the chapel, peering into the clawing smoke until finally he was able to make out the shape of a man in dark robes standing on the other side of the ward. There was something familiar about him but also something eerily incongruous in the way he was just standing there, calm yet watchful, as if the brutal pageant in front of him had been staged purely for his entertainment. And he wasn't alone. Standing in front of *him,* Father Nimbus could just make out the struggling, terrified figure of a child around whose neck the man's hands were tightly clamped.

"William!"

Father Nimbus ran as he had never run in his life, pushing his way through the surging, panicking crowds of people and animals, stumbling over the blood-smeared flagstones, never once taking his eyes off the boy and the monk.

"Let him go!" he pleaded when he reached them, sinking to his knees, his hands pressed together in supplication. "In God's name, let him go! He is just a child."

The monk smiled and cocked his head to one side curiously, then tightened his grip on the boy and with his free hand gestured to the old priest to rise and come closer.

Father Nimbus did so, inching toward them while all the time speaking softly to the terrified boy: "Don't be frightened, dear one," he told him, although he was trembling himself. "No one will hurt you." But beneath the suffocating hand William was screaming, begging him to turn back.

"All will be well," Father Nimbus said, as he held out his hand. For a moment William felt the monk's grip loosen and was about to wriggle free and run to safety when the blade of a dagger flashed inches from his face and plunged into the old man's chest.

Father Nimbus sank to his knees for the last time.

"I'm so awfully sorry, William," he said.

AS FATHER NIMBUS DREW HIS last breath Gwil and Alan were fighting back-to-back on the other side of the bailey with barely enough room to raise their swords in the cramped chaos of battle.

They had been woken, along with the rest of the garrison, by the sound of the great hall's roof crashing to the floor through its burning rafters and had rushed to see what was happening.

From the window of the guardroom the situation looked bleak indeed.

The men now standing on the battlements, silhouetted against the skyline by the light from the flames below, were strangers, not a Kenniford guard in sight, and below the ramparts, the enemy force outnumbered the defenders by at least two to one.

Without a word both men ran down the keep's narrow staircase, swords raised, shields clattering intermittently against the stone pillar, expecting, at any moment, a rush of men toward them. Instead, however, halfway down they came across Penda who was cursing broadly and trying in vain to pull a hauberk over her dress.

"No you don't," Gwil said, grabbing her by the arm and forcing her back up the stairs toward the solar. "Ain't no call for the likes of you down there, this is hand-to-hand stuff. Now, do what you're told for once and get back."

She argued with him bitterly, as he knew she would, angry tears spurting from her eyes, but when he explained that the solar was defenseless without her, and that Lady Maud and the others were in greater need of her help, she capitulated.

"What about the other men?" she asked.

"Out there fighting," Gwil said. "What's left of 'em. Now get."

She turned reluctantly and made her way back toward the solar.

Gwil watched until she was safely out of sight.

She would not fight again while there was a breath left in his body. He had made that promise to himself the day she had lain so close to death in the solar and now he would guard this place with his life to prevent anyone ever reaching her. God willing, and if he kept his wits about him, there was a chance he could do it, too. After all, the keep was the most easily defended part of a castle. Even if everywhere else was overrun or burned, the keep, built of stone and for self-sufficiency, could be sealed off and protected for as long as supplies allowed, though only God and possibly Sir Bernard knew how long that might be.

But first he must fight.

He reached the bottom of the stairs and plunged through the door to the inner ward.

So far the fighting was confined to the outer bailey but even here the noise was deafening and the air so fume filled, thick and acrid, that he was forced to cover his mouth and nose to prevent himself from choking.

When he reached the gate he stopped to take in the disorienting, unfamiliar landscape that faced him on the other side of the curtain wall.

Almost nothing remained of the ramshackle buildings that had once lined the bailey, their occupants either dead or dying or fighting for their lives before him.

Smoke was pouring through the windows and roof of the great hall, and further along, where a burning yew had toppled against it, the chapel was engulfed in great orange flames that leapt high into the night as they devoured it. The mews and stables had gone, too, reduced to untidy piles of charred wood and rubble, and the horses, or the few to have survived, were careering up and down in panic, trampling bodies underfoot.

Within a few feet of the gate, their backs to him, stood a thin line of Kenniford men, the last bastion between the invaders and the keep, and beyond them, getting closer all the time, was a whirling, screaming tangle of men, swords and axes.

UP IN THE SOLAR MAUD paced the floor.

"What are we to do? What are we to do?" she repeated over and over, beating her sides with her fists.

"We wait," Milburga said. "We stay here and we wait, ain't nothing else we can do."

Maud stopped suddenly and turned toward her, her face deathly pale. "But we have to do *something*!"

She cast wildly around the room looking in desperation from Milburga to Penda and Tola and back again, hoping for some shred of comfort, but they returned only blank stares, their own shock numbing them into the same state of helplessness as their mistress.

She turned to the window and began to beat the sides of her fists on the stone sill. There must be *something* she could do! This impotence would destroy her as surely as Stephen would. Standing here waiting was torture and she could not bear it. If only she had a sword, if only she could fight, if only . . .

"But you cannot, my lady, and you will not," Alan had told her moments before he left her to join the battle. "We are fighting for you and Kenniford. Put yourself in danger and we're all lost."

It had been agony to accept, to watch him leave, and she had begged him to take her with him, but deep down she knew he was right and eventually she let him go. Like it or not, she *was* their figurehead, and if Kenniford was slighted only *she* could negotiate their surrender and save their lives.

"Sweet Mary, help us!" she cried, imploring the ceiling as though the Madonna herself were sitting in its rafters. "How in God's name did they get in?"

She sank down onto a chair, suddenly dizzy as the waves of an old memory washed over her.

She was a little girl again shivering with cold and fear, standing beside her father outside the Wormhole on that other fateful night.

"Will there be traitors, Father?"

"There are always traitors. Trust nobody."

But it was too late. She had not listened to him. She *had* trusted, and just as he had prophesied, Kenniford had been betrayed.

She stood up, her mouth framing a silent scream, and staggered helplessly toward Milburga, who reached out and folded her into her arms like a child.

OUTSIDE THE KEEP ANOTHER CHILD was screaming, his voice lost, too, swallowed up in the noise of battle. Nobody noticed him, or, indeed, the figure beside him who melted into the shadows, slipping as easily as autumn mist through the doorway and into the keep itself.

CHAPTER 38

MILBURGA CLUTCHED HER MISTRESS TO HER.

"Got to be brave now," she whispered. "Got to be as brave as you've ever been."

It was the call to arms Maud needed. She must do her duty. If there was one thing Sir Robert had drilled into his only daughter it was this.

Her responsibility now was to her men, to the people of Keniford and to these women standing so anxiously around her. And then, of course, to William, for whom she must send immediately.

She had last seen him earlier that evening. He was angry with her still, had refused to speak to her when she put him to bed, turning his face to the wall as she bent to kiss him good night. No doubt he had woken to the sounds of the invasion like everybody else but was either too proud or too angry to come to her. He would be alone now, unprotected and frightened, and he would need her. She must pull herself together and act.

But as she started toward the door Milburga blocked her path.

"Where do you think you're going?"

"To get William," she replied, trying to sidestep her.

"No you don't." Milburga blocked her path again. "Won't have you wandering around on a night like this. I'll fetch him. You're to stay put. You heard what Alan said." The standoff between them was broken only when a calm voice sounded from the corner.

"I'll go." All eyes turned toward the speaker. "Well, makes sense, don't it?" Penda shrugged. "I can look after myself and he'll be more likely to come with me."

Without waiting for a response she got up and walked out of the room. Once outside she took her baldric from its hook above her mattress and strapped it across her chest. She was unlikely to need the poignard it contained—the keep, at least, was safe for the moment—but it would be a comfort to have it with her just in case.

Milburga appeared in the doorway to hand her a rushlight.

"Here," she said, pressing the metal holder into her hand: "Be careful, mind."

Penda nodded and set off.

William's chamber was on the opposite side of the keep from the solar looking out not over the bailey but the river and woods behind the castle. It was little more than an alcove carved into the thick stone wall, providing just enough space for a small hand basin and a bed. And although Maud had offered him a much larger room when he first arrived, he had chosen this one especially because, he said, he liked its coziness and its view toward the river.

It was a good deal quieter on this side of the castle, undisturbed by the everyday bustle and business of the bailey, and tonight, as she rounded the corner, Penda noticed that even the noise of fighting had receded. It was darker here, too; the fires in the bailey that burned so fiercely, illuminating all the rooms on the other side of the keep, were invisible from here, and she was forced to rely entirely on the flickering rushlight to guide her. It was also bloody cold and she was cursing herself for leaving her mantle behind; never mind, she consoled herself, she'd be back for it in a bit when she'd fetched the boy.

The journey seemed to take longer than usual in the dark and on her own but eventually she reached William's chamber. Somewhat to her surprise, she found the door already open, yet some instinct made her reluctant to go inside; so instead, standing on the threshold, holding the rushlight out in front of her, she craned her neck to peer into the darkness.

"You there, William? It's me, Penda." In the eerie, absent stillness of the room her voice echoed back to her, increasing her feeling of unease; too loud, too conspicuous.

"*William,*" she whispered, shrinking back from the doorway. "*William!*"

Still nothing. Not a sound. Damn!

She stepped reluctantly into the chamber, her rushlight at arm's length. He could be hiding somewhere, too frightened to come out, and who would blame him tonight of all nights? And yet, other than an untidy pile of sheets and blankets strewn across the floor, there was no sign of him at all.

Her heart sank.

There was only one other place he *could* be, and to fetch him from there would mean immersing herself even further into the darkness on the long climb up the winding staircase to the turret. She had never set foot there before, never had reason to, thank God, but had heard enough about the place from Maud and Milburga not to relish the prospect. Neither did she welcome an encounter with Kigva, especially not on a night like this.

She had only ever glimpsed the woman scuttling around the castle late at night, to steal, or so it was presumed, water from the font or plants from the kitchen garden, but she had heard enough dark mutterings, among the servants, about scrying and spells and various "goings-on" to convince her, as they themselves were convinced, that she was, indeed, a witch.

On the other hand, if the only terror she faced tonight was Kigva, then she would have got off lightly; besides, it would give her something constructive to do, take her mind off Gwil, for whom she'd been worrying herself sick.

He was out there now facing goodness knew what, maybe even wounded, maybe even . . . She shuddered and crossed herself. It didn't bear thinking about.

She stopped for a moment and took a deep breath as she formulated a new plan.

She would fetch William just as she had promised, and deliver him to Maud, but after that she was done. She'd be damned if she was going to sit in the solar twiddling her thumbs with the other women all night waiting for deliverance. No, she had made up her mind. The minute William was safely back in the solar and her duty was done, she would creep out to join the battle alongside Gwil. It was where she belonged, not up here running stupid errands playing hide-and-seek with a little boy.

When she reached the foot of the staircase leading to the turret, she stopped and looked up.

The darkness was impenetrable, a dreadful, cloying, empty void whose peculiarly malignant stillness was only emphasized by the distant sound of battle. She shuddered and then remembered Gwil. For him, if for no one else, she would brave whatever horrors the turret held. And so, with the now-dwindling rushlight in one hand and the hem of her skirts in the other, she began to climb.

The staircase seemed interminable and became increasingly narrow the higher she climbed, as though the rough, stone-flagged walls were closing in around her, catching at her clothes like wicked hands. Something wet dripped from the ceiling onto her forehead; a spider's thread tangled itself in her eyelashes; small, invisible creatures scuttled at her feet; and from a wall crevice a cat hissed, batting at her skirts with its paw as she passed.

"Pssst!" she spat, stamping her foot, feeling a little braver when the creature screeched in indignation and ran away. And when, to her great relief, she reached the top, she found herself on a dimly lit, narrow landing outside a large wooden door.

What she had expected of the infamous turret she didn't quite know; the odd dragon, maybe, a witch or two or any of the other unmentionable horrors with which her imagination had been conjuring on the way up. What she hadn't expected, though, was silence.

There ought to have been voices, some murmur of life, and yet the darkness of the stairwell was superseded by an equally palpable hush. It smelled strange, too—cats' piss, musk and damp . . . And something else . . . Some awful, indefinable yet strangely familiar smell evoking a fear so powerful that it threatened to spin her round and send her scurrying back down the stairs.

Damn it! She pinched herself. Ridiculous! She was Penda, the arbalist, the girl who had stared death and its arrows in the face and won. She was made of sterner stuff than this, and yet . . . and yet . . . there was something in the air up here that terrified her inexplicably.

She blew out the rushlight, hoping to vanish into the darkness, and then, as quietly, as deftly as she could, though her hands were shaking, lifted her dagger from its sheath and pushed open the door.

In the dim light from the flickering sconces dotted around its walls, she saw an enormous room running almost the entire length and width of the keep, and apparently empty.

Ashamed at the sense of relief she felt not to have to venture any further in, she was about to turn around and scurry back down the stairs to report William missing, goodness only knew where, when she spotted a small pile of rags in the far corner.

It moved.

"William! That you?"

The bundle stopped moving: Silence. Then a moment later she heard a strange keening sound emitting from it, filled with such pain and anguish that she forgot her own fear and rushed across the room toward it.

William was lying on the floor half slumped against the wall like a child's discarded doll, so pale and still that if it hadn't been for the low, agonizing sounds he made she would have thought he was dead.

She knelt beside him, placing her dagger on the floor as she took his face in her hands. "You hurt, darling?" she asked, turning him toward her.

But there was no response; instead, as she scooped him up into her arms, he lifted a trembling hand to point at something behind her, and as she turned her head to follow the direction of his finger, she immediately wished that she had not.

On the other side of the room the tattered curtains around a large bed fluttered in the breeze like the fingers of a raven's wing; and from the window above it, a path of moonlight shone across the prostrate figure of a man.

At first glance he looked as though he was asleep, but when she looked again, cursing herself for having done so, she saw a large hole where his belly ought to have been and a glutinous skein of entrails arranged purposefully beside him like a grotesque spider's web. On the floor beside him lay a woman, naked and bleeding from a wound in her neck so wide and deep that it had partially severed her head.

She turned back to William, clutching him tightly to her chest.

"I'm going to get you out of here," she whispered, but as she reached for the knife beside her, a figure stepped out of the shadows and the toe of a boot pressed heavily onto her hand.

"I've been waiting for you," it said.

CHAPTER 39

OUTSIDE, THOUGH THE BATTLE CONTINUED, Kenniford was all but defeated, the castle guard driven back to a cramped corner of the inner bailey in a last, desperate attempt to defend the keep. And as the king's men swarmed the gatehouse, the portcullis rose and the drawbridge lowered, the last flames of hope stuttered and died.

Gwil glanced up at the allure, where a great phalanx of Stephen's men stood silhouetted against the night sky, bows raised, arrows tensed against their strings, watching and waiting for the inevitable command to unleash their storm.

Enough. There must be no more bloodshed.

He raised his arm, put his horn to his lips and blew. At its sound the fighting stopped, a hush fell and from somewhere toward the gatehouse a jubilant trumpet blew as William of Ypres and a score of knights galloped across the drawbridge and into the castle.

It was Sir Rollo who broke the news to Maud that Kenniford was lost.

He entered the solar ahead of Alan, Gwil and Sir Bernard, who were carrying Father Nimbus's body.

"William of Ypres awaits our surrender, madam. I am so sorry," he said.

There was an awful silence as Maud stared into the faces of the men, registering the same look of ashen defeat on each. It was over. She nodded, then turned her attention to the body of the priest.

"If you would be so kind as to put him on the bed and leave me for a moment," she said.

They did as she had asked, lowering him gently onto the bed before filing out of the room; Milburga and Tola followed behind, weeping silently.

Maud watched them go and, as soon as they had disappeared, knelt beside Father Nimbus's body, caressed his forehead and gently lifted his hand to her cheek. Then she bent her head onto his shoulder and wept.

A little while later she stood up. Duty dried her tears. There would be time enough to mourn the priest, the rest of her life perhaps, but now she had other lives to save if she could. She walked over to the basin, washed her face, straightened her skirts and went to join the others.

HALFWAY DOWN THE STAIRS ON their way to meet William of Ypres Gwil realized that Penda wasn't among them.

He grabbed hold of Tola, the nearest person to hand, and swung her round to face him: "You seen Pen?"

She shook her head, startled by the urgency of his expression.

"N-not for a bit," she stammered, pulling away from him. "Went to fetch William for Lady Maud. Ain't come back yet."

He let her go, pressing the heels of his hands to his eyes in despair. He needed to think . . . She should be *here;* she *must* be. When Kenniford surrendered she had to be as close to Maud as possible because only the lady of Kenniford could ensure their safe passage out of here. Anyone left behind would be hanged.

With a gesture to Alan, he dismissed himself from the company and made his way back up the staircase.

She was in here, *had* to be. After all, they had been fighting only feet from the entrance; even in all the chaos somebody, surely, would have noticed if either she or the boy had tried to slip out. Besides, he consoled himself, even Penda wouldn't be stupid enough to leave the safety of the keep, brave little bugger though she was. No, she was in here somewhere and he would find her.

"Penda!" he called, but each time his voice echoed back to him unanswered in the darkness.

By the time he had exhausted every floor, every corner of every room, he had reached the staircase leading to the turret and his rising anxiety was making him irritable. To keep his mind from darker thoughts he had begun to compose the chiding he would give her when she turned up. Oh, she'd be in trouble all right. He'd brook no excuse for all the worry she'd caused him; instead he would take her by the shoulders, shake her firmly (but gently of course) and say something along the lines of: "Now, look here, Pen. Frighten me like that again and . . ." Which was when it dawned on him that those were the words of an anxious father, an irony that made him laugh out loud.

"Didn't bargain for that, Lord, did I? Didn't expect to love her like my own. But You knew, didn't You? Right from the start You knew, crafty old bugger." For a rare moment or two he felt the warmth of his love for her and the serendipity of God's inimitable plan flood through him . . . until something stopped him in his tracks: it was almost nothing, just a scent; but it was the faint though unmistakable scent of asafetida and as it reached him he turned cold and began to run.

He was panting heavily by the time he reached the top of the stairs, but what he saw when he plunged into the middle of the room knocked the remaining breath out of his lungs and made him retch and then, as he reached instinctively for his sword, he heard a familiar voice:

"Well, well, Gwil," it said. "It *has* been a long time."

Gwil turned around slowly and saw Penda, her eyes wide with terror, her head tilted back as she strained desperately away from the knife the monk was holding to her throat. As calmly as he could Gwil reached inside his cloak and took out the quill case.

"This what you're looking for, Thancmar?"

The monk nodded and held out his hand. But Gwil stepped backward away from him.

"Not yet," he said quietly. "Let her go first. Then you can have it."

At that moment Penda felt a sudden spasm of rage shoot through the body behind hers, and the flesh around her throat puckering as the monk tightened his grip on the knife.

No, actually, it wasn't *the* knife, it was *her* knife! She was about to have her throat slit with her own knife! The shock of discovering William, the horror in the room and the appearance of the monk, which had initially knocked the stuffing out of her, was beginning to wear off; besides, if there was a single trait running through her like a seam through a rock it was her sense of pride. After all, hadn't Gwil admonished her about it often enough? And suddenly, the idea of being dispatched in this way seemed not only ignoble to the point of ridiculous but extremely unfair and was the impetus she needed to jerk herself backward and ram the top of her head painfully into his chin. There was a gratifying yelp as he loosened his grip just enough to allow her to slip from his grasp and slide headlong to the floor at Gwil's feet.

"You all right, Pen?" Gwil looked down, extending his hand to help her up, but as he reached out there was a sudden flash of metal and a brutal thud as the monk's sword scythed onto his wrist. She heard Gwil cry out and saw the quill case he had been holding drop to the floor as the fingers of his injured hand unfurled from around it like broken strings.

The quill case!

She had never understood its significance; all she knew for certain was that it was a talisman to Gwil and that whatever power it held he would need now more than ever. The fact that the monk so desperately wanted it, too, made it imperative she find it first.

With one eye on Gwil, as he reeled from his injury, she shuffled across the floor on her knees to where it had fallen, her hands sifting and scrabbling through the filthy rushes as she went until, at last, she felt a familiar shape beneath her fingertips. She clutched it tightly in her fist and was about to scramble to her feet when a shadow fell across her.

"Give it to me," a voice hissed.

She shook her head but dared not look round; instead, her eyes screwed shut so tightly she thought they were going to burst. She began to pray—for Gwil, for William, for her own quick and painless death, for the safe deliverance of Kenniford—but even as her mouth moved around the litany she heard a sword rend the air above her . . .

"Our Father who art in heaven" . . . concentrate . . . concentrate . . . Damn! . . . What was it? . . . Oh yes, "Hallowed be Thy name . . .'

Any moment now the blade would fall . . . *God! Let it be sharp! Oh, let it be swift!* . . . Any moment now . . . But instead of the blow she expected, the soft thud of metal on flesh, she heard Gwil's voice summoning the monk, silence and then the clashing of swords.

By the time she had risen to her feet and got her bearings again the men were on the other side of the room, where the rushlights, burned almost to nothing, flickered so dimly that the two circling, feinting figures merged almost completely into the shadows. Only the occasional gasp, and the brutal beat of sword against sword, broke the silence. Even William, standing beside her, his face buried in her skirts, had stopped his dreadful keening, too frightened even to breathe . . . Then suddenly there was a cry, the clattering of a sword as it tumbled to the stone floor and a shriek of vicious jubilation from the monk.

Gwil!

He was unarmed now and helpless . . . She must *do* something! But what? Without a bow and arrow she was useless, worse than useless, she was nothing; besides, William was clinging to her so tightly that she could barely move.

"I have to go," she pleaded, trying to prize herself free of the small arms around her waist. "I have to go to Gwil!" And as she struggled from his grasp, she pushed him toward the open door. "Run!" she screamed over her shoulder as she sprinted across the room.

WHEN SHE WAS CLOSE ENOUGH to see clearly in the gloom, she saw Gwil lying in a pool of his own blood struggling against his failing strength and the slipperiness of the rushes to get up, the monk hovering over him, stabbing at him viciously every time he tried to scramble to his knees.

"Hey!" Penda screamed, holding up the quill case. "This is what you want! This, not him!"

The monk turned very slowly toward her.

"See!" she called, waggling it at him like a rattle at a baby. "*I've* got the bloody thing!" And, raising it high above her head, she started edging slowly backward, luring him away from the stricken man on the ground. For a moment, the tactic seemed to work and he teetered on the brink of following her until, with a sudden change of heart, he wheeled back to Gwil with one last devastating thrust of his sword.

Penda heard a scream, a primordial howl of such profound grief and suffering that her hands flew to her ears to block it out; only when she tasted the blood it had scoured from her throat did she realize it was hers.

"Gwil!" she called, slumping to her knees. "Gwil!" But he made no response, even as the monk turned again and began advancing on her.

She could only watch as the harbinger of death came gliding across the floor toward her, each footstep drawing her inexorably to the conclusion of her life yet she felt strangely unafraid, enveloped in a peculiar numbness, as though such close proximity to her own demise inured her to all other emotion—the last blessing of the condemned, she thought; or was it simply that without Gwil, nothing mattered anymore?

He was close now, so close, in fact, that she could smell him. He was grinning at her as though they were playing a game, a deadly cat-and-mouse—except that she refused to play. If these were to be her last moments on earth she was going to spend every last damn one of them avenging Gwil, or at least die fighting.

He stopped within a yard of her, black, pitiless eyes boring into hers, but she glared back, steadfast, unblinking, and thought she saw, just for a moment anyway, a flicker of confusion cross his face.

The grin faded.

"Run," he hissed, jutting out his chin in a feint toward her, but she stood her ground, unflinching, flexing her arm instead to throw the quill case high into the air above his head, and, as his eyes flicked briefly from hers to follow its trajectory, she launched herself at him with a punch. There was a sharp exhale of breath as the surprise and force of it rocked him backward, but just as she prepared to hit him again, he hit her back.

It was a blow heavy enough to send her flying across the room but not so devastating that she had no time to wonder—before the flagstones rose up to meet her—why he hadn't killed her. Why, instead of running her through with his sword as he could so easily have done, had he deliberately turned his arm to clout her with the flat of the blade instead? That he intended to kill her eventually she had no doubt; yet twice now he had deliberately stopped short of it and she wondered why . . .

At that point, the back of her head hit the floor and the room went black.

SHE LAY WHERE SHE HAD fallen, drifting in and out of consciousness. When she opened her eyes everything seemed distant and confused: the room, the monk, Gwil, William, tiny, fuzzy specks on a shifting, undulating horizon, one minute there, the next not. But when she closed them it was as though she were no longer even in the room but back on the desolate fen, the beat of horses' hooves drubbing in her ears and the ghost of the little girl who had died and been reborn there running through the marsh.

She remembered that child so vividly now, the terror and loneliness, but most of all the overwhelming sense of shame she had felt as she cowered helplessly beneath the monk while he raped her . . . And there was something else . . . something about her hand! . . . She had been holding something then just as she was now! Only this time it was not the quill case but a cold, heavy object that another small hand was fervently pressing into hers.

She opened her eyes. A small shadow knelt beside her imploring her to wake up as it tried to manipulate her fingers around the hilt of Gwil's sword.

"I came back," William whispered. "I got this for you." She took the sword from him, scrambled to her feet and tucked it quickly into her belt at her back.

The room was even darker now, if anything—the candles and rushlights had burned to nothing—but as she blinked away the darkness, she could just make out the monk standing in the middle of the room, perfectly still but for his hands, which were working methodically around a knot in the belt at his waist.

So that was why he hadn't killed her! Suddenly an instinct she had assumed long dead began to stutter and spark to life inside her like the embers of a fire after a breath of air.

"Get out," she hissed at William. "Get out! Now!" And she saw her transformation reflected in his eyes as he flinched from her like a frightened animal. She watched him retreat toward the door out of the corner of her eye, fighting the urge to call him back, to give him one last reassuring hug, but in the next moment he had vanished from the room and she turned back to face the monk.

The moon had reappeared, shining through the narrow windows onto the grotesque panorama of the room, its pale light delicately silvering the congealing pools and sprays of blood, the mutilated corpses and the now-naked figure of the monk.

"Come," he said, beckoning, and she nodded, lowering her head meekly as she stepped over the rushes toward him.

"Here I am," she said softly when she was close enough to hear the groan of pleasure as he reached out to her, long fingers quivering like tendrils as they stretched to touch her hair.

"Still red," he murmured, caressing the curls that fell around her face with his fingertips, eyes half closed in ecstasy.

"Doesn't come much redder," she muttered, slipping her arms behind her back to grip the sword. "Red as blood, in fact," she added, as, in one deft movement, she slid the blade from her belt, swung it out in front of her and plunged it into his chest.

For a moment they stood like lovers, conjoined by the blade in her hands.

"This is for Gwil," she whispered, forcing the weapon deeper in to his flesh, her breath caressing the side of his face. "And this is for me," she said, twisting the hilt before wrenching it free.

She watched dispassionately as he crumpled to the floor and then sank to her knees in exhaustion.

A sudden movement behind her made her jump and she leapt up, turning abruptly to see Gwil swaying on unsteady legs, peering at the monk's body over her shoulder.

"Bastard dead, is he?"

"Gwil!" she cried throwing her arms around him.

"You all right, Pen?"

"I thought you were dead," she said, weeping into his neck. "Oh God, Gwil, for a moment back there, I thought you were dead."

"Nah, not me, Pen," he said, but even as he spoke his legs buckled and he too collapsed.

"Gwil!" She knelt down beside him and tenderly lifted his head onto her lap, and in the cold dawn light that was now seeping through the windows, she saw the mortal wound in his chest.

"Just need a little rest is all, Gwil," she said, clutching him to her as she rocked him like a baby. "Just a little rest, now, and then we can get out of here. You'll be right as rain in a day or two if I know you."

He nodded, smiling up at her, but she turned her face away to hide her tears.

"That's it, Pen," he said, his voice not much more than a whisper. "Just a little rest . . ."

"Just a little rest," she repeated, wiping roughly at her eyes with the back of her hand. "Because we're going to get out of here, you and me, and then we're going to go and live peaceful like we planned. Remember? The fens, remember? . . . Remember what we planned, Gwil?" She was speaking quickly, urgently, almost gabbling, as she reminded him of the plans they had made, hoping that their memory could somehow tether his soul to his body forevermore. But he only smiled and nodded, murmuring something she couldn't hear.

"What's that, Gwil?" she asked, craning toward him, her tears dripping onto his chest. "Can't hear you too well."

"Christ's blood, Pen!" He grimaced. "Not . . . going . . . to . . . make me repeat it, are you?"

"Hush now," she said, stroking his face. "No need to go tiring yourself out with talk, plenty of time for that later."

But Gwil shook his head.

"Got . . . to . . . say this now, Pen . . . Got to tell you that . . . might've took a while . . . but truth is . . . *the truth is* that I couldn't have loved you more or been more proud of you if you was . . . well . . . if you was my own." Then he smiled and sank back into her lap. She saw him blink, as his eyes grew tired, and she lifted his hand to press it against her lips.

"Don't you ever say that, Gwilherm de Vannes . . . Don't you *ever, ever* go saying stuff like that . . . You're just tired is all . . . Wouldn't be talking like that 'less you were."

But Gwil was no longer listening; instead he was looking beyond and through her, as though at some invisible presence above her head.

"She safe now, Lord, is she?" she thought she heard him ask. "I do right by her in the end, did I?" And then in response to a reply audible to no one but him, Gwilherm de Vannes, bravest of men, gave one last contented sigh and closed his eyes.

CHAPTER 40

AD 1180, Perton Abbey

BRAVEST OF MEN. BRAVEST OF MEN," the abbot murmurs.

Outside the storm has cleared, the wind and rain have ceased their battery of the abbey roof and the trees on the rise stand upright and still again.

With the little strength left to him, the old man rises on his elbows to peer through the window, his rheumy eyes squinting into the light as he searches for something. When, at last, he finds it, he drops back onto his pillows with a sigh. "Well, well," he says.

The storm has blown the last leaf off the old oak tree . . .

He smiles sadly as he turns toward the scribe. The once upright, eager young man now sits slumped and bowed on his stool, tears dripping indecorously off the end of his nose onto the tablet in his lap. The abbot's face clouds with pity.

This is a misery I have inflicted, *he thinks, and is sorry for it, yet he cannot waver now.*

"So Gwil is dead," the scribe says quietly.

"I'm afraid so," says the abbot. "And Father Nimbus and countless other brave souls besides. Death came to Kenniford that night, as I warned you he would, and did not leave alone."

The scribe is silent for a moment, then he turns to the abbot.

"But who admitted him, my lord? Who was the 'serpent' you spoke of, 'the betrayer of Kenniford'? I must know . . ."

Silence again. The abbot is looking through the window once more.

"My lord?" Perhaps he has not heard him. "The one who betrayed them all? You have not named him."

"Have I not?" the abbot replies eventually. "It was William, you see, in the mistaken belief that the monk could cure his father. Kigva had so convinced him of the restorative powers of the monk's prayer that he resolved to get him back by any means, so on the day they met—as if by chance—on the riverbank, it was all too easy for Thancmar to persuade the boy that his motive for returning to the castle was pure. William was just a child, after all, and, besides, he loved his father."

"He must have suffered greatly, though," the scribe says softly. "William, I mean."

"Indeed," says the abbot, wiping away a tear, relieved that the scribe is too busy writing to notice it.

The scribe looks up. "And the others, my lord? What became of them?"

The abbot cannot speak, lest his tone betray what he dares not; instead he raises his hand to motion for some water, which the brother infirmarian brings quickly, administering the sips with his usual care while scowling his eternal rebuke at the scribe above the old man's head.

The abbot sips the water gratefully and is once more revived by it. Death's fingers may be tightening their bony grip but he will resist them just a little longer . . . He sighs again: "The terms of surrender were reasonable, as these things go; the survivors were, at least, granted safe passage out of the castle, along, of course, with all Maud's 'useless mouths'—she insisted on it. They left that very morning for Bristol, turning their backs forever on Kenniford, which, from then on, I fear, became an important stronghold for the king as his main crossing on the Thames."

"And Penda? And William?" the scribe asks, leaning forward anxiously. "What became of them?"

"They survived," the abbot replies. "And now, if, that is, you will indulge me just a little longer, we must head to Bristol."

CHAPTER 41

WILLIAM OF YPRES HAD BEEN in a very good mood on the morning of the surrender. The invasion had gone rather well—better than expected actually. His casualties were minimal, the king had his longed-for crossing on the Thames and, to be perfectly honest, he simply didn't have the appetite for a mass hanging that day. No, all things considered, he would happily grant Lady Maud of Kenniford—although she would have to forget the "of Kenniford" epithet from now on—a safe passage out of the castle, along with all those who wanted to leave with her.

A cock crowed as he watched the party of dispossessed ride across the drawbridge for the last time. He yawned; all this munificence was making him sleepy.

THE JOURNEY TO BRISTOL TOOK the ragged cavalcade through a landscape punctuated by the marks of war, every other village a ruin of burned houses, flattened crops and slaughtered animals. Alan led the way, retracing the route he had taken with the empress, traversing the uplands by day, seeking refuge in the cover of woods and forests by night, their movements trammeled at all times by an acute awareness of the gangs of outlaws who famously roamed the countryside preying on unsuspecting travelers. Not, as Milburga was quick to point out, that there was much worth stealing: a few half-lame palfreys, a couple of flea-ridden hounds and a rickety old cart containing the few casks of water and stale loaves Gorbag had managed to smuggle out of the kitchen before they left. Other than that there were only the clothes they stood up in, although, judging by the odors emanating from *some* she could mention, most of those could probably stand up and run away all by themselves.

"Right bunch of tatterdemalions we are," she said to Maud, turning in her saddle to cast a critical eye over the caravan of dejected souls following on behind. "Look too poor to be worth robbing; wouldn't give us a second glance if I was them."

Maud smiled weakly but said nothing. She had barely uttered a word to anybody since they left Kenniford. For which Milburga blamed Father Nimbus. Not that she wasn't grieving for him herself, mind, it was just that getting cross—as she always found anyway—was a good deal more enervating than feeling sad. Not to mention there being a certain irony, about which she felt rather bitter, in the fact that the only person who had ever been able to truly comfort Maud was the late priest himself.

It was late morning on the second day of their journey and they were riding through a beech wood, carpeted in bluebells, its canopy interspersed with shafts of warm golden sunshine. The scene, the scent, the whole enchantment of the place made Milburga smile with pleasure, and she glanced sideways at Maud to see whether it had lifted her spirits, too, and saw—if the bowed head and listless droop of her shoulders were anything to go by—that it had not.

Milburga sighed. It pained her to look at her mistress, who looked as if all the stuffing had been knocked out of her—not that you could blame her, of course; what with losing poor old Girly and the castle and everything, she had every reason to be miserable. Nevertheless, it shouldn't be allowed to go on too long, and Milburga vowed then and there that the moment they got to Bristol, she would set about putting it right. In the meantime—and this would be difficult—she would hold her tongue, leave Maud to her sorrows and give her time to grieve, poor love.

She sniffed, then turned her head away to dab surreptitiously at her eyes; these were dreadful times right enough, and they didn't even end with Maud. There was William who looked like a wraith these days, so pale and skinny and refusing to eat or drink or talk to anyone, either; but then, God only knew what *he'd* suffered! Penda, too, for that matter, smothered in a pall of grief just like the mistress, only hers, if that were possible, was even thicker and more impermeable.

Oh well, Milburga comforted herself, *not too much longer now.* They would be at Bristol any day, and in the meantime, there being nothing she could do for any of them at the moment, it was probably best not to look.

On the fourth morning, as dawn broke, cold, hungry and almost blinded by exhaustion, they arrived at last on the outskirts of Bristol, where an enormous golden castle rose out of the early morning mist like a miracle to greet them.

"Wait here!" Alan held up a hand, as he drew rein by the ocher banks of a huge river. A murmur of relief rippled through the procession like a breeze as they watched him clamp his heels hard against his horse's flanks and gallop off toward the gatehouse to announce their arrival.

WELCOME, WELCOME, MY POOR, POOR darlings!" Countess Mabel, Earl Robert's doughty wife, stood beneath the portcullis holding out her arms as they staggered wearily over the drawbridge toward her.

"You must be Maud," she said, clutching her to her bosom. "So sorry, so terribly, terribly sorry to hear what a beastly time you've had of it, my dear; I do know how it is. Robert and I have had such trouble in the Marches. Quite, quite horrid, I do know." And before Maud could respond or, indeed, extricate herself, she felt the countess's mighty chest rise against her cheek as a pair of enormous lungs filled like bellows and a voice that could doubtless be heard in those distant Welsh Marches shouted: *"Matilda! Matilda! They're here. Come quickly."*

It was all too much.

Perhaps it was relief that they were safe at last, a belated reaction to what they had endured, extreme fatigue, maybe, or simply the idea of the empress being so unceremoniously summoned, but whatever it was—and even Maud herself didn't know for sure—she began to laugh, quietly at first, an easily suppressible shuddering counterbalanced, in its early stages anyway, by Mabel's solid bulk, against which it rose like a voluptuous wave gathering mirth and momentum, until finally—just as the empress came gliding into view—she was so convulsed by it that the countess was forced to let her go. And there Maud stood, to the openmouthed amazement of everyone else, insensible with laughter, tears spurting helplessly from her eyes as her body shook like one of Gorbag's jellies.

Milburga came to the rescue, although whether Maud's or the countess's nobody knew.

"My lady is tired," she said, taking her mistress's hand and giving its palm a sharp, surreptitious pinch. "A rest perhaps?"

"Indeed," said the bemused countess. "What a very good idea."

Once Maud had composed herself—a few sharp words from Milburga later—they were led to the keep through three enormous baileys, each one lined not with the ramshackle timber buildings of Kenniford but stone-built constructions gleaming with modernity. Every spare inch of every quarter of the place bristled with well-ordered industry, a cacophony of sounds and a dazzling array of people.

As they walked into the inner bailey an invisible wall of warm air blasted their faces like the breath of God from a vast kitchen housing three ovens, each one large enough to roast two oxen side by side and around which scores of cooks, bottilers, bakers and scullions buzzed like bees around a hive. Further on, beyond the great hall, teams of masons and painters were putting the finishing touches to a glorious chapel whose curved, painted ceiling met the arches of its walls in a frieze of sculpted marble punctuated by windows of colored glass. Milburga had never seen so much glass, or so much color, come to that! And in the wards, among the many huntsmen, herdsmen and verderers who populated the place, groups of outlandishly dressed people darted bearing exotic silks and hides, furs and spices.

"Merchants," Alan explained, amused by her openmouthed wonder as they passed. "Foreigners."

DESPITE THE GRANDEUR OF BRISTOL and its assault on their senses, Penda remembered almost nothing of her early days and weeks there, just as she remembered nothing of the flight from Kenniford; everything from Gwil's death onward was blank, a bit like living in a fog. Only the sharp pangs of grief reminded her that she was still alive; everything else was buried and apparently quite dead.

"Alan it was come back to find you," Milburga told her later, although she had not asked. "And there you was, weeping like a baby and clinging to Gwil's dead body, and poor little William there clinging to you. Dragged you both away, he did, and you making all kinds of fuss and then not speaking nor eating, not for days and days, and I was affeared as how you was going to die of a broken heart."

Left to herself she would have done so but Milburga simply wouldn't allow it. And it was she who undertook to chide and cajole the girl back to the living, reminding her of the necessity of food and rest, coercing her back to the rituals of life, which, left to herself, she would otherwise have neglected.

"Ain't no sense in all this flopping about," she would say, as she took a comb to Penda's hair or tied the belt around her kirtle to prevent it falling around her ankles like a sack round a stick. "Ain't going to bring 'im back is it?" And Penda would smile and shake her head, pretending, though only for Milburga's sake, that it would not.

Him . . . Gwil . . . Her grief for him was unremitting, sucking her to unholy depths like an unsuspecting traveler into a bog, only to spew her out again just as she prepared to drown. His memory infused everything she did and became the prism through which she was reluctantly discovering a world without him. She thought constantly about how much he would have loved this castle, its opulence and elegance, and especially the calm order imposed throughout by the venerable Earl Robert.

"You'd really like him, Gwil," she said, lifting her face to the heavens—despite Milburga's chiding that a dialogue with the dead wasn't healthy, she persisted. "Nothing like his sister; real charming he is, kind, too, clever like her but nowhere near as haughty with it." Gwil would have approved, too, of Countess Mabel, another of those redoubtable, aristocratic females by whom Penda was surrounded.

Whether he would have noticed the change in the empress, she wasn't sure. He had never observed her quite as keenly as she had and the changes were subtle; nevertheless, she had changed, as they all had.

She was still beautiful, of course, in that glacial way of hers, but her hair was a little more gray flecked nowadays, and although her presence was still intimidating, somehow its ferocity had calmed, lending an impression of increased contentment. And the reason for it? By all accounts an unkempt, stocky, russet-headed boy of about William's age who ran hither and yon all day with an energy that even Penda found aging—her son, Henry.

She got her first glimpse of them together in the hall at breakfast one morning, the empress's still elegance a sharp contrast to the fidgeting, chattering scruff of a boy beside her who leapt up from his stool every so often, as some new idea or another struck him, only to be forced back down by his mother. It was exhausting to watch but however badly he behaved—and his tantrums were infamous—the empress would merely incline her head and patiently entreat him to do as he was told, wearing, at all times, an expression of such indulgent amusement that it was obvious to all who saw it that she adored him.

"Future king. That's what they say," said Milburga, who had followed Penda's gaze. "Little sod more like! Bright, though. Very. They say it's his brains what singed his hair red."

Indeed Henry's precocious thirst for knowledge was such that his pursuit of his tutor—a certain Master Matthew, who was reputed, under normal circumstances, to have the wisdom of Solomon and the patience of saints—bordered on persecution. Henry was often seen chasing him around the castle battering him with question after question until the poor man appeared near to collapse.

And yet, however exasperating Henry could be, Penda was grateful to him for his kindness to William, whose grief, like hers, seemed boundless. The bright, self-possessed child of Kenniford days had dwindled to a listless shadow of himself. According to Tola, who attended him, he wet his bed nowadays, beset by night terrors in which he cried out in his sleep begging his dead father's forgiveness for some imagined crime.

"Blames hisself for what happened, poor little devil. Always the innocent what suffer, ain't it?" she said with a sorrowful shake of her head after one particularly bad night. And Penda could only agree that it was and yet, to her shame, found herself unable to console him. To be reminded of that night when they had clung together while the devil did his work was more than she could bear and she could not speak about it.

Fortunately, however, Henry Fitzempress had decided, quite unilaterally, that he and William were going to be friends.

He appeared out of nowhere at Mass one morning, shuffling noisily into the pew beside Penda, whom he acknowledged with a broad grin, before leaning across her to engage William, who was sitting beside her, in an astonishingly loud whisper.

"What's your name?" he asked, unabashed by the tutting and shushing that had struck up around him.

"William," William mouthed back, anxious not to offend his inquisitor but equally nervous about invoking the disapprobation of the other worshippers.

"Good," said Henry cheerfully. "Well, I'm Henry. Do you know much about Vegetius?"

William, bemused, turned to Penda, who could only shrug.

"Oh, it's all right," Henry added quickly, sensing his discomfort. "Not many people do but when I'm king all my soldiers will study him because he was very clever."

"Oh," said William.

"Don't worry," said Henry. "I'll teach you all about him, if you like." Then he picked up the book he had brought with him and spent the rest of the service reading it. Penda, who knew very little about letters, was, nevertheless, fairly certain that whatever the book was, the Bible it wasn't.

After that the two became inseparable and Penda watched them, with a mixture of relief and gratitude, scampering out of the hall after breakfast every morning to go either to the tiltyard, or hunting, or to the dreaded "vegetable lessons"—as William referred to them—with Master Matthew.

TIME PASSED. A WARM SPRING and a fine summer led to an exceptionally early harvest, and for several days at the end of July the air in the wards hung thick with trailing clouds of chaff and dust, and echoed with men sneezing as grain-laden carts trundled over the cobbles, bringing in the crops.

One particularly glorious afternoon, Maud was enjoying a rare moment of peace, standing at the solar window overlooking the river, watching a kingfisher dart through the willow trees, its iridescent blue wings sparkling like sapphires in the late afternoon sun.

For the first time since their arrival in Bristol, nearly three months ago, she had managed, for almost an entire day, not to think about her future nor dwell too much on her past and was feeling unusually happy. Of course she still grieved for Father Nimbus and for the loss of Kenniford, always would, and knew that at some point she would have to address her future—not that Lord Robert and Lady Mabel hadn't been hospitable—they had, uncommonly so. It was just now that she was feeling better, she also felt redundant and bored and it didn't suit her. Just for the moment, though, just this afternoon, she would refuse to think about anything . . .

It was remarkably warm for so late in the day; a haze of spent sunshine still hovered on the horizon and she yawned, leaning dreamily on the windowsill, her chin in her hands, tasting the sweetness of the air.

An unexpected knock on the door made her jump and she turned around, surprised to see the room empty. She must have nodded off while the other women left and was about to call out "Come in" when the door opened of its own accord and the empress walked into the room.

"No, don't bother," she said as Maud's hands flew to her head in a futile attempt to straighten her circlet. "It looks rather fetching drooped over your eye like that. Who knows? We might all be wearing them that way soon. Besides, I shan't be here long. There was just a little matter I wanted to discuss with you." Then she stalked toward a chair in the middle of the room and sat down. Maud's heart sank.

"Now," said the empress when she had made herself comfortable, her elegant hands folded neatly in her lap. "I remember you asked me once not to marry you off . . ." She was looking up with that enigmatic faint, cold smile that had chilled Maud's spirit once before. "Remember?"

Maud nodded, a fearful anticipation rendering her speechless. She had dreaded this moment since that terrible night, all those months ago, when they had waited together in the postern and she had made her plea.

"Well, I'm afraid," the empress continued, looking beyond her, through the window, "I have bad news . . ."

Maud opened her mouth but before she could say anything the empress shook her head and raised her hand. "It's no good remonstrating," she said firmly. "You are a prize, madam; even without Kenniford your dowry is considerable; besides, you have other estates, and the fact of the matter is that one of my knights is in need of a reward, a rather substantial one, too, so I'm left with no alternative but to give you to him."

Maud, by now leaning against the wall for support, clamped her hand to her forehead. In a single stroke her beautiful afternoon, her *life,* had been ruined, and she was powerless, once more, to do anything about it.

"Oh, don't look so glum." The empress tutted, rising from her seat and turning to the door. "It's not as bad as all that; besides, Sir Alan of Ghent would make a rather pleasing husband I would have thought. Better than your last one anyway."

Maud's legs began to buckle under the shock. "*Sir* Alan!" she echoed, gaping like a fish at the empress's retreating back.

"Indeed," Matilda replied over her shoulder. "Hasn't he told you? I knighted him this morning."

S'POSE IT SHOULDN'T 'AVE COME as a shock," Milburga confided to Penda later that evening as they prepared for bed. "But it did."

"But I thought she wanted to marry him," Penda said, frowning; after all, or so it seemed to her, it was fairly obvious that they were in love.

"Oh, she did!" Milburga replied. "Does! It's just the way the empress done it come as a bit of a shock, poor little love." She sniffed loudly, wiping her eyes with the back of her sleeve, and for the rest of her life would regale anyone who would listen with the story about how her beloved mistress broke her heart forevermore when she broke the news that she was to be married again and whisked off to France.

The days passed quickly after that in a flurry of prewedding preparations. Milburga, with Penda as her underling, established herself at their forefront, setting about them like a whirlwind even though the slightest mention of the impending day sent her into a fit of sobbing.

"Just give me a moment," she would say, her face raised to the heavens so that she could breathe deeply of whatever it was that sustained her until the next bout. "Be all right in a moment." At which point Penda would put her arms around her and hold her until she was.

Before they knew it, Lammas Day was upon them, the eve of the harvest festival, and that evening, in the dwindling heat, as swallows swooped above their heads picking off the last of the day's midges, they all sat down to a banquet on the lawn.

Penda sat beside Maud on the dais, opposite Henry and William, who, like many of the other diners, proudly sported the cuts and bruises sustained during the course of that morning's game of football. It had taken place on a large strip of land on the demesne—ostensibly, a contest between two rival parishes who were bitterly disputing the rights to a local stream, but it actually involved almost every able-bodied man and boy for miles around. Its aim, as far as Penda could make out, was to chase a spherical object the size of a large pumpkin, made from a leather-clad pig's bladder stuffed almost to bursting with dried peas, the length of the field and pass it, by any means possible, between two posts at either end. It was both brutal and anarchic—she lost count of the number of bloody-nosed, broken-limbed casualties dragged past her during the course of it—but utterly compelling, somehow reminiscent of the Kenniford ramparts during the siege, and she had longed to join in.

"What you fidgeting about like that for?" Milburga asked at one point, as bored and disapproving of the game as Penda was excited by it.

"I want to know what's going on," she replied, stretching her neck as she jumped up and down to see over the head of a tall man who had blocked her view. "I don't understand the rules."

"Rules!" Milburga spat. "What bloody rules? Ain't no rules. That's it, that is. You watch! Them'll chase that bloody thing 'til they're nearly all dead of exhaustion and then they'll want feeding." Which turned out to be a pretty accurate assessment of the proceedings.

"D'you see that really *huge* fellow I got the ball off?" she overheard Henry ask William excitedly over supper, but William shook his head. "Oh, come on! You *do* remember! *Must've* seen him! The giant! 'Bout seven feet tall?"

"Nope," William replied blithely, a mischievous smirk on his face as he loaded his trencher from the enormous plates on the table in front of them. "I didn't actually. I only noticed when you got flattened by the little short one what looked like a girl." There was a howl of protest as Henry suddenly lunged at him, grabbed him around the waist and wrestled him to the floor, then shrieks of helpless laughter as they disappeared, tussling like puppies underneath the table.

"Boys!" Maud said, looking on with indulgent incomprehension. "They're just so . . . so . . . *different*, aren't they?"

Penda laughed.

"But it is good to see William enjoy himself again," she added. "He was such a worry when we first arrived, but a different child entirely since Henry came along." By now both boys had clambered back onto the bench and were eating quietly; she lowered her voice and leaned closer to Penda. "Actually, I have great hopes of that friendship, you know?" she said, inclining her head toward them. "When Henry becomes king—*if* he becomes king, that is—I'm rather hoping he will find some sort of position for William in the Church. Somehow I have always thought that the ecclesiastical life would suit him." She stared thoughtfully at them for a while before turning to Penda. "And you," she said, squeezing her hand gently. "I've been just as worried about you, you know? But you also seem a little happier these days, am I right?"

Penda didn't trust herself to reply, suspicious of the lump that had risen in her throat as it often did whenever there was a reference to Gwil, however oblique.

"Oh, I do know how you feel," Maud continued gently, as if she had read her mind. "But it will get easier. You'll always miss him, of course you will, but it will get better with time and you do have a future, you know, a bright one, too."

Penda shook her head, hardly daring to look up in case she unraveled completely.

"Come now," Maud said, taking Penda's face in her hands and turning it toward her. "You do, you know? And I would like to help you. When I'm—when *we're* married, Sir Alan and I . . . we will be leaving for France. But there's this manor of mine in the fens . . ." She paused, dabbing gently at the tear that had plopped onto Penda's cheek. "Somebody told me once—Gwil, it must have been—that you came from there? . . . Anyway, it's not a huge place—well, as far as I can remember, I haven't seen it since I was a child—but I want you to have it as a token of my gratitude for all that you did for Kenniford . . . for William . . . and for me."

Overwhelmed by a sudden roster of conflicting emotions, Penda opened her mouth to speak but no sound would come out.

"Shh now." Maud put a finger to her lips. "You're not to say anything. It is done, and as soon as it is safe enough, Earl Robert has agreed to provide an escort to take you and Milly there."

"Milburga!" Penda gaped incredulously.

"Yes, Milburga!" Maud replied, delighted by the enormous grin that had spread across the girl's face. "Oh, I'm so glad you're pleased. I begged her to come with me, of course, but she absolutely refuses to set foot either on a boat or in France. Says she's too old; besides, deep down, I think, she might be happier with you."

TO PENDA'S ENORMOUS SURPRISE Maud asked her to be one of her bridesmaids and on the morning of the wedding she and several other girls—"borrowed" from among the empress's ladies-in-waiting to make up the numbers—attended her in the solar, all wearing matching blue pelisses, as was customary, to confuse any evil spirit who might yet be abroad to bedevil the marriage.

It was another beautiful day and Cousin Lynessa, who had arrived from Godstow only the night before, sat on the bed, swinging her legs, marveling at all the jostling, primping, preening vanity while Milburga, unusually dry eyed today of all days, put the finishing touches to the bride.

"Stop it!" she chided, grabbing Maud's wriggling shoulders in an attempt to hold her still while she dabbed saffron powder on the end of her nose and rosewater on her earlobes. "Never known such a fidget as you."

Maud grimaced. "Nerves!" she mouthed at Cousin Lynessa over Milburga's shoulder.

"There!" Milburga said when she had finished, standing back to admire her work. "You'll do."

"I'd better," Maud said, grabbing her nurse in an enormous hug and kissing her all over her face. "Because I'm not going to do this again."

When the time came they processed out of the keep into an afternoon of blazing sunshine across a pristinely swept bailey toward the chapel, where a huge crowd was awaiting them. If it hadn't been for the familiar faces breaking through the throng of people every so often, the sheer numbers might have been overwhelming, but every couple of yards there was a reassuring glimpse of either Sir Rollo or Sir Bernard, or Gorbag, Tola or Sir Christopher elbowing their way to the fore to wave at them as they passed.

Just before the bridal procession reached the chapel doors, where the bride and groom were to exchange their vows, Maud, overcome by a sudden rush of nerves, stopped abruptly. The rest of the women appeared not to notice, carried away by their own excitement, but Penda, who was walking beside her, saw that all the color had drained from her face and that she was trembling. Without a word, she reached out and took Maud's hand and gave it a gentle, reassuring squeeze.

"Thank you," Maud whispered, squeezing back. "I don't know what's wrong with me . . . It's just that . . . oh, I don't know . . . It's just I'm not sure I deserve such happiness after . . . you know . . . everything . . ." But, before Penda could respond, the crowd parted to reveal Alan.

He looked astonishingly young all of a sudden, bereft of his usual self-assurance and quite as nervous as his bride as he shuffled from foot to foot, and yet the moment he looked up and caught sight of Maud his face was suddenly lit with an expression of such tender adoration that Penda deemed it safe enough to release her hand.

"Bit different to the last one," Milburga whispered, smearing away her voluptuous tears with the end of a soggy sleeve, as Maud knelt to take her vows. "True love this, see, no knife to 'er throat this time." And Penda laughed, infused, suddenly, with the deep sense of joy that was enfolding them all like a warm summer breeze.

CHAPTER 42

AD 1180, Perton Abbey

*A*ND THE WAR, MY LORD, *was it over then?" asks the scribe. The abbot is silent for a moment, staring through the window at the bare oak bough that taps against the glass in the breeze like impatient fingers.*

"My lord?" The old man is so still, so quiet . . . Oh, please, not yet! Not now! *He rises abruptly from his stool to peer at the body on the bed beside him and in so doing accidentally sends the wax tablet in his lap to the floor with a resounding crash. A wizened head pivots at the sound and a quick pair of eyes root him to the spot.*

"Sit down!" the abbot says testily. "We haven't finished yet."

The scribe recoils and does as he is told—though his buttocks ache from so much sitting. Nonetheless he is relieved by the admonishment. He has come to know the abbot well: where there is temper there is yet life.

"I'm sorry, my lord."

"Never mind, never mind," the abbot replies, gulping down a wave of rising irritation. Has the boy learned nothing? Must he continue his tutelage of him to the very end? . . . Ah well, not too much longer . . . He takes a deep breath.

"No," he continues, although his tone is more gentle now. "The war wasn't over, not by any means, not for another decade or so, but—and this I grant you—from then on something had changed . . . You see, by then it was no longer simply a dispute between Stephen and Matilda; the empress had all but given up her claim. Instead, the real battle now was for the future accession: Henry Fitzempress or Prince Eustace. Stephen, of course, wanted Eustace to succeed him, but the boy died suddenly in 1153—the summer of that year if I remember correctly—struck down mysteriously; divine vengeance, or so they say, for the wanton destruction he spread through Cambridgeshire and, in particular, the terrible damage he inflicted on Saint Edmunds Abbey. But whatever it was that killed him, when he died Stephen lost all resolve and agreed that Henry should inherit. In return, our dear Fitzempress, still very young, remember, and with a good deal of business to attend to in Normandy besides, consented that Stephen should rule until his death, which actually wasn't too long afterward."

He is breathing hard—it has been a long speech for a dying man—yet the scribe, greedy for the information, like a beggar for bread, allows him no respite.

"My lord," he says, ignoring the irritable sigh and raised eyebrows that accompany his prompt. "I was wondering . . . I know they were married, as you said . . . but what became of Maud and Alan? Did they go to France?"

"They did indeed," the abbot replies, smiling at last, "and were blessed with many children. They are both quite elderly now, of course, but live happily still, or so I believe."

The scribe nods, diligently jotting the words upon his tablet and—hoping that it might go some way toward securing his place in heaven—allows the abbot to take a rest.

"And Penda?" he asks eventually.

"Penda." The abbot's voice is soft, almost a sigh now, caressing her name with a familiarity the scribe has not noticed before. "She returned to the fens with Milburga, to the manor Maud gave her . . .

never married, but is quite wealthy, or so I hear . . . sheep farming or some such . . . I forget . . ." His voice trails off as, once again, his gaze drifts back to the window.

"And the quill case?" He must not lose the old man's attention now. "Did she keep it? Did she ever learn its secret?"

"Oh yes, she learned it," he replies. "But not immediately . . . Kept it on a string around her neck and wore it always, to remind her of Gwil—it was all she had of him, you see . . . And then one day, many years later, when he was able, William translated it for her."

"William!" The scribe frowns, confused. "But I thought he would become a knight as his father had wanted. What business would a knight have with Greek?"

"None at all," the abbot replies. "But William did not become a knight. Fortunately his childhood friendship with Henry endured, just as Maud had hoped, and when he took the throne, Henry gave him a position in the Church."

"Oh, I see," says the scribe, head bowed over the tablet in his lap as he writes furiously. "And do you think they ever knew it was William who betrayed them?" He does not look up from his labors as he asks his question and therefore cannot see the look of desolation cloud the abbot's face; only the sound of muffled sobs disturbs him eventually, drawing his attention back to the old man, who has hidden his face beneath the sheet.

"My lord!" He leaps up from his stool like a scalded cat, casting anxiously around for the infirmarian, but the room behind him is empty, no sight nor sound of anyone other than the distant rhythmic munching of contented pigs beneath the window.

"A moment please . . ." The plaintive, tear-muffled voice rising from the bed is barely a whisper and the scribe, overcome by a sudden rush of pity, sinks to his knees and reaches for the abbot's hand.

"We need not continue, my lord, if it pains you," he says tenderly, trying to stroke the gnarled fingers back to warmth. "Another day, perhaps . . ."

But the abbot shakes his head. He will continue . . . He must . . . There may not be another day.

"Kenniford's betrayal was never discussed, certainly not with William, but I think somehow they always knew, and forgave him, too, such was their goodness; even Penda, who, I believe, suffered most of all." He pauses for a moment, his gaze drifting back to the oak bough. "And yet they were all so very kind to him, far kinder, in fact, than he ever deserved . . ."

"No, my lord!" The words rush out of the scribe's mouth in a torrent before he has time to censor them, surprising even himself with the strength of his objection to the calumny. "You are too harsh! William was just a child, after all, and what he did was out of love for his father! Besides, from what I've learned, he must have suffered for it terribly."

The abbot stares at him for some considerable time, observing, with a peculiar satisfaction, the crimson-cheeked indignation on the young man's face. So you have learned something after all, *he thinks.* If nothing else, there is, at last, compassion.

"Of course he suffered," he continues, eventually. "And suffers still, although not, perhaps, for too much longer."

It is the scribe's turn to be silent.

"I see," he says at last, because suddenly he can, with a clarity as if a veil has been suddenly lifted from his eyes. "Of course," he murmurs softly as it dawns on him that the man beside whom he has kept vigil for so long is not quite as old as he thought at first and that his years are not so numerous that he should, perforce, be dying of them; and yet . . . and yet . . . he is *dying, although not from the physical corruption of extreme old age, but rather from a lifetime's malignant culmination of grief, guilt and loss.*

I have been so blind, *he thinks, as he leans across to press his lips against the abbot's hand.*

"William," he whispers.

The abbot turns slowly toward him, his eyes sparkling with tears.

"It is such a long, long time since anyone has called me by that name," he says. "Thank you."

"For what, my lord?"

"For listening, for judging me kindly, for hearing my confession . . . But now, if you'll excuse me, I have another matter to attend to. Our business here is done, I think . . ."

He smiles fondly as the scribe struggles stiffly to his feet.

"Good-bye, my son," he says.

"Good-bye, my lord," the scribe replies, clutching the wax tablet tightly to his chest as he takes his leave and walks wearily across the room. The old man watches him go, his eyes moistening with pity. I could call you back, *he thinks, and longs to, yet there is no comfort he can offer.*

When he reaches the door the scribe pauses for a moment, turning back to the room one last time, and as he raises his hand in a final salute, the sun appears from behind a cloud, sending a shaft of light through the window onto the abbot's face, bathing him in a golden benediction.

ACKNOWLEDGMENTS

Emma Norman, Harry Clifford and Charlie Clifford, and Helen Heller for all their help and support and simply for being there for both of us. Also to Rachel Kahan at William Morrow who championed this book through thick and thin and has been a most astute and assiduous editor. Ditto Emma Buckley whose editorial help and friendship were also invaluable. Many thanks are also due to Adrienne Kerr of Penguin Canada.

ABOUT THE AUTHORS

ARIANA FRANKLIN was the award-winning author of *Mistress of the Art of Death* and the critically acclaimed, bestselling medieval thriller series of the same name, as well as the twentieth-century thriller *City of Shadows*. She died in 2011, while writing *The Siege Winter.*

SAMANTHA NORMAN is Ariana Franklin's daughter. A successful feature writer, columnist, and film critic, she lives in London.